For Paul

And with thanks to my mother,
who has always made me think

D1321635

PART ONE

Living it Up

1

As hostess, Catrin Howden didn't actually mind her guests playing Russian roulette — it was just the thought of the mess it made on the towels.

It was twenty minutes to midnight on New Year's Eve.

Across the bright debris of the table, where candles were flickering through empty champagne bottles and crystal flutes reflected rainbows of light, the guests had fallen silent.

Catrin, too, was silent.

She played with a long strand of her fine dark hair and looked across the table at her white-knuckled husband.

William's calm, fine-featured face stiffened. He glanced at her for a second but before she could react he looked away and with a sudden jerk he pulled the thin pale string viciously. Instantly there was an explosion of sound and out of the emerald party popper that he was still clutching flew a large quantity of aubergine dip. It hit the side of his head with force and trickled down his temple slowly, a clotted mass, grey as brains.

Gunpowder smoke lifted pungently upwards.

There was a deafening cheer and the table began bouncing beneath pounding fists, setting the china ringing and making the glasses dance sideways on the damask cloth. Catrin could feel it shuddering under her bare forearms as in the din she kept her gaze on her husband. She began to smile – William's handsome face was still impassive and the dip had splattered into his fair, wavy hair. She watched him touch it briefly and wipe his fingers on the tablecloth.

He stood up suddenly amidst the noise, the legs of his chair screeching on the polished floor, and he picked up the silver tray which held the weapons of war.

'Your turn, Hugh,' he said, handing the tray across the table towards his friend and colleague.

Hugh, chief reporter at *Media News*, was a large man whose dark eyes were fringed with white eyelashes which hid his eyes as he stared at the tray. He stroked his palms down his white shirt front through which his stomach showed pinkly but it was impossible, just by looking, to tell which of the party poppers had been refilled and which were empty. His hand hovered for a moment and he chose a blue one and tossed it in the air.

Then, with a grimace, he aimed it at his forehead, narrowed his eyes and pulled recklessly. There was a small explosion and a puff of sulphurous smoke but that was all. He did a thumbs-up sign in response to jeers from around the table and the tray was held out to Catrin. Choosing red, to match her dress, she lifted up the party popper, pointed it towards her forehead and pulled the string.

The smoke stung her nose. Another blank. The plastic was hot in her hand and she dropped it on the table

4

with relief and blew a strand of hair away from her eyes.

'I'm going to get some towels,' she said, glancing at William, and she reached over for her glass to take up with her. She sipped her champagne as she went upstairs, smiling as she heard another cheer. She went into the bathroom and sat down on the cold edge of the bath, feeling . . . happy.

She loved New Year's Eve. She loved the feeling of having the old year all wrapped up and done with, survived, and what was more, enjoyed. She liked the thought of a new year stretching out before her like a stream of computer paper waiting for input.

As Sales Controller of South East Television, her new year wasn't exactly a blank; but still – a New Year held promise. It smacked of infinite possibilities and surprises.

She stood up and finished off her champagne, enjoying the sensation of it prickling her tongue. She put the glass down on the chilly windowsill and, remembering why she was there, she walked over to the airing cupboard where the towels were kept. As her fingers touched the chrome knob she hesitated; she'd heard something, some sound that didn't belong to the house. Frowning, she stood for a moment listening, her fingers loosening themselves from the cold chrome. The echoey bathroom was silent. Not even the taps dripped.

She was mocking herself gently as she opened the cupboard door. For a split second she had a faint impression of subdued life inside the warm darkness. There was a slight movement in the gloom and she jerked her head, startled. Suddenly from the top of the pile of pastel towels there came a great flurry of movement and as it swept towards her she felt a swift flash of pain in her hand.

Instinctively she banged the cupboard door closed. It shook, bounced slightly and then the latch caught, containing the harsh chattering within.

Panic had made the adrenalin burst under her skin like pin-pricks and swearing softly she looked at her hand. A bead of blood had welled up and she turned on the tap and rinsed her hand under the cold water, wincing at the sound of wings dashing and flapping against the door. Her heart was thumping but as she patted her hand dry the flapping stopped, replaced by jittery, clicking noises of distress.

She glanced at the windowsill and wished she hadn't drunk all her champagne.

She knew who to blame – Roger, she thought bleakly, looking warily at the airing cupboard door; Roger Elsworth, the St Francis of Stanmore. He actually fed pigeons on bird seed despite the fact they preferred Big Macs. William had joked that the three days that Roger, Sarah and their daughter Lottie had stayed with them had convinced him of the benefits of divorce and contraception. So she'd hit him with *The Times*. And secretly agreed.

'And on my towels,' she muttered as the magpie kept up the barrage of noise. Well, the Russian roulette victims were going to have to have old ones. She whipped three crumpled, white hand towels from the rail and hurried back downstairs.

The game was still in progress.

The shock, she thought, must have sobered her up

because suddenly it didn't seem so much fun anymore. She reached for a bottle and refilled her glass.

The weapons tray was half-way round again, having passed Hugh, and Jean, Hugh's naturist friend, and presumably Roger, because it was now being offered to Sarah who was stretching back from it with an expression of distaste and fastidiousness.

'I don't have to, do I?' she pleaded to her husband.

Roger, his bald head tanned from skiing, smirked at her. 'Go on,' he said, 'you might be lucky.'

Sarah narrowed her eyes at him malevolently and then she turned to Catrin, reaching over to rest her hand on her arm.

'I don't have to, do I, Catrin?'

Catrin put thoughts of the bird in the airing cupboard out of her mind. 'Of course not,' she said loyally.

'Yes, you do,' Roger said.

'Do you know how much this dress cost?'

'Aim it at your head then, darling,' Roger suggested.

Sarah pouted. 'You think the hair was free?' Still, she stretched out a manicured hand and let her fingers dance for a moment over the tray. She picked up the orange party popper and fired at herself, changing her mind at the last moment so that a high-velocity charge of camembert and fresh cream skimmed her head and exploded on the wall behind her. She giggled nervously and turned to look at the wall.

'Give her a yammer as a forfeit,' Hugh said, banging the table with his glass.

Tim, an old schoolfriend of William, was sitting diagonally across from Catrin. He smoothed back his thinning hair with one hand and cut a piece of stilton with the other.

'I'll do it.' He mixed champagne, port and stilton in a small glass and handed it to Sarah with a grin. Sarah took it and looked at it distastefully.

'I can't drink this,' she said.

Hugh banged the table with his glass again and the base snapped off. 'Oops.'

Sarah had shut her eyes. She jerked her head back, swallowed the contents of the glass and gagged for a moment on the cheese before looking at them through watering eyes that finally settled on Roger. 'I hope you're happy,' she said.

William glanced at Catrin. Her eyes caught his. He gave her a faint conspiratorial smile. From within their own happy marriage they saw signs of upheaval in others as a weakness.

'Make one for Roger,' he called across the table. 'He gloated.'

'You all gloated,' Roger protested.

'We cheered. It's not the same.'

Sarah looked mollified but suddenly, as though in a fade-out, the room fell silent.

Catrin had her back to the stairs and turned as a small voice behind her said with pompous indignation: 'Can't you all go home? I'm trying to sleep.'

Sarah and Roger's daughter, Lottie, was standing on the stairs wearing non-sexist striped pyjamas.

Sarah, still sporting a quiff of camembert and cream, leapt out of her chair with a frantic look in her eye, no doubt wondering how Penelope Leach would have played it.

'Now look what you've done,' she said to Roger through gritted teeth, and in a soothing, insincere voice to Lottie, 'We'll be quiet, darling. Let Mummy carry you back upstairs.'

'Not with that yucky stuff on your head,' Lottie said, retreating indignantly. Sarah followed her.

The table erupted into giggles.

'Thirty-three is not at all old for a woman,' Catrin said to no-one in particular, 'but four is.'

'What's the time?'

'Ten to.'

Catrin got up, pushed her chair back and followed Sarah to the bathroom.

'Hair all right?' she asked, glancing at the airing cupboard. All was quiet.

Sarah ducked her head for Catrin to look. 'Is it all off?'

'Spotless. Oh, just a dab of camembert there, I'll wipe it off for you.' She dabbed at Sarah's blonde hair. 'That's it.' She lifted the lavatory lid up and put the tissue in. 'By the way, what on earth is in the airing cupboard?'

Sarah looked at the cupboard door rather sheepishly. 'Ah,' she said. 'The magpie. We found it under the bridge this afternoon. Roger thought this was a great way to teach Lottie about death in a controlled environment.'

Catrin looked at her wryly as she washed her hands. 'What's Roger going to do, strangle it?'

'Is it still alive?' Sarah said, touching her earring uncertainly. 'Isn't it amazing, you're here in Central London and you have magpies in the garden.'

'Amazing is finding them in the airing cupboard,' Catrin said. 'You country types, we're going to have to use towels with magpie shit on them. Come on, let's go back down or else they'll have yammed in the New Year without us.'

They went into the kitchen and Catrin took two bottles of Bollinger out of the fridge and gave them to Sarah. She took two herself and they returned to the dining room where Hugh was accepting raucous advice on how to solve a puzzle that had fallen out of a cracker.

'It's nearly midnight,' Catrin said as they put the bottles on the table. William got up and started taking the foil off.

'Put Moira Stewart on,' Tim said.

'Isn't she the newsreader?' his wife, Lisa, asked irritably.

'No, that's Moira Anderson.'

'You always get them mixed up,' she said, hitting him with a spoon, and they tumbled into the sitting room which was full of balloons and switched the television on.

Catrin and Jean distributed glasses. The grandfather clock began to chime midnight.

They lapsed into silence as the seconds sounded by. On the eleventh stroke Hugh gave a premature shout. On the twelfth, to the shout of 'Happy New Year' they toasted each other and tipsily joined hands to sing 'Auld Lang Syne'. Catrin, as always, found she'd forgotten the words.

'Let's do the fireworks!' William said, as whichever Moira it was launched into the second verse.

'He's always been a pyromaniac,' Catrin said to Jean, out of the corner of her mouth.

Jean wrinkled her nose and gave William a sideways glance. 'Pervert.'

They went out into the dark, cold garden. Frost glistened on the grass from the lights of the house.

Catrin, Sarah and Jean huddled together under the trees that sheltered them from London's alien orange sky. Behind them Lisa grumbled at having to come out at all. A dark shadow that was William crouched over the fireworks, lighting the touchpapers.

He hurried away as with a hiss the fireworks agitated, spewing out sparks in a rush of light that coloured their faces red.

'Aaaaahhhh . . .'

Someone handed Catrin a glass of Armagnac. It blazed through her as she watched the sparks from the fireworks burst in the sky, spreading themselves wide as they scribbled down the night like glitter thrown across black paper.

Hugh came and stood next to her and he put his heavy arm around her shoulder. 'I wonder what's in store for us all,' he said reflectively, holding his glass up to the showers of light.

'That's up to us,' Catrin said.

'Ah! You think it's as simple as that?' He sounded amused.

'And isn't it?'

When he didn't answer her she linked her arm in his. 'Life is what you make it,' she said. 'It's a script that you write for yourself. You choose what you want from life and then you make it happen.'

'I'm sure you do,' Hugh said lightly. 'And where does fate come in?'

He sounded amused and Catrin felt a flicker of annoyance. She wondered whether he was mocking her. 'Our fate is in our own hands, don't you think?'

Hugh sipped his drink. 'You make it sound so simple.'

'But?'

'Oh, no buts –'

He started to say something else but his words were drowned out by staccato cracks from white blazing stars that lit up the sky and drifted, spent, over the emptiness of Regent's Park.

Catrin glanced back at the house. Through the half-open curtains she could see the lights of the Christmas tree. She looked at the garden sheltering their guests, their friends; the fireworks were lighting it up like a grotto. She smiled to herself. Fireworks; for celebration.

Later, when they were saying goodbye, a red balloon that had broken free shied away from the gust from the opening door. It scooted in a circle and drifted out with Hugh and Jean, floating around their ankles anxiously. They laughed and caught it and got into a chugging cab.

Catrin watched with William until the rear lights of the taxi disappeared down the road and then she heard a small voice behind them. 'Catrin? Where's my mummy?' Lottie's small hands fiddled with a loose red button on her pyjama top as William closed the door.

'Hello, Lottie. She and Daddy have gone to bed, I think.'

'Have I missed the fireworks?'

'Yes. But William's kept some sparklers for you.'

This information was accepted in silence. The button was tugged harder. 'I didn't have a story tonight,' Lottie said.

'Didn't you? In that case you'll have to ask Mummy to tell you two tomorrow,' Catrin said treacherously. 'Come on, let's get you to bed.'

She picked up the small, warm figure and took her back to the guest room.

Lottie got into bed reluctantly and leaning back on her stiff little arms she stared at Catrin. 'I can't sleep without a story,' she said, matter-of-factly.

'Oh.' Catrin sat on the edge of the bed. 'I could tell you a poem,' she capitulated. 'It's a poem with a story in it.'

'Is it *Hiawatha*?'

'Is it *Hiawatha*? Do you know what the time is? Right, this is the poem. ''For want of a nail, the shoe was lost. For want of a shoe, the horse was lost. For want of a horse, the rider was lost. For want of a rider, the battle was lost. For want of a battle, the kingdom was lost, all for the want of a horseshoe nail.'''

Lottie continued to look at her expectantly.

'That's it,' Catrin said, getting up and smoothing the creases out of her dress.

'It was very short.'

'Yes. It's enough, though, isn't it? From losing a nail to losing a kingdom?'

'It's silly.'

'I quite agree. But that's the olden days for you. Goodnight, Lottie.'

'Goodnight.'

'Sleep well – and – Happy New Year.'

Catrin went back downstairs and found William at the dining room table up-ending the last of the champagne into a glass. A streamer was draped round his neck.

He smiled up at Catrin and passed her the glass.

'Happy New Year, you,' he said.

'Happy New Year.'

'Come here.'

Catrin smiled and sat on his knee, curling her hand around his neck. She pulled her dark hair away from her face and put her cheek to his, feeling his bristles prickle against her skin. She stroked them with her finger, making them rasp.

William held her finger and kissed the tip of it with his moist mouth and pressed his nose against hers. 'You know Hugh's Jean, she said naturists refer to us modest people as textiles,' he said. 'Seems to think it's we who are odd.'

'I expect she felt a bit over-dressed.'

They grinned at each other. Catrin looked closely into William's slightly unfocused eyes. His irises were huge and she tried to see herself in them but it was like looking into the black lagoon. She moved her head back and let the flickering candlelight reach them.

'Your eyes are the colour of wet slate,' she said softly.

'Ah, Catrin, it's the Welsh in you. How many English women would know the colour of a decent piece of slate?' His hand was on the tiny red buttons at the back of her dress.

Catrin felt his fingers climb down them slowly, each in turn. She felt her red silk dress loosen until it slithered down around her waist. The heat from her body made her perfume drift up in a warm scent and she shivered.

With gentle hands, William held her hair away from her face and began to kiss her. Catrin shut her eyes

14

and felt his mouth move to her temples, eyelids, cheeks, lips; the warm moisture cooling on the places he had left. William's mouth moved to her neck; he nuzzled the place where the blood throbbed through her artery, his warm breath stroked her skin moments before his lips rested on her throat and moved down to her chest, breasts, thorax, her navel.

He put his hands underneath her bottom and lifted her up to ease off her dress. As she stood in her underwear, one eye on the door, she felt goose-bumps tingle on her skin as her kissed her abdomen, moved his warm mouth to her pubic hair underneath her panties, then to her thighs, and her knees, and down to her ankles, to her toes and their red nails, to the back of her knees, her bottom, the small of her back. . . He stood behind her and held her tightly, his arms folded across her.

'Time for bed,' he said, his warm breath in her ear.

Catrin looked at the party poppers, the streamers, the bottles, the glasses, the end of the party.

'I love you,' William said, his mouth pressed against her ear.

Catrin twisted her head to look at him, took his warm hand and kissed it, feeling it furl around her face. It smelled vaguely of his woody aftershave. She picked up her dress from the floor and blew out the candles. Their smoke swirled palely in the air.

On their way to bed, dragging their clothes in one hand and holding hands with the other, William lifted up their joined hands and asked her how she'd cut herself.

'There's a magpie in the airing cupboard,' she said, tossing her hair away from her face.

Death in a controlled environment. On their towels. She smiled at his expression and squeezed his hand gently. 'Just one. For sorrow,' she said.

2

It was twenty to midnight and Jonathan Wade, Chief Executive of Midlands Television and so he'd often been told, every woman's idea of a romantic hero, strode into the kitchen to find, to his dismay, that his wife was still on the phone.

'An ovarian cyst, darling,' she was saying, swinging a sheer-, black-stockinged leg. 'The size of a grapefruit, but of course they always tell you that. No, of course they didn't let me keep it. Anyway, the point is, everything is fine and we're staying in tonight to conceive.'

Jonathan opened the fridge after first checking his reflection in its black-lacquered door.

'We'll have a maternity nurse, then a nanny. Maybe two, for shift work. Jonathan? He loves the idea.' She put her hand over the mouthpiece and called to Jonathan who was still crouching by the fridge, 'It's Henry, darling.'

Jonathan looked over at his wife. 'Bloody Henry,' he mouthed and she gave him an encouraging smile.

He took a beer out of the fridge, closed the door and stared at the can. Beer? On New Year's Eve? He looked at himself in the fridge door again and opened it and replaced the can.

'Of course we hadn't been trying for long when they

17

found it. Terribly common apparently; one just doesn't realise it because they're hidden.'

Jonathan, still staring into the fridge, raised his dark eyebrows. It was true; damned right they were hidden. You couldn't conceal a grapefruit-sized cyst just anywhere.

He took out a bottle of Chardonnay and closed the fridge door. As he passed his wife he brandished the bottle at her.

She smiled at him briefly and he took the bottle and two glasses into the sitting room, negotiating the obstacle course created by the many tables that were dotted around, and sat down with a feeling of relief.

He liked the room. He liked the whole house, despite the tables, which were covered in what he always thought of as trinket boxes but his wife always referred to by name as though they were pets: 'my Limoges, my Doulton.' The house was carpeted throughout in green and reminded him of the golf course. The only room he disliked was the black kitchen, which didn't matter because he hardly ever went in there. Nor, for that matter, did Amelia.

He poured himself a glass of wine and leaned back on the sofa to drink it.

It was New Year's Eve and they were going to conceive a child. He'd estimated that he had, milling about inside him, two hundred and forty million sperm ready to fight for the honour of fertilizing Amelia's egg; two hundred and forty million sperm which had been saved up over the last month for this one night, The Night of the Red Asterisk. Amelia had taped her ovulation calendar to her bathroom door and when he'd passed it earlier it had seemed to wink at him in encouragement. Soon the nursery – 'All pastels darling, don't want it to suffer over-stimulation in the early months.' – would have his child in it, a small child, hopefully a boy, hopefully a small version of himself.

He crossed his ankle over his knee, pushed away his dark hair from his tanned brow and smiled. He hoped the boy would have a dimple in his chin, as he did. And dark hair. And blue eyes.

He looked at the ceiling reflectively; looks mattered.

He was suddenly aware that the wine glass was cold in his hand and with a tanned thumb he carelessly wiped the condensation away and went back to his thoughts.

Life was so much easier with good looks.

He was still, even after five years of marriage, his wife's idea of the perfect man. He knew it because she told him so. She told him that he was straight out of a Mills and Boon. Blue-eyed, dark-haired, lean and naturally muscular . . . Jonathan tensed his stomach muscles automatically and put the wine glass to his lips again. Arrogant . . .

'Darling, Henry sends his best,' Amelia said, coming towards him with an empty glass. 'I told him all. He wanted to know why we were staying in.'

'I heard you,' Jonathan said, pouring her the wine.

'He is a dear.' She cocked her head and looked into his deep blue eyes. 'He thought that after the baby was born we should go away. Say, November? He's still got that place in Antigua; he went there himself after his sons were born.'

Probably why his wife left him, Jonathan mused.

'Yes, why not,' he said. It might be nice once they had a baby. Correction; if.

'You're looking at me strangely.'

'No, darling, we'll go.'

'You think I won't conceive,' Amelia said coolly, stroking her thumb and forefinger down the stem of the glass. 'You think it's my age.'

Jonathan jerked upright and the wine spilt out of his glass and on to his trouser leg. He plucked the cold, wet fabric away from his leg. 'Don't be ridiculous,' he said sharply, 'you're only thirty-eight. That's not old.' Because if it was, thirty-nine would be old too. And he was thirty-nine. 'It's young. Look at what's her name, that actress – forties, wasn't she?'

Amelia continued to look at him intently. Then she sank down onto the floor at his feet. He patted her short hair vaguely. Then, deliberately, as it wasn't a night on which to fall out, he traced his finger along the continuous line from her forehead to her nose.

'I love your head,' he said.

'You say the nicest things,' she answered.

'Look – I only thought – I mean, if it doesn't happen –'

'It will happen.'

Jonathan smiled. He believed her. It was true, things always happened the way Amelia wanted, she made sure of that. Their marriage for instance; it puzzled him now, the way he had got married to Amelia, almost as if he'd had no hand in it. Of course, it was not that he hadn't wanted to, but she was rather too, well, rather too ugly for what he'd had in mind for a bride. A buzzing came into his head again. Well yes, all right, he'd also imagined someone younger.

'I hope it looks like you,' Amelia said.

'Yes.' He said it rather too fervently. He'd heard someone describe Amelia as '*jolie laide*', which as far as he knew meant jolly ugly. He was aware of Amelia looking up at him again.

He smiled, showing his white teeth. It was his practised, romantic hero smile but he suddenly wondered if he looked ingratiating.

'Let's go to bed,' he said. Put those two hundred and forty million sperm to the test. 'Whatever happens, it's nobody's fault.'

The phrase, since the discovery of the cyst, had become Amelia's motto.

And as he got to his feet and took her hand he was rewarded by the sunburst of Amelia's rare smile.

They went to Amelia's room to make love; she insisted. Amelia's room was all blue apart from the carpet and it could get disconcerting, it felt like being at sea. Jonathan was still holding on to the Chardonnay, reasoning that champagne was a little premature.

He undressed and got into her cool bed and looked up at the blue canopy overhead. It was like lying outside under the sky. He shut his eyes for a moment and awoke with a start as Amelia slipped into bed next to him.

Jonathan rolled over and leaned on his elbow to look at her.

'Are you ready for this, Wade?' she asked him easily.

'Ready? I've been ready for the last four weeks.'

'A quickie, or a slow one?'

Jonathan grinned. 'Can't make a baby with a

quickie,' he said, easing himself on top of her. Her slim body always felt fragile underneath him and never more so than now. He moved tentatively inside her and tried to think of golf swings. Why had he said it would be a slow one? The month's abstinence wasn't conducive to a leisurely pace.

Amelia wriggled beneath him. 'Don't do that!' he said with alarm but even as he spoke the race was on – more of a sprint, really – and with a swift burst of sensation in his groin he fell heavily onto Amelia. She began to laugh in his ear.

Jonathan raised his head. 'Did you catch me up?'

'No. But it doesn't matter.'

Jonathan rolled off her and looked up at the blue canopy.

He'd done his bit. All those sperm . . . it was up to her now.

'Give me five minutes,' he said, grinning, 'and I'll make it up to you.'

She gave him another glimpse of her smile and touched his cheek in a rare gesture of intimacy. 'Give me a pillow.'

Jonathan pulled one of his from beneath his head. Amelia raised her bottom off the bed and wedged the pillow under her hips.

'What's that for?'

'To help things along,' Amelia said. She patted her abdomen. 'Bon voyage,' she said softly.

The words made Jonathan think of the sea again. He lay on his back, staring at the canopy which was dancing before his eyes. 'Amelia – if it doesn't work – I don't have to wait another month, do I?'

'Of course not,' Amelia promised. There was a

pause before she added, casually, 'Is five minutes up yet?'

He awoke, frightened and disorientated with a cold, dead thing lying across his chest. To his relief he realised it was his arm.

He sat up in bed and rubbed it vigorously until it began to prickle with pain as the blood returned.

Amelia was asleep beside him, on her back, her lower body making a mound under the bedcovers. She was still lying on the pillow.

He gently touched the bedclothes over her abdomen. That was what she would look like when she was pregnant. God, he loved her.

He looked at her for a few moments before slowly easing himself out of bed.

It would be New Year's Day, now, he thought nostalgically. He was sorry to have missed the celebrations.

He went to the window and pulled back the drapes and looked out. The garden was vast and dark and silent. He loved the garden. Sometimes he saw foxes listening there, heads cocked before dashing away; city foxes, streetwise, searching rubbish as a way of life. But tonight the garden was still and strange.

He closed the drapes, happy to be back in the warmth of the room.

She hadn't moved. He would have liked to have woken her, talked to her but he didn't really dare.

He pulled on a bathrobe and went into her bathroom. The red asterisk winked at him again from the door.

He went down the hall and into the unfriendly

darkness of his own room and he looked at the clock's luminous hands and saw to his amazement that it was not yet midnight.

A swift thrill of happiness spread through him and he hurried down the stairs into the entrance hall where the Christmas tree stood. He switched on the lights and they twinkled in the draught.

And as he stood there the small clock on the console table began to chime.

Ting.

Jonathan listened to the hollow ring that measured time gone.

Ting.

He thought of First Footers and pieces of coal.

Ting.

Of parties reaching their peak without him.

Ting.

Of drunken kisses and 'Auld Lang Syne'.

Ting.

Of guests getting peckish for fried-egg sandwiches.

Ting.

Of avoiding reproachful looks from the one to drive.

Ting.

And the mystery of the lost shoe.

Ting.

And the first close look at the appalling sum on the off-licence bill.

Ting.

The sad return of the egg sandwich.

Ting.

And the hopeful search for the Resolve.

Ting.

Of wives' threatening calls to Al Anon.

Ting.

He was going to open that champagne. A New Year was something to celebrate, it really was.

He hurried to the kitchen and found a bottle of Louis Roederer. It wasn't chilled but he opened it anyway, a little carelessly. Some of it bubbled onto the black marble worktop and he traced a heart in it with his finger as an antidote to his fear that underneath the marble in gold lettering he'd find engraved the initials RIP.

He sipped and shuddered as the bubbles burst in his mouth. He felt light-headed and oddly happy.

He took the champagne back into the entrance hall and stood by the Christmas tree and looked at himself in a red glass ball, all fish-faced and rotund. He reached out to touch the ball and a shower of pine needles pattered to the floor.

He, Jonathan, Chief Executive of Midlands TV, was a lucky man.

Hugging the bottle to him, he left the fairy lights on and went back up the stairs to bed.

3

Marilyn Northcott, Catrin's cleaning lady, was spending New Year's Eve in the Duke of Wellington for only one reason – it was that she fancied her married neighbour, Harry Blake. If it hadn't been for Harry she would be locked in the relative comfort of Catrin's bathroom instead of sitting where she was on the lid of a lavatory in the pub. They hadn't even been out and he owed her one.

Suddenly she paused with her finger still in her pot of Dermablend as she heard someone come into the cloakroom. She held her breath until she heard the door close on the cubicle next to hers and then she relaxed and continued to cover up her freckles laboriously. Freckles, she thought disgustedly, wasn't the word for them. They were huge brown daubs that covered her fine, even features as hideously as graffiti.

She angled the mirror and frowned. As the walls were decorated in a shrill shade of pink she was finding it hard to decide whether her face was terribly flushed or whether it was merely the reflection of the paintwork.

The sound of energetic vomiting came from the next cubicle.

Marilyn grimaced and carried on with her task.

The door of the cubicle opened and the sound of

gargling joined that of a running tap. The tap was switched off. There was a final, dismal groan, and the cloakroom door opened and closed.

For a moment all was quiet, but then the cloakroom door opened again and a familiar voice called her name.

'Marilyn? Are you in there?'

'Won't be a minute, Theresa.'

'Hurry up, will you, I'm desperate.'

'Use the other one,' Marilyn suggested, not wanting to be rushed.

'Can't. There's sick on the floor.'

Marilyn, tilting her mirror again, decided the high colour was, after all, just the walls.

'Coming,' she said, dabbing at her face. She put her make-up back in her bag and came out of the cubicle to check the state of her complexion in the speckled mirror on the wall.

'About time,' Theresa said, dashing past her.

Marilyn leaned over the washbasins towards the mirror and was satisfied. Her glossy copper-coloured hair swung around her face and she hooked it back behind one ear. Her red hair and freckles were the blessing and curse of her Irish father and to disguise the curse she always wore make-up. Even her ex-husband had never, in five years of marriage and during the birth of twins, seen her without it. Her one great relief after having the boys was to find that they'd inherited their father's opaque, cream skin.

She looked at her watch. It was twenty to twelve.

'Any sign of Harry yet?' she asked.

Theresa groaned from inside the cubicle. 'How would I know? You can hardly move in there.'

27

'Yeah, great . . . he'd better come. I only came because of him. I could have gone to Catrin's, you know. She was having champagne, the lot . . .' Marilyn, watching herself talk, was not quite happy with her lips. She opened her make-up bag again and took out a lip pencil. She outlined her well-shaped mouth carefully and reapplied her bright red lipstick. She put the cap back on it. 'I could have taken a guest.'

'Me?' Theresa asked hopefully.

'No, not you, you twit, a man.'

Theresa snorted from inside the cubicle. 'She only wanted you there so that you would help her clean up afterwards.'

Marilyn looked at herself thoughtfully. 'No, she didn't. She likes me, in her own way. For instance, she never refers to me as her cleaning lady. Not to my face, anyway.'

Her last words were drowned out by the sound of the lavatory flushing.

Theresa emerged and washed her hands. 'She makes you work though, doesn't she? I mean, mine's not bothered about her oven. I squirt Mr Sheen in the air and make a cup of tea and watch Cable.'

Marilyn laughed and moved away from the mirror for Theresa. 'So?' she said. 'Perks of the job. I'll tell you something, though – she might have a good job but Catrin's hopeless at housework. She didn't even have a mop until I started working for her. I told her I'd only work for her on condition she bought one.' She took out her perfume and sprayed the air. 'That sick is making me sick.'

'Yeah.'

Theresa was looking at herself as though she wasn't

the person she'd expected to see in the mirror. She tugged forward strands of gelled hair.

'Have you seen Terry yet?' Marilyn asked her as she licked her fingers and twirled the edges of her fringe.

'No.' Theresa sniffed glumly. 'Great night this is going to be, New Year's Eve and no men around.'

Marilyn nudged her out of the way, glanced in the mirror, gave her hair a last flick of the comb and shut her handbag. 'I bet they'll come,' she stated confidently. 'We've dropped big enough hints. Come on, let's get another drink. Are you still on the Pils?'

'I thought I'd have a short. Port and lemon.'

They opened the door that led into the bar, entering yeasty warmth, noise, and the thick haze of cigarette smoke which muted the flashes of green and red from the tinsel overhead. Marilyn coughed and being taller than Theresa looked over the mass of heads to see if she could see Harry in the crowd.

The pub was festooned with Christmas decorations. They hung, bobbing, from every inch of the ceiling, making the bar seem smaller and more cramped than usual. The DJ in the corner was playing old Christmas songs and occasionally voices would lift in tune with it, singing a few remembered lines over the shout of multiple conversations.

'Can you see Terry?' Theresa yelled in Marilyn's ear.

'No.' But Marilyn could see Harry. Her heart gave a kick of recognition.

He was leaning on the bar; a huge man with short curly dark hair and a mole on one ear that made him look as though he was wearing a stud. He had on a pale blue denim shirt over a white T-shirt and he looked like a lumberjack.

29

Marilyn, staring blankly so as not to give the game away, wondered what it would feel like to be held in those massive arms. She was pretty confident that, sooner or later, she would find out. After all, she didn't have to go far to look for him. He lived in the flat above hers; he lived in the flat above hers with his wife, Debbie; the fly in Marilyn's Dermablend.

Marilyn watched him turn to someone by his side and recognised the bleached white-blonde of Debbie's short hair and the excitement that the kick of recognition had set off in her evaporated as quickly as it had come. He'd brought his wife along with him. He hadn't taken the hint after all.

Marilyn's spirits fell. Great. How was she supposed to seduce her neighbour when he'd brought his wife along?

'Harry's over there,' Theresa said helpfully, jumping up and down like a little Jack Russell and pulling at her arm.

'I know. So is Debbie.'

'Well,' Theresa shouted philosophically, 'it is New Year's Eve. He couldn't really leave her at home, could he?' Her voice softened in admiration and was almost drowned out, but Marilyn heard her breathe: 'Look at those muscles.'

'Harry's?'

'No, Debbie's, you fool. She's still doing that weight training then.'

'Yeah . . .' Marilyn swept her coppery hair back from her face. Maybe, she thought wretchedly, she didn't stand a chance with Harry after all. A 'hello' from time to time wasn't really anything to get excited about. It was just that she sort of had a thing about married men – there were so many pluses – they could never stay the night for a start, so she didn't have to worry about waking up minus her make-up . . .' Are you going to get us a drink?' she asked Theresa half-heartedly.

'You go. You can stand by him and chat him up.'

'No, I'm not going. You go, go on, here's the money.'

As Theresa pushed through the crowd Marilyn looked indifferently at the faces round the bar, some of which she knew, some of which were strangers'. She didn't fancy any of them. What a waste of a New Year's Eve, she thought bleakly. She could have been at home with the boys, watching a video. Or at Catrin's with . . . a guest. Despite what Theresa thought, Catrin was all right, really. And she paid well.

She saw Theresa sidle to the bar right next to Harry. Harry was looking at Theresa now and there was Debbie bending forward and – Marilyn let her face go a blank as Harry lifted his eyes from Theresa's to look straight over at her. She flicked her gaze away, looked at the decorations on the ceiling, half of which seemed to be falling down, and felt a blush burn up her neck and through her face. She hoped the Dermablend would hide it. She'd kill Theresa, though.

And there was Theresa, coming back through the crowd towards her, leaving disgruntled expressions and spilled drinks in her wake, with two large glasses of port and lemon held up over her head.

'Harry bought them,' she said triumphantly, holding them like trophies. 'I told him you were here.'

Marilyn turned her back to the bar. 'Subtle, aren't you,' she said, looking into her drink. 'What did he say?'

'I think he does fancy you, you know.' Her pale face was curious. 'Has Debbie had a boob job?'

'Why? Does it look as if she has?'

'Weight trainers are usually flat-chested, aren't they.'

'Maybe Harry likes boobs.'

Theresa looked at her, shocked. 'Marilyn! Don't you even know THAT?'

'I hardly know him . . .' It wasn't his brain but his size, she supposed, that she went for. Her ex-husband Dave, for all he was a nice bloke, was a weedy-looking sort who always got into fights. Tough, but weedy-looking. A terrier sort of a person; whereas Harry was more your St Bernard. 'Anyway, I've got to start somewhere. You think he was interested?'

'Doesn't double port and lemon sound interested enough? At least he's here. Not like Terry.'

'Did you tell him the right pub?'

'Ha ha.' Suddenly Theresa jabbed her. 'Harry's looking at you again.'

'Don't stare at him! Hey – there's Terry over there –'

'Where?'

'Look for the space and you'll see Terry's head below it.'

'He's not that short.'

Marilyn shrugged. Being five-ten, most men were short, to her.

'He's probably been here all the time,' Theresa said, pleased. 'You don't mind if I have a word with him, do you?'

'No. I think I'll go home.'

'Don't go – it's nearly midnight.'

And as Theresa pushed her way through the crowd the DJ began announcing the last record before the countdown to the New Year.

In the steaming pub the air of excitement grew. Marilyn clutched her glass and realised she had finished her drink but now that Theresa had gone there was no-one to fetch her another.

The music stopped and in the relative quiet the DJ started the countdown and was joined by a roar of voices.

'TEN!'

'NINE!'

'EIGHT!'

'SEVEN!'

'SIX!'

'FIVE!'

'FOUR!'

'THREE!'

'TWO!'

And suddenly, unexpectedly, the whole room plunged into darkness.

Being blind shut everyone up.

It was eerie that it all should go black just on the last stroke. It was as if the end of the world had come.

Marilyn made a whimpering noise in her throat; she didn't like it.

There was a surge of hot bodies and for a moment she found herself squeezed and lifted off her feet. She stumbled, strange sour breath on her face, and a small pale orange flare flashed from a match and burned bravely above the dark bobbing heads, and another and another, and an approving murmur began above the cursing and jostling.

There was a drunken shout: 'Put the bloody lights on, will you?'

A woman squealed, but the sound was muffled. The murmur grew. Someone pushed Marilyn in the small of the back and she threw her hands out in front of her, afraid, in the middle of the anonymous crowd. She touched a wool jumper, itchy under her fingertips. 'Oi,' came a voice from it.

Marilyn felt the gloom in her nose and her mouth, gagging her. She tried to keep her eyes on the flickering flames from disposable lighters – the matches had kept burning out.

'Hey!' shouted a voice from the smoky dark, 'what's going on?'

'The electricity's gone,' the DJ shouted back. 'Happy New Year, anyway!'

And they suddenly remembered why they were there. A small scattered cheer went up.

'Give us a kiss!' came a camp voice nearby.

'Marilyn?' whispered a voice in her ear.

She jerked her head around, hope lifting her spirits. 'Harry?'

'Happy New Year . . .'

With unerring aim the dark shape of Harry dipped towards her and his lips touched hers. She felt her heart begin to race. His lips were sweet and firm. He broke off the kiss for a moment, and then kissed her twice more, quickly, his hands on her shoulders as large as she'd hoped they'd be. Marilyn felt suddenly dreamy. It was lovely kissing Harry in the dark. She raised her head for more.

Harry's mouth met hers again and she kissed in the smell of him, her tongue retreating from his tenuous touch, his saliva sweet in her mouth, his breath smelling sugary, almost medicinal.

'What are you drinking?' she whispered to him.

'Cherry brandy. Come here.' He gave her a last quick kiss and then he was gone.

Marilyn looked towards the centre of the pub where a small circle of lighter flames burned erratically.

Everyone, to her, seemed to be kissing in the gloom.

'Happy New Year, girl,' said a voice next to her.

'Yes,' she said vaguely and all of a sudden the power came back on and they stood blinking at each other in the harsh brightness, startled at being exposed again.

Marilyn looked towards the bar. Harry, miraculously, was back on his seat as though nothing had happened. Her heart was still beating faster, it hadn't slowed down yet.

Slowly Harry turned, looked at her once and turned away.

Well, Marilyn thought; not *quite* as though nothing had happened. Even from that distance she could see that Harry's mouth was branded with gashes of bright red lipstick.

'No luck, then?' Marilyn asked Theresa as they flooded out of the pub at closing time, two women in the early hours of New Year's Day getting ready to walk home alone.

Theresa sniffed in disgust. 'Terry said he was going back to being a good Catholic.'

Marilyn shivered and fastened her coat. The night was cold and frost glittered on the pavement like discarded tinsel. She pushed her hands deeper into her pockets and made fists of her hands. She wished she'd brought her gloves. 'What's that supposed to mean?'

'He'll see me, but no sex.'

Marilyn sighed. 'A waste of time then.'

Theresa folded her arms and tucked her hands under her armpits. 'Oh, I don't know,' she said. 'I thought I might become a Catholic too, then we can have sex legitimately.'

They both looked up as a convoy of cars came past, horns blaring.

'HAPPY NEW YEAR!'

'Same to you,' Theresa shouted back hopefully. 'Anyway, what do you think?'

Marilyn finally fastened the top button of her coat. Her breath was misting in the cold air as she considered the question. 'If you became a Catholic and you and Terry had sex, it would mean you were both sinning. In other words, if you became a Catholic it would be twice as bad.'

Theresa stamped her feet to warm them. 'I wish we'd had another port and lemon,' she said. 'It would have warmed us up.'

'I wish I'd had a cherry brandy.'

In the absence of any taxis they began to walk together along the road.

'All right, then,' Theresa said. 'I'll tell him what you've just said, and then say that as I'm not a Catholic it's only half as bad as it could be. What do you think?'

Marilyn made a face and shrugged. 'It's worth a try,' she said.

She looked up at the orange tinted night sky, thinking of Harry. A new year had begun. It was looking, so far, much the same as the old one, she thought wryly.

A small commotion behind them made her stop and turn.

Theresa retraced her steps and came to a stop beside her. 'Isn't that Harry?'

'Yes. And Debbie.'

'Why don't you walk home with them?'

Marilyn, hearing the word 'lipstick' feature heavily in the conversation, pulled her sleeves down over her hands. Her fingers were freezing.

A new year. The frost on the pavements took on a new sparkle. Maybe not quite the same as the old one after all.

'I'm safer by myself,' she grinned. She tugged Theresa's jacket and they hurried, giggling together, up the road.

4

He bought me Poison, Frances Bennett, one of SETV's business managers, thought morosely.

She swung her blonde hair away from her face and looked around the small Italian restaurant with distaste.

More than one male diner was watching this glum, beautiful blonde who was sitting alone but she was used to that. She stared over their heads, hardly noticing them. She had more important things on her mind. Alex had bought her Poison and she was about to find out why.

Strings of fairy lights were hooked up on the wall and, looking up, she found she was sitting directly below a green bulb, the glow of which made her look like Frankenstein's bride. Frowning, she moved her seat forward. It wasn't that she cared what Michael Zephyr thought; she wouldn't have let anyone see her looking green.

She twisted her blonde hair into a hank and let it go. It fell into shape like in a shampoo commercial.

She leaned forward to look at the candle flickering raggedly in the Chianti bottle and her gaze drifted to the wax-blemished label. It wasn't the kind of place she cared to be seen in, far less spend the last few hours of New Year's Eve, but Michael Zephyr, private investigator, had said he had some good news for her and it wasn't something she felt could wait.

'Anything to drink, Madam?'

Frances looked coldly at the waiter. 'No,' she said. She glanced at her watch. Zephyr was late.

She stroked her fingernail up the dark blonde curve of her widow's peak and wondered how to play it when she heard the news – should she scream, cry, faint, look tragic? How did people usually react when they found out their boyfriend's lover's name?

A few tears, she decided, might be nice. Not a faint; that indicated shock and it was no longer a shock, as she'd suspected it for months. So tears, certainly, with maybe an option on a small scream.

She couldn't believe it of Alex. To cool off, and then to buy her Poison. If she'd had any doubts then the Poison had confirmed them as surely as if she'd caught them together. To buy her Poison when the only perfume she ever wore was Gio . . .

The waiter came back to the table, smiling his relief. 'Madam? Your host has arrived,' he said, pulling out the chair opposite her for Michael Zephyr, private investigator, to sit on.

And Michael Zephyr sat, smoothing his blond hair down with the palms of his hands.

'You took your time,' Frances scowled. 'I've been here hours.'

Michael Zephyr grinned. He looked ill at ease and younger than he had in the familiarity of his own office. He put a cardboard folder on the table in front of him and jumped as the waiter placed a fake green leather menu on top of it, open.

'Oh,' Zephyr said, looking at the menu and then raising clear eyes to Frances. 'Have you decided?'

'Just a beer,' Frances said, 'I've lost my appetite.'

'Two beers,' Zephyr said to the waiter, who shook his head impatiently. 'This isn't a bar, this is a restaurant. You have to eat,' the waiter said, holding his small writing pad in front of him pointedly.

'Anything,' Frances said impatiently, waving a careless hand. 'Just bring whatever you like. Silly little man', she added to Zephyr under her breath.

'Spaghetti?'

'Whatever.'

'Me too,' said Zephyr, worried that the waiter had heard the not-so-quiet comment and would take his revenge when making out the bill.

'Now,' Frances said as the waiter walked away, 'tell me the news.' Her voice seemed to tremble gloriously and she felt it was the right touch. She leaned forward, away from the sinister green glow of the light and her blonde hair slithered against her shoulder and hung forward, skimming the table. 'Tell me it all.'

'Oh.' Zephyr opened his file up and turned over a couple of printed sheets of A4. He smiled. 'As I said, it's good news.' He looked up from the papers. 'Basically in the last four weeks Alex Martin has not seen any woman at all outside of work. That is, apart from you.'

Frances stared at his young, pleased face and a sense of disappointment began to drag inside her. She felt as though she was being pulled down somewhere she didn't want to go.

She braced her feet under the table, trapping

40

Zephyr's foot. 'What do you mean?,' she asked him sharply. 'That there isn't anyone else?'

'No, there's just you, that's all.'

Frances looked beyond him into the restaurant. 'Just me.'

Zephyr was disconcerted. He picked up his papers and looked at them again, carefully, as though he might have misread them. 'Yes,' he said finally, 'work, home, work, home. That's it, really. The only time he goes out is with you. Apart from that –' He shrugged briefly.

Frances leaned back in her seat, momentarily forgetting, in her shock, about the green light bulb. She glanced upwards and moved forward again.

'You know what he bought me for Christmas? Poison,' she said bitterly.

'Poison?' Zephyr looked troubled.

'I wear Gio. He knows I wear Gio. Who wears Poison? That's what you should have been finding out.' She looked with contempt at the report. 'I could have done better myself,' she said, pushing his file away from her. 'I want my money back.'

Zephyr swiftly steadied the old Chianti bottle which she had almost knocked over with the folder. Hot wax splashed onto his hand and he peeled it off with his thumbnail carefully. 'You haven't paid me anything yet,' he said reasonably.

Good judgement on my part, Frances thought shrewdly, and was forced to lean back quickly as two bowls of steaming spaghetti were put down in front of them.

'Pepper? Parmesan?'

Frances waved her hand. 'Look,' she said to Zephyr,

'he wanted to marry me. If there's no-one else then why should he change his mind?'

'I don't know,' Zephyr said.

'I'm his ideal woman,' Frances said. 'He loves blondes, he loves independent women, he loves women with a mind of their own. I'm his ideal woman . . .' her voice tailed off. The dragging feeling began again. Sadly, it wasn't unfamiliar. 'I was bald until I was three,' she said suddenly, looking at Zephyr intently. 'Then my hair grew like the golden fleece. I appeared in a Weetabix ad with my father. He ran off with the actress who played my mother. It put me off breakfast cereal, I can tell you . . .' Her voice tailed off again.

She stroked her hair with her pampered hand and looked away from the table to the other tables in the restaurant where people were eating New Year's Eve Celebration Dinners. Seven courses. All she could think of was Weetabix. Seven courses . . . she felt ill at the thought. It was no wonder, she thought contemptuously, that they were so fat.

She sipped her beer and looked at Zephyr who was chopping up his spaghetti with his knife. 'So you don't think there's anyone else. I wouldn't have come,' she said, 'if I'd known.'

Zephyr looked hurt. 'I thought you'd be glad it was good news,' he replied indignantly.

'Well it isn't, is it?'

She could have spent the evening with Alex. They would have gone out to a party hosted by some ex-member of an Australian soap. They could have gone to bed. Instead, here she was with some blond low-life of twenty-five who, although he'd come recommended by a couple of divorcees of the 'my-wife-from-hell' brigade, had not by any means come up trumps.

Thinking of the wives from hell reminded her suddenly that they'd both claimed to have been seduced by Zephyr.

Strange, she thought, watching him scoop up the remains of the chopped spaghetti with his spoon.

He looked up on the last mouthful and raised his eyebrows as he noticed her still full bowl.

'You haven't eaten yours.'

'I'm food combining.'

'Can I have it?'

Hovering on the verge of outrage, Frances found herself feeling suddenly touched by his question. There was a certain intimacy in having your food eaten by someone else. And of course it was the ultimate dining-out experience in dieting terms – she wouldn't put on a gram.

'Help yourself,' she said at last.

She stroked her hair. He was cute – his face looked newly-washed and shiny. Perhaps he didn't even shave yet. He looked innocence itself; couldn't be, of course, since the divorcees had been at him, but he looked untouched.

He had begun chopping her bowl of spaghetti with his knife. It was like being out with one's little brother, she thought; and a frisson of incestuous lust shivered through her.

'You're not supposed to chop it up,' she said. 'You wind it round your fork, look, I'll show you.' She leaned across and wound it as promised and held it to him for him to eat. His mouth closed around the food and she slid the fork out of his mouth and put it on her side plate.

She could see him looking at her.

Then with great concentration he wound his own fork around in the tangle of spaghetti, and although some ends flicked free on the journey to his mouth – a well-shaped mouth, she noticed – that was how he ate the rest of it. A quick learner, Frances thought. She was impressed.

Zephyr put his fork and spoon together in the bowl and looked at her with a shy smile. 'I thought you would be busy with it being New Year's Eve,' he said.

'I would have been.'

'Where did you tell Alex Martin you were going?'

'I didn't have to tell him anything. We had a blazing row and I walked out. That bloody perfume.' She sniffed thoughtfully. 'He would have come after me, once,' she said.

Zephyr nodded. His gaze rested on the empty bowl which had been his and which he'd now put in front of her.

'Would you like anything else?' he asked.

'Would you?'

Zephyr looked at her closely.

Frances put her hands behind her neck and lifted her hair up, gathering it all on the top of her head and letting it fall again.

Zephyr shivered.

'Is your office open?' Frances asked him. Her voice was playful, teasing, seductive and she bit her lower lip gently with her perfectly capped teeth.

Zephyr put his hand into his pocket and took out a

set of keys. He held them up and they jingled together softly. Frances stood up.

'I'll see you outside,' she said and she went to the cloakroom to repair her make-up while Zephyr paid the bill.

Michael Zephyr's office was functional – he liked the word. If the furnishings reminded one of a dentist's waiting room, well, that was because he'd bought them from a disillusioned dentist who was moving to Holland.

They weren't the sort of furnishings that a beautiful, tall blonde with a widow's peak that made her look like the angel of death should be seen in, but nevertheless, here he was, pressed against a blue, dirt-engrained, simulated-leather bench, being seduced, condomless, on New Year's Eve.

He'd slept with quite a few women since becoming a gumshoe. They usually wanted to sleep with him for revenge.

He'd thought, having told Frances Bennett that her man was, in fact, faithful – the first one ever – that revenge sex would be out of the question.

He was wrong.

He shivered as her cold hands slid under his pants and eased his Chinos down.

For a frighteningly long moment he thought he was going to be unsuccessful but suddenly it was all right and as she held him, gasping, he breathed deeply beneath her peppermint-smelling hair and, as he put it to himself afterwards, didn't let himself down.

He thought what a wonderful job it was, being a gumshoe.

It was just like in films. As far as sex was concerned, you couldn't lose.

Frances had never been one to feel guilty but she panicked as she stopped a cab just after midnight and gave the driver Alex's address.

The lights were off when she reached his flat. She kept her hand on the bell, convincing herself that he was out. He wasn't. His voice came over the intercom and she answered back defiantly in the chilly night,

'It's me!'

Instantly the door release catch buzzed and she smiled to herself.

He was waiting at the door as she stepped out of the lift. All he was wearing were the Calvin Klein boxer briefs she had given him for Christmas before he'd given her the wrong perfume. His dark hair was rumpled.

'Hello,' he said softly, 'I was hoping you'd come back. I've been trying to call you.'

Frances smiled a slow and secret smile. 'Aren't you going to let me in?'

Alex grinned suddenly. 'What a good sight you are,' he said, putting his arm around her.

As he closed the door behind her a clacking sound came from his living room.

'The Christmas cards keep falling over,' he said. 'Haven't got round to doing anything about it. Will you have a drink?'

Frances nodded. She needed one. And even more than that, she wanted a shower. The condomless seduction of Zephyr didn't seem such a good idea now.

The thought of pregnancy flashed into her mind and out again.

Alex poured the gin and tonic while she showered, and came rather damply into his bedroom and looked at the navy sheets that Alex had returned to. He was watching her, his hands behind his head as she got into the warm bed with a sense of relief and leaned over him to kiss him. Her golden hair covered them both like a canopy. In one swift movement she straddled him and watched his eyes widen in surprise.

'Just a minute,' he said, 'we'd better be careful, we wouldn't want –' He stretched out his hand to the chest at the side of his bed and took out a condom and tore the foil open with his teeth. He gave the condom to Frances and she put it on him reluctantly, wondering if she could surreptitiously split it with her nail.

If she were pregnant, Alex would marry her, she was sure of that. And no contraceptive was one hundred percent safe, was it? She smiled slowly and sweetly at Alex.

Zephyr might have done her a favour after all.

Alex pulled her to him.

'You're so beautiful,' he was murmuring in her ear, 'I love you, I love you, you know . . .' and with his whispered words her thoughts of abandonment and Weetabix and rejection drifted away.

She rather recklessly told him later, as he drove her home in the early hours of New Year's Day, that she'd hired a private detective to follow him.

He smiled as he listened to her, knowing the story might well not be true. He knew she had little regard

47

for the truth whether telling it or recognising it. It was what made her such a good negotiator at SETV but was, however, also the reason she was still only a business manager. And it made her hell to live with.

When he wasn't with her he thought of nothing but her, and when he was he knew he would be happier never seeing her again. She was self-centred but she obsessed him; he looked at every blonde woman he saw and they all failed, next to her.

He could smell her perfume, overpowering the Limes toilet water that he wore. Gio, of course it was. How had he got it wrong?

He pulled up in front of the Knightsbridge mansion block where she lived and suddenly wished she'd said she'd stay, but she got out of the car with the same alacrity with which she'd got out of his bed and she bent her head to look at him through the open window.

'I'll ring you. Perhaps tomorrow.'

Alex realised he was being dismissed. 'Oh,' he said, surprised. He'd hoped for a coffee, and maybe bed again.

'Bye, Alex,' she said, and with a toss of her hair she began walking swiftly away from the car into the night.

'I love you,' he called after her through the window and there was a note of fervour in his voice which amazed him; what if it were true? 'Goodbye,' he added softly but by now she was too far away to hear.

He started the engine and waited for her to wave. She didn't. The door of the building opened and let out a knife-edge of light before closing again. She'd gone.

As he drove off, pulling his hand in from the icy air, he realised sadly that not once that night had anyone blessed him with the optimistic promise of a Happy New Year.

PART TWO

For Want of a Nail

5

New Year's Day was coming to an end. Catrin pulled the bedroom curtains to against the city night and sat on the edge of the bed.

The house was quiet again; quiet and theirs once more.

Roger, Sarah and Lottie had left, and so had the magpie — Roger had finally caught it in a towel and released it grudgingly. He seemed to feel it had let them down by not dying.

'Lottie should have seen the majesty of death,' he'd said, peeved, as it flew away.

'You should have put it in the fridge,' William had said. 'Putting it in the airing cupboard must have revived it.'

Catrin had thought William was crazy even to suggest it.

'He would have, you know,' she said suddenly.

'What?'

'Put it in the fridge.'

There was a grunt from William who was lying on his side in bed, almost asleep. His face was lit by the lamp that curved over the bed and in its light Catrin could see his eyelids glistening like a child's.

On her bedside table was a goldfish bowl full of daffodils all closed up, a thank-you from Sarah.

Catrin took off her jeans. The house was quiet and still and William's breathing had relaxed into the hypnotic rhythm of sleep. She took off her sweater and undies and pulled her long hair to one side so as to take off her earrings. The butterfly on one of them was always stiff.

Hooking her buffed pink fingernail behind it she pulled hard but it didn't give; the butterfly continued clinging firmly to its gold stem.

Catrin felt her nail tear.

'Damn,' she said under her breath and held out her finger to inspect the damage. It was torn almost to the quick.

The emery boards were in the bathroom but she was naked now and William looked so warm and the bed so inviting . . . she slipped into the sheets and cuddled up to William.

He moved at the feel of her beside him and put his arm around her waist, pulling her nearer.

Catrin smiled and kissed his mouth gently and watched him blink in the light and smile as he shut his eyes again.

'Goodnight.'

'Mmmm.'

Traces of his bristles were catching the light like threads of fine gold wire. Catrin looked at him. She loved his face, loved the way his cheeks hollowed away from his fine cheekbones, the dark eyebrows that curved above his translucent eyelids.

He smiled again, not quite asleep. 'Your breath is tickling my face,' he said drowsily and he reached for her hand and threaded his fingers through hers.

She stretched out her leg and laid it across his and

they shifted, adjusting to each other, getting comfortable under the cool sheets.

Catrin reached up for the light switch. She snuggled down in the bed and in the warm and comfortable tangle of William's limbs she fell asleep.

Later, in the cold unpromising dark, she woke uneasily from a dream, disorientated and aware that some strange sound had disturbed her.

She reached for her watch and saw by its luminous hands that it was twenty past three.

She tried to remember the nightmare but the lingering threads of it trailed away from her memory and faded out of reach. Rolling onto her stomach she hugged her pillows to her; they were hand-plucked Polish goosedown pillows, bought at half-price in Harrods' sale. They felt soft and airy against her body, comfortable pillows, comfortable but not comforting.

She was aware of her forgotten dream dangling still in the back of her mind and she had the feeling that in it she'd neglected something – neglected a baby, put it somewhere and forgotten where.

Pop.

Jerking her head up, Catrin listened, motionless. The sound had come from somewhere very close. The house was full of sounds; the central heating, the fridge, traffic from the street, but this sound, the one in her ear, was new and unfamiliar. There was, she was sure, something in the room with them. Fragments of the dream returned, and with them the sick feeling of neglect, and she strained to see but the only thing visible was the glowing face of her watch.

She felt for William and her hand touched his back

and she felt his hot body moving slightly with every breath.

'William?' she whispered and even her voice was strange.

Pop.

She froze. The sound was very close to her. The thick darkness of the bedroom filled with menace and she felt hurriedly for her bedside light and switched it on. Her tired eyes ached in the light but the ordinary yellow and blue familiarity of the room reassured her and she was relieved and felt foolish for feeling relieved.

'I blame it on the cheese,' she murmured, thinking of William's mother who would never eat cheese after lunchtime.

Pop.

'William?'

William shifted slightly in his sleep.

Catrin turned her head to look at Sarah's closed-up daffodils beside the bed. In the warmth from the central heating they had started to open and the brown papery coverings that protected the bud had given way, to reveal the golden yellow of petals about to break free.

The sound came again, just by her ear. She watched in surprise as a tightly packed head loosened itself. Pop.

She started to laugh gently.

'William – William,' she whispered, 'wake up.'

'What?' he said squinting at her and pulling the sheets back over himself.

'Listen to the daffodils, they're opening up.'

He closed one eye. 'The daffodils are opening up?'

'Can't you hear them? Listen carefully.'

'Catrin?'

'Yes?'

'You listen carefully. Put the light out or . . . else. We've got work in the morning.'

Catrin reached above her for the light switch. It was just the daffodils, she thought; it was as simple as that.

She switched the light off and shut her eyes and pulled up the sheets. Scrunching them between her fingers she felt they were already losing their crispness and she wondered fleetingly whether a duvet might, after all, be better. But they liked sheets. Sheets were good, if inconvenient. They liked the best.

She lay with her eyes open and listened to William breathing in the dark. She could feel her blood beating through her ears, and suddenly she thought how fragile they were, how mortal, nothing but small machines that would eventually wear out.

She swallowed the saliva that had shot into her mouth with the fear and she made to open her eyes, but they were already open in the darkness and she looked for the luminous face of her watch in case she'd gone blind. She saw the second hand beating its way round, and she lay back on the pillow and the blackness settled on her face and she felt a new rise of panic in the pit of her stomach.

She felt as if she were no longer in the blue and yellow room.

She felt suddenly as if she had lost contact with the rest of the world; as if she wasn't real, as if she had been cast adrift in the dark. Fear closed up her throat as she tried to swallow and with a surge of panic she sat up and tried to find the light switch. Finally when her thumb found it and the light came on the whole room jumped back into place as though it had never been away.

She looked down at William who was flinging back the sheets and struggling to sit up.

'Catrin? What's the matter? Can't you sleep?' he asked her, smoothing her hair away from her face with his warm fingers. She kissed them briefly and dryly as they passed her mouth.

'I'm scared,' she said. 'I had a bad dream.'

'Come here,' he said, putting his arms around her, but she didn't want to be held, she wanted to get away.

'I'm going to make myself a drink,' she said, getting out of bed and reaching for her dressing gown. It was a heavy one, a German one, white velour; when it was wet it stopped the washing machine from spinning. She pulled it on and tied it tightly around her. A friend had told her that when her husband had reached forty he'd started wearing pyjamas and now she understood why. It felt a lot safer, being wrapped up.

William was asleep again and she felt irritable at his peacefulness. She switched the bedside light off and went downstairs.

She opened the doors to the dark garden and stood on the doorstep and breathed in the cold night air gratefully. It made her feel alive.

After a minute or two she went into the kitchen to make herself a weak – very weak – coffee, and she took it back out onto the patio. The path was painfully and reassuringly cold under her feet, so cold that it made her calves ache.

She couldn't shake off the feeling of unreality. I'm just tired, she thought, watching the steam and her breath mingle in the cold night air.

She looked at the burnt patches on the lawn where the fireworks had been only a night ago.

She felt unutterably sad. It's all right, she told herself, but it wasn't. Because from somewhere, nicely hidden, the knowledge that she wouldn't always be there had bubbled up, malevolent as marsh gas, and made itself known.

No, she wouldn't always exist.

She had only come into being thirty-three years ago. The year before that she hadn't existed at all and one day she wouldn't again. And despite the Welshness of her she didn't want peace, perfect peace nor eternal anything, she just wanted to stay here where the patio stones were cold and painful and real beneath her feet. Where the traffic never stopped and drunks argued and birds sang.

She shivered and tightened her grip on the hot mug and sipped the coffee again.

She'd had a dream, a bad dream, that was all. The mortality business — well, that was true, but then it always had been.

Everything was all right. She and William, they would live a long time yet. They had money. They had a good marriage. They were happy. They would live forever.

When William came down later, rubbing his eyes after a battle with the alarm clock, Catrin was shuffling cue cards for the presentation she was giving at Cleveland Foods that day.

'The following graphs show the usage of airtime by brands in terms of the transmission hours of contractors,' she said with a grin. 'Morning, William.'

'Is the coffee hot?'

'It's instant.'

'Make me some, will you? And give me a hug.' He squinted at her. 'How long have you been up?'

'A couple of hours,' she said, getting up to put her arms around his hot body. William had the hottest body of anyone she'd ever known but he never sweated or got uncomfortable in the heat. She looked up into his grey-blue squinting eyes and smiled.

They were both short-sighted. They'd found out that they'd both chosen the same NHS glasses when they were adolescents and never worn them. A myth propagated by her mother at dinner parties, and totally untrue, was that they had once shared a pair of contact lenses. She seemed to think this showed their compatibility, although when William had mentioned that they did share the same toothbrush, she'd been appalled.

Catrin rested her cheek on the hairs of William's chest.

'Are you feeling better?' he asked, stroking her cheek and letting his hand drift down the thick dressing gown along the ridge of her spine. 'Did you say you had a bad dream?'

'Yes, I did,' she said, pulling a face, 'but I can't remember it properly, I can only remember the taste of it, if you see what I mean.'

'And how did it taste?'

'Like bad crab.'

He laughed into her hair. 'That's not a dream, that's a nightmare.'

'Yeah . . . do you ever think about dying, William?'

He didn't answer for a moment, then he said, 'We're all going to, aren't we?'

Catrin sighed. 'You're a big help.'

She moved out of the heat of his arms and turned on the kettle. 'Let's go out tonight,' she said lightly. 'Let's go to Odette's. I don't feel like shopping and there's no food left.'

'Does that mean we've finished all the turkey?'

Catrin made a face at him. 'Seriously,' she said. 'I'll book. Eight o'clock?'

'If you like. I thought you'd want some time in after the New Year and all that.'

Catrin wrinkled her nose. 'Here's your coffee. I'm going for a shower,' she said.

'Howden's Law,' she muttered under her breath as she looked for a pair of tights in her drawer after her shower. She'd been up hours and she was still going to be late for work. She found a pair at last and took them out with some relief.

Sitting on the bed she started to ease them onto her smooth legs.

'Have I got a white shirt?' William asked her, popping his head round the door.

She'd have to take them to be done, she thought guiltily.

William thought she ironed all their clothes herself. In fact she took them to the laundry in batches, and spent hours afterwards peeling all the laundry labels off.

61

The trouble was, she had a sneaky feeling that if William found out she was faking the ironing he would think it was as bad as faking orgasms.

'And have you seen my silver cufflinks?' William asked, coming into the bedroom, towelling his hair dry.

'In your stud box.'

William draped his towel around his shoulders and looked on the dressing table. 'No, they're not,' he said.

'They are, William.' Suddenly she felt her broken nail catch in the leg of her tights. Holding her breath, she tried carefully to unpick the fine mesh that had caught in the jagged edge but it made no difference. Like a whisper, the hole became a ladder, travelling up her leg towards her thigh with the gentleness of a whisper.

She turned to William but he had gone out of the room.

Annoyed, she took the tights off and flung them in the bin under the dressing table.

And suddenly, triumphantly, she remembered that Marilyn had given her a pair for Christmas and that they would still be under the tree.

She ran down the stairs to fetch them and reading the packet as she took them back up, saw that they were stockings rather than tights. But it didn't matter – she knew she had a suspender belt somewhere.

Back in her room she looked through the drawer and found it tangled up with a black bra. She began to dress and looked at herself in the mirror – black suspenders, black panties, black bra, Barely Black stockings. She heard William come out of the bathroom as she slipped her black shirt on and she was stepping into her skirt as he came back into the bedroom.

She looked at him in the reflection of the wardrobe mirror and instinctively he raised his eyes and for a second they looked at each other. His gaze flicked to her legs. She pulled up the skirt and fastened it.

'Did you find your cufflinks?'

'They were in the stud box.'

Ho-hum, Catrin thought, pulling on her jacket. She restrained herself.

'What time is it?'

'Quarter past eight.'

'Oh, help, I'm late,' she said, 'and I need petrol. How long will it take me to get to Hemel?'

'Forty minutes or so. Depends on the traffic. Maybe longer.' He threw the towel onto the bed. 'You can take my car if you like. I filled it up yesterday. The keys are on the table.'

'Thanks, William.' She looked at herself in the mirror, brushing her hair into place. She put on her lipstick. 'Do I look all right?'

'Too good for work,' he said. 'Come here.'

She went to him obediently and tilted her head so that he would not smudge her lipstick. She was going to be late.

'You smell good, too,' he said, stroking her bottom through her skirt. His fingers caught on the knob of a suspender.

Catrin turned around suddenly. She threaded her fingers through the hair on his chest and the same feeling of apprehension came over her. 'I love you, you know,' she said seriously, frowning at him. 'You don't mind, do you, going out tonight?'

'Of course not.'

Catrin hesitated. Her briefcase was on the table. She did a mental check — briefcase, William's car keys, her house keys — she had everything. Still, it was as if there was something she'd left unsaid, something neglected. She wondered if it was just the aftermath of the dream.

'I *do* love you,' she said.

William looked surprised at the emphasis.

'I know,' he said gently, holding her shoulders, 'I know that you love me.'

Catrin straightened her jacket. 'That's all right then,' she said but still felt reluctant to leave.

'You're going to be late,' he said and he gave her a nudge.

'I'm going.'

She went downstairs and left her own keys on the kitchen table for him and picked his spares up. She shifted the briefcase to the other hand and finally left the house.

As she got into his car she remembered she still hadn't filed her nail.

She was going to be late.

6

Alex Martin reached for his watch which was on top of a pile of midnight blue towels in the bathroom and tried to ignore Frances.

'You don't love me like you used to,' she was saying plaintively, hugging her arms around her.

'I do,' he protested lamely, trying unsuccessfully to convince himself. 'Look, I haven't got time to argue now. I've apologised and I don't see what else I can do.'

'Poison,' Frances complained, tying her blonde hair up with a red ribbon, ready for a shower. 'I've never worn Poison in my life.'

After a great night of great sex Alex remembered why he'd decided that he couldn't put up with any more. It was because Frances thrived on argument whereas all he really wanted was a bit of peace.

He looked at his face jadedly in the steamy mirror which he wiped with the palm of his hand and his blurred and dripping reflection stared back at him blankly. He thought he must be getting old. He had the perfect woman, the loveliest female he'd ever seen, sitting naked in his bathroom and all he could think of was how to get rid of her painlessly.

Poison, he thought suddenly, watching the mirror slowly cloud up again; how very Freudian it would be if Poison turned out to be the one thing that got rid of her.

'What are you thinking, Alex?' Frances asked, her head to one side.

'Nothing,' he said, tying a towel around his waist.

'Men always say that,' she pouted. 'They're usually thinking about their cars.'

'Not guilty.'

'Do you ever get jealous, Alex?

Alex splashed on his Limes toilet water, by Floris, and wondered, as his face stung, what was coming next. 'Sometimes, I suppose,' he said. 'Why?'

'Nothing.'

He began to brush his teeth vigorously, aware of Frances staring at him. She often ended conversations like that. He would have pursued them once but now he preferred to pretend he hadn't heard.

He rinsed his mouth out and turned to her, dabbing his face with the towel. 'You have remembered that I'm doing that presentation with Catrin this morning? It's in Hemel Hempstead. You'll have to get the tube in.'

'And get molested?' Frances untied her hair and it fell loose on her naked shoulders.

It was a gesture, he thought, that he had seen before but he still felt a jerk of lust, despite himself.

'What time will you be back in the office, Alex?'

'Lunchtime.' He looked at her face and his gaze drifted wistfully over her slim body. How could he give her up? And yet he knew it wasn't Frances the person that he loved, but the sight of her, her perfection, her ability to make heads turn. She was so beautiful it hurt.

A lock of damp, silky hair fell over his eye and he began to rub the heel of his hand against his jaw. He was expecting the usual rasp but as he'd just shaved it was like the sound of stockings brushing together and he abandoned the gesture instantly.

'Can we have lunch?' Frances was asking in a small voice.

'I'll have to check my diary,' he said briskly.

Frances went to the shower and turned on the taps.

Out of the corner of his eye Alex could see her stretching out her arm under the shower head, dancing her fingers under the onrush while she adjusted the temperature with the other hand. The spray was landing on his back, fine cool droplets of water and it irritated him.

'You're making the floor wet,' he said sharply.

Frances took her hand out of the flow of water and straightened up, drying her hands on the dark blue towel.

'You don't love me,' she said. It was a statement in which there was no room for denial.

Now, he knew, was the time to agree with her, to be honest and let her go. 'Cheska,' he began but she cut him off.

'Frances,' she said, 'my name is Frances.'

'Frances makes you sound like some sort of nun,' he said, hoping to jolly her out of it and hating himself for his cowardice.

'You make me wish I were one. Who is she?' Her voice was trembling a little. 'Just tell me her name.'

'Listen,' he said, 'there's only you and you know it. I bought you the wrong perfume and I'm sorry it upset you. Whatever happens, there is no-one else. I would have thought your private detective would have been able to tell you that.'

She was looking at him steadily with lie-detector eyes.

He looked steadily back.

'Home – work – home. Ah!' Frances's eyes lit up. 'She works with you and she's married.' She tossed her hair triumphantly, looking happy for the first time.

Alex looked at her helplessly for a moment, then shrugged. As he did so he felt his towel slip. Instinctively he made a grab for it and then thought, what the hell. He whipped it off and slung it over his shoulder.

'I'm going to get dressed,' he said, walking slowly out of the steamy bathroom. Frances's eyes would be on him, he knew, all the way to the door. Or maybe they wouldn't.

He closed the door of his bedroom and selected a shirt from the boxed pile in his wardrobe. Wide blue stripes. Daniel Hechter. He liked stripes.

Poor Frances, he thought, only momentarily diverted by the process of getting dressed; he had been cool with her lately. Maybe, after all, he shouldn't give her up. She was his ideal woman – what was he saying, she was every man's ideal woman. She was beautiful, he loved being with her, looking at her, touching her. Everything she did looked beautiful, graceful, desirable and she never seemed awkward or out of place.

But what he really wanted was a peaceful life. He looked at himself in the mirror.

'Thirty-five is not old,' he said aloud, but not too loudly.

It wasn't; for a man.

Frances, on the other hand, was thirty; a dangerous age for a woman. She wanted marriage. He'd found himself wondering in the past whether he shouldn't marry her and have done with it.

He shook out his freshly laundered shirt and felt that right now he would settle for anyone who actually liked him. And laughed at his jokes.

He put on his shirt and as he buttoned it he realised he couldn't hear her moving around the flat. It worried him. Having Frances there in a mood was like having a small time bomb around the house. He wondered what would have happened if he'd bought her Gio – would they have gone on as they were, he getting cooler, she getting more desperate? Gio. He frowned.

Personally he liked light perfumes on women, nothing too strong and sexy. He liked perfumes he could believe came from their pores or from their hair, clean-smelling perfumes rather than knock-them-dead ones, but he knew that knock-them-dead ones were sexy. Everyone knew that.

He glanced at the clock on his bedside table. It was later than he'd thought.

Frances came into his room and stood in the doorway, hugging a red kimono around herself. 'Why did you buy Poison?' she asked casually, as though, in the end, if she persisted, she would catch him out.

Alex turned and gripped her by the upper arms. She didn't say a word, just looked at him. He was deadly serious suddenly and he knew it wasn't because of what she'd said but because he was late for work. Still, he let himself get angry.

'Frances, why did I buy Poison? Nearly all the

women I've been out with have worn it, that's why I bought it.' He paused and stared at her beautiful face. He was going to be late. 'Don't mention it again.'

'I love you,' she said, as if it explained everything.

'No, you don't. I don't think you even like me.' The truth seemed to open up inside him. He felt as though he couldn't get his breath. 'Let's leave it at that, shall we?'

Frances looked at him, her beautiful mouth slightly open. 'Leave what at that?'

'Us. We're finished.' And he believed it. He let her arms go and they seemed to fall limp by her side. He stared at them, he couldn't believe how easy the words had been to say. 'I have to go,' he said. 'I'm going to be late.' He knew he should have felt relief but instead his head throbbed with the tightness of a headache about to begin.

Frances raised her limp hands to her face and he saw she was crying.

Remorse welled up in him but there seemed little point in apologising. 'I'll see you,' he said.

She didn't reply.

He left the flat and closed the front door behind him.

As he walked to the car he sighed, his breath clouding in the cold air. His headache was deepening. He got into the icy car and leaned his head on the steering wheel. He knew she wouldn't set the burglar alarm. He knew she'd cry in work and tell the receptionist what had happened and the receptionist would spend the day issuing bulletins on it. He knew it was the end.

He thought of the times he would see her in work, briefly, just in passing, and he knew that he would long for her in the way people long for something rare they've lost.

He opened the car window and looked up at his flat.

He could go back up there now – he'd done it in the past – he could go back and apologise and fall into those lovely arms and kiss her perfect unsmiling face and smooth the hair of her widow's peak. He could do that. He could do that but he knew it wouldn't put things right. Together they'd never been right.

Regretfully, he closed the window again. Funny how it hurt, he thought.

He couldn't imagine them being friends. She wouldn't know what a friend was, she only knew how to get her own way. But not this time. Not with him.

He started the engine, not daring to look at the clock. With tyres screeching he headed towards the motorway.

What the hell.

He put his foot down, making up for lost time.

The M1 northbound was comparatively clear.

Catrin heaved a sigh of relief. It would have looked bad if she'd been late.

It was a good morning for driving; the sky was blue and cloudless and cold and the sunlight was making the winter landscape vivid.

She glanced at the clock on the dashboard and frowned. It seemed to be dimmer than usual; looking at it again she found she could hardly read it.

Still, she must be making good time. The road ahead was clear and she put her foot down. Expecting the usual powerful thrust forward she was surprised to find that the accelerator was not responsive and as she pressed her foot right down she realised that the car was actually losing speed.

Checking the mirror she indicated and changed lanes and as the loss of power became alarming she steered the car onto the hard shoulder where it rolled a few dozen yards before finally coming to a stop by some stunted shrubs.

Catrin stared out of the window and tried to keep calm. SHE WAS GOING TO BE LATE. She switched the ignition off, cursed, and turned the key again. There was no response. She tried the hazard lights but nothing happened. The car was dead.

She thumped the steering wheel in anger. Great, she thought, moving over to the passenger seat to get out, why did it have to be today? And William didn't even have a car phone.

She got out of the car and stood beside it uncertainly, deafened by the drone of cars as they sped past. The wind billowed her hair out behind her as she wondered which way she should walk to find the nearest phone.

Suddenly a car pulled up sharply in front of her.

Startled, she opened the passenger door to get in again but realising that the central locking system wouldn't be working either she hurried round to the boot where William kept his cricket kit. She took out the bat and held it in both hands and as she emerged threateningly from behind the lid of the boot she saw that it was not a stranger who had stopped his car for her but Alex Martin.

She put the bat down and grinned. The grin wouldn't go and she felt insane with relief.

'Having trouble?' Alex asked, grinning back at her. His silky dark hair shone in the winter sun.

'No, just thought I'd stop for batting practice.' She threw the Duncan Fearnley back in the boot. 'The car's broken down.'

'Right, we'll sort that out later. Do you want to lock it?'

'The locking mechanism's gone,' she said as she reached into the car to take the keys out of the ignition.

'OK.' Alex looked at his watch. 'We've got fifteen minutes to get to Cleveland Foods.' He took her briefcase from her and with long-legged strides they ran together to his car.

Once they'd got in and shut the doors they looked at each other, pleased, and sat for a moment in the comparative silence of the citrus-smelling car.

Catrin smiled. 'I'm awfully glad you saw me.'

He smiled back and adjusted his tie, although it didn't need it. 'Me too,' he said as she fastened her seatbelt. 'I wouldn't have recognised the car, but I recognised you.'

He edged back onto the road and accelerated violently.

Catrin smiled to herself. Alex Martin had been research manager at SETV for three years and she felt suddenly as if she was seeing him for the first time. She wondered, modestly, whether the macho driving was for her. She thought it was.

'You're married, aren't you,' Alex asked her suddenly and as he turned his head his silky dark hair fell over one eye.

'Yes, I am,' she said, surprised.

73

He glanced at her again; a swift, appreciative glance. 'You don't smell married.' He was smiling.

Catrin laughed. 'How do married women usually smell?'

Alex thought about it. 'They usually smell of, you know, hairspray and deodorant, that kind of thing.

'And not perfume?'

'Not perfume, no, not perfume. Why is that, do you think?'

She glanced at him sideways. 'Perhaps they like to keep it for their husbands.'

'Yeah.'

But she wasn't keeping it, was she. She wondered if that was what he was thinking.

He pulled out, overtaking a lorry so fast that the slipstream made the car swerve.

'What are you wearing?'

So they were still on the subject.

'Sheer Scent,' she said, amused. 'Ultima II.'

He was silent. Her thoughts were elsewhere when he said softly, 'I like it.'

They reached junction eight and left the motorway. As they came to the first roundabout she saw, with sinking heart, a line of traffic stretching as far as the eye could see, a chain of brakelights glowing like rubies. She looked at the clock and her heart sank with disappointment. They weren't going to make it after all.

'Don't worry,' Alex said. 'I know another way.' He swerved the wheel to take a left-hand turn. Jolted against the door Catrin almost grabbed the dashboard, but stopped herself and was glad she had, liking the

74

feeling of being cool with this dark-haired man she hardly knew.

The road had hedges either side.

Catrin looked at the speedometer. They were doing forty.

Uneasily she gripped her seat.

The lane was too narrow, surely, for that sort of a speed. As Alex approached a bend he pressed the horn.

Awaiting them was an undulating mass of black and white and as she realised that they were cows and that they were blocking the road she swung her arm out at him as though to make a barrier that would stop him. Her voice seemed calm and still.

'Alex.'

He swung the wheel, rode a ditch and saw the hedge close over the bonnet, heard it scratch with squealing fingers his beloved car. There was a moment of weightlessness, a moment that was all, amidst the din and confusion.

And then there was silence.

In the silence, Catrin was hanging upside down.

I knew it, she thought, I knew it, I always knew that this was how I would die, through not saying something, through not speaking up. He'd been going too fast.

The silence was humming loudly, hurting her ears.

She opened her eyes.

All the windows were broken. Through them, in the incredible quiet, came the muddy green scent of crushed grass.

She turned her head carefully to look at Alex. He was upside down too, wedged in his seat.

'Alex, are you all right?'

Stupid question.

He groaned gently. 'Winded,' he whispered after a moment. 'Hold my hand.'

She reached for her seatbelt and unlocked it. Unharnessed, she fell on her head and screamed sharply with the sudden pain. Tears began to roll down her cheeks.

'Catrin?'

'I'm here.' She scrambled round, kneeling on the roof lining, wiping the tears off her face. 'How can I get you out?'

'Hold me, will you?'

She knew he was winded, his voice sounded strange, he couldn't get his breath. Crouched next to him, she touched his hand.

He began to grunt rhythmically. It was an ugly noise and that frightened her more than anything because she knew instinctively that he was a vain man. His silky dark hair was hanging down and she pressed it flat against his head for him in an attempt to put something right.

'Hello?' came a voice.

Surprised that this new world should contain someone other than them, Catrin crouched to look through the hole in the crazed window.

She saw a youngish man who was lying flat in the field in his effort to look in. His face was whiter than seemed natural.

'Are you all right?' he shouted.

'Yes.' What a question, what an answer. 'My friend – he's hurt.'

The man got up and tried to pull the door open and the car began to rock.

Catrin cried out in some alarm. 'Don't – please –'

'Someone's gone for help. What can I do?'

'Nothing – don't touch –'

The man went away.

The humming silence came back. Catrin felt happier. It was so quiet. Alex had stopped shuddering and groaning. It was nice and quiet now.

'Alex? Are you all right?' She found she was holding his hand and she rubbed it to warm it.

He opened his eyes to look at her. Brown eyes, wide, how strange, she'd remembered them as being blue. 'I think we should go to the party,' he said.

Catrin smoothed her fingers against his palm. It was brick red and still cool. 'Yes, let's do that,' she said.

'Please will you hold my head?'

'Oh, yes,' and she moved up to him and let his silky, hanging head rest upon her shoulder. He felt so heavy and fright filled her up. 'Alex? Is that all right?'

'It's lovely.'

She rested her cheek against his. He smelt citrussy, like limes, and every short breath that he took wafted it over her eyes.

'We ought to go soon.'

'Yes.'

Time didn't pass. There was no beginning and no end to it; it seemed as though she had always been there, and always would be, crouching, holding the weight of his head on her shoulder.

'Has there been an accident?' he asked after a while. 'It's still daytime. I'm all muddled.'

'It doesn't matter,' she said softly, 'at least you know you are.'

'It's not much help.'

'No.' She stroked his face gently. It was cool and smooth. She had grown used to the quickness of his breathing but despite that she didn't notice when it stopped. It was just that suddenly she knew he was dead.

She heard a siren in the distance and was sad for other souls as battered as they.

'It will be all right,' she said steadily to him.

She heard voices, noisy, and faces appeared at the window and she wanted to tell them to be quiet, that there was someone dead in here, though she knew it didn't matter.

The car seemed to lift. The door was jerked open and strangers spoke to her and took her out.

They put her on a stretcher. She could see the man who'd appeared earlier sitting on the grass, his arms folded around his head.

'She was married. Now she's a widow,' she heard one of the men say.

Unsurprised that catastrophe had also befallen William she said nothing. She lay with calm acceptance where she'd been put, before slipping away into an empty sleep.

7

As editor of *Media News* William was usually the first in the office but because he'd decided to fill Catrin's car up on the way in to work he found Hugh Gascoigne, his chief reporter, in before him for once.

'An unprecedented honour, Hugh,' William said with a grin. 'This earliness is the result of a New Year's resolution, I hope?'

He sat at his desk and Hugh leaned over him, wearing a tie that was easily large enough to be a forgotten napkin still tucked in from breakfast.

'Sarcasm, William, is sad in one so young. And don't mention the New Year –' he gave William a sideways glance, '– my head's still thumping.' He paused. 'Must have been the fireworks, old chap.' He then looked across the office over William's head.

William looked in the direction of his gaze and saw Jeff, gofer and office junior, lighting up despite the office ban on smoking. William stared at him. Jeff looked lean and – cool. He was in his early twenties and he put the glamour back into smoking. One look at him and William felt prematurely old.

Hugh looked at William and grinned. 'I've just seen her,' he said, 'talking to Jeff.'

'Who?'

'The new receptionist. Oh, my poor old hormones . . .'

William leaned back in his chair. 'Go and drool elsewhere,' he said, 'I've got work to do.'

'William, William —' Hugh lowered his voice conspiratorially, '— she's wonderful, just a little blonde thing, you could put her in your pocket. Petite,' he added, for William's benefit. 'And she's just gone to the machine for a coffee.'

William switched his computer on, ignoring him.

'Well?' Hugh said.

'Well what?'

'Well, don't you want one?'

'Hugh, I am a very happily married man,' he said. 'But now you mention it, a coffee would be great.' William got up out of his chair and took his jacket off.

Together they crossed the office and sure enough, at the coffee machine stood a small figure dressed in black. Her hair was a fluff of white-blonde frizz and William felt a pang of sympathy for her. He'd known, once, what it was like to have hair like that.

As soon as they reached the machine William could see that she still hadn't managed to work it.

'Look, you pull a cup down from here,' he said, reaching past her. 'Then you press this red button.'

The coffee came gushing out into the plastic cup. The girl looked up at him thankfully and all William was aware of was a pair of startling blue eyes, the bluest eyes he'd ever seen, set in a pale face. And Hugh had been right — she was tiny, even smaller than Catrin, he thought with surprise; and she had hair so much like his – naturally curly and fair. He kept his short but she must, he thought, brush it, because it looked like candy floss.

He realised that he was frowning at her.

'Thank you,' she said shyly, holding the cup at the rim.

'Oh, that's all right,' William said diffidently. 'Coffee, Hugh?'

'Get me two, will you? One doesn't make much impression any more.' He turned to the girl with a lecherous smile. 'I'm Hugh and this is William. What's your name?'

'Jenna,' she said. 'Jenna Greenwood. I'm new.'

She smiled at them, showing small white teeth. They looked to William like milk teeth. Then she turned and walked towards the lift, away from them, holding her cup in her outstretched hand and not spilling a drop. They watched her until the lift doors opened and swallowed her up.

'What do you think?' Hugh said. 'Is she permanent?'

'No, just tempting. Temping,' William amended hurriedly. 'She looks awfully young.'

'You need them young, at my age,' Hugh said.

'Oh yeah? What about Jean?'

'We're just good friends,' he said, straight-faced.

They walked back to their desks with their coffees. William sat down and got out his Mont Blanc pen.

He looked at some copy that had been put on his desk. 'Hugh,' he called across, 'this isn't true, is it, about some wonderful crystal trophy being dropped at LTV's golf tournament during the presentation because the MD was drunk?'

'It is true. He tried to play it down by saying it was

81

a spoof and that the smashed bowl was from Woolies. However, another one was ordered immediately from Mappin and Webb.'

William grinned. 'You could dine out on that one.'

The phone rang and he picked it up. 'Have we heard what? When?' Another merger, or rumoured merger. He thought for a moment and scribbled on a pad. 'Jeff,' he called, 'check this out, will you?'

Jeff came over and William felt a new pang for the William he once had been. He'd never be that lean again. Jeff took the note without a word.

William was surprised, a short time later, to find Jenna standing awkwardly in front of him.

'Mr Howden?' she asked tentatively, her blue eyes awash with some expression he couldn't fathom.

'Yes.' Call me William. He was distracted by Hugh in the background who was grabbing his heart and pretending to faint. Hugh would give himself a heart attack one of these days.

'There's a phone call on the switchboard for you. It's a hospital in Hemel Hempstead.'

Some mistake, obviously, William thought. He wondered how to tell her. She looked as if she were going to burst into tears. 'It's for you,' she urged. 'I didn't know how to put it through.' Her blue naked eyes never left his in her attempt to convey the urgency that wasn't reaching her gentle voice. 'Will you come and take it?'

He hesitated, then heard himself say, 'Yes, of course.'

He followed her towards the lift, past the incredulously grinning Hugh, past Jeff who had his back to them and who was drinking his coffee out of a china mug. A china mug? Why hadn't William thought of bringing in a china mug?

When the lift came he stood in the centre of it and watched the dark brown door slide closed in front of him. Jenna pressed the button without a word. William felt inside him a quiver of fear that seemed to have come from nowhere. He stared at the dark brown door. He was in a box, he thought, a metal box supported by nothing but cables. People went up and down in this little box every day without so much as a second thought. But he was having second thoughts. He felt perspiration break out on his forehead. For the first time in his life he realised that he hated lifts; he was afraid.

The lift jerked to a halt, shuddered, and slowly the doors opened. He stepped out with a great intake of breath and felt the sweat on his brow grow cold. That was the last ride, he vowed, the very last one he would ever take in a lift.

'Mr Howden,' said Jenna's gentle voice, 'this is the first floor.'

He stepped back in again.

Upstairs he had almost said William. Call me William. But he wasn't William now, he was Mr Howden, just like she'd said.

The lift bumped to a halt again, adjusted itself and allowed them out.

He followed her round to the desk. She sat down and he stood facing her nervously.

She handed him the phone. 'I haven't had my training yet,' she said.

William nodded to show he understood. He put the

phone to his ear. 'Hello?' He cleared his throat. 'William Howden here.'

A very clear voice replied, matter-of-factly, 'Your wife has been involved in an accident, Mr Howden. She's unhurt but in shock. We are keeping her in under observation.'

William hugged the receiver in the crook of his neck. He grinned slightly. 'This is a joke, isn't it.' The grin went, he didn't know where it had come from in the first place. 'Should I come right away? I'll come. I'll come now. Thanks.'

He put the phone down and looked at Jenna. Her clear, unlined face, dimmed by her bright blue eyes, looked back. Or were there, yes, shadows underneath her eyes, slight ones, small signs of dissipation on her young face. He loved signs of dissipation, loved them on Catrin. Smudged mascara . . .

'It's my wife,' he said, 'a slight accident.'

That was what she'd said, wasn't it? A slight accident?

'Shall I get you a cup of tea, Mr Howden?'

'No, no thanks. I'll get off there. I'd better let Hugh know.'

He went back upstairs in the lift and bumped into Hugh who was hovering around the lift doors.

'Sorry, Hugh. Listen, I've got to go out for a bit.' He frowned, feeling like an actor who'd been cast in a part he wasn't up to. 'Catrin's been involved in an accident.' Without the word 'slight' it sounded more real. 'She's in the West Herts in Hemel.'

Hugh patted his shoulder. Then: 'Do you want Jeff to drive you?'

'No.' Pause. 'Actually – yes. If the car's not too –

you know – I don't know exactly what's happened but if it's a small bump, if the car is driveable – Jeff could bring it back.' He picked up his jacket. 'I've got some copy on my desk.' He pinched the bridge of his nose between his thumb and forefinger. 'Will you –'

'Go on. I'll get Jeff. Don't forget your keys.'

William and Jeff went down in the lift and out to the car park.

As they walked to the car Jeff asked: 'Are you all right to drive?'

'Yes. You can bring my car back if it's –'

He drove in silence, a happily married man whose wife was suffering from shock.

William was first to see his car deserted on the hard shoulder. A weak reflection of the winter sun shone off its roof.

'There it is!' he said, pulling into the inside lane. He slowed down as they passed it. 'The back looked all right,' he commented with relief. He'd been imagining a pile-up.

Jeff twisted round in his seat. 'Front looks OK too,' he said. 'Couldn't have been that bad.'

'She wasn't hurt, just shocked.'

Jeff took a pair of sunglasses from his inside pocket. Ray-Ban Wayfarers, William guessed, but glancing at Jeff he could see they were small round John Lennon ones.

Jeff wiped them with a linen handkerchief. 'Shock can be dangerous,' he said. 'My old lady had a friend, a nurse, who witnessed a car crash. She helped with the casualties then dropped down dead herself.'

William looked at him. 'Thanks.'

'Your wife will be all right. The hospital will see to that.'

'She's brave,' William said.

Jeff put on his shades. 'Women are.'

They must be born New Men these days, William thought wryly. The lad couldn't fail.

After the onrush of doctors, nurses, police, registrars, Catrin found herself momentarily left alone in the narrow peace of her hospital bed.

She lay with her arms outside the sheets. A drip stretched from one of them.

She stared at her hands then slowly she lifted one up to her shoulder where she could still feel the heavy warm weight of Alex's head. Her hand felt not Alex's soft dark hair, which she could still feel tickling against her cheek, but nothing, just her own cold skin.

She put her hand down again and stared at the cream ceiling.

The police had gone now. They'd been kind enough in their questioning; they'd not actually said Alex had been to blame – how could they blame the dead? – but they'd had about them all the time an air of tiredness.

She'd told them about the presentation at Cleveland Foods. As she'd talked she'd known that a death was far too high a price to pay for her car breaking down and for them almost being late.

And the fear of being late was the reason for the speeding that had led to Alex's death next to her, crushed and hanging, his citrus breath against her nostrils, his wasted breath, and she knew that the alternative, which they'd been so anxious to avoid, was having to apologise for being late.

She tried to remember how mortifying the idea of being late had seemed. She'd thought that terrible things would happen: lost accounts, embarrassment, altered schedules.

Catrin shut her eyes.

It hadn't been life or death, after all.

It needn't have been.

She could have stopped him except that she'd liked being cool, she'd liked sitting next to that dark-haired man in his dark car who wanted to know what perfume she wore. She'd enjoyed it and she'd wanted to impress him. She would have died rather than ask him to slow down.

No, it was he who died.

Hold my head, she heard him say in her ear.

Frightened, she sat up in the hospital bed, she could feel the weight of him in the hollow above her collarbone and when she felt for him she could feel the indentation of him on her shoulder despite the thick brushed nylon of the borrowed hospital nightdress.

Hold my hand, he'd said.

She looked up sharply as the ward door opened and saw William looking down the ward for her.

'William!' she called anxiously.

'Catrin!' He came and crouched next to her, his face troubled as he looked with grave concern into her eyes. He pushed her hair away from her face. 'Catrin, are you all right?'

'Yes.' She nodded to back it up.

'What's this?'

'It's a drip.'

'You're suffering from shock,' he said.

'No, I'm all right, I wasn't hurt.'

She felt her throat closing up as if it was being squeezed. William took her hand and started stroking it. She wanted to pull away.

'What happened?' William asked her, holding her hand tighter in both of his own as though he knew he was keeping it captive.

'Alex Martin died.'

William raised his eyebrows. He looked shocked. 'Alex Martin?' he asked, confused. He looked towards the ward door and back at her. 'Did you – did you run him over?'

'No.'

'A heart attack,' William said quickly, 'it was a heart attack, was it?'

'No, he died in the car with me.' Catrin heard her voice swing octaves. William had let her hand go and she put it under the bedcover.

'He died in the car with you?' William's face slowly altered, fear whitened it before her eyes.

'Your car broke down and he gave me a lift and crashed.' That was all that had happened, she could say it in a few small words.

William stared at her.

Catrin looked down at the frayed black velvet ribbons on the front of the borrowed orange nightgown. A phrase from some distant time past was repeating itself in her head: 'the majesty of death'. An utter lie.

'He just went,' she said, and it frightened her. 'William, I feel strange.'

William took her other hand and moved the needle that was taped under the skin.

'My car broke down?' he asked her in confusion as

though trying to find something in the story he could understand.

Catrin nodded. She thought of the relief and the innocence with which she had greeted Alex from behind the car, the cricket bat in her hand.

'There were cows in the road –' Tears sprang from her eyes without any warning.

William jumped to his feet. He felt in his pockets and shook his head and stared at her and then put the edge of his palms under her wet cheekbones to catch the flood and gave up and cupped her face with his cold hands.

'Catrin, Catrin.' He straightened up again and pulled his shirt from his trousers and mopped her face with it. 'Don't cry, it's all right. Catrin . . .' He gave up the mopping and held her head, hands pressing against her tangled hair, and he crushed her against his chest.

She pulled free from him in a panic. 'Don't squash me –'

'It'll be all right,' he said helplessly. He let her go and tried to smooth some hair away from her face but it stuck to his damp hands.

He looked at her, his face baffled. 'I can't understand why it would break down,' he said, still trying to make sense of it.

The ward door opened and a nurse came in, brisk and normal. 'Lunch, Catrin?'

Catrin shook her head and the tears flew off her face.

'I'll bring you some to try. You're not vegetarian or anything, are you?'

'BUPA, we're on BUPA,' William said, getting to his feet.

He straightened himself and for an instant he looked rather pleased.

They were on BUPA. It was the only thing, at the moment, he knew for sure.

When the doctor came to look at Catrin, William went to find Jeff.

Jeff had got a handful of change and he bought two coffees from the machine in the waiting room and they stood next to it, drinking the weak coffee, two men of the world.

'How is she?'

'She's OK.' Nurses swept through and looked at them. 'I should get flowers. Jane Packer. Catrin uses Jane Packer.' William felt confused. Flowers. Or was it grapes? 'The doctor's in with her,' he said.

'What do we do now?' Jeff asked.

'We'll wait. See what the doctor says.'

Jeff glanced at his watch. He did it discreetly, but William saw him all the same.

'Give me a minute,' Jeff said, and he went to talk to a pretty nurse with pale pink lips.

William stood awkwardly drinking his coffee. After a few minutes he glanced hopefully at Jeff but Jeff was still deep in conversation with the pretty nurse. William finished his drink. He wanted to join them but bought another coffee instead with the change that Jeff had left.

As soon as he'd taken it from the machine he knew he didn't want it but it was too late now so he sauntered over to a stand with leaflets on it and looked at the ones on Breast Examination and How To Stop Smoking. For a minute or two he lost himself in the world of nicotine patches but as soon as he stopped reading his troubles came back. His head ached. He was hurting for Catrin. He wanted to go through those plastic doors and take her away. He wondered if she'd stopped crying and what he should do about it if she hadn't. He was afraid of her tears.

'Doctor out yet, William?'

William jumped at hearing Jeff's voice so close to him and spilt a little of his hot coffee on his hand. He shook it wildly and realised he was being uncool in front of Jeff so he thrust it in his pocket where it continued to burn fiercely, heating up the silky lining.

'Not yet,' he said.

'I've just been told about Alex Martin. Poor bloke.'

William's hand throbbed in his pocket. He looked at Jeff.

'Did they say what happened?'

'He wasn't killed outright, you know. Catrin watched him die. I rang up Hugh while you were in there – thought I ought to keep him up to date. That little nurse has been very helpful.' He gave William a wink.

William looked at him.

'Are you all right with that coffee?'

William nodded. The enormity of what had happened hit him again. It had been a perfectly ordinary morning, then bang, his life was knocked sideways. He felt vaguely outraged.

Jeff went to the coffee machine and bought another cup. When he came back he asked, 'What's the news on Catrin's car?'

'It broke down. The dead man – he gave her a lift.'

'It broke down?'

'Let's see if we can get it moving.' Having an aim made him strong again. He was glad to have something to do, something to get to grips with. He threw his cup towards the wastepaper bin and it went in. He felt triumphant.

Jeff's cup was still full. He put it carefully on the table on the way out.

William drove southbound, came off at junction seven and rejoined the northbound carriageway.

'There it is,' he said as they came to it again. He switched on the hazards and pulled up behind it.

'You stay here,' he said to Jeff, getting out of the car. He ran, half crouched against the whip of the passing traffic, and began, with his spare keys, to unlock the door. He was surprised to find the car hadn't, in fact, been locked.

He slid into the driver's seat and pulled the door closed. The car seemed to bounce slightly in the slip-stream from the road. William breathed deeply. He had the impression he'd been holding his breath for quite a while.

He put his key into the ignition and turned it. The car leapt into life and he felt a flicker of pleasure because it had always been a reliable car. He had been surprised, although he hadn't said so, when Catrin told him it had broken down.

William stared out of the windscreen.

But it hadn't, had it?

It hadn't broken down, but she'd still gone in a car with Alex Martin.

William rested his head against his arms and shut his eyes.

The image came to him again; Catrin wearing suspenders and catching his eye in the mirror. She never wore suspenders for him.

He loosened his tie and opened the top button of his shirt to cool himself down. He felt fevered with shock.

He suddenly remembered Jeff was waiting in the car behind him. He looked into his rear-view mirror and made, for Jeff, a gesture of victory, fist raised. He put the car into gear and he drove himself home.

8

After waiting in vain for Alex to come back and apologize, Frances went into his bedroom purposefully.

He had a two-drawer pine chest next to his bed. She pulled the drawers out and emptied the contents of them onto the floor.

It was like emptying out the Tardis, she thought in amazement. The floor was heaped with junk; rugby programmes, pieces of Lego, cufflinks, foreign coins.

She tossed the drawers onto the bed and looked with satisfaction at the chaos she had brought about. It was, she knew, something she was quite good at.

With her foot she prodded Alex's possessions. What was she looking for? She wasn't sure, but she was confident that she'd know it when she found it. Some sort of evidence, she thought, something that would point her to the woman who wore Poison. Proof of infidelity. Letters, locks of hair, that sort of thing.

She crouched down to take a closer look at a small china bulldog. Picking it up, she looked at the underside for a signature but found it was some cheap thing, something from a Christmas cracker. With an expression of distaste, she held it away from her.

'That can go,' she said firmly and she went to the kitchen to fetch the bin.

Going through Alex's drawers was cheering her up. She loved going through other people's things.

She laughed to herself at an ingot on a chain. Very seventies. There was a champagne cork with a sixpence mounted on the top – naff, she thought; and rugby programmes, yuk; postcards from his parents – what was the point in keeping them when his parents had been dead for years? There were photographs of himself taken in a photo booth; a broken model of a Cessna; receipts for things bought long ago; guarantees no longer valid. She inspected them all and few passed muster. Soon the bin was full. Frances eyed critically what was left. She'd kept his wage slips, hallmarked cufflinks, two bottles of Limes, by Floris, and a tie-pin in a box. It all fitted easily into one drawer.

With a self-satisfied sigh, Frances replaced the drawers in the chest and imagined what Alex would say when he saw them. She'd saved him a job.

She found it strange that she hadn't come across any evidence after all.

She sighed and flung herself down on the bed.

Where was Alex? She wanted him to come back as he always did. She wanted him to apologise and hold her close until she forgave him.

She would forgive him, of course, eventually. She always did.

She stretched lazily and wondered whether she might be pregnant. What a stroke of luck it would be if she were because she was sure it would nudge him into marrying her.

She would keep her fingers crossed.

Men needed a nudge.

* * *

She arrived at the office at eleven-thirty and dumped her briefcase on her desk with a thud.

'Anything been happening? Anyone been looking for me?' she asked James, one of her execs, casually.

'Actually, yes, er . . .'

'Alex?'

'Er, no; Blackwall Carsons have been on. Their ad didn't go out last night.'

Frances looked at him expectantly. Then she said: 'Is that it?'

'Well – yes.'

'Shit,' she said. 'I'll ring them later. No sign of Alex?'

'Isn't he doing that presentation with Catrin at Cleveland Foods?'

Frances looked at him, then gazed over his head into the distance. She thought for a moment. 'I hoped he'd be back by now. I'm starving. Fancy an early lunch, James?'

'Me? Now? Yes.' He straightened his tie.

Frances felt a surge of contempt. 'OK,' she said. 'And do me a favour, would you? Get on to Blackwall Carsons for me.'

As he dialled, Frances leaned back in her chair. She had been out with a lot of men. She'd also been left by a lot of men. She'd never really understood why. She did all the right things like never showing her true feelings; she tried playing hard to get and she tried playing fast and loose. She dressed like a nun and she dressed like a tramp. When men declared their love, she never said she loved them. And when they didn't, she did. And where had it got her?

She stared at the ceiling. She would never understand men, just as she had never understood her father, leaving her just when she had got beautiful. It seemed unfair, when a man was all she wanted. Or rather, a husband was. It was as simple as that. She wanted someone who would appreciate her looks. Someone who would look after her.

She looked coolly at James who was talking into the telephone, lying for her. They all did that, to start with. James was too young to be husband material but he wore Cerruti suits. Or at least, he wore suits with the Cerruti label inside them. True, rumour had it that the label was in fact the only Cerruti thing he did own and that he transferred it from suit to suit, but it was, after all, only a rumour.

She stood up as he put the phone down. 'Ready?' she asked.

She watched him take his jacket off the wire coathanger – wooden ones obscured the label and the Cerruti people hadn't given him one of their own – and slip it on.

'Let's go,' she said.

Frances looked round at the rest of her group. 'We're going to the Green Man,' she said. 'If Alex comes looking for me, let him know.'

James's shoulders seemed to sink a little, momentarily, but he rallied.

The Green Man was across the road from the office. In the heady days of the eighties it had been a wine bar called L'homme Vert but had now reverted to being a foodie pub called the Green Man.

James held open the door for her and Frank, the manager, who had been Franco in the L'homme Vert days, greeted her enthusiastically.

''Ello, darling,' he said. 'Lunch?'

'Please. And get me a Kir Royale, will you.' She looked at James. 'Frank's champagne is disgusting on its own.'

They took the menus from Frank.

James opened his and looked through it once, swiftly, and then more carefully.

Frances handed hers back. 'I'm not hungry,' she said.

James raised his head, a startled look on his face.

'You have what you want,' she said, like a bored godmother on a duty outing.

James gave the menu one last, lingering look before he handed it back. 'Just a beer, thanks.'

'A beer,' Frank sneered at them both.

Frances didn't care. She was the expert. She could out-sneer the best of them.

Twelve-thirty came and went.

Frances, on her third Kir Royale, wondered what exactly had happened to Alex; she wondered whether the argument had been serious, after all. She had accused him to be reassured. Men knew that, most of them, unless they were guilty.

Her gaze shot to the door every time it opened. She felt she had spent a long time waiting for Alex. She glanced at James who was beginning to look slightly the worse for wear. They had long since given up making conversation.

'We'll give it another five minutes,' she said. She was beginning to feel the awful hollowness that desertion brings, and thoughts of Weetabix flickered through her mind.

Frank had become very tight-lippèd by now and once more she sensed him hovering over them. He wanted their table. Frances stared at him blankly and looked away.

'Haven't got a cigarette, have you, James?'

James looked startled, as if he'd forgotten where he was.

'I thought you'd given up?'

'I've given up giving them up.' Yeah, she thought, so only pensioners and adolescents smoked now, so what.

'Frances!'

She lifted her head hopefully and although she knew the voice was not Alex's at least it was a diversion.

'Frances!' Through the crowded bar the robust shape of Hugh Gascoigne sailed towards her. He paused en route to speak to Frank, then pushed his way to Frances's table. He leaned on it heavily, like a presiding judge.

'Mind if I sit down?'

Frances stared at his enormous tie for a moment and then waved her hand towards a chair. 'As long as you're not after gossip,' she said.

'No,' Hugh replied. He watched as Frank put three brandies on the table in front of them. 'This isn't business, Frances. Drink,' he said, rather loudly.

'I don't want it,' Frances said. She hated being told what to do.

Still, something about Hugh's presence made her look at him again. He had about him the air of a hunter who had tracked down its prey.

She noticed that his fair eyelashes hung straight down like fringing on a lampshade. There was something attractive about him but she'd often wondered whether Jean was a cover and whether in truth he was gay. It would be a pity for women, she thought, if he were.

'Drink,' he repeated softly, turning his back on James.

No-one ever bossed her about. Still, she reached out for her glass and noticed with surprise that her hand was trembling.

Hugh's voice was gentle. 'I have some bad news. Your friend Alex Martin is dead.' He was watching her carefully. His eyes were not friendly eyes, she could see that now; they were reporter's eyes, reporter's eyes in a friendly face.

She put her undrunk brandy back on the table. 'Have you got a cigarette?' she asked.

Hugh raised his hand and shortly, she wasn't sure how, cigarettes were put in front of her with a book of L'homme Vert matches.

Frances opened the packet and took a cigarette out and lit it. Her hand was now, she noticed, remarkably steady. She sucked in deeply and exhaled the smoke with a tired sigh.

On the next table a group of men, probably former smokers, turned around to frown. She looked at them and they turned back.

Your friend Alex Martin is dead.

Frances looked at Hugh through the smoke.

'He's not getting away with it that easily,' she said.

And suddenly she saw that the future which she

had so neatly planned had crumbled away, torn from her despite the fact that it had been within her grasp. She threw down her cigarette, clenched her fists and screamed.

Hugh Gascoigne was already back at the office when Jeff returned brimming with news.

Hugh sat himself down and helped himself to one of Jeff's cigarettes. Giving up, to Hugh, meant never having to buy his own. He studied the end of it before tapping it against the back of his hand.

'So he's not coming back in today?'

Jeff gave a smirk. 'Would you?'

Hugh put the cigarette in his mouth and leaned over for a light. He pulled on the cigarette and exhaled with deep satisfaction before returning his thoughts to the conversation in hand. 'I don't see why not,' he said, 'he's done nothing wrong.'

'*He* hasn't,' Jeff said.

'Nor has she. There's no harm in getting a lift with someone.'

'Oh, come on . . .' Jeff regarded the filter on his cigarette with amusement. 'It doesn't make sense. She told William the car had broken down.'

Hugh leaned back in his swivel chair. 'All right, old man. Let's say they were having some sort of clan-destine liaison. They could meet anywhere. Why choose the hard-shoulder of the M1 half an hour before a presentation? It won't wash and I can't see it, myself. Alex Martin's not even married, they wouldn't have been stuck for places to go.'

'What about Frances Bennett?'

'What about her? She wasn't living with him. She's

got her own flat in Knightsbridge. No, you're on the wrong track.' He tapped his ash into a crystal ashtray. 'This yours?'

Jeff nodded.

'Nice.'

'Some people get their kicks from doing it in strange places,' Jeff said.

'Yes, but they weren't doing it, were they? There's no proof they were doing it anywhere.'

'Their car crashed into a field. Cleveland Foods is on the main drag into town.'

'That's hardly the point, is it? The point is, if they'd been going to consolidate their friendship in a field then they would have arranged to meet there, not that I believe they did. But no-one parks their car on the hard shoulder.'

'Unless she was chasing him? Flagged him down?'

'She couldn't have been both chasing him and ahead of him. Jeff, you're making too much of this. I know Catrin. You're on the wrong track.'

Jeff almost smiled. 'Hugh, there's a story in it.'

'Not as far as *Media News* is concerned. We'll do an obit. on Alex Martin but there's no need to mention Catrin at all.'

'What about Frances Bennett?'

'Frances. Yes. Funnily enough, she took it badly. It surprised me; she's always seemed hard as nails. Well, you can never tell. She seemed –'

'Seemed what?'

'Ah, never mind. They're friends of mine. Just concentrate on Martin. We'll need a copy of his CV.'

Jeff stood up. They're friends of mine . . . enough

said. But they weren't friends of *his* and he had a reputation to build. And another to demolish, he thought with a smile.

9

After a restless night in the hospital, Catrin wanted to go home. She lay rigid and unmoving on the hospital bed as though she was on a mattress of broken lightbulbs.

On the locker in a polythene bag lay her clothes. They smelled of limes. The ward seemed saturated with the smell, even though the bag was knotted up. Catrin could smell it as nurses and doctors and the food trolley punctuated the twisting ribbon of images of the time before the crash: Alex Martin's dark hair flying as he walked towards her; she and Alex running together with long-legged strides back to his car; sitting with him in the citrus-leather silence; his white-toothed smile and the gleam in his brown eyes. She could smell the smell of him because he had been real, twenty-four hours ago.

And then he'd gone.

It was like a trick; like a glove puppet someone had taken their hand out of.

'Catrin? Doctor to see you.'

Catrin sat upright and kept the sheets neck-high as the doctor and his entourage gathered around her bed.

'How are you feeling?' he asked her, indifferently.

'Fine,' she said.

'Good, you can go home this afternoon.'

She watched them as they moved off to the next bed. And having been pronounced well, she wearily went to phone William.

Catrin saw William before he saw her.

As he approached the bed she looked at him gravely, searching his face for landmarks.

He gave her a curious, thoughtful look and smiled briefly, dropping the holdall onto the floor.

As she watched him there was something about his eyes that bothered her; they seemed pale as mercury, their gaze somehow out of reach. She knew he hated hospitals, he'd always told her that.

'William?' she said softly, so that he would look at her.

His eyes met hers for a fleeting second. 'That nightdress,' he said, 'where did you get it from?'

'It belongs to the hospital,' she said and she rubbed the pile lightly with her thumb. 'Someone left it behind.'

'Died in it, more like,' William said.

Catrin looked down at it. The huge, fuzzy tangerine flowers at the neck were like a wreath and the shrivelled piece of ribbon under the bust became something terribly sad. Even as she stared at the pattern the petals became blotched with dark orange tears.

William touched her shoulder awkwardly, his voice contrite. 'I'm sorry,' he said, 'I didn't mean to upset you.'

'It's all right,' Catrin said and put her hand over his, but he took it away and reached for the holdall and hoisted it onto the bed.

'I put some clothes in here, as you asked. Didn't

know what to bring that would be comfortable, so I chose these because they were both green.'

He opened the bag for her and took out a lime green sweater and a pair of olive green trousers. Catrin looked at him and his eyes caught hers and held. And still that same, curious light was in them.

'Thank you,' she said. 'Did you bring any underwear?'

William looked at once startled and defensive. 'You didn't ask me to,' he said. 'Couldn't you wear the old stuff?'

'No,' she said steadily, 'I'm going to burn it.'

'All of it?' He looked at the clothes in the polythene bag and suddenly a look of awful understanding crossed his face. 'They've got blood on them?'

'No,' she said softly, 'he didn't bleed. It was internal, it was all internal. If he bled, you couldn't tell.'

'Considerate of him.' His voice was strangely hard. He glanced at her and pressed the bridge of his nose between his thumb and forefinger. 'I'm sorry,' he said miserably.

'It doesn't matter.' She picked up the sweater.

'Nice colour,' William said, as if to make amends. He stretched out his arm to touch her and by accident knocked the jumper away. 'Sorry.'

'It's all right.' She picked it up again. 'Will you help me move the screen?'

Together they pulled the coral curtains and stood awkwardly inside the privacy of the orange glow.

Uneasily, Catrin turned her back on him as though he were a stranger and she took off the fuzzy nightdress and picked up the green trousers and pulled them up over her bare bottom. Hurriedly, she pulled on her sweater and freed her hair from the crew neck. Then she turned around to face him.

Caught unawares his face was dull with misery and Catrin, watching him, felt as though she was drowning.

'Ready?' he asked her.

Suddenly the smell of limes was all around her and with every breath she took it grew stronger, she could even taste it in her mouth, sharp and bitter and clear. 'Can you smell something?' she asked him urgently, and in agitation she cupped her hands over her face but the smell was in her nostrils, in her hands and in the air, sourceless. She pressed her hands on her husband's face and he shied back from her, alarmed, but she said: 'Smell them. What can you smell?' and she felt him press his face obediently against her palms.

'Soap,' he said, his voice muffled. 'Soap or perfume, that kind of thing.'

'Limes?'

Her palms cooled as he inhaled deeply. 'Maybe,' he said uncertainly, 'I don't know. I can't smell anything, really.'

'I can smell limes,' she said despairingly.

'It'll be lemon. Hospital disinfectant,' William assured her.

'Really?' She stared at him. Her unease was contagious.

'Come on.' He picked up the holdall and with a fleeting glance at the polythene-shrouded suit on the locker he headed for the door and Catrin hurried after him.

It was strange to be out. Standing in the doorway Catrin blinked in the weak sunshine that glittered on the cars in the car park. She folded her arms against the cold and ran to catch up with her husband, stopping in surprise as she saw that he had come in his own car. 'It's been fixed,' she said. 'That didn't take long.'

William bent his head to unlock it. When he straightened he looked at her warily across the roof.

Catrin narrowed her eyes against the sunshine. She pulled a strand of hair away from her face and shivered. 'What was wrong with it?' she asked.

'Get in,' William said.

Catrin got in and pulled her door closed. The sun had warmed the interior and she leaned back and felt her shoulders loosen. She turned her head slowly to look at him.

'Catrin.' In the intimacy of the car his voice was low but he sounded tired. His hands were resting on the steering wheel as though they were too heavy for his arms. 'There was,' he said, 'nothing wrong with it at all.'

Catrin laughed, glad it was something she could so quickly clear up. 'It broke down,' she said, 'all the power went, starting with the clock. The glow went –'

'Maybe you stalled it,' William said carefully, but there was a request in his eyes that Catrin couldn't miss.

She looked at him steadily and felt her heart beat faster. After a moment she shook her head. 'I didn't stall it.'

William turned his head away from her and looked straight ahead through the windscreen. He pressed his lips together. 'Catrin, watch this,' he said, 'watch.' He switched on the ignition and the car flared into life. He pressed his foot on the accelerator with increasing pressure so that the vehicle reverberated and roared until the noise was unbearable and as Catrin covered her ears, he let it subside into silence.

'It broke down,' Catrin said slowly as though it was something she was trying to memorise. 'The car broke down and Alex Martin saw me and gave me a lift. I wish,' she said, and her voice flew suddenly from strong to fragile, 'more than anything else, that he hadn't.'

'Jeff was with me,' William said softly, spacing each word as though it mattered. 'Jeff was with me when I went to try it and it started first time.'

Catrin stared at him without seeing him. We're not immune after all, she thought. We who are not old, not poor, not sick, can die just the same. She felt exposed and afraid. Someone, something, had picked on her, had collared her skipping self and said look! Look at Alex! You're not safe at all!

'Of all people,' William said.

'Yes.' She hardly heard him. It could just as easily have been her. She felt tiny, minuscule, insignificant; but despite that, fate had seen fit to get her in its sights. She shuddered in the warmth. She was right to be afraid.

William didn't speak to her again until they reached the house. He pulled up outside it but made no move to get out of the car. 'I won't come in,' he said, 'but I'll be back early.' He held out his keys for her.

She took them from him reluctantly. They felt cold and heavy in her hand.

William, seeing something in her eyes, added, 'Listen, I'll take the car in to the garage. I'll get it checked.'

She didn't know why it should make her want to cry. 'Thanks, ' she said.

'Go on inside,' he said. 'Have a cup of tea.'

She got out and stood on the pavement reluctantly, still holding on to the car door.

'See you,' he said and as he began to move off she banged the door shut and watched him as he drove away.

She went to the front door.

It was not at all like coming home.

Inside the house, all was quiet. She seemed to have been away for a lifetime.

She walked into the living room. The sun was shining through the patio doors, showing up smears and fingerprints on the glass. The beam of sunlight was settling on the grey carpet and dust was dancing and bobbing along it, suspended by the warmth.

The Christmas tree was barer. As she slammed the door shut behind her she heard the dried-up needles patter to the ground. The draught from the door disturbed the tinsel which waved its fronds like the legs of dying flies.

She went into the kitchen, switched on the kettle and opened the fridge.

It was empty except for a pale green cabbage. She took the cabbage out and put it on the chopping board where it lolled for a moment. She opened the cutlery drawer and took out the chopper. There was no need for her to be chopping cabbage, she knew, but it was something constructive and mindless to do and she held the knife steadily in her hand and sliced through the base of the cabbage.

Out of the corner of her eye she saw something small and translucent fly up strangely at an angle, spinning like a helicopter propeller. On the cabbage, minus one wing, an insect struggled. 'I'm sorry,' she said to it harshly, through clenched teeth.

She felt her face screw up. Suddenly the smell of limes was in her kitchen, suffocating her. She felt her stomach contract and she rushed to the bathroom and held on to the toilet bowl and was violently sick.

10

Marilyn had completely gone off the Duke of Well-ington.

'Why, what's he done to you?' Theresa asked, play-ing with her beer mat.

'Ha bloody ha.' Marilyn sipped her cherry brandy and wondered what it reminded her of – apart from Harry's New-Year's-Eve kiss.

'I wish you'd said you were going to be like this. I'd have gone out with Cathie instead,' Theresa com-plained. 'Being in love is supposed to make you happy, or hadn't you heard.'

Marilyn took her Body Shop mirror out of her hand-bag and checked her make-up with a worried look. Relieved that it was doing its job, she put it back in her bag. 'I'm not in love,' she said.

'Why do you keep going on about him then?'

Marilyn looked at a man in the corner of the pub who was playing the fruit machine. She could see his elbow go back and forth as he jabbed the button. The machine was singing away electronically, a merry little tune, while the man looked as though he was fighting for his life. 'I don't keep going on about him,' she said. 'He's nice, that's all.'

'They're all nice, aren't they,' Theresa said with sat-isfaction. She had good reason to feel smug. Terry had argued with his priest and had gone off religion completely, to the extent of giving his precious statue of the Virgin away. Since it normally stood on a window-sill half-way up the stairs, making Theresa feel a trifle nervous at having to pass it on the way to Terry's bed, its absence came as something of a relief. And to Terry, too; his sign of the cross had always looked more like a nervous twitch than a blessing when he went upstairs in a state of lust. 'Anyway,' she said, turning her thoughts to Marilyn's troubles, 'he *is* married.'

Marilyn looked at her disgustedly. 'Religion's rubbing off on you,' she said.

'There's nothing wrong with religion,' Theresa said stoutly. There wasn't, now that it wasn't affecting her. 'The trouble with you is, you want a bit of excitement.'

'So would you, if you were me. Two kids and no man.'

'You shouldn't have got rid of Dave.'

'I had to,' Marilyn said, 'you don't know what it was like, living with him.' She picked up her drink and sipped it again. It tasted as if it would do her good, like expectorant. She'd never expected to order a drink she didn't much like just to feel nearer to someone.

Theresa was looking at her expectantly. 'Was he – you know –' she jerked her head hopefully.

'What?'

'Did he want to do things?'

Marilyn looked at Theresa and curled her lip. 'That's all you think about, isn't it?'

Theresa looked half hurt at the accusation and half proud of it. 'It's all anyone thinks of, isn't it?' she said. 'Oh, don't bother,' she added, 'it's not as if I tell you everything, is it?'

113

Marilyn knew she'd overstepped the mark, forgotten to play the barter system of information. She ran her tongue over her teeth. They felt bumpy, coated with cherry brandy. Her tongue tasted of it too. I'll have a lager next time, she thought.

She looked at Theresa who was looking at the floor. 'All right, I'll tell you,' she said.

Theresa continued to stare at the floor. It didn't do to give in too easily.

'Dave,' Marilyn said, 'always slept with his eyes open.'

Theresa's head snapped up.

'It's true,' Marilyn said. 'I know it doesn't sound much.' It was, though. She wanted to shudder. 'I'd get in late and open the bedroom door and leave the hall light on and I'd see his eyes staring at the ceiling, all pink. I mean, I'd put the light on and he'd be asleep.'

'Urgh,' Theresa said.

'I mean – how can you dream if your eyes are open?'

'I don't know,' Theresa breathed.

'I don't know, either. It's not natural, is it,' Marilyn said to her glass.

Theresa shrugged.

'I tried not switching the light on,' Marilyn went on, 'but it was no use, because I knew he was lying next to me with his little pink eyes staring at nothing at all. He was like the undead.' Poor Dave, it wasn't his fault. 'He was all right in the daytime, though, but at night – it gave me the creeps.'

'Yeah, it would,' Theresa said. 'It would give me the creeps too. I mean, it sounds a bit like God, doesn't it,

114

you know, all-seeing. That used to give me the creeps, when Terry would say that.'

'Never stopped him, though, did it,' Marilyn said.

'Well, he decided that God probably wouldn't mind.'

'Try telling the priest that,' Marilyn said, who knew about Catholics.

'He did. That's why they had an argument.'

The lounge bar door opened and a head popped round it.

Marilyn looked up as the head withdrew before reappearing again. 'Oh God it's Harry,' she said, scrabbling for her handbag underneath the table. She found it, and hit the back of her head as she tried to straighten up. Red in the face and forcing herself not to rub the bump, she emerged from beneath the table and pretended not to look at Harry who was rolling towards them, looking pleased. She opened her bag and took out her mirror quickly but Harry had reached her and he snatched it out of her hands and held it up in the air out of reach.

'Harry —' she protested, grabbing his arm, '— give it me back.'

And Harry did.

He sat on the stool next to her, dragging it nearer to hers. 'You don't need that to tell you you're beautiful,' he said, 'believe me. You are.'

Marilyn raised her eyebrows.

'I'm serious,' Harry said, his voice warm and kind. 'I don't know what you wear all that make-up for.'

Marilyn looked at him.

'Don't mind me,' Theresa said, her hand around her empty glass.

'Hello,' said Harry, and he held out his hand.

Theresa shook it, taken aback by the gesture, and blushed.

'I've been looking for you two everywhere,' Harry said.

'You should have looked here first,' Marilyn replied, unimpressed. 'You know we always come here.'

'I thought you might have been at home.'

'Wife out, is she?' Theresa asked meaningfully, rather bitchily, Marilyn thought. She kicked her under the table.

'Yeah, flexing her muscles,' Harry replied.

'You'd better watch yourself,' Theresa said, rubbing her shin.

'I do.'

But he was looking at Marilyn. It was *that* sort of a look – it said he fancied her and he wanted her to know it and he wanted to know what she was going to do about it.

Marilyn looked back. Her look said she was interested and what was he going to do about that?

'She's a DaCosta to her fingernails,' Harry added offhandedly.

Theresa gave him a sympathetic smile but Marilyn knew that the message was for her.

'I'll have a lager,' she said, moving a beermat with her fingertip.

'Me too,' said Theresa.

They both watched Harry as he got up to fetch the drinks.

Marilyn didn't need the cherry brandy now – she'd got the man. She knew she'd got him because of the warning he'd given her but she suspected the warning was Harry's way of making himself look brave.

The DaCostas didn't frighten Marilyn. Arnold DaCosta was a boxing promoter with bigger people than her to make trouble for and she wasn't scared of Debbie, muscles or not.

Anyway, she was entitled to a bit of fun.

She glanced at Harry who was still at the bar, his back towards her. She still had the Body Shop mirror in the palm of her hand and she lifted it to her face and made a swift but careful check for freckles.

'"You look beautiful,"' Theresa said, mimicking Harry's words.

Marilyn snapped the mirror closed and slipped it back into her bag.

She tossed her dark red hair away from her face.

'I know,' she said, and grinned.

11

On the morning of Alex's funeral Catrin went out into the garden and sat on the cold step, her mug steaming raggedly in the breeze.

She was looking forward to the funeral.

The fact that she was looking forward to it troubled her. It seemed as if the focus of her mind's eye had altered so that the only important things were those relevant to the accident. Only twice in the ten days since it had happened had she felt alive: at the inquest and there on the step, with the thought of the funeral in her mind. Like the inquest, it was proof of Alex's death.

After the accident she'd found herself sitting in the bath surreptitiously checking herself for injuries, wondering whether she was sick as she searched for something more than a bruise, longing for her aches to be something serious so that she could say – yes! It really happened! I was hurt too! To be able to suffer the relief of a physical pain to replace the bleak fear that lurked intrusively behind every thought.

She had nothing to remember him by. Never really having known him, she couldn't say she'd lost him – he had never been hers. But he had died on her and the only person she could share it with was him and he was gone.

It wasn't that no-one cared. She knew that in the office they would have collected for a wreath for him, sincerely sorry and shocked as they were at what had happened. 'Shame about Alex. Nice chap,' they'd say. It was the sort of thing she would have said herself. And she knew that, had she died, they would have done it for her. And their expendability frightened her.

'He should be grieved for,' she said aloud, and she put the palm of her cold hand on the rim of the mug beside her and felt a fading warmth like a last gasp that couldn't touch the chill inside her.

'Catrin?'

William's voice coming unexpectedly from behind her startled her. He should have been in work, he'd left that morning as she'd stared at the ceiling in the cold comfort of their bed.

'William – what's wrong?' She automatically looked at her wrist but she wasn't wearing her watch. 'What are you doing home?'

'I couldn't talk to you from the office,' William said. 'Come inside, it's cold out here.'

Catrin followed him in, uneasiness churning her stomach, and sat on the sofa.

William sat on the arm of the chair, towering above her. He gazed speechlessly at his knee for a moment, pinching the trouser crease where it had smoothed out.

'I've just picked up the car from the garage. They can't find anything wrong with it,' he said at last, and looked at her wearily.

The uneasiness in her stomach seemed to spread through her, she could feel it seeping through her veins with her sluggish blood and she felt as though it was something she'd been through before. Something bad. She shut her eyes to clear her head.

'I suppose we shouldn't be surprised at that,' she said.

'Oh?' The word seemed to jerk itself out of William's pinched face.

'It worked again, didn't it, practically straight away,' she said softly, almost to herself. 'As if it had served its purpose.'

'The killer car,' William said with a loud, bitter laugh. 'It breaks down and then it mends itself. What am I supposed to think, Catrin?'

There was a long silence. In the background she could hear the slow inexorable tick of their kitchen clock, time passing.

'The best of me,' she said at last. 'That's what husbands are for.'

William rubbed his hand across his eyes and kept it there for a moment. 'So what do you think happened?' he asked her, his voice deader now.

Catrin stared at the carpet. It seemed to dance before her eyes. 'I can only think it must have been a loose connection,' she said, lifting her head, 'which has righted itself again.'

William nodded his head slowly, his expression a mixture of hope and scepticism. 'A loose connection,' he said.

She'd forgotten what it must be like for him.

She got up and put her arms around him and her lips touched his wiry, shampoo-smelling hair. He didn't move for a moment, but the stiffness went out of his hot body and then he rested his head against her.

They'd been so distant, she thought, in these last few days.

Her gaze wandered to the clock. She should be getting ready for the funeral.

Her spirits rose again with expectation. She kissed her husband's hair absently and was surprised; she'd been expecting it to be silky, black and smooth.

Oh, Alex.

'I'll take you,' William said, coming into the bedroom as she pulled on her black leather gloves. She didn't reply at first, merely kept her eyes on the pores in the grain of the soft calfskin. Her killer gloves, William had called them in the days when death was still a joke.

'I can take a cab,' she said.

'No, it's no problem,' he said.

Catrin looked at herself in the mirror. She felt oddly happy, as if she were going to a wedding; she felt that same sense of expectation inside.

'I can stay with you, if you like,' William added, he who hated funerals, hospitals, any indication of man's mortality, 'unless you think you can manage on your own.'

She smiled, grateful to him not for asking but for showing that he didn't want to go.

'Thanks, there will be people from work there, I can sit with them.'

There seemed to be a trace of citrus in the air. She breathed in but it had gone.

'Are you ready?' William asked her as she picked fluff off her black coat.

'Yes.' She wanted to be early. She wanted to sit

peacefully somewhere near Alex to say goodbye.

'What are you thinking?' William asked as he picked up his keys.

'Just – I suppose we ought to go.'

They got into the car and she put her handbag on the dashboard while she checked the *A – Z*.

They saw the church spire from quite a way off but reaching it was not quite as straightforward.

William, cursing, did another three-point turn while she found her place on the map.

'Sorry, next right,' she said, and laughed. The sound of it, so unexpected, played back in her head. She always used to laugh. She pulled down the sunshield and looked in the mirror. The lighted frame illuminated her face and she pushed up the sunshield and sat back.

'Third on the left,' she said, keeping the page of the *A – Z* open with her leather-clad finger.

Presently they pulled up alongside the church. William looked past her at the lych gate, his face close to hers.

'Sure you don't want me to –' he gestured towards his door.

'No. Really. But thanks.' She looked at the church too, and opened the car door.

'I'll come and pick you up later,' William said.

'OK,' she replied, hardly hearing him. She got out of the car and pushed the gate open. The wind blew her hair and she was so glad that the elements were unrestful. Her father had been buried on a sunny summer's day and she'd hated the weather for its disrespect; the beauty and the sunshine had been a sacrilege. Now, she was glad of the wind.

She reached the door half expecting it to be locked, but the latch lifted easily and when she pushed, it opened.

The inner door was already ajar and Catrin stepped through it into the church. It was vast and cool and dark.

At the front of the church, near the altar, she could see the coffin shining in the steady, unwavering gleam of two candles.

She walked down the aisle towards it, her heels tapping on the cold stone floor.

When she reached the coffin she could see it was made of polished pine. It was on a brass trolley. In the old church it looked rather new and self-conscious.

She tentatively put her hand on the wooden box. It was hard to imagine Alex in there. He should have had a sarcophagus, she thought; gold leaf and perhaps a hologram of him on the front.

Tears rushed hot and unwanted into her eyes and she brushed them away and took off her gloves. With her forefinger she touched the brass name-plate gently. ALEX EDWARD MARTIN. She hadn't known his middle name before. Taking her hand away she saw that she had left a fingermark on the brass. She felt for her handkerchief and realised that she'd left her handbag in the car. Reaching out her arm she tried to get the mark off with her sleeve but before she was able to she heard the clatter of the door-latch and a wedge of light grew larger as the outer door opened.

Tiny heels, heels like hers, tapped along the stone floor towards her and broke into a run.

Catrin saw Frances Bennett, blonde hair tucked into a huge black-and-white-hooped hat, run down the aisle towards the coffin, a cry trailing behind her like a banner.

She stopped rather abruptly on seeing Catrin. 'Oh,' she said, and her large eyes filled with unshed tears as she, too, laid her hand on the coffin lid. In the other hand she held a red rose scarred up the stem where the thorns had been pressed off. 'I loved him,' she said tremulously, looking from the name-plate to Catrin. 'He was going to marry me.'

'I'm sorry,' Catrin said. Their voices echoed in the cold church.

Frances put the rose on the coffin and looked at it. It seemed rather forlorn and she picked it up again.

'Why did he have to die,' she asked Catrin, 'when he knew I loved him?'

'I don't know. I'm so sorry.'

Frances frowned and tried again with the rose, which was beginning to wilt. She placed it above the name-plate and looked at it with her head to one side.

'I should have bought a bouquet of them,' she said. 'I was going to drop it in at the burial. Drop it in, do you think? Or it might be nice to have it on the top through the service. I mean there are no flowers.'

'His parents didn't want them?'

'His parents are dead. He's just got an uncle. He wants donations to go to the Cheshire Homes.' Her normally inexpressive face screwed up in a way that would have appalled her had she been able to see it, and Catrin put out her hand.

'I'm so sorry,' she said again as Frances's tears spilled down her face.

'Why did he have to die?' Frances demanded and Catrin didn't and couldn't begin to answer.

People were beginning to come in now, taking their seats and talking in whispers.

'I suppose we ought to sit down,' Catrin said, but Frances shied back towards the polished pine.

'I belong here,' she said, 'next to him.' She took a small silk handkerchief from her sleeve and dabbed under her eyes and stopped suddenly, mid-dab, as though something had just occurred to her. 'You were with him, weren't you, Catrin, when he died? Did he mention me? Do you remember his last words?'

Catrin saw the undertaker hover in the aisle. She rubbed her temple and remembered only too easily, how could she not? They were embedded in her for life, those gentle, lime-scented words, that he thought they should go to the party.

Was that how death had seemed to him, like a party about to begin? Was that what had made it so terribly easy for him to go?

'What did he say?' Frances demanded of her, jerking her sleeve.

Catrin was startled. 'He said he was muddled,' she said, drifting back into remembrance. And what had she replied? That at least he knew he was.

'It's not much help.'

She was aware of Frances staring at her with sudden understanding. 'It was you . . .' she said.

Catrin looked away into the steadily filling church. She saw William standing near the font looking for her, her handbag in his hand.

'It was you,' Frances repeated, and her voice contained not grief, not pain but a rising note of triumph. 'You are the Poison.'

Catrin's eyes met William's across the church. He lifted her bag up to show her why he was there.

'You've got your own man,' Frances said, her eyes gleaming, 'why did you have to kill mine?'

And William was walking towards them now, his tired face stretched into a smile as he held out the bag, and Frances, aware only of her own small drama, asked in her strident and spoilt and piteous voice: 'Why couldn't you have left him alone?'

William had never felt so clear-headed in his life as when he pulled away from the church.

He drove calmly until he saw an empty phone box and although he hadn't intended to, although it hadn't been planned, he stopped the car and got out.

He pulled open the door and stepped inside. He jingled coins in his pockets, remembering that he'd decided to ask Catrin to sew them up. Still, just as well he hadn't. He placed the coins in a small pile, largest at the bottom, on the telephone, and thought briefly of Catrin and was caught in a spasm of hurt for his lovely wife.

Wives asked for New Man, he thought, and when they had him, this was how they treated him. Well — no more.

He stared at the phone.

What women didn't realise was that beneath every one-hundred-per-cent cotton shirt was a primitive man trying to beat his chest.

William Howden, primitive man, read the instructions for obtaining the emergency services. Suddenly he heard someone cough exaggeratedly outside the phone box. It was a 'hurry up' cough and surprisingly effective. He huddled around the phone and put in his money and dialled.

Behind him the coughing continued, making him edgy.

In his ear the phone rang unanswered.

He pressed the follow-on button and tried again. This time, in his ear, a soft and unperturbed voice announced herself as *Media News*.

'Jenna?' he asked, his voice almost a whisper. He cleared his throat. 'Jenna?' Better. 'William Howden here.'

'Oh, Mr Howden.'

He cursed himself. He should have said, William here. And then she would have said, mortifyingly, William who? Now he was Mr Howden.

'Any messages for me?' he asked.

'Just one moment please, I'll put you through to your secretary.'

'No!' he yelled before the click, 'Jenna, are you there?'

'Mr Howden?'

A fierce banging broke out on the glass of the booth. He hunched further over the phone.

'Jenna?'

'Mr Howden, there's a terrible noise, I can hardly hear you –'

'Yes, I know, I'm covering a –' What was he going to say? A riot? 'Never mind that, Jenna, I was wondering –'

'Yes Mr Howden?'

'I was wondering whether you were free –'

The banging broke out again. The glass sounded insecure in the door.

'For lunch sometime?' Jenna asked softly in his ear.

William stared at the Instructions for Use. It was as easy as that, he thought. Or it could be.

The realisation made him giddy.

Behind him the banging started afresh.

'Er, actually,' he said, thinking quickly, 'I meant, were you free to pass on a message to Hugh, to tell him that I'll be in later?' But he smiled as he said it; people could detect a smile in a voice.

He replaced the phone and turned to fight.

On the other side of the door stood, to his relief, not an angry mob but a small middle-aged woman who was pointing at his car. 'It's blocking my drive,' she said as he came out, 'and I've got to pick up my grandchildren.'

'I understand,' he said. He did. He got into his car and drove it slowly up the road away from the telephone kiosk.

He thought about the call and about Jenna's young voice.

It was as easy as that.

So why did he feel so disapproving and so pleased? Because whatever Catrin had done, he himself was made of sterner stuff. He was not like Catrin and he was not like his father. Primitive man might have made himself known, but new man, surprise, surprise, still had some life in him yet.

12

That evening Marilyn, fully made up, was lying on her purple sofa watching television. Watching was the word; she'd long lost track of the film's storyline but, as she put it to herself, it didn't matter because there wasn't anything else on.

Evenings always dragged for her when she had the boys.

Evenings were the loneliest time of the day.

In the early days of her divorce from Dave she'd kept the boys up to keep her company but after regularly finding them sleeping on a camp bed outside the classroom at going-home time she'd reconciled herself to her lonely nights.

She didn't hear the knock on the door at first; or rather, she did hear it, but thought it was part of the film. It was only when it became more persistent that she sat up, got up off the sofa and went to the door warily. Usually people buzzed the outside bell . . .

'Who is it?'

'It's Harry. Harry from upstairs.' There was a pause. Then he added, 'Have you got any sugar?'

The drowsiness she'd felt watching the film cleared like bubbles in salt water. 'Just a minute,' she said, and she ran to the bathroom to check her freckles. All covered. Good old Dermablend. She ran back to the door and opened it.

Harry was standing there, his permanently pleased smile shining up his face and a sugar bowl, held out like a burnt offering, in his hand.

'Hello,' he said.

'Hello. You'd better come in.'

'Thanks.' Harry made for the sofa and sat in it as though it was his. He took up most of it. 'Debbie's gone weight-training,' he said. He looked at Marilyn appreciatively and his face suddenly dropped. 'It's like living with Arnold Schwarzenegger.'

Marilyn tossed her red hair away from her face. 'Most men would like their women fit,' she said teasingly.

'Fit for what?'

For a moment their eyes met. Marilyn was the first to look away. She was smiling to herself. 'Cup of tea?' she asked.

'If you're making one,' Harry said enthusiastically, putting his sugar bowl on the arm of the chair. He said it with the appreciation of one who usually has to make his own.

'Won't be a minute.'

Marilyn went into the kitchen with a grin on her face. She waited while the kettle boiled and she made the tea in a teapot, rather than putting a teabag in a mug as she usually did.

'How many sugars?' she called as she poured it.

'Don't take it,' he called back.

She came back out with the mugs and as she handed him one she said: 'So why did you want to borrow some?'

130

Harry didn't even seem abashed. He looked carefully at the pattern on the side of the mug and smiled, showing he thought she had good taste. 'I don't suppose you remember what happened in the pub New Year's Eve,' he said.

Remember? It was all she'd thought about ever since.

'I wasn't drunk, if that's what you mean,' she said coolly.

Harry smiled to himself and looked straight into her eyes. 'That red lipstick,' he said reflectively. 'You haven't got it on tonight.'

'No.'

'You look nice without it. You knock spots off anyone around here.'

The make-up knocks spots off, if only you knew, she thought lamely.

'Where do you work?' she asked him, changing the subject.

'British Telecom.'

'Oh.'

'Where do you work?' asked Harry.

'I do cleaning jobs.'

Harry's eyebrows lifted in flattering surprise although they all cleaned for someone, her lot. Still, it seemed as though he'd marked her out as being something else.

'But what's your dream?'

Embarrassed, Marilyn looked away. 'Don't be daft, I haven't got one.' She poked the carpet with her toe and then looked up at him. 'I can't afford dreams.'

'Dreams are free,' Harry replied. 'Everyone should have a dream.'

The idea amused her. 'Okay.' She stretched her arms out and yawned comfortably. 'What would my dream be? I suppose I'd like to open a sandwich bar.' Yes, that was her dream. 'Ten till three, lunchtime service only, so that I could still take the twins to school and pick them up.' She liked the sound of that. 'I'd have it done out in red checks.'

'Better than bouncing ones.'

Marilyn smiled at him. She wanted to hit him, in a friendly way. 'Are you always like this?' she asked.

Harry shook his head. 'Not really,' he said. 'Not when Debbie's around. That woman's taken the shine off me.' He rubbed at a mark on his trousers reflectively. 'She makes me feel all tarnished.'

'You're mad. Why don't you leave her?' Marilyn asked curiously. She liked getting down to practicalities.

'She's a DaCosta, isn't she,' Harry said.

Marilyn gave a laugh. Arnold DaCosta, gangster with a reputation, wore bright tracksuits and shades, constantly. It was quite helpful for those who wanted to steer clear of him – it made him easier to spot.

'You're not scared of them, are you?' she teased.

'I'm scared of Arnold,' Harry said ruefully. 'He makes bloody sure of that.'

Marilyn looked at the man-mountain on her sofa, half-amused. 'I can't imagine you being scared of anyone,' she said. 'And DaCosta's only small.'

'Small but evil.'

He didn't seem inclined to say any more.

'Still,' Marilyn said, 'you should be allowed to leave her. I mean – if you told her you didn't love her she wouldn't want to stay with you anyway, would she?'

'You don't know Debbie. She likes to see me suffer.'

Suppressing a laugh, Marilyn said: 'You? You don't know what it is to suffer, look at you.'

Harry grinned. 'Yeah, nothing much affects me.' He added: 'But you do.'

He put his mug to his mouth.

Marilyn was reminded once more of a St Bernard dog. Harry had that St Bernard heaviness, the solidity, the friendliness. You could curl up with a man like Harry, she thought.

Harry finished his tea. He looked at his watch.

'What time does she get back?' Marilyn asked, jerking her head upwards in the direction of Harry's flat.

'Any time she wants,' Harry said. 'I'd better go.' He stood up reluctantly and gave her the mug. Their fingers touched around the handle.

'Come again if you like,' Marilyn said diffidently but her eyes flickered to his lips. She couldn't help but remember that sweet, medicinal kiss in the thick smoky dark of the pub.

As though he was reading her mind he bent his head swiftly and brushed her lips with his so lightly that they hardly touched. 'See you,' he said.

She wanted to shiver with that small thrill of excitement but she folded her arms and watched him go out of the door. Moments later she heard his footsteps on the floor above her.

She picked up his mug and saw the dried drips of tea on the side, where his lips had been. She put it to her lips but it was cold. Unlike Harry.

He'd left his sugar bowl.

Which meant a return journey.

She sat down and looked at the flickering television again. So she wanted to own a sandwich bar, did she? Well, why not? As Harry had said, dreams were free. And he'd kissed her. Sort of.

Altogether he'd kissed her twice.

She wondered what DaCosta would have made of that.

13

The day after the funeral William was in his office looking through *Newsdesk* with the concentration of an examiner. Jeff – it was personal with Jeff, now.

William found that he was the only trade editor not to have included in his paper the wonderful story about Alex Martin's mysterious death in a field with married Catrin Howden by his side. Strange, really, because it was a good story, full of innuendo and well-written.

The fact that they were on their way to a presentation had not been mentioned despite the fact that it would have been natural for them to have shared a car. And of course an ordinary explanation was superfluous to the story; what's more, it would have ruined it. As an editor he could, of course, see that.

William dropped the paper on his desk.

It was as a husband that he hated Jeff, not as a boss.

He looked through the window towards Jeff who was sitting at his desk smoking languidly with one hand and writing with the other.

Traitor, William thought. That he should have taken Jeff, of all people, to witness Catrin's lie about the car having broken down – he could hardly bear to think of it.

He stood up, agitated with resentment.

Jeff moved too; he was now sitting on the edge of his desk, leaning forward a little, his eyes narrowed against the smoke from the cigarette in the crystal ashtray. It was a pose, William could see that; he knew that that amount of careless style could only be contrived.

William's face twisted with a sudden dislike.

He had never felt out of control in his life but now, for the first time, he felt the clinging unease of the weak. Things seemed to be moving independently, out of his grasp, changing of their own volition. Catrin started it, he thought. She'd weakened him. The Delilah syndrome had got hold of him. He wiped his hand across his eyes.

Suddenly he saw Jeff move away from his desk. A flash of red, quickly obscured by Jeff, caught his eye but William knew that it was Jenna. Couldn't miss that dress. It had caught his eye that morning. 'Hi,' she'd said to him with a shy smile as his eyes had drifted across her dress to her face. Hi. Not, 'Good morning, Mr Howden,' as she had at first.

William felt a jab of irritation as he saw Jeff offer her a cigarette. Who was on the switchboard while she was up here, distracting his staff?

He saw Jeff swinging around with a look of annoyance on his face. The cigarette packet dropped onto the table.

Jenna was walking towards him. William sat down hurriedly and stared at the papers on his desk.

There was a tap on the door. A light tap. The equivalent of a gentle cough.

'Come in.'

She came in, no smile now, and stood wistfully in

front of his desk, her large, mascaraless, sad blue eyes resting on him. She's got a lovely mouth, he thought reluctantly, still holding her responsible for his wife's accident – why not blame the messenger? – although he knew, of course, Catrin had only herself to blame.

He didn't say anything at first. Something in him shied from what she was going to say. It was bound to be something troublesome. She was handing in her notice or she wanted holiday leave or time off for a dentist's appointment, i.e. a job interview. But as the silence went on he leaned back in his chair and raised his eyebrows queryingly, wondering what was going on in the mind behind those brilliant, sad blue eyes. They seemed hardly real. But strangely enough they made him feel interested again.

'Yes?' he said at last, with the air of one pretending to offer his full attention.

'We –'

She stopped after the one word but it reminded him of how young her voice was. And she looked stricken. She was going to hand in her notice. Great. Why tell him? The advertising chaps did the hiring and firing. He wished she'd get on with it.

'What is it?' he asked abruptly.

'We've had a collection for your wife and bought her a basket of fruit.' Her eyes were sadder still, and full of understanding. They were the impossible blue of picture-postcard skies. 'I'm so sorry for you.'

For a moment he hardly knew what he had heard and then he thought, "for you." She'd actually said that.

He realised suddenly that the office was very quiet,

that he could smell her perfume even from this distance.

He raised an eyebrow wryly and unexpectedly told her the truth. 'I feel sorry for myself.'

She nodded and put her hand to her hair, smoothing it back. It was so much like his, slightly coarse, that as she stroked it again he could feel it as though he was doing it with his own hand.

'Is she out of hospital yet?'

'Yes, she is. Yes. She's going back to work tomorrow.' William was aware during this exchange of talking about his wife as though she were an old relation, someone distant. Yes. Catrin *was* someone distant, prowling around with wide-open eyes so as not to miss anything else fate might throw at her. Prowling around on the alert all the time, as if it would help.

Jenna smiled sympathetically. The smile had a funny effect on him. It was a smile with a message. 'I'd better go,' she said. 'The basket is downstairs. It's got things in it like figs and pomegranates and lychees.'

William ate apples and oranges, himself. But Catrin would probably like it. 'Thank you,' he said and looked at her again. He wasn't sure whether he usually looked directly at people or not, and if he did, why looking at Jenna should seem such a personal thing to do.

He felt as though he must, some time recently, have stopped looking people in the eye.

Jenna lowered her head and her face was immediately hidden by her hair.

Pow!

William, married and cheated on, felt, for no particular reason and with no particular joy, that he had scored one against his wife.

It was raining that afternoon.

William wondered if it was the rain that had brought him there as he stood, wet and cold, outside his parents' house waiting for his mother to open the door.

He'd been thirteen when he'd first realised the spasmodic unhappiness in the house was caused by his father's 'little indiscretions'.

He'd heard his mother, once again, crying in the bathroom. He'd thought that was where women did their crying – he'd grown up with it, the sound of sobbing against running water. She must have thought it drowned it out – it did for her, of course, but not for him, standing stiff and troubled outside.

'It means nothing,' he'd heard his father protest, not just that time but over and over across the years, like a sort of motto.

Then, the thirteen-year-old William had thought, why do it? And it was what the thirty-five-year-old William thought now. With Catrin's infidelity, his greatest fear had been realised. He could feel his marriage crumbling under his feet like arid soil. He could feel his life breaking up.

He hammered on the door again, soaking wet and cold.

Finally the door opened and his mother greeted him with her well-bred lack of surprise. 'William,' she said, 'you're soaking. Come in. Is Catrin with you?'

'No.' All his desperation seemed to go into the word but he waited, dripping, while she took off his jacket.

'Tea? Brandy?'

William wanted neither but his mother based her life on formalities.

'I'll have an Irish,' he said.

'Ice?'

'Just water.'

He waited for her to get it and looked at the photographs in their silver frames. Next to his parents' wedding photograph was one of him and Catrin. Catrin looked calm and terribly beautiful in her straight, cream wedding dress. He, proud and tall, stood next to her, his arm around her waist. They were both looking at the camera with the eyes of those who have nothing to hide.

'Your father's not in at the moment,' his mother said, coming back. 'He's gone to play chess with Boris.'

'Fine,' William said and wondered where to go from there. It was his mother he wanted to speak to. Why, at thirty-five years of age, did he want to talk to his mother about something real? 'It was you I wanted, as a matter of fact.'

He felt, rather than saw, her apprehension. A pause. 'How can I help you?' She was always polite.

'You and Pa –' he began. There was ice in his drink after all. He swirled the fluid around the glass and the ice cubes chinked gently. ' – I know things haven't always been –'

His mother looked at him gently. 'We've been married for almost forty years, you know.'

'Forty years?' he said, grasping the phrase as though it were a rope with which to swing himself out of trouble. 'Special anniversary I suppose,' but he didn't know when – he would if he thought about it. Forty years.

She was his mother.

'It's not always easy,' she said, 'for anybody.'

He knew then that he hadn't come for sympathy but for advice.

'You know my thoughts on marriage,' she said, 'and it was in church, too. You'll have to be strong for both of you.' There was the merest touch of disappointment in her voice.

William drank his Irish all in one go and felt worse than ever. 'How did you manage?' he asked. 'How did you cope? You and Pa –'

'There was never,' she said firmly, 'anyone else for either of us.'

William put down his empty glass. His mother was still looking him in the eye. He could hear the rain smattering the window. Against the sound of running water from the gutters outside he could hear her crying, behind the bathroom door.

'Thanks, Mother,' he said.

Back out in the rain his isolation grew as he repeated her denial in his head while he knew for sure she was lying.

That night he returned home late to find all the lights on in the house and Catrin in bed. The house was tidy, not out of care but out of a lack of use.

Catrin was sitting up in bed hugging her knees.

'How was your day?' he asked her as he took off his jacket.

'Fine,' she replied brightly.

He took a coat hanger out of the wardrobe to hang

his suit on. As he undid his tie he looked at the daffodils in their goldfish bowl. They were dead, yellow trumpets transformed into brown paper, crumpled much as they'd been to start with but without the promise of glory to come. He fancied that the water, sulphur yellow, was beginning to smell.

He undressed quietly and got into bed. 'You're going in tomorrow?'

'Yes. Back to work. Back to normal,' Catrin said and turned over, pulling the sheets with her.

He switched off the light and turned too and clung to his side of the bed. He tried to breathe steadily and finally he fell asleep to dream of Jenna and hesitant smiles; of a world which was controllable and of emotions understood.

Later that night Catrin woke briefly. She sought warmth not against the hot smooth surface of her husband's back but in the sleepy memory of disconnected words: would you hold my hand, my head.

And smelling the scent of limes in the room, she sank back into sleep.

14

When Catrin had said she'd be back to normal she'd genuinely believed it.

It was a matter of the will, that was all. And work was balm, wasn't it?

Wearing red for confidence Catrin walked into the quiet buzz of office conversation punctuated by ringing phones and knew that she'd done the right thing. She smiled to herself. It felt good to be back.

But as she was striding towards her office, something happened. The murmur of voices ceased. She stopped in mid-stride, surprised, and looked round to see what was happening. Somewhere close to her a phone began to ring and continued ringing, unanswered.

She looked at the bank of faces. She was aware of a few eyes on her, but not all, by any means. Heads were averted, some in embarrassment and a couple in sympathy; she felt her heart begin to thump.

In the still workplace the ringing continued persistently and intrusively and no-one made a move to stop it.

For what seemed like a long time she stood there, afflicted by the same paralysis that had seemed to come over the office.

She swallowed hard, and felt her saliva negotiate

what felt like an extraordinary obstruction in her throat.

'Someone get that phone,' she said loudly and the paralysis that had momentarily come over her left her; she carried on to her office and opened the door.

Once inside she closed it behind her and leaned against it, her breath coming in short jerks. She could hear the office hum rise behind the door in a sort of crescendo, and settle.

It's all right, she told herself; it wasn't that bad. A job wasn't like death, a job was just a job.

She sat down at her desk and after a moment she picked up her phone for her secretary. 'Fiona? Could I see you, please?'

Fiona came in seconds later holding a box file in her hand as though for protection. She looked slightly sheepish and her plump face was flushed.

'Sit down,' Catrin said.

Fiona looked disconcerted and sat on the edge of the chair as if ready to make a quick getaway.

'Um,' she said before Catrin could continue, 'we weren't expecting you to return so soon. Frances isn't back yet, you know.' Her eyes flashed at Catrin. 'She's heartbroken, she's wearing black.' Fiona's expression showed the slightest possible sign of distaste as she added: 'And hats.'

That figured, Catrin thought.

'She has been in, obviously.'

'Yes,' Fiona said, and added hurriedly, 'but she had to be sent home.'

Catrin nodded. Frances in hysterics in the office was not unknown.

'How,' Fiona asked, her voice suddenly gentle, 'are you feeling?'

Surprised by the question, Catrin didn't answer for a moment. 'Oh,' she said, 'all right.'

Fiona nodded, taking her at her word. She pushed herself further back in the chair and breathed in deeply as though bracing herself for something. 'You might as well know, Frances is saying you and Alex had a thing going,' she said quickly, glancing towards the door as if there might be eavesdroppers. 'She hired a private detective to follow him. You have to feel sorry for her –' she folded her arms defensively, ' – she was so upset by the news.'

The mention of Alex's name, so casually used, was like a gift to Catrin. It brought him back to her, real and warm.

'I mean,' Fiona continued, 'no-one had ever even caught a whiff of gossip. I hope you don't mind me mentioning it. Of course, it's none of my business what you do.'

Catrin raised her eyes. They felt heavy, she would have liked to have closed them and rested her head on her arms and slept. Hopefully to dream. Hopefully to escape.

'No,' she said with effort, 'I'm glad you told me. There was nothing between us.'

Fiona nodded. She looked full of satisfaction. 'I said we would have known. I'll put them right,' she said. 'Coffee?'

Catrin shook her head, sick with a sense of having betrayed Alex.

Nothing between them? It wasn't true what she had said, it wasn't true at all. Because when she thought of Alex, of the touch of him in the car with her when he was going, she knew without a doubt that in those moments she had loved him.

That afternoon as she was preparing to leave for home, there was a knock on her door.

Whether Fiona's counter-gossip had been unsuccessful or not-yet-embarked-upon she didn't know, but the caller was Alex's ultra-efficient secretary, Enid, a middle-aged woman with a correct manner and a warm heart.

'These were in his drawer,' she said. 'Thought you might know what to do with them.'

And she placed on Catrin's desk, like offerings on an altar, a spare set of house keys, a bottle of Mont Blanc ink and Limes, by Floris.

15

Two weeks into the new year Jonathan Wade was still playing with his Christmas presents.

His attitude to golf clubs was almost the same as his wife's was to cosmetics – the newer the better. As a result, Amelia's bathroom was studded with gilt-lidded jars and Jonathan's jeep was bristling with clubs; all crying out to be used.

The thing was, new clubs really could make a difference.

He glanced at himself in his mirror wardrobes, smoothed down his hair and stood back to practise his swing with his latest driver.

He was favourably impressed by it. It was strange really how much better his swing was in the privacy of his own room. It was, he had to admit, well nigh faultless.

Now all he had to do was to persuade Amelia to let him go down to the driving range.

He tossed the club onto the bed and turned back to the mirror. He tried his swing without the club and it still looked good – he had the rhythm, he really did.

He popped his head into Amelia's room. She wasn't there and he walked to her bathroom door.

'Amelia? Are you in there?'

Instead of a reply there was a sort of choking sound.

Jonathan raised an eyebrow. He often did that sort of thing, as though he was in a film. It was, he supposed, a habit. It was something he'd learned at school and it had taken a great deal of practice to perfect. The secret was to hold the inactive eyebrow down and raise the other until one got a sense of which muscle was involved — it had taken days to learn and he was still quite pleased at having mastered it. He forced his attention back to Amelia.

'Darling?'

'Jonathan . . .'

The word came out as a broken cry, followed by the choking sob again.

Jonathan stepped away from the door.

Crying was always trouble. It meant she needed him and if she needed him he wouldn't be able to go to the driving range and the Day of the Perfect Swing would pass and he might never have quite such a good chance again.

He took another step backwards.

'Jonathan?'

She made it sound as if she could see him! He hurried back to the door. 'Darling?'

'Come in, will you?'

So he reluctantly pushed the door open and saw Amelia sitting on the low-level WC that they'd had put in to replace the genuinely ancient one that had been there before, and she was crying silently into her hands, as though the world had come to an end.

'What is it?' Jonathan asked, frightened.

Amelia took her hands away.

'My period,' she said.

Jonathan felt himself go weak with relief. Nothing serious! He could be out within the hour!

He was aware of Amelia's pink, wet eyes on his and he adjusted his expression as best he could.

'You don't care,' she said flatly, wiping the tears away with toilet roll.

'Of course I do,' he retorted. 'I care a lot. But we can keep trying.' He reached out and put his hand on her bare knee. It seemed rather a daring thing to do. He'd never touched Amelia while she was sitting on the lavatory before. Or anyone else, come to that.

'What if it wasn't the cyst? What if it's just me?'

'Ah, well. You've still got me,' he said consolingly; but surprisingly she didn't seem to be consoled.

'I was so sure,' she said, 'so sure, this time.' The tears started afresh. 'What if I've left it too late?'

Jonathan felt a trifle more alarmed. Amelia wasn't into soul-searching of any kind, probably because she didn't have one.

'Too late? People have them when they're ancient now,' he said. 'You've got another twenty-odd years yet.'

The thought of only twenty-odd years to antiquity struck him, once he'd said it, as a little off-putting; but he'd meant for women, of course. It was different for men. Oddly enough, though, Amelia was looking more cheerful now.

'I do love you,' she said. It sounded rather endearing.

'And I love you.' He patted her on her bare knee. This was his chance. 'Er, Amelia – mind if I pop out?'

Amelia blew her nose. 'Golf I suppose? No, I don't mind. I think I'll ring Henry.'

'You do that,' Jonathan said, going back to the bedroom for his club. He looked at himself in the wardrobe mirror and grinned. He'd handled it rather well. He could be very sensitive when he tried.

And where women were concerned it was something to be proud of.

16

Three weeks after the crash, on a sunny Saturday afternoon, Catrin splashed herself with Limes, by Floris, left a silent William reading *Wisden* and headed for the gym.

The air was crisp and the sky was blue.

She parked her car near the health club and she took out her bag and hoisted it over one shoulder. The weather made her feel optimistic; it was an optimistic sort of day, bringing with it thoughts of spring.

She breathed deeply and let it out like a sigh. Her breath clouded finely in the chill air and she walked into the foyer with her face tingling from the cold.

'Hi,' she said to the girl behind the desk, dropping her bag at her feet. 'Are the toning tables free?'

'I'll just check,' the receptionist said with a smile of recognition. She traced a manicured finger along a line in her appointments book and looked up. 'Sure,' she said.

Catrin picked up her bag.

'Did you have a good Christmas?' the receptionist asked.

Catrin hesitated for a moment, then she said, 'Yes. Yes, thanks, I did. You?'

'Great. Put on a few pounds.' She looked at Catrin. 'You look as though you've lost a bit.'

Catrin smiled wryly. 'You never know,' she said, and headed for the changing room.

It was something, wasn't it? She'd discovered the secret of effortless slimming. She could write a book about it – *Losing Weight the Howden Way*.

First, kill a colleague . . .

Not funny.

She took a pink T-shirt and leggings out of her bag and changed into them and strolled into the toning-tables room. She liked toning tables. No more aerobics – no more going into the class looking like Jane Fonda and coming out like Henry. No; exercising on her back was definitely more her style. Since she wasn't getting any exercise with William.

She gathered up her dark hair and tied it with a pink towelling band.

'If you're ready, Catrin,' said a familiar voice.

'Hi, Louise,' Catrin said, getting onto the warm-up bed.

'Nice to see you back.'

'Nice to *be* back.'

Louise switched the machine on.

Lying on the rhythmic bed, her tense muscles soothing themselves by relaxing and contracting against the machine, Catrin began to feel a certain release. The whole world didn't, as she'd begun to think, revolve around the accident. It was time, now, that she put it behind her. What was done was done, there was no putting it right, no going back, only forward.

And William . . .

She and William would have to talk. They were

married, they were supposed to be on the same side. She hadn't paid him enough attention, she knew that; Alex Martin's death had used up all her resources, leaving nothing for her husband. But they'd be all right.

She tensed her muscles against the machine and relaxed, tensed, relaxed.

It was so nice to be back, she thought, looking at the prints on the walls. After the session she would shower in the pale lilac shower stalls and wrap herself up in one of their fluffy lilac bathrobes and have a facial, or perhaps a body wrap, Frigi Thalgo, all that camphor and menthol smelling so strongly you knew it was doing you good.

And fortified, pampered, she would make it up to William.

She heard a familiar voice against the churning sound of the machine.

'Hi guys!'

She would make it up to William, start afresh.

'News, darlings –'

Put things right, get life back to normal, not mention the past again.

'– Catrin's been having an affair. And she was in a crash and this guy was killed –'

Catrin raised her head, a chill creeping up her body, freezing her, she could feel her hair stiffening, going brittle, snapping off.

'– in a field!' the voice ended triumphantly, Sarah's voice, gleeful, scornful, confiding. 'So much for the perfect marriage!'

Catrin felt herself being humped about by the bed; it was like trying to get off a bucking bronco, the machine was shoving her around like a sack of potatoes. She landed on her feet, put her hand out to steady herself.

By the desk Louise was looking at her, stricken, over Sarah's shoulders. Sarah, still leaning over the desk, suddenly straightened and turned in the direction of Louise's horrified stare, a wide smile congealing on her face until it was a mockery of itself, not a smile; there wasn't a trace of humour. All that was left was a grimace.

'Catrin.'

Catrin didn't reply.

By her side the bed bucked, riderless.

'Oh, shit,' Sarah said.

'Upside-down,' Catrin heard herself say in a low voice. 'You forgot to say that we were upside-down.'

A momentary flare of interest betrayed the fact that Sarah hadn't said they were upside-down because she hadn't known it. But she knew now.

'Look,' Louise said, 'maybe it would be best –'

'I'm not leaving,' Sarah said, 'I don't see why I should. I'm sorry, Catrin, but I was only telling the truth. It's not as if it isn't common knowledge.'

For a moment Catrin could only stare at her. 'Sarah, there was no affair,' she said finally. 'You, of all people, should know that.'

Louise, at the edge of her field of vision, was edging towards the bed, unsure whether to turn it off and thus get in the line of fire, or whether to stay where she was.

Catrin was looking at Sarah's face. It was smooth, unlined, familiar and hard. She'd never noticed the hardness before.

Sarah flicked a strand of blonde hair behind her ear. 'Catrin, you're human like the rest of us. There's no point in acting so holier-than-thou. If you don't talk, how are we supposed to know the truth? I thought we were friends,' she said, aggrieved.

'The accident wasn't something I wanted to talk about.'

Sarah's face softened. 'Look, everyone goes through a bad patch. I've had a couple of flirtations myself. To get back at Roger. I know what it's like.'

Catrin didn't say a word. She was too stunned to reply.

'You poor thing,' Sarah said. Her voice was sweet with pity and regret, she could afford it now that the damage was done. She made to put her arm around Catrin and for a moment – for a moment Catrin would have given anything to have a good cry.

Right beside her, the bed continued to rock and toss.

Catrin knew that the balance of power had shifted, that the tables were turned.

She had always been so proud of her marriage. It seemed to her now that she and William had given dinner parties so that it could be seen by others in its perfect setting, while all along her friends were ignoring their standards and having affairs.

'Of course, we came out of it,' Sarah was saying.

Meanwhile Louise had come to a decision. She strode over to the bed and switched it off.

Sarah let her arm drop from Catrin's stiff shoulders.

Louise was looking at her. 'Shall I get you a cup of tea?' she asked.

'No, thanks. Another time.'

Was that her voice, strong and ordinary? She was

surprised. She went to the changing room and put her jacket on over her leggings and T-shirt. The rest of her clothes she put into her bag.

Sarah came in. 'Look,' she said, 'these things happen. Couples stop getting on, but it's not the end of the world. Come round and we'll talk about it. You know how much Lottie likes you . . .'

Catrin put her bag over her shoulder. 'It might have happened to you but it's not going to happen to us,' she said.

She walked past Sarah. The sound of Sarah's exasperated sigh pursued her to the door.

Catrin got home and found William in the garden, bowling a baseball at the wall with tense ferocity.

She stood in the doorway, watching him.

He threw it over and over again, always catching it despite the force with which it rebounded.

She should have been able to go over and stand by him, ask him if he wanted a coffee. He hadn't changed, he was the same man. Neither had she changed; so why couldn't she remember how to say it naturally?

She went inside to get a sweater and came back out, pulling it on. William had stopped bowling and was sitting on a garden chair, his arms on his knees, his hands dangling, his damp hair sticking to the sweat on his forehead.

'I'm just making a coffee,' she said, walking across the grass to him.

He didn't raise his head.

'Sarah was at the gym. She was saying all sorts of things about their relationship –'

William looked up, a ghost of a smile on his face.

'Sarah would.' He gave a quick laugh. 'That's discretion for you.'

'William, it's not funny,' she said, anger flaring up out of nowhere.

His smile died away. 'I know.'

She felt disadvantaged, standing up. 'Our marriage is all right, isn't it?'

For a moment she thought he was going to fudge it, pretend he hadn't understood the question, but he didn't.

'I don't know,' he said quietly.

She felt a cold hand close around her heart. 'You don't know?'

Funny how everything else seemed to drift away, even the traffic seemed quiet.

'We always said – if one of us ever was unfaithful – that it would be the end –' William rubbed his cheekbone with his thumb and came to a halt.

Catrin fell to her knees in front of him on the cold damp grass. 'Yes, but we haven't been, have we? I know how you feel about it, that's what's made ours so strong –'

He looked at her, disappointed, and was silent.

It was cold, out in the garden. The sky above them was still blue and the sun still shone but it was low in the sky and feeble.

William's eyes met hers. He stood up. 'Come on,' he said, 'get up. You'll get cold.'

He held out his hand for her and she took it and he pulled her to her feet.

The knees of her pink leggings were muddy.

He brushed at them, knocking away stray blades of grass.

They went back into the house.

'It's so chilly,' William said and shut the doors. 'Oh, Catrin, why?'

He hugged her violently, squeezing the breath out of her and she felt her knees buckling under his weight. He straightened, let her go, and as she staggered, he put his hand beneath her chin and raised it.

She let her face be lifted to his. He began to kiss her, hard, for the first time since the accident. Her lips were pressed against her teeth, he kissed her unrelentingly, angrily. She felt the taste of blood in her mouth and pushed him away.

'Stop it,' she said, 'you're hurting.'

He stood back from her helplessly and wiped his mouth with the back of his hand and stared at the trace of blood on it.

'What's going to happen to us?' he demanded angrily.

Catrin felt herself shaking. How was it that they didn't know how to behave with each other any more? She ran her tongue around the inside of her lips, feeling the torn skin.

Where had the trust gone? she wondered. Perhaps it had never been there at all. Perhaps they'd come into the marriage without it, two innocent souls relying on the magnanimity of life to keep them together.

And it wasn't being magnanimous any more.

Things were going wrong.

And now it was up to them.

She'd show them.

'Let's have a party,' she said softly, watching him. 'We'll invite the usual crowd, make them see we're OK. Sarah, Roger . . . are you listening?'

William shook his head. 'I can't listen to this,' he said.

Catrin put her hands on either side of his face, and turned his head back so that he was looking at her, turning him towards her as he used to do with her when he wanted to kiss her, when he wanted to make love.

'Yes, you can. We can put things right if we want to,' she said softly, 'it's up to us. Things will be all right from now on. We'll go back to being how we were. We'll start again . . . pretend that the accident never happened, that Alex never existed.'

William straightened and she let her hands fall. He was taller than she, he moved away from her. He looked at her briefly; just a brief glimpse of pain.

'All right,' he said wearily, 'we'll have a party.'

'A survivors' party.' Because they would survive; she would make sure of it. 'A survivors' party,' she repeated, liking the words; pretending to herself it was as easy as that.

PART THREE

For Want of a Shoe

17

At the beginning of February Frances was rinsing out
an empty Gio bottle, a frown corrugating her forehead.

It had just been the once, she told herself; so she
couldn't be.

She took the bottle with her into the lavatory of her
Knightsbridge shoe box. It was always cold despite the
radiator which got so hot there was a risk, when
seated, of her burning her knee on it. There were some
copies of *Hello!* on the floor but still it wasn't the kind
of place in which to spend any length of time – maybe
it was the heart-attack blue of the walls that she found
chilling or maybe it was just the effect of the window
of frosted glass that never saw the sun.

So as quickly as she could she sat on the lavatory,
fingers fastidiously raised away from the bottle, and
put-put-put-spluttered in the small hole in the top.

Frances put the bottle on the shelf.

She couldn't be, she thought angrily; that was all
she would allow herself to think. She couldn't be.

Because if she were it would be too annoying to
know that if Alex hadn't got himself killed, she would
have had the means to nudge him into marriage. Why
not? Men got nudged into marriage via pregnancy all
the time.

She sighed and looked at the bottle. She couldn't

be. Not after doing it just once without protection. No-one could be that unlucky.

The clinic was private and homely and civilized. The pale winter sun was beaming dustily through the window and coming to rest warmly on the chintz arm-chairs.

Frances couldn't relax. She stood in an elegant pose by the fireplace until she felt the dried flower arrangement in it catch her stockings and she moved to the window irritably and pulled the pale blue curtains closed. The sun was giving her a headache.

Spread underneath the window on a small coffee table was a kettle, cups and individual packets of coffee. There was a jug of milk and a sugar basin. Frances looked at the coffee hopefully but almost instantly she felt her stomach churn.

She turned on her heel and looked at her watch. The clinic was very quiet. Swiftly, she poked herself in the abdomen with a pink-polished nail in the hope of dislodging a few cells here and there.

'Frances Bennett?' came a female voice from the doorway.

Frances picked up her handbag and walked into the consulting room.

This was the real thing, she thought, looking round. No intimations of country life here, but an examination bed, a desk with a blood pressure monitor and stethoscope, kidney bowls, plastic gloves and a tube of lubricating jelly.

Frances sat on the edge of a leather chair. She looked at the doctor unsmilingly.

'You think you might be pregnant,' the doctor said,

her voice calm and encouraging. 'Have you tried a home test?'

'I couldn't bear to,' Frances said, 'I couldn't face that sort of thing on my own.' She allowed her voice to tremble.

'I see. You've brought with you an early-morning sample of urine?'

Frances didn't bother to reply but opened her bag and brought out the perfume bottle wrapped in a cream silk handkerchief. How ghastly if it had leaked.

The doctor took it over to a table. She came back with what looked like a strip of plastic.

'It's positive,' she said tonelessly. 'You're pregnant.'

Frances looked from the strip of plastic to the doctor.

'Are you sure?' she asked. 'Is that test reliable? It was only once . . .' How could Alex have done this to her? It had been such a good plan. It would have worked . . . tears of genuine self-pity came into her eyes. She covered her face with her hands.

The doctor, well-prepared, handed her a box of pale green tissues and when Frances didn't take it she placed it in her lap.

'It's come as a shock,' she said dryly.

Frances felt for the box and pinched a tissue out, dabbing her eyes carefully so as not to smudge her mascara. 'It's come as an awful shock,' she agreed.

'Are you on good terms with the father?'

It was the first time that Frances had considered Michael Zephyr's role in the matter.

She balled up the tissue and thought of his clean grin and his folders full of good news, and she wondered where toy boys came in the scheme of things now. She was sure they were still around but under another name. Younger men, perhaps. She thought she'd read that Joanna Lumley had one. In fact, probably all the glamorous actresses around were married to younger men. They certainly weren't married to older men because older men only married young girls.

'Not really,' Frances said, 'I don't know him awfully well.' She looked at the doctor in sudden despair. 'What am I going to do?'

'You can have the baby,' the doctor said practically, 'or you can choose not to have it. What was the date of your last period?'

Frances pulled her blonde hair away from her face and reached into her bag for her Filofax. 'The seventeenth of December.'

'All right. Take off your pants and stockings and lie on the bed.'

Frances did so, still crying. She felt the tears drip into her hair. She climbed onto the roll of paper that was spread along the bed and she lay down stiffly. The doctor advanced with polythene gloves and examined her inside and out.

'Quite early,' she said, 'which ties in with your dates.'

'What happens now?'

'Dry yourself. What happens now is entirely up to you.'

Frances got off the bed. 'I want it not to have happened,' she said. 'The father . . .' she stopped suddenly. The image of Michael Zephyr looking pleased with himself burned into her mind. She wasn't sure if it was the done thing to have a baby by a younger man. She suspected they were only meant for enjoyment. Tears for herself and for her thwarted plans rolled again. 'I've never seen myself as an unmarried mother,' she said.

The doctor laughed briefly. 'We don't have unmarried mothers any more,' she said, 'only single-parent families.'

Frances put her undies on slowly. 'Well I don't think I want to be one.'

The doctor was writing something in a file. 'So what do I do if I don't?' Frances asked.

The doctor raised her head. 'You see two doctors and we book you into a clinic.'

Frances stared at her face, trying to read it for clues. She knew nothing about babies, she was an only child. She hadn't wanted a baby, only a husband. The tears began again.

'Would it hurt?' she asked quaveringly.

'Everything hurts,' said the doctor, staring back. Her hazel eyes were clear but her eyelids drooped and the shrug she gave was a tired one.

'You've seen this before,' Frances said.

The doctor smiled. It was a smile that said there was little to smile about. Perhaps she was right.

Frances left the room one perfume bottle lighter and one pregnancy heavier. Still, she'd always believed that a trouble shared was a trouble halved. Even better than a trouble halved was a trouble offloaded.

She took her mobile phone out of her bag.

Michael Zephyr had got her into this mess and he could get her out of it.

She was feeling better already.

*　　*　　*

Michael Zephyr, gumshoe, was making a career move.

He'd seen the films where the good guys got run out of town – gumshoes were always the good guys – but this good guy wasn't going to wait for the bailiffs to come, he was going of his own accord. Mostly because his year on the Enterprise Allowance Scheme had come to an end.

He pushed his hands into the pockets of his jeans and looked around his empty office fondly.

Easy come, easy go, he thought.

He hadn't lost money on it – he'd sold the dentist's chair to a massage parlour and the bench to a pie and eel shop. He was glad they'd gone to good homes.

Now he was looking forward to his next job, as a driving instructor. He'd got himself the job because what sort of people learned to drive? Girls.

He smiled and smoothed back his hair, imagining his hand on theirs on the throbbing gearstick.

He'd got bored with being a gumshoe. He'd had it up to here with glamorous wives panicking about their husbands. He was even beginning to feel sorry for the men. He hadn't understood at first why a man would cheat on a blonde, stunning wife – and not necessarily cheat on her with another blonde, stunning woman, but with dark, homely types, mousy types, the quiet ones – but he understood it now. They did it just for a change. Nothing personal. He'd tried to get his women clients to understand that, that it was no reflection on them.

Suitably convinced, their egos restored, they usually then pounced on him.

It had been fun at first but really, it wasn't natural for women to pounce on men. They didn't realise a

168

man had his pride. He hadn't realised it himself until the driving job came up – and by that time he'd begun to feel a certain sympathy for the husbands who were getting it elsewhere. Even to the point of lying to protect them.

There was, of course, always one exception to every rule and his was Frances Bennett; he would have given her one again anytime, but then, her bloke hadn't left her, had he?

The memory of New Year's Eve came back strong and sweet. The contents of his filing cabinet, all his cardboard folders, lay scattered on the dusty windowsill – the cabinet itself had gone to a mini-cab firm – but before he started looking through them for her number he picked up the phone and put it to his ear. It was dead. He dropped the receiver onto the floor. Ah, well, it had been just a thought.

Easy come, easy go, he mused again.

He looked around.

It had been fun while it lasted. He had no regrets. He was looking forward to being a driving instructor . . . all those seventeen-year-olds, little bitty girls who wouldn't know a clutch if he got them in one . . .

It would be good, being a driving instructor.

He couldn't lose.

That afternoon Catrin was at her desk, still trying to shake off a dream she'd had about her father. She'd dreamed she'd gone to visit his grave and found the coffin exposed in a bank of mud, one end of it split open.

She picked up her polystyrene cup and finished the black coffee, shuddering at the memory. She felt tainted by it. Hard as it was to believe that these things had happened just by chance – her nail breaking, the car stopping – it was harder still to believe they'd been prompted by the just and impartial hand of fate. Justice had seen her basking on the warm, sunny rock of life with William, and just like that had flipped it over. And now she was in the dank dark on the underside of the stone. She could smell the dampness. It smelled of the mud in the dream.

Once she would have rung William and he would have cheered her up. No chance of that now.

She picked up her cup again and saw that it was empty. She was standing up, about to get another, when Frances rushed back into the office in a state of agitation.

'Got a moment?' she asked, waving a magazine. A small flutter of inserts slid out onto the floor.

'Of course.' Catrin waved her towards a chair.

Frances sat down heavily and slapped the magazine down on the desk. It skimmed across towards Catrin and she caught it and turned it the right way up.

Mother and Child.

She glanced at Frances, recognising at once the expression on her face: Frances was building herself up for a drama.

'Has this got something to do with your morning off?'

Frances' eyes became miraculously tear-dampened. She seemed to hover uncertainly between hysteria and grief. Grief won; she let the tears roll and pointed with trembling finger at the magazine.

Catrin looked down at the cover. A little fair-haired girl was sitting on her impossibly young and stress-free mother's knee. They were both laughing at something just over the photographer's shoulder. The photograph made her feel strange, excluded not only from motherhood but from the joke as well.

The child reminded her of Lottie and she looked at Frances thoughtfully. 'You're pregnant,' she said.

Frances' face screwed up. Suddenly she slammed her hand down on the desk, hard but not too hard, not hard enough to hurt. 'I just can't believe this is happening,' she wailed, 'what have I done? What have I ever done to be hurt like this?'

It seemed to Catrin to be an echo of what she herself had wondered but that modesty had prevented her from expressing.

She didn't reply, but she looked at Frances' slim waistline and inwardly marvelled.

'It's your fault, you know that, don't you?' Frances asked, her voice rising, 'it would have worked if it hadn't been for you. It's your responsibility too, you know.'

Alex's baby, Catrin found herself thinking. A baby with Alex's dark hair, its small head bobbing uncertainly beneath her chin, its warm body held close. She could feel it as though it were there in her arms.

'Alex's baby,' she said aloud. She felt herself smile at the thought of it.

Frances looked at her uncertainly.

'Congratulations,' Catrin said warmly. A baby, a little thing, she could feel it in her arms, feather-like, tiny spider's legs for eyelashes, hands like little starfish, nails like small pink shells. Someone to make even the most fragile person seem strong, something to heal the loss of Alex, a baby to put things right. 'You must be thrilled.'

Frances dragged the magazine back to her side of the desk and stared at it as though suspecting that Catrin had seen something in it that she had missed.

A baby, Catrin thought. There were times she'd thought she was pregnant, before she was married. Despite the pill there was always the superstition that she would get found out – she blamed it on her Methodist upbringing. She'd rush to the loo every five minutes to see whether her period had started and when finally it did – oh, thank you, thank you, to her Methodist God.

And after she and William had married there'd been one occasion then too, when she'd thought . . . this is it. She'd bought a pregnancy test, half hoping . . . but glad, on finding the result, that she wasn't. They weren't ready . . . they wanted time together . . .

She looked over at the magazine again. Even upside-down it made her yearn.

Frances was still staring at it. 'I didn't want a baby, I wanted a husband,' she said reflectively. 'I wanted Alex. I'm not keeping it, I'm going to have an abortion.'

The shock made Catrin jump to her feet. It wasn't the sense of her arms being emptied, it was more than that: it was the shock of someone opting for death, for another death, as though in these circumstances it was a valid choice.

'I don't want to be a one-parent family,' Frances said plaintively. 'I don't have to have it.'

Catrin, who had once campaigned for a woman's right to choose, who firmly believed in it, felt as though she had been hit.

'But I want it,' she said.

Frances looked at her. 'Why?' she asked curiously, hooking her long hair behind her ear, 'Is it because you want a piece of Alex?'

'I can't bear for there to be another death,' Catrin said and the dream and her father's mud-engulfed coffin came back again, and the smell of the earth.

Frances was looking more cheerful now.

She got up and went to the door. She stopped, her hand on the doorknob, and looked back at Catrin.

'I'll bear it in mind,' she said.

18

That evening Marilyn was back at home, letting herself into her flat, when she heard Harry come down the stairs from his own. She smiled, unable to help herself.

'You're back,' he said, coming up behind her, his voice half pleased, half shifty. 'Where are the boys?'

'They're with their dad. Come in.'

'Debbie's out,' he said, following her inside. He seemed satisfied, as though it was his doing. 'I've missed you, you know,' he said, settling himself on the sofa. 'Where were you last night?'

'Busy.'

'Too busy for me?'

She hung her coat up and didn't answer him. She went into the kitchen and switched the kettle on, thinking how nice it was to have someone to make tea for. As she waited for the kettle to boil, Harry came up behind her, making her jump.

She didn't turn around, she just stood still, watching the steam begin to cloud from the kettle spout.

She felt Harry's mouth against her red, shiny hair, and felt the warmth from his breath. Her heart began to beat faster.

'You're bloody beautiful,' Harry said.

Marilyn stiffened as Harry continued, 'You're the most beautiful girl I know. I don't know why you want to wear all that make-up. You don't need it,' he whispered, his breath blowing on her hair.

The kettle switched itself off.

'Why do you have to spoil things?' Marilyn asked irritably, pouring water from the kettle into the teapot to warm it. 'I didn't ask you to come here, you know.'

'I'm only telling you the truth, girl.'

'Are you?' She threw the water into the sink and slammed the teapot down a little too hard. 'How do you know I don't need it? Go home, Harry,' she sighed. 'This isn't going to work.'

Harry folded his arms and leaned back against the washing machine, a hurt expression on his face. 'I'm only saying,' he said.

Marilyn picked up the teapot and looked at the base; she was sure that she'd broken it. Along the bottom she could see a crack, like a fine strand of hair. 'Now look what you've done,' she said impatiently. 'Listen, what's it got to do with you whether I wear make-up or not?'

'I love you,' Harry said.

He said it so abruptly and so loudly that it seemed to Marilyn she could hear the china ring. Still holding the teapot, she looked at him, her mouth open in shock at the words. It was too soon for him to say that; he hardly knew her.

Marilyn bit her lower lip and looked at the teapot.

Harry was shocked himself, and slightly defiant.

After a few seconds of silence, he added, 'I do,' as though she'd argued the point.

Marilyn turned her back to him. She made the tea anyway, in the cracked teapot.

'Makes no difference,' she said at last. 'If you think

you can come in here and tell me what to do – in my own flat –'

The note of finality in her voice got through to Harry and he looked at her, puzzled. 'Don't you want me to come round again?'

'Not if you're going to talk about make-up, I don't. Now bugger off, Harry.'

Harry was looking hurt. He was better at looking hurt than anyone she'd ever met, including the twins.

'One last kiss to remember you by?' he asked her in a small voice.

'Go home.'

Harry turned, his shoulders drooping with misery. He looked over his shoulder at her and walked slowly through the kitchen door.

Marilyn watched him with no sense of victory. It was like telling a dog off – if Harry had had a tail it would be tucked out of sight, in defeat. Those big eyes, that puzzled, remorseful look, tugged at her heart as he slunk away back to Debbie.

She knew that one word from her and he would bound back, panting.

With a sigh she picked up the teapot, pouring the tea into one mug and putting the other one back on the mug tree.

It didn't matter about the teapot now anyway. She'd go back to a bag in a cup again.

The thought was so dismal, so final, so frighteningly real that, putting the mug down, she ran to the front door and shouted up the stairs: 'Harry! Harry!'

Harry looked over the banister, his face a picture of gloom as though he hadn't yet dared himself to hope.

'Yes?'

'Come here,' she said.

He came back down the stairs slowly and looked at her on the landing.

'What?'

'I'm not saying it out here,' she said, 'come back inside.'

Looking dignified, he didn't make for the sofa this time. Instead he leaned against the table, his eyebrows raised.

'What?'

Marilyn's heart was beating faster with fear than it ever had with love.

She didn't know what to say. She touched her cheek. Her make-up was the only thing that stopped her from feeling a freak; her freckles were ugly, big brown blotches; she looked as though someone had taken a paintbrush to her. At school a new teacher had told her once to go and wash her face.

She flushed hotly. 'I'm a freak,' she said.

'Mental, more like,' were Harry's encouraging words. 'What are you on about?'

'I have to wear make-up,' she said in a low voice. 'That's all I can tell you.'

Harry grabbed her swiftly in one move, picking her up around the waist with his huge arm.

At first she thought he was going to kiss her but as he began to run with her towards the bathroom she started to struggle.

'Harry, put me down, I'm serious,' she said angrily, hitting him hard on his head. 'Harry –' for a minute they got stuck in the doorway. She landed a blow on his cheek but in doing so hit her elbow on the door. Harry flinched and grabbed her arm and as she raised the other, he grabbed both her wrists in his big hand and picked up a flannel in the other. Marilyn, furious, began to kick. Harry jumped back a little but didn't let her go. He held her tight against his chest and rubbed her face with the flannel.

Sobbing angrily from frustration she tried to move her head but Harry was strong. Her face was stinging, it felt raw, some soap from the flannel had gone in her eyes, and Harry became gentler, patting her face as she cried. Then he let her go. She flew at him, landing a punch on his eye and although he flinched, Harry seemed hardly to notice.

'You've got freckles,' he said, surprised.

She was poised to kick him but something in his voice stopped her in mid arc.

'They're lovely,' he said, reaching out to touch the brown marks with his finger. 'They suit you.' He stroked her sore and scorching face with his cool hand, and searched for words. 'They suit you,' he said again, wonderingly; 'you look like a cross between a red setter and a Dalmatian.'

Although her face was still burning as much from humiliation as from the scrubbing, Marilyn suddenly felt something inside her shift, settle and be calm. She felt light and airy as though something awful had left her.

Tears came back into her eyes and she smiled waveringly.

Harry would never know what a difference those words made to her.

She loved dogs, and Harry had made her freckles acceptable in the one and only way she could understand.

A cross between a red setter and a Dalmatian, she repeated to herself slowly. She felt terribly proud. She was touched, and what was more, she was grateful.

'Harry,' she said softly, and the way she said it told him he was forgiven. More than forgiven.

He picked her up, and, after a bit more trouble getting through the bathroom door, he took her into her small bedroom and put her on the smooth cover of her neat pink bed.

They undressed rapidly and urgently on their backs and Harry got under the duvet and pulled her to him and hugged her passionately in the dark, pressing his cool face against her still-burning cheek.

And for the first time ever in her life, Marilyn found herself in love.

They were making too much noise to take in the new voice that was calling to them from the lounge.

It was only when the light suddenly went on that they came down to earth and heard the echo of the word that put an end to their passion.

'Ha-ree . . .'

19

That evening Catrin put her key in the door just as William opened it.

'Sorry,' they said together, like strangers, at finding themselves face to face.

'I'm going for a jog,' William said.

He was wearing a navy sweatshirt and navy jogging pants, which she hadn't seen before.

'I thought maybe we could talk,' Catrin said, still standing in the doorway. Even as the words came out she knew it was a futile thing to say. It was a phrase that struck terror into every man's heart. Men could think of nothing worse than having to talk about problems – their solutions involved adrenaline, fight or flight. In William's case, watching him look longingly over her shoulder at the outside world as though he was seeing Shangri-La, it looked as if flight was more what he had in mind.

'There's nothing to talk about,' William said politely.

For a moment Catrin considered not moving. 'Why do you want to jog?' she asked, surprised at the note of desperation in her voice, 'You never jog.'

William glared at her and finally she stood aside.

'You've brought all this on yourself,' he said as he began his run.

*　　*　　*

Catrin went to sit by the gas fire. She watched the flames writhe and twist and leave the logs untouched. Moses had probably worn the same expression of incomprehension when he came across the burning bush; hers was over William jogging.

She stood up. The room seemed dark. In the broom cupboard there were a couple of l50-watt bulbs and she fetched one to replace the old one and sank back into the sofa.

Suddenly it was as if she could see cracks every-where. The ceiling seemed crazed with them and still the room seemed dim. There was not enough light. She'd put the brightest bulb in the socket but she was still sitting in the gloom. It occurred to her that some-thing inside her had dimmed and all the 150-watt bulbs in the world weren't going to scare away the black shadows in her head, but knowing that made no difference because she couldn't put it right.

She used to be able to. She used to be good at solving things, she used to be able to see them clearly.

Another shadow jostled in with all the rest. It was the shadow of William jogging.

William never jogged.

Not even before the start of the cricket season.

But he was jogging now.

Just another little thing to separate them; another little thing to keep them apart.

William came back from his jog gasping for breath and looking a lot less fit than when he'd left.

Catrin caught him before he went upstairs, surpris-ing herself with her speed. She stood on the bottom step, barring him from climbing up.

'We've got to talk,' she insisted; it was the only thing she could think of to say.

'Excuse me,' William said, still panting, and leaning one arm on the banister, 'I'm going to have a shower.'

'You can have a shower afterwards.'

William glanced up the stairs. 'There's nothing to talk about,' he said, using the standard first defence tactic. He tried to edge past her.

'Oh yes there is,' Catrin said. 'For a start, Frances is pregnant and she can't look after the baby herself.'

William rasped his stubble. 'And what's that got to do with us?' he asked, genuinely puzzled.

Catrin pushed her fingers through her hair. 'Well – I thought maybe we could look after it for her.'

As soon as she'd said it she felt her neck turn a fiery red and the heat spread to her face as though she'd proposed something indecent.

'Fine,' William said, taking advantage. He stepped forward.

Catrin retreated up onto the next stair. 'Is it really fine?' she asked him. 'What are you trying to walk away for?'

'Of course it's not fine. Why would it be? How could you imagine it might be?' he asked her, pushing past, at last, and looking down at her from the top step.

'She'll have an abortion otherwise,' she pleaded up at him.

William looked down at her and rebelled. 'It's ridiculous.'

As she heard him say the words, somewhere inside herself she began to cry. Why wasn't she able to put something – anything – right? She'd been able to, once. She'd been able to control things. Now they were crumbling.

Why didn't he do something?

She wanted him to kiss her and she wanted him to fight her and she wanted to cry angrily and be overcome and sob on him and for him to make things normal.

But what he did was turn his back on her and close the bathroom door.

She stared at it as though it had swallowed him up.

Perhaps he could see it all more clearly than she; perhaps he, unlike her, was under no illusions about a person's ability to put things right.

20

'Ha – reeee . . .'

It was soft and almost musical, the way that Debbie said it.

Even above the grunts of lovemaking they heard it, that lyrical cadence of contempt floating through the dark and stopping just as the light went on.

From beneath the soaring humidity of the pink duvet, Harry reared up off Marilyn like a frightened horse. As he did so his whole weight rested on Marilyn's lower half, so that her first concern was not that they had been discovered by Harry's wife, but that her pelvis had been crushed.

Exposed to the chill evening air, the sweat on her body turned cold and hot again.

Above her, Harry's arms went rigid as he continued to pin her to the bed.

'Harry,' Marilyn groaned up at him desperately but Harry was busy turning to look at his wife, turning his head towards her so slowly that Marilyn heard his neck creak. Then, as his eyes rested on his wife, it was as if he had caught sight of the Medusa; he gave a deep sigh and fell heavily down on top of Marilyn, knocking the breath out of her.

Marilyn's world went black as she panicked beneath Harry's cold and flabby chest.

Struggling for air, she prayed that Debbie would pull him off. It was going to be an awful way to die. As pinpoints of light flashed inside her eyelids she heard Debbie call, 'Harry!' in a voice that was no longer the least bit melodious, but Harry didn't respond. Straining her neck muscles Marilyn moved her squashed face so that her nose was in Harry's cleavage and she breathed rapidly through it, although, being squashed, it squeaked piercingly with the effort.

Thankful that she probably wasn't going to die, she wondered what Harry was playing at. She tensed her legs and managed to struggle her way from under his chest and push her face out into the open air above his shoulder. She felt a sudden sympathy for the newborn. Suddenly across her line of vision floated the mean, lean features of Harry's wife and Marilyn wished she'd stayed where she was.

Debbie was looking at her with disgust written across her face. 'You slag,' she said. 'Harry, get off her.'

Marilyn was momentarily hopeful, but Harry didn't budge. She wished he would. She wondered whether her ribs were broken. She couldn't breathe. She sucked some air in. It reminded her of her childhood, when she drank through paper straws that went soggy and made her feel she'd suffocated.

'I think he's fainted,' she croaked using her small lungful of air.

'Fainted?' Debbie rubbed at her short white-blonde hair. 'I hope he's dead,' she said viciously. 'I hope the shock's killed him and you have to lie there rotting beneath him until you're dead. You're dead anyway,' she said through tightened lips. She poked her finger towards Marilyn's face. 'I'm going to bloody well leave you to it. You're welcome to him.'

Marilyn heard her stride to the door and stop.

'He was like a lifeless corpse when he was alive, you probably won't notice the difference.'

Marilyn thought that was a bit strong. She struggled under Harry, assuming it was the parting line.

'Harry, get off me,' she said urgently, 'she's gone. Get off me, Harry, you're crushing me, bloody fool.'

Harry tentatively raised himself and rolled onto his back on the bed, blowing out air through his pursed lips, like a whale through his spout. He felt his heart.

'She'll do for me one of these days. Feel that,' he said, taking Marilyn's hand and placing it over his left nipple. The hairs on his chest tickled her palm. Sure enough, under the heel of her hand she could feel his heart thudding like a drum.

She looked at Harry, propping herself up on her elbow. There had been a touch of admiration in his voice. She rubbed his chest absently and flopped back on the bed and began feeling her ribs. She breathed deeply and felt them ache as they expanded. She put her hands on her hips and rotated them slowly. It was no thanks to Harry that she was still in one piece.

'You nearly crushed me,' she said sorrowfully, 'I thought I was going to die.'

'I fainted, it was the shock,' Harry said earnestly, raising his head off the pillow. He looked suddenly offended. 'And what did she mean, I was like a lifeless corpse when I was alive? She's never had anything to complain about with me.'

'I don't know what she meant. You'd better get

dressed before she comes back.' Marilyn got out of bed and looked at the door. 'How did she get in?'

'I might have left the door open,' Harry said sheepishly. He looked glum. 'I suppose she came to look for me.'

'What are we going to do?'

'Maybe she'll leave me,' Harry said hopefully, 'then I could move in with you.'

Marilyn, so recently besotted, felt her heart melt again. She smiled. 'You could come with me to Catrin's survivor party on Thursday,' she said. 'We could come back home and fall into bed.'

'What have you got to survive? Her cooking?'

Marilyn grinned.

It was no time for complacency though. 'Come on,' she said, 'or Debbie'll come looking for you again.'

They got dressed hurriedly. She kept glancing at Harry – Harry looked different in clothes – he looked stronger, taller. She fancied him like mad; more so, now.

Feeling her eyes on him, Harry buttoned up his shirt and pulled a face. 'She always had bad timing. I was nearly there, you know,' he said ruefully.

Marilyn picked up the duvet and shook it, puffing it up before letting it settle on the bed. 'You'd better go home,' she said softly.

Harry chuckled gently. 'Best contraceptive you can get, your wife's voice when you're with someone else. Stopped me in my tracks.'

Marilyn looked at him across the bed. She began to laugh as well. It suddenly seemed very funny. They laughed the laughter of survivors, triumphant in the happy knowledge that the worst had happened and that they were still alive.

Harry walked around the bed to her and pulled her to him, wrapping his arms around her and resting his chin on her head.

'If she's thrown me out we can get married,' he said magnanimously. He touched her freckles with his huge finger. 'Would you like that?'

Marilyn looked up at him through her tangle of red hair. 'Like it? Of course I'd like it.' The thought of a twenty-four-hour Harry and no more Dermablend made her smile. 'The boys would like it too. Maybe she's done us a favour. Maybe she'll take the hint . . .' Her voice tailed off. Or maybe she wouldn't.

Harry nuzzled her neck and she pushed him away. 'Harry, you'd better go.'

Just as she'd said it, the door opened again and Debbie came back in.

Her reappearance was not quite as unexpected as her first entrance had been, but they sprang apart as though Semtexed.

'Glad to see you're decent,' Debbie said sarcastically. 'Harry, I've been waiting for you. I thought your faint would pass off if I left.'

'I think I've got epilepsy,' Harry said, checking his buttons.

'Epilepsy.' She spat the word out scornfully.

She walked across the lounge and stood in front of Marilyn like a sergeant major on parade. 'And what's wrong with you?' she asked, staring at Marilyn's face. 'Leprosy?'

'They're freckles,' Harry put in helpfully.

'Freckles?' Debbie took a closer look. She was so

close that Marilyn could feel her breath on her eyes.

Harry looked at her too. Thanks, Harry, Marilyn thought, staring back at Debbie.

'They're big for freckles. Are you sure they're not some sort of skin cancer? You use a sunbed a lot.'

'Not on my face,' Marilyn said.

'What's that?'

'I don't use the sunbed on my face. I put a towel over it.'

'Yeah.' Debbie tilted her head at an angle. She was looking at her with the enthusiasm of an amateur entomologist. 'I'd keep it there if I were you.'

'Ha, ha,' Harry laughed.

'Creep,' thought Marilyn.

Debbie folded her arms and stepped back to look at them. 'So you two are in love.'

Marilyn nodded her head at the same time as Harry denied it. She looked swiftly at the man who had proposed to her moments before.

'No, no,' Harry said, sounding shocked.

'No, no,' Marilyn heard herself say.

Their voices died away like a Greek chorus and they waited for Debbie's verdict.

This is my house, Marilyn told herself, feeling defiant; but not defiant enough to say it aloud. It's my house but at least it's all in one piece, she thought. She stared at Debbie. As in an encounter with a mad dog, she knew the one thing to remember was not to show fear.

Debbie was still scratching her head. Her hair looked almost like a judge's wig; not so much blonde as grey.

Marilyn stood motionless as Debbie scratched and scratched with thought.

'Well, that's different, isn't it,' she said finally.

Marilyn felt her knees wobble with relief. It might be her house, but Debbie was in control.

She'd heard that Debbie was hard but she'd never seen it at first hand before, the manipulation, the ability to make people afraid.

'What you're saying,' Debbie said, as though she was getting it straight, 'is that you don't love each other but it was just a quickie.' Her black eyebrows were raised like sideways question marks. 'Just a quickie, was it?'

'Yes, yes,' said Harry as Marilyn shot him a glance. He was really getting the hang of it. He'd have been marvellous in pantomime. Marilyn didn't move.

'Just a quickie,' Debbie repeated sorrowfully.

As she looked at her, Marilyn felt her own face drop into sorrowful lines. She had no doubt that Harry was sorrowful, too, very sorrowful.

'JUST A QUICKIE?' Debbie's scream bounced off the walls and shocked Marilyn to the core. She could hardly understand where it had come from. Where had the anger been hiding all that time? 'AND YOU – HOW COULD YOU SLEEP WITH HIM?' Her voice dropped and she looked baffled. 'It's not as if you don't know him.'

Marilyn's jaw had gone slack with shock.

The scream had made her ears ring and she wanted to rub them.

'Debbie,' Harry's hands were flapping around her as if he'd set light to a stick of explosive. 'Debbie, I love you, love.'

'You do?'

'You know I do.'

Marilyn braced herself. She'll never believe that, she thought.

Debbie's teeth were clenched and her jaw muscles showed clearly through the smooth skin on her lean face. 'Do you? Do you, Harry?'

'Of course I do, I'll make it up to you, I'll sort it out . . .' he was choosing his words tentatively as though he was using a magic incantation for the first time. '. . . see you right . . . work things out . . . make an effort . . . come home early . . .' the spell went on and on.

And against the background of Harry's mumblings, Marilyn watched Debbie's teeth slowly unclench until she looked almost normal. 'We'll sort it out between us, will we Harry?'

'Of course we will, I promise you. You know me.'

'Yes, I know you, Harry. So I won't have to ask my brother for help?'

'Of course not. This is between us.'

'Right. Come on.'

And with that one command she declared her ownership. Perhaps it had never been in doubt.

Marilyn looked at Harry, willing him to return her gaze. His eyes flickered but they did not make contact with hers.

And so Debbie walked slowly to the door with Harry trailing behind her like a cowed cur.

Marilyn watched them in case Harry turned round, but he didn't. He shut the door behind him. Presently Marilyn heard their footsteps on the floor above.

She hurried to the door and locked it, too late. They wouldn't be coming back. Looked like he wouldn't be coming to the party, either.

Fully clothed, she got back into bed and pulled the duvet tightly around her.

She felt stunned by Debbie's noise and power. And Harry hadn't even said goodbye.

Poor Harry. Debbie would kill him. She didn't need DaCosta to look after her, she could do it all by herself. Marilyn rubbed her cheek against the pillow. See? No make-up.

She moved to where Harry had lain but the warmth of him had gone and the bed was cold.

She wanted to cry. She was missing him already.

21

The following Thursday afternoon William was standing by his office window, looking out onto the busy London street at people scuttling home from their jobs in more-or-less straight lines, unaware of the turmoil in the mind that was looking down on them.

William was thinking of the survivors' party.

Catrin might believe she'd survived but he was still drowning, he was still drowning and she hadn't seen it. Just as he'd begun to tread water she'd ducked him again with the suggestion they keep Alex's baby and he'd found himself in the dark waters once more.

William stared down at the street.

Once, they'd agreed on things. It seemed a very long time ago.

He put on his jacket ready to go home and was astonished as he opened the door to see Jenna at Jeff's empty desk, sobbing.

He felt a rush of compassion and warmth, nothing like the way Catrin's tears made him feel. Catrin's tears made him helpless and anxious but this small person weeping at an empty desk simply aroused his sympathy. He walked up to her and crouched down next to her and took his handkerchief out of his pocket, a crumpled handkerchief, a handkerchief that Catrin had not bothered to iron.

'Hey,' he said softly, pushing it into her hand, 'it can't be as bad at that.'

Who was he kidding? He knew how bad it could get.

Jenna lifted her head to look at him, her tear-washed eyes sparkling like the Ceylon sapphires that Catrin admired. Her hair was paler and wilder than ever and she pulled a strand between her fingers and her mouth turned down as the tears began to roll again.

'My boyfriend,' she said, 'has finished with me.'

William almost laughed aloud. She thought that was a tragedy? He could give her tragedies. His wife in stockings in someone else's car was a tragedy. Lying about the car breaking down, that was what tragedy was all about.

'Has he,' she asked, 'mentioned it to you at all?'

'To me?' William was surprised at the very question then suddenly, sharply, he guessed and was pleased at his perspicacity. 'It's Jeff, isn't it.'

'I thought you knew,' Jenna said, her voice trembling.

'I guessed,' William said. Jeff! It would have to be Jeff, wouldn't it, who got to Jenna first. Jeff, the bastard. He couldn't leave anything alone.

He straightened from his crouch, his knees aching, and looked down at her tousled fair hair. He wanted to smooth it down. He wanted to help her. He wanted to show her what a good man was like – he wanted to put her off Jeff. He wanted something to happen.

'Would a drink help?' he asked her suddenly, hoping that if she refused he could pretend he'd said something else.

Jenna's enormous eyes showed that one would. 'Would your wife mind?' she asked in her quivering, upset voice.

William detected something in her phraseology that made him do a mental double-take. Despite the quiver, he thought she was issuing a challenge. She was seeing whether or not he was answerable to his wife. If he said no, then it would be a lie and she would know it, and if he said yes, and went ahead, it would be deception.

'Probably,' he said finally.

Jenna rewarded him with a bright and brilliant smile that should have made a rainbow; and they went for a drink.

William had forgotten how much fun pubs were with their dark smokiness and air of bonhomie.

He was enjoying watching Jenna draw her wild mane of blonde hair back from her face first one way and then the other. It kept on springing back and falling into her eyes. Occasionally she looked at him with her mascaraless eyes and his heart would jolt at their nakedness.

'Will you have another?' he asked her, to distract himself.

'G and T, please.'

William pushed his way to the bar again.

He hardly ever went into pubs. When he and Catrin went out it was to eat.

He stood behind the crowd at the bar and tried to catch the barman's attention. The barman caught his eye and served someone else.

William looked back at Jenna who was sitting

impassively at the table, twirling the stem of her glass. She looked up suddenly and caught his eye and he winked at her and turned back to the bar, amazed with himself; he wasn't the winking type. He seemed, since the New Year, to be turning into someone else entirely.

'A gin and tonic and a pint of lager, please,' he shouted to the barman who nodded and picked up a glass. His heart leapt. It was like a sign! This is it, he thought; this is power. It had been taken away from him but now he was getting it back again. Here he was, comforting Jenna, paying back his wife and Jeff in one fell swoop.

He'd never agreed with men who called women 'castrating', but now he wondered if there mightn't be a grain of truth in it. Jenna was letting him do – and appreciating – what came naturally to men – buying drinks. Whereas if he'd been with Catrin, she would probably have bought the drinks herself.

With Jenna it was a case of primitive man and primitive woman – she was no more likely to buy a round than she was to say something of interest. No! That was a sexist statement! Yeah, well, primitive man was allowed to be sexist, wasn't he.

'Thanks, mate,' said the barman, taking the money.

'Have one yourself.'

'Yeah, go on. Thanks, mate.'

William returned to Jenna triumphant, carrying the spoils of war.

'So what is your wife like?' Jenna asked him as she stirred the ice around with her little finger and put that same little finger into her perfect mouth.

'She's . . . er . . .' William looked away from the

196

finger sinking into the little pink mouth and felt the hairs on his body rise. 'She's very nice.'

Jenna frowned and the smooth skin of her forehead creased like crumpled velvet and smoothed out again without a trace.

'Nice?'

Of course, she would know the whole story about the car that hadn't broken down from Jeff. She knew the truth. It was a comforting thought.

'She's very different from you.'

He was relieved to see Jenna smile. Her blue eyes were warm and confiding and admiring.

William picked up his drink. It felt heavier than the previous two. He put his mouth to the glass and felt the foam tickle his upper lip.

'Not as se —' aware of the foam on his mouth and worried that he looked as though he had a white moustache he wiped it off, worried also that 'sensitive' wasn't a very complimentary description.

'Jeff used to think I was sexy, too,' she said, looking momentarily sad. 'William . . .' she looked shy. '. . . I've never been out with a married man before.'

He was irrationally pleased to be the first. He would initiate her into the delights of married men.

'I lost my virginity when I was fifteen,' she said twirling the glass, 'to a friend of my father. He looked a bit like you.'

'Only older,' William said, and laughed to show that he knew it was a joke.

'You're thirty-five, right? He was thirty-five.'

'How old are you now?'

'Twenty-three.'

'How old is Jeff?'

197

'How did you know about Jeff?'

'You told me.'

'Did I?' She giggled and fished the lemon out of her glass. Her giggle faded away. 'Look,' she said, 'it's the one I had in my last drink. Those are my teeth marks.'

William bent forward to look at the lemon slice in the palm of her hand and then he looked at the selection of glasses on the table.

'Can't be,' he said, 'all our glasses are here.'

Jenna, her palm still outstretched, pouted.

'They must be someone else's toothmarks then.'

'Yes, they must be,' William said encouragingly.

'Yuck.'

She opened her bag and took a crumpled white handkerchief out which William saw was his, the one he'd given her when she'd cried. She wiped her hands on it and then rubbed her mouth as though she'd been kissed by a bristly aunt. Then she gave him his handkerchief back.

William took it and saw it had on it a smear of pale pink lipstick. He made to put it in his pocket but surreptitiously dropped it on the floor. He wouldn't, even now, want Catrin to see it with pink lipstick on it.

'You've dropped it,' Jenna cried and picked it up for him.

He took it from her and looked at his watch. He was shocked to see the time. He remembered the party that Catrin was giving to prove they were happy, the survivors' party, and he got to his feet. 'Listen, I have to go,' he said. 'Where do you live?'

Jenna looked at him with huge blue eyes.

'Finchley.'

Miles away. He would have to get her a cab.

'You know,' Jenna said in a small voice, 'I've always been in love with you. Ever since the coffee machine.'

William, once the pang of alarm had passed, felt rather pleased, as if that was how it should be. The survivors' party would have to wait a little longer for him.

'Come on,' he said. 'I'll drive you home.'

22

Catrin interrupted her unpacking of the Marks & Spencer bags to ring William's office again.

She counted ten rings and slowly replaced the receiver. The disquieting thought that he had forgotten went through her mind again and she stared at the phone, wondering why she'd so readily convinced herself it hadn't been necessary to remind him that morning.

She picked the phone up and tried the number again just in case she'd misdialled the first time.

At each burr she imagined the phone being answered. She found herself smiling so that she wouldn't come over as anxious when he picked it up. Burr. Burr. With each ring the tone seemed to get more hollow so that she could almost hear it echo in the empty office.

She put the phone down.

She went back into the kitchen and arranged all the foil dishes with the starters in a row and all the main course dishes behind them. The vegetables were ready prepared in their bags and with nothing left to do she went into the dining room and walked slowly around the table set for ten. The white damask cloth glowed, the glasses sparkled, the candlesticks shone, the silver gleamed so hard it dazzled. She pulled out a chair and sat down and stared at the table.

There was nothing wrong with it. It was perfect. Why should the sight of it depress her?

She leaned on the table and pushed her hair away from her face and rested her forehead on the palms of her hands. She knew what was bothering her. It wasn't a table set for friends, it was a table set to impress.

She rubbed her eye with the back of her hand and stared at the unlit candles, their wicks still encased in virgin wax.

But that was what it was all about, wasn't it; impress them, impress them with their happy lifestyle and mock anything that went against the grain. They were all guilty of it, they all played by the same rules.

Except she hadn't, had she.

The rules had been broken. She'd broken them. See, an accident would have been all right, it would have had a certain cachet; it was the death that had been in bad taste. But even bad taste could be overlooked; the whole point was, she hadn't shared it. Best to have lunched with Sarah straight away and said, William thinks we were having an affair – can you believe it?! Gossiped, made a joke. Instead she'd kept it to herself, worse than that, kept it for herself like a secret, leaving them, the supposed insiders, to speculate.

In keeping them out she'd made an outcast of herself.

'Ridiculous,' she said aloud, and gave a laugh, but she knew, now, that she'd put it into words, that it was the truth. They'd drawn their own conclusion because she'd neglected to draw it for them. 'The survivors' party!' she said, staring at the table, astonished at her own self-deceit.

And William wasn't playing any more.

I've messed it all up, she thought.

She crossed her arms and hurried into the kitchen for a gin and tonic to numb the panic. A few sips made her tense shoulders start to ache. She ought to get ready. She took the drink upstairs with her and sat on the side of the bath, put the bath taps on and squeezed bath gel into the steamy running water.

Maybe it was another case of self-deception, she thought, watching the water foam, but it might yet be all right. There was always the possibility that William was, even now, on his way home.

William pulled up outside Jenna's house and looked up at it through the car window. Jenna's hand came to rest gently on his arm.

'Thanks, William,' she said softly in her young voice.

Net curtains, William thought, hardly hearing her as he looked at the filtered light shining through the window. They reminded him of his student days. Student houses always had net curtains. He glanced at Jenna's expectant face half hidden in the shadows and wondered why he hadn't imagined her living in this rather seedy semi-detached. A studio, then? No. He realised he'd thought she would still be living at home.

'There's a light on,' he said, looking at the house again.

'That'll be Alvin,' she said dismissively. 'He's my flatmate. He's harmless. Do you want to come in?'

William imagined himself going up the path into that net-curtained house. He didn't allow himself to speculate on what might follow if he did; better to go now. He wasn't going to emulate his father, not at this stage of his life, not ever.

'I'd better be getting back,' he said, still staring at the house. He knew she was looking at him and he turned towards her. Her face was raised; even sitting down she was small, so small. He could see the light catch on her pale lipstick, highlighting her lips while the rest of her face remained in shadow.

'Thanks for –' Jenna paused. 'You know,' she continued hesitantly, 'listening and stuff. And for the drinks.'

William knew he hadn't done much listening. He'd done the talking, talked about *Media News*, about stories, about Hugh. Avoided, of course, saying anything about Jeff.

'That's all right. Get some sleep,' he said, 'and I'll see you tomorrow.'

'OK,' she said and leaned towards him suddenly and kissed him on the cheek. She was up and out of the car before he could respond and he saw her run up the path, her hair, one pale frothy mass, bobbing behind her.

He saw her stop and bend her head to look in her bag for the keys but the door opened suddenly and she went inside. He saw her hand flutter briefly like a white handkerchief and the door closed.

He started up the car.

He could do with a drink. Correction; he could do with a few drinks. He didn't know whether it was to maintain a high – the high, he told himself, of comforting Jeff's girlfriend – or whether it was to bring him back down to earth.

He would call in to the pub by the canal once he was home. He'd park the car and pop in, have a drink before the party.

He'd need a drink, to survive.

Eight for eight-thirty, she'd told them.

At eight o'clock precisely, just as she'd put her earrings on and fastened her plain black velvet dress, the doorbell rang.

She hurried to answer it, her spirits lifting, sure that it was William.

She opened the door.

A tall figure in a cloak stood there.

She tried to hide her disappointment.

'Marilyn! Come in! You're the first! Are you alone?'

Marilyn tossed back the hood of the cloak. Under the security light her hair shone darkly. 'Harry's too afraid of Arnold DaCosta to come,' she said with disgust. 'Or too afraid of his wife. Wimp.'

She stepped inside and undid the cloak and handed it to Catrin who took it automatically, her eyes fixed on Marilyn's dress which fitted like a second skin. It was covered in copper sequins which looked like scales and the effect was as some exotic lizard or chameleon. Under her gaze Marilyn laughed and tossed her hair away from her face. Copper sequinned earrings caught the light.

'Guess how much?' she asked.

'They – you – look a million dollars.'

'Thanks. Camden Market,' Marilyn said, pleased, tossing her head again.

'Harry must be mad,' Catrin said with a grin.

'Nah, he leaves that to his wife.'

'Come and have a drink.' Catrin hung the cloak up and went through to the kitchen. Marilyn followed her and leaned on the worktop. She lifted the lid of one of the foil cartons and sniffed appreciatively.

'Got the caterers in, I see,' she said.

Catrin grinned. 'Good old M & S. What will you have to drink?'

'Haven't got any cherry brandy, have you?' Marilyn asked her hopefully.

'Wouldn't be surprised. We went through that cocktail thing, you know . . .' They'd been through all the 'things' in their time, the wok thing, the ice-cream-maker thing, the pasta-machine thing, the espresso-machine thing. She hunted around at the back of the cupboard and her hand closed round the rather sticky neck of a bottle. She looked at the label and brandished it. 'Here you are.'

She poured it and as she handed the glass to Marilyn she looked again at Marilyn's face. What she had thought was some sort of dappled effect on it, caused by the light bouncing off the sequins, wasn't that at all.

'You're not wearing make-up,' she said, surprised.

'I've given it up. Harry likes me natural.'

'I can see why. Marilyn, I didn't know you had freckles.'

'You weren't supposed to, were you,' Marilyn said, keeping her head lowered in embarrassment.

Catrin was fascinated. She reminded her of a skew-bald pony she used to ride after school, during long summer evenings.

'You look heaps younger,' she said. 'Lucky you!'

Marilyn sipped her drink and looked towards the sitting room. 'William still changing, is he?'

Catrin picked up the Gilbey's and added more gin to her drink. 'I wish,' she said as she turned back. 'He's not home from work yet.'

'He's late, isn't he?'

Catrin's drink was too strong now, too gin-y. The fumes were making her eyes water. She pulled a face and drank it anyway.

'Something must have cropped up.' She looked at Marilyn and raised her eyebrows. 'It happens, doesn't it.'

Marilyn looked at her curiously, her head to one side. 'Does it?' she asked softly.

Catrin put her glass down and opened the fridge door. She took a lemon off the shelf and began to slice it. A fine spray of juice fell over her velvet sleeve. She picked up the teacloth and dabbed at the fabric and dropped a slice of lemon into her glass, where it keeled sideways like a dead goldfish.

Catrin picked up the glass and lifted it to the light.

'Yes,' she said, shaking the glass in circular movements in the hope of blending in the taste of the lemon. 'Oh, you might as well know, it's a mess really. I don't know what's happening to us. We haven't slept together since the New Year.' She gave a dismal laugh. 'I'm beginning to dream about it.'

'You know it's bad when you start doing that,' Marilyn said sympathetically. 'I wonder how he's coping?'

The doorbell rang. They both stiffened but for a moment neither of them made a move to answer it.

'Might be William,' Marilyn said.

'Might be.' For a minute she didn't move, dreading finding out that it wasn't. She put her drink down and took a deep breath as she went to open the front door.

It was Hugh and Jean.

She tried to mask her disappointment and greeted them with awkward hugs. As Jean went through, she grabbed Hugh's arm. 'You haven't seen William, have you?'

'Isn't he here? Of course he isn't, you wouldn't be asking. Haven't seen him, Catrin. Sorry.'

'Just thought I'd ask,' she said lightly, walking with him towards the sitting room and looking away from his curious white-fringed eyes. 'What will you have to drink?'

'Scotch.' He smoothed the front of his shirt with his huge hands and his eyes met hers again. 'Better make it a large one,' he said.

By half-past eight they were all there apart from William: Sarah and Roger, looking smug; Tim and Lisa looking anxious; Hugh looking for the Scotch and Jean looking as though her clothes were strangling her.

Marilyn took away Harry's place setting. She left William's alone.

'He's bound to turn up soon,' she said.

Catrin shrugged and lit the candles which spread a soft-focus pool of light across the table.

The herby smell of the cooking food drifted through.

No-one had asked where William was although it was the only thing they were really interested in.

She heard the cooker timer go off and she went back into the kitchen and took the dishes out of the oven.

207

The surge of heat on her face made her feel weary and she crouched tiredly, her teacloth in her hands.

'Need a hand?' Marilyn asked her brightly, coming in.

'Thanks – will you put it out? I'll take the plates through. Supper's ready!' she called as she carried them into the dining room.

There was an air of carnivorous excitement as the guests took their seats, as if the smell of blood was in the air.

Catrin sat down at one end of the table and faced William's empty chair at the other end.

She saw Sarah catch Roger's eye and glance meaningfully down the table. There was a trace of a smirk on Roger's face.

'Red or white?' Catrin asked.

Sarah looked at her sympathetically. 'Roger will do that for you, darling,' she said, taking the bottle from her. 'I mean, it's a man's job. Here, Roger, see who wants what, will you?'

Catrin allowed the bottle of red to be taken out of her hand.

She picked up the white wine bottle and poured herself a glass.

Sarah picked hers up and saluted Catrin with it.

'To survivors?' she asked, cocking her head.

Catrin took a mouthful of wine without replying.

The phrase was unfortunate and they began to eat in silence. In the glow of the candles the faces around the table were calm. The only sound was of silver ringing against china, and of glasses picked up and put down.

Catrin put a forkful of food in her mouth and found

she couldn't swallow it. Her napkin was still on her side plate and she unfolded the starched damask with effort and put it on her velvet-clad knee.

She realised her heart was beating madly, loosely, wildly as though it had come free of the muscles holding it. It was clattering around so loudly inside the cavern of her chest that she could hear it resonating in her eardrums, be-boom, be-boom. William had left her, at least for this night. She didn't dare think any further ahead and still, be-boom be-boom, the heart rate that couldn't have gone any faster accelerated with fear.

Bad luck was like a cancer; it tended to spread out of control.

As she picked up her glass again the front doorbell rang.

'I'll get it,' she said sharply, getting to her feet. The napkin dropped to the floor. 'Excuse me.'

She had ceased to hope it might be him, and was hardly surprised to find a complete stranger at the door, asking for Marilyn and taking off his jacket happily.

'Come on in.'

The dining room was silent as they walked in. Catrin hadn't realised before that there were degrees of silence; this one was fairly buzzing. She knew that they, like she, had expected William and instead, here was this large newcomer, dressed in black denims. She put the coat on the chair and sat down.

A thrill of excitement seemed to vibrate above the table.

Harry went straight to William's chair and sat down. 'This is Harry, Marilyn's friend,' Catrin said and introduced the others to him whilst serving him his food. She sat down again and saw Marilyn give him a contemptuous look.

Harry ignored it and began to eat, looking rather pleased with himself. 'Nice house,' he said. 'Garden?' he asked conversationally. 'It's important to have a garden.'

The last traces of animation brought on by his entrance leaked away. There was no response to his statement at first, but with effort, and due to his self-appointed position as surrogate host, Roger rallied.

'Have you got a garden, Harry?' he asked politely.

'Got a balcony,' Harry said. 'I'd like a garden.' He looked around the averted faces at the table and promptly joined them in keeping quiet.

Catrin cleared the plates and retreated into the kitchen and rested her head on the cool fridge door.

Marilyn came in after her. 'Bundle of laughs, aren't they? Sorry about Harry, I didn't know he was going to show up.'

'I'm glad he did, I couldn't bear looking at that empty chair, it made me want to scream.'

They took the main course through. A gloom had descended over the table. The guests seemed to take it in turns to look surreptitiously at their watches. It was like a meal hosted by a silent order. Roger asked her where the wine was kept and fetched two more bottles of red and one of white, but the sight of them seemed to subdue the guests more, threatening, as they did, to prolong the evening further.

Even Hugh was silent as he stared at his plate thoughtfully.

When the doorbell went again they'd sunk into such apathy that the sound deafened them.

Roger, who was still pouring the wine, put the bottle down and said that he would get it.

Though Catrin carried on eating it was impossible not to listen to the voices at the door, one raised, one more controlled. And she knew the raised one was William's.

She seemed to be glued to her seat. She tried to spear a sugar snap pea but just then the door swung open and William appeared, swaying, in the doorway.

He wasn't wearing his jacket. A red and white life-belt hung diagonally from the shoulder of one arm and went under the other, like an ammo belt.

'Hello,' he said loudly, with an unfamiliar air of bon-homie, 'so this is the survivors' party. You don't look much like survivors to me.' He laughed and put his other arm through the lifebelt, holding it around his waist. 'Should have been prepared.'

'William –' Catrin said, her voice ringing out a warning.

'It's all right, I'm not staying. Not hungry,' William said firmly, 'but you carry on.' He waved his hand benevolently at them. 'Enjoy yourselves.'

He hoisted the lifebelt over one shoulder again. They heard him walk unsteadily to the stairs and climb them slowly.

Mortified, Catrin glanced at her guests and then ran up after him.

When she reached the bedroom William had fallen onto the bed and was taking his trousers off.

He smiled when he saw her and he reached for her but fell back again.

211

'William, what's happened?' she hissed, trying to keep her voice down so that she wouldn't be heard.

He leaned forward and tried to reach for her hand but missed, and started laughing. 'Out. Pubbing. Enjoying myself.'

Catrin stared at him. She'd never seen him drunk before, never like this. She knew that what she should do was go back downstairs, face their friends and ask them all to go home. Apologize.

William gave his trousers a last tug and they came off. He threw them across the room joyfully. The red and white lifebelt was on the floor and as he stood up his foot caught in it and he stumbled onto the bed again.

Catrin grabbed his shirt as he fell and there was a tearing noise as the cotton gave. It sounded violent and William pushed himself up and tugged at the shirt to look at it.

'You've ripped it,' William said slowly, in a small voice, 'you've ripped my best shirt.'

'It isn't your best shirt –'

'Ripped my shirt,' he said, sitting up. 'Don't look at me like that.'

'No.' Catrin turned away from him.

They would wonder what was happening. They would be straining their ears, speculating on what was being said, on whether there was going to be a row.

'How are they surviving down there?' William asked, and giggled.

She looked at him with a sudden surge of anger. 'You've given them what they wanted,' she said, 'look at you. You've played into their hands – we were supposed to be showing them that things are all right. What are they supposed to think now?'

'The truth,' William said, sounding horribly sober.

Catrin ran back downstairs and paused at the bottom with her hand on the banister.

'Bloody poor taste,' Tim was saying, swirling a Shiraz in his glass, 'turning up late and pickled.'

'It's against the law to remove lifebelts, you know,' Roger pointed out. He picked up the bottle and looked at the label. 'He was lucky to get away with it. Of course, it doesn't help that Catrin's cracking up. It's post-traumatic stress disorder, anyone can see that.'

Catrin walked back into the room. 'Our sort don't get depressed, do we?' she said. 'We have to have designer illnesses.'

She ignored the glance that Roger and Sarah exchanged.

They had drifted away from the table and Hugh was pouring himself another Scotch, his arm resting lazily against the mantelpiece above the unlit fire.

By the window, Harry was stroking Marilyn's arm. 'Let's go upstairs,' he suggested hopefully, 'while we've got the chance.'

'You must be joking,' Marilyn said, offended. 'I thought we were supposed to be staying away from each other?'

'Only when we're at home. We're safe here, aren't we?' He slid his hand down her sequinned bottom. 'You feel like a mermaid.'

She pushed his hand away. 'I'm going to the toilet,' she said, tossing her hair away from her face.

There was something a bit off about Harry being so scared of his wife. He was going to have to stand up to her sooner or later – she didn't like the thought of him being scared of anyone, even if they were DaCostas.

Disgruntled, she ran upstairs to the bathroom but it was only when she'd shut the door that she remembered there was no longer any need to check her make-up. She stared at herself in the mirror anyway and flushed the lavatory. Coming out again she stood by the window at the end of the landing. It opened out onto a small balcony at the side of the house, overlooking waste ground formed by a triangle of walls belonging to the house next door and the house that backed onto William and Catrin's.

She climbed through the window and stood, leaning on the balcony, glad of the cold night air, and the wind blew her hair gently so that it tapped and fluttered against her back. She shivered suddenly and ducked back inside again. As she closed the window she heard the lavatory flush and the door opened and William came out wearing a white T-shirt and a pair of grey tracksuit bottoms.

'Hello, William,' she said, amused to see him. 'You're not dressing for dinner then.'

He looked at her blankly for a moment and then broke into a smile. 'I know you,' he said, pointing a finger at her.

'Marilyn.' She'd never noticed before what nice teeth he had. He was quite good-looking in his own way, it was a shame he wasn't getting any.

'You look,' he said, waving a hand, 'like leaves on the water.' He side-stepped to pass her to go down the stairs and Marilyn stepped the same way.

'Oops,' she said with a laugh and swung her hair away from her face.

'Lovely dress,' he said.

Marilyn laughed again. 'Thanks.'

'You're welcome.' William was staring at her fixedly.

Nice eyes, Marilyn thought. She'd never really looked at him before. There again, he'd never been available before. If Catrin wasn't sleeping with him then he was fair game, really.

'Marilyn,' came Harry's voice from the bottom of the stairs, 'are you up there?'

Marilyn pulled William's hand impulsively and took him into his own bedroom. She shut the door and leaned on it.

'I'm hiding from him,' she whispered conspiratorially.

William smiled. 'Me too.'

Marilyn lifted up her arms and put them round his neck. He didn't move and she kissed him on his cool, beautiful mouth, teasing her tongue between his lips to open it. Suddenly he responded and slid his arms around her waist

There, Marilyn thought; easy. Catrin really was a bit of a fool to let her husband go to waste . . .

Marilyn broke off the kiss and put her cheek against his, making small, sighing noises near his ear. She leaned against him and he lost his balance and they took a few staggering steps together before they fell onto the unmade bed. He was still holding her and she fell with a bounce on top of him, her knee between his thighs.

At that moment there was an enormous shout from

outside and a crash, followed by a dull thud that stopped her in her tracks.

She looked down at William who seemed to have noticed nothing.

'What the hell was that?' she asked him.

'What?'

Marilyn got off the bed and straightened her dress.

'It sounded like Harry,' she said and ran out of the bedroom.

The balcony window was open and the curtains shivered in the draught. Marilyn climbed onto the balcony and looked down. William followed her unsteadily. She could hear groans coming from the darkness below.

'Harry?' she called to the pale shape of Harry's face that was visible, 'is that you? Are you all right?'

A groan came rising up out of the dark.

Catrin climbed onto the balcony behind them, her face drawn, her lipstick long gone, a glass held tightly in her hand.

'What's happened?' she asked William who was holding his head. 'Has someone been sick?'

'Harry's fallen off the balcony,' William said conversationally. 'He's down there somewhere. Do I know him?'

'I'll get an ambulance.'

The guests were all climbing onto the balcony now. At last the evening was livening up. They made room and they leaned over to look into the dark triangle of undergrowth, shouting advice. It was getting crowded and they pressed against the wrought-iron railing to get a glimpse of Harry.

'Hey!' Roger shouted to him, 'Can you move?'

There was a sharp scream and they all fell quiet.

'Lie as still as you can,' Tim said. 'There's an ambulance on its way. The important thing is to keep calm.'

From the darkness Harry's voice rose up. 'You must be joking,' he said, 'there are things moving down here.'

'Harry!' Marilyn cried. 'Are you hurt?'

'The bush broke my fall and I've landed on a mattress or something. It's all damp. And there's something soft down here –' his voice started to rise in panic.

Marilyn felt let down by this show of cowardice. All that fuss and he wasn't even hurt. 'Yes, Harry,' she said coldly; 'it's you.'

In the distance the thin wail of an ambulance siren came closer.

'Shall we send it back, Harry?'

'No, I think I've broken my neck.'

Someone began to guffaw.

The sound of breaking branches came from below and there was another squeal.

A ripple of laughter broke out on the balcony. They had all seen Harry come in; it was funny to think of the squeals coming from a man like that.

'Something's just fallen on me,' he shouted up.

A bottle of Scotch was doing the rounds. It came to Marilyn and she took it, annoyed by Harry and by the amusement he was causing, and swigged it from the bottle and almost choked.

The ambulance arrived and the small crowd on the balcony was lit up spasmodically by its blue flashing light.

Marilyn watched a ladder being passed over the wall. Harry appeared on the ladder and got over the wall with alacrity. 'I think I've broken my neck,' they could hear him saying earnestly.

Satisfied and sated they all milled back into the comfort of the house. William looked at Marilyn. 'Do you want to go with him in the ambulance?'

Marilyn saw the reflection of the blue light fade. 'Harry'll be all right,' she said and went downstairs where Catrin was staring at herself blankly in the mirror.

Catrin then hurried upstairs to the bedroom to put some more lipstick on. She smoothed it over her lips unsteadily, brushed her dark hair quickly and glanced back at the unmade bed.

It was strange how things turned out. Harry had given them all something else to talk about. He'd given the party quite a festive air with his dramatic plunge.

She giggled and straightened out the sheets.

His screams really had been quite funny; so shrill.

She smoothed her hand over a bump and pulled the sheet back to see what it was.

And she could see what it was easily enough. It was one of Marilyn's copper-sequinned earrings.

Catrin picked it up and stared at it, perplexed.

She wasn't a jealous wife – why should she be? but she had noticed earlier that Marilyn had been gone for ages and for a while Harry had been calling her. And William had been – where?

In their bed with Marilyn.

She felt crushed, as though a block of concrete had been dropped on her, not because of William's treachery but because of Marilyn's. The things she'd done for Marilyn! Bought her a mop, never referred to her as a cleaning lady to avoid hurting her feelings . . .

Catrin staggered back down the stairs with the earring in her hand.

The party was in full flow. It was, incredibly, and thanks to Harry, a success. The candles flickered in soft-focus, the conversation was lively, buzzing!

'Look what I found in my bed!' Catrin said loudly, animatedly to Marilyn, her voice ringing out across the room. 'Your earring.' The coppery sequins glittered against her open palm.

Anger powered through her then and she threw it wildly at a surprised Marilyn and it missed, hitting the wall and rebounding with a 'ting' against a glass on the sideboard.

The 'ting' seemed to hush them all up. The guests fell quiet, avid for the latest spectacle, this newest piece of entertainment.

'And *you* –' she turned to William. SLAP.

Her hand stung hotly. William reeled. A smile stretched across his face as though everything, really, was all right; or maybe in his drunkenness he just hadn't felt it.

Catrin, incensed, disbelieving, outraged and drunk, stared at her guests like an unbalanced MC. She searched for words to explain her behaviour and found no nice way to put it.

'He's slept,' she said, in utter disbelief, 'with our cleaning lady.'

A thrill of horror went through the room. It was all that was needed.

As they gathered around her, consoling, helpful,

marvellously outraged themselves, she was surprised to find that, through this latest violation of good taste, she'd been forgiven.

23

Amelia's second period had come and gone.

The consultant gynaecologist's room was an odd shade of beige; it was the colour, Jonathan thought, of old porridge.

As every woman's – or at least his wife's – idea of the perfect man, he disliked beige intensely. Real men didn't like beige. Still, it was all right for a consultant, he supposed.

He narrowed his deep blue eyes at the consultant's head as he watched him flick through a file on the highly polished desk before him and he reached out his arm and put it around the shoulders of his trembling wife.

Poor Amelia, he thought, nuzzling her sweet-scented hair. It must be awful for her, knowing she was in some way deficient.

The feeling of pity moved him even now and he tightened his arm around her shaking, cashmered shoulder and stroked it with his thumb. Capable, energetic, strident Amelia for once in her life, hadn't got her own way.

Poor Amelia, insisting that it was no-one's fault and every twenty-eight days placing a new packet of Lillets on the cistern like a flag of defeat.

He moved his hand to her hair and stroked it gently.

She didn't move. She was staring at the consultant as though he was a guru, a mentor, a man with the power of life and death. Poor Amelia.

The consultant took a propelling pencil out of his pocket and underlined something heavily. And, apparently satisfied, he looked up at them. Now,' he said, 'we seem to have discovered what the trouble is. It's something that is far from uncommon these days, and no reflection of course . . .' he looked down again and followed the line of print with his finger.

Beneath his arm Jonathan felt his wife quiver. He pulled her closer to him.

The consultant looked him in the eye, man to man. 'You,' he said accusingly, 'have a low sperm count. And therein lies the problem.'

Jonathan felt as though his head had come unbolted. It's a lie, he said inside his head. He snatched his hand away from his wife's shoulder as though she'd burned him. Bloody cheek, he thought resentfully.

'Now as to treatment –'

'Just a minute,' Jonathan said, cut to the quick by the unjustness of the accusation, 'I think you'll find that it's nothing to do with me.' He was every woman's idea of – well, never mind. 'Look,' he said, wanting to be reasonable and remembering the embarrassing trip down the corridor with a sterilised container, 'I'm sure you'll find there's been a mistake. My wife – she had a cyst removed, the size of a grapefruit –' he didn't look at her, he didn't like to embarrass her, but didn't that tell them something?

'Twenty million sperm per millilitre of semen,' the

consultant said rather loudly as though to drown him out.

'Twenty million? Well there you are then.' It was a fortune in sperm. 'One of them – I mean, it only takes one –'

The consultant was looking at him rather severely. 'Sperm have a big job in front of them,' he said. 'The wastage is appalling but it is a necessary wastage. You have a low sperm count.'

Go on, rub it in, Jonathan thought. Twenty million sperm per millilitre of semen?

'You're probably wondering what we can do,' the consultant said ponderously, looking at him indifferently for a reply.

Twenty million sperm per millilitre of semen. How many millilitres were there in an orgasm? It was like one of those maths questions he'd always rather liked at school.

He was suddenly aware of Amelia again.

She hadn't moved, in fact, it was as though she'd seen a vision. Her wonderful, ugly face looked more aristocratic than ever and as Jonathan followed her gaze he found she was staring at the consultant. The Oracle.

He would solicit her help.

After all, she knew it couldn't be him. It had never even been considered. It was her, they'd always known it was her, she'd had to have a cyst removed.

'Amelia?'

She turned her head towards him. Her face was so happy and joyous he hardly recognised her. She seemed surprised and dazed as if something wonderful had happened. She was smiling – smiling! and her smile turned suddenly into a happy laugh. 'It's you!' she said gaily, 'it's your fault! It's not me at all!'

He was shocked at her treachery. 'It's no-one's fault,' he said indignantly, 'we always agreed that.'

Amelia turned to the consultant, 'It's his fault, isn't it?'

The consultant looked disapproving. 'As you both want children you can only see it as a joint problem.'

'But you never really wanted them, did you Jonathan?' Amelia said with a hypocrisy that took his breath away. She leaned over the desk and took the consultant's hand and shook it warmly. 'Thank you.'

'Now as to treatment,' the consultant said, 'there are things –'

'Bye,' Amelia said, leaving the consultant in midflow, leaving him, leaving it all behind with a spring in her step.

Jonathan got to his feet and rushed past the consultant. He suddenly wanted to hurt back and, mid-stride, he said the only awful thing he could think of.

'I hate beige.'

He made it his parting shot and he hurried to catch up with his wife.

'It's nobody's fault,' he said as he rushed after her to the car.

For the first time ever, he sounded as if he meant it.

24

The morning after the party William woke with a metal bar lying across his eyes. He forced them open nevertheless, and through his eyelashes he caught a glimpse of his alarm clock, ticking loudly, too loudly near his ear.

The clock said twelve o'clock.

The clock said twelve o'clock; or one of the hands had dropped off.

Twelve o' clock when? He peered towards the curtains and saw a crack of light between them. It was lunchtime. It was a weekday! He should be in work!

He struggled with the sheets that had wrapped round him tightly, bound him, and the struggling made his head pound harder and he gave up and lay back on his flattened pillows, exhausted.

What had he done? Alarmed, he opened his eyes again and remembered Jenna, that he'd gone to the pub with Jenna. He'd – he'd gone to the one by the canal – and stolen the lifebelt.

Both these things were bad enough but lurking about in his subconscious was something worse, something darker. He'd never realised before what a painful thing thinking was but he realised it now as he sweated the memory out of his head. And he remembered that the dark lurking thing was Marilyn and that she'd been at their party and she'd pushed him on the bed and that Catrin had made a scene.

'My head,' he groaned, and sat up with the sheets still wrapped around him. What with his head and the iron bar it seemed best to keep his eyes closed, so he sat and waited to feel better. The taste of alcohol was in his mouth and he jutted out his lower jaw and tried to breathe out and upwards and yes, he could smell the alcohol on his own stale breath. Still.

It meant the worst was yet to come.

The scene at the party continued to hover darkly in his mind; so darkly that he couldn't actually picture it, but he remembered Catrin shouting and being aware of all the others looking on. He tried to remember that he'd defended himself, but couldn't. He did remember seeing Marilyn leave, seeing her turn once, red marks showing up against her pale face.

Shit.

It had been serious. It was serious. However drunk he'd been, he'd known the seriousness of being accused of sleeping with his cleaning lady.

So why was he feeling vaguely proud?

He managed to unwind the sheets and saw that he was still wearing his clothes – his T-shirt and his grey tracksuit bottoms from the night before. He eased his legs out of bed and put his feet on the carpet. He didn't feel at all well. He stood upright with effort and swayed slightly and walked gingerly to the guest room.

The bed was rumpled and slept in. So now he knew where Catrin had spent the night.

Shit.

He went into the bathroom and squinted at himself in the mirror. His lenses! What had he done with his lenses? Fumbling, hopeful, he opened his lens case and found it was empty.

He felt ill. He fell on his knees and lifted the lavatory seat and bent over it, heaving dryly. The effort made his head pound harder.

He swallowed and stood up.

Jenna.

The memory of her ... the memory of her came cool as snow; soothing to him. He wanted to bury his hot head in her and be healed by her freshness.

But first, he had to face his wife. Maybe it would do them good, he told himself optimistically, to clear the air.

He got downstairs and found to his relief, that she had gone to work. The relief was momentary; if she'd gone to work then she hadn't been as drunk as he and her memory of the previous night's proceedings would be clearer — not at all a good thing when his own muddled memories were clearer than he cared them to be.

Hopefully he felt the kettle but he found that it was cold. Not only had she gone to work but she'd gone on time.

It bothered him to the extent that he needed to talk. He needed to talk to Jenna. He hurried to the phone and found that bending made him ill. So, crouching by the side of the sofa he dialled his office and heard Jenna's young, sweet, breathless voice answer him.

'Media News.'

'It's William.'

There was silence. Then: 'Where are you? I thought you would be in. I thought you'd want to see me.'

'I know, I – I'm in trouble.'

'Oh, William. Is it anything terrible?' she asked and he could hear her voice quiver over the line.

Suddenly it all seemed rather fantastic. It didn't seem like his life at all; he felt he'd been given the lead part in someone else's.

'Catrin found our cleaning lady's earring in the bed,' he said, and, despite the headache, he felt he said it pretty casually.

Silence.

'Jenna?'

'Your cleaning lady's earring?'

It was the contempt in her voice that made him realise his mistake, his gaffe. Because Jenna, now, felt she had a stake in him too. He vaguely knew he should be pleased but it left him with no-one to share the *frisson* of his confession with. Damn. Two women jealous of him. He knew that he ought to feel pleased but he didn't.

'It was a mistake, of course,' he said. 'I mean, on my wife's part.'

'And on mine,' she said. And hung up on him.

He kept the receiver to his ear for a moment as though she might come back.

There was a noise at the door and he saw that Catrin was standing there – how long had she been there? He scrambled to his feet, holding onto the sofa to do so and wondering what she thought, if she thought he was hiding.

'Just ringing the office,' he said, putting the phone back on the table.

Catrin had a carrier bag in her arms. Her dark hair was tied up but strands of it had strayed free and she looked young and familiar and uncomplicated.

And suddenly all he wanted was her.

She turned and went into the kitchen, her hair swinging behind her.

He followed her, pushing his hands into his pockets. 'Catrin . . .'

She swung around again. 'What?'

'I'm sorry about – you know –' he took his hands out of his pockets and shrugged. 'I was drunk.'

'So that's all right, then,' she said coldly, putting the bag on the worktop.

'Well no, but –'

'Wasn't it enough, just to be late? No, you have to pick at our marriage in public like some scab, look, look what's happened, so that everyone can see it –' her face flushed and she turned back to the shopping.

William's head was pounding again. He frowned. The thought of picking a scab made him ill. 'It's not like that,' he protested feebly.

'Then what is it like?'

He decided he would be better on the attack. 'You should know,' he said, 'you started all this.'

'What?'

'I think you heard me.'

Her face altered suddenly before his eyes. Such anger!

'You bastard,' she said and it shocked him. She never swore; she never ever swore and he tried to think what he'd said to make her so fierce. His head was pounding and he wanted to wedge it in a vice and squeeze it to keep it still. He felt as if his brain was going to burst out of his skull.

'Don't you ever blame this on me again,' she said and he watched her grab her jacket from the cupboard.

'Where are you going?'

'Back to work,' she said, banging the cupboard door closed.

He winced. 'Why? Can't you stay home with me?'

She stepped right up to him, so close that she stood on his foot. 'You're only hung over,' she said in his face. 'Don't be pathetic.'

He felt the tendrils of her hair waft against his cheek and she turned and picked up her keys and walked out, slamming the door hard behind her.

He pressed his head with his hands to ease the throbbing.

'Pathetic,' he said. 'If only she knew.' Somehow it didn't seem convincing, even to himself.

So much for clearing the air. The black cloud settled itself above his head as though the rain was there to stay.

'Headaches,' Harry explained to Marilyn from his hospital bed in a self-satisfied way. 'I keep getting them. They're still doing tests.'

Marilyn stared him in the eye until he began to shift uneasily. 'What?' he asked her nervously.

'There's nothing wrong with you,' she said loudly. 'Look at you.'

'I could have broken my skull.'

'So? There's nothing inside it.'

'Shh,' Harry said, making patting motions with his hands, 'the nurses will hear you.'

'I knew it.'

Harry put his hand on the back of his neck. 'I have got a headache,' he said, 'it's a killer, I can tell you. Seriously.'

'It's from the wine, Harry, from the wine.'

Harry looked hard done by. 'I didn't drink that much,' he said, 'I didn't get the chance.'

Marilyn felt for her earrings. She had gold studs in and since last night was paranoid about losing them.

'How did you fall off the balcony, Harry?' she asked him coolly.

Harry pushed himself up in the bed and groaned pitifully. Seeing that she was totally unmoved he jerked his head towards his locker. 'Pass me my cigarettes, will you?'

Marilyn reached for them.

'You're not allowed to smoke in here, are you?' she asked him suspiciously.

'Oh, they don't mind. They smoke themselves, half of them.'

Marilyn passed him the packet and he tapped one out. There was something about the way he did it that made her replay the conversation in her mind.

'How did you fall off the balcony, Harry?' she asked again.

Harry sucked deep on his cigarette and looked at the end of it closely, then he looked at Marilyn, straight-faced. 'Where were you when I fell?' he countered.

Marilyn stared back. 'In the bathroom.'

'No you weren't. I looked.'

Silence settled over them. A portable television in the corner of the room announced the news.

'You were in the bedroom with him,' Harry said, taking a fleck of tobacco off his tongue.

'With who?'

'Him who owns the house. The man with the lifebelt.'

Marilyn folded over the cuff of her shirt more neatly. 'How do you know?' she asked, without looking at him.

'I climbed over the balcony onto that little ledge to take a look.'

Marilyn raised her hand and hit him on the head. Harry dodged back against the pillow but it was too late. He looked surprised and hurt. 'What was that for?'

'You've got a cheek,' Marilyn said crossly, feeling for her earrings again.

'What do you mean, I've got a cheek; you were the one in there with him. I saw you pushing him onto the bed. He didn't stand a chance.'

'Yeah?'

'Yeah. Then I fell.'

They glared at each other, unsmiling.

Into Marilyn's mind came the memory of that terrible scream. She wanted to giggle. 'You're daft, you are,' she said, softening. 'How did you fall?'

'I lost my footing.' Harry still looked stern. 'I thought my end had come. I could have been killed.'

'No you couldn't, you landed on an old mattress.'

'I could still have been killed,' he insisted.

'It would have served you right. How long would you have watched us for?'

'How long would you have gone on for? I was going to burst in and thump him.'

'Well, you took your time.'

'I wasn't sure what he was up to, to start with. Might have been innocent.'

232

'Very nice of you to give him the benefit of the doubt,' Marilyn said sarcastically. She looked at her watch and stood up. 'I don't know why I bothered coming,' she said.

'Don't say that.'

'It's the truth.'

'I still don't like you saying it. Don't you love me?' Harry asked her anxiously.

She returned his gaze impassively. 'I suppose so. Shall I come this afternoon?'

Harry looked suddenly uncomfortable. 'Debbie's coming to pick me up.' He attempted to smile. 'But just wait till I get out of here, I'll make it up to you. It's worth everything to be with you, you know that, don't you? But we just have to be careful.'

'Still scared, aren't you, Harry?'

'Only for you,' Harry said.

Marilyn looked at him carefully. Then she gave him a little contemptuous wave.

'Bye, Harry. You're all talk,' she said.

25

Two weeks after the consultant's unjust accusation Jonathan Wade was sitting, desolate, in his study.

The study had distressed oak panels in it like a library in an Agatha Christie novel and it had been soundproofed; so why could he still hear Amelia order the removal men about?

Jonathan slumped over his desk in misery. He held the pose until he began to get pins and needles in his leg and even then he carried on holding it a little longer, just in case Amelia should come in.

Finally forced, through pain, to his feet, he rubbed his leg vigorously and thought, *I will show her!*

He was Chief Executive of Midlands TV; he was a success, a success! With his black hair, trimmed every six weeks by John Frieda, and all his own teeth and the dimples in his cheeks, every woman's – apart from Amelia's – romantic hero, he wouldn't be alone for long.

The truth was, he didn't want to be alone for a minute.

He hated being alone.

He flexed his leg; the pins and needles had drifted away. Pleased about that, he returned his thoughts to his loneliness and heard a knock at the door.

'Jonathan? I'm coming in.'

He knew it was too late to resume his slumped position so he hurried to the window and stood looking through it. The light would blacken out his features when he turned and Amelia would never be quite sure –

'Amelia,' he said as she came in, her hair perfect, not at all the hair of anyone who was moving house.

'Jonathan.' Her voice rang out bossily, without, he noticed, a hint of regret in it.

'This is the number of Henry's private line. He hopes we can all be civilized.'

Jonathan turned. He imagined the figure he made – a handsome, black silhouette against the light. 'Ah,' he said, 'Henry thinks wife-stealing is civilized, does he.'

Amelia sighed. 'He didn't steal me. And he happens to like me.'

Jonathan frowned. But then, he'd never thought much of Henry's judgement. However, Amelia was his wife and he loved her, in his own way.

'Amelia,' he pleaded, 'don't go.' The words came out in a rush. 'What can he give you that I can't?'

'A baby,' Amelia said, ever practical. 'You've never loved me anyway, you've always thought me ugly.'

'It's a lie,' he said, lying. 'Don't go!'

Amelia came up to the window to stand next to him. She took a bit of fluff from his polo shirt; probably the last wifely thing she would ever do for him, and he kissed her quickly on top of her short hair. 'Please,' he said passionately.

She took his hand and put a card into it and folded his fingers over it as though he were a boy being given a birthday fiver. 'If things get too terrible for you, ring me,' she said, 'but I shan't come back. We've had good times, haven't we?'

It was like being sent back to prep school: shut out of the warmth of everyday life and sent into a sort of busy, regimented emptiness. He imagined going into the office and not having her to come home to.

'I liked being a husband,' he said.

Amelia sighed. 'I know,' she said sympathetically, 'it's just that you were never very good at it. I mean, when you put yourself as the first five people you'd most like to be with, a wife can't help feeling it.'

She went on tip-toe and kissed him on the nose. ''Bye, darling.'

At first he didn't move, liking the idea of a noble silence. Then, suddenly, something occurred to him and he grabbed her arm.

Startled, she turned to him, her lips apart, surprise glowing in her dark eyes like a light. 'What is it?'

Jonathan looked into the deepest depths of her eyes as though he was searching her soul. 'Amelia,' he asked her earnestly, 'apart from this sperm business, am I still your idea of the perfect man?'

After she'd gone he prowled around his huge house, alone.

It looked quite bare, stripped of all the little tables that had been scattered around like islands in a sea of green.

He stood by the sitting-room door and narrowed his eyes. He blurred out the Regency-striped wallpaper and the watercolours she'd left him by artists he'd never heard of, and he smiled with sudden pleasure at the thirty-five feet of clear run across green Wilton

236

that he had just designated as his putting green.

He would make the most of being single. It was a state he was unused to, looking as he did. He knew he was good-looking because he'd been told so at regular intervals ever since he was sixteen, when he had made love to the neighbouring girls' school's most popular prefect against a tree.

Jonathan went for his putter and came back and tried out a few practice shots towards the window.

He was distracted more than once by the absence of all those little tables. Why Amelia needed so many he couldn't imagine.

He stuffed one hand in his pocket and frowned in a manly way and tried to remember what had been on top of them all but the only thing that came to mind was a vast urn of dried roses in the corner. He'd once suggested that had Amelia remembered to put water in they wouldn't have got so parched.

The look she'd given him had withered him to the same state as the roses.

Women.

He looked a little forlorn as he swung his putter again.

He put a fluorescent golf ball on the Wilton and nudged it gently towards a gadget he'd bought from Lillywhite's which, when hit spot-on, ejected the ball back to him. Wonderful thing.

He slicked his hair back from his face boyishly. That was the idea, anyway. He could still feel boyish at thirty-nine, couldn't he?

He changed his putter for an iron.

It seemed rather pointless having thirty-five feet of clear space and only using a yard of it.

He walked down to the large windows and opened them. There were no curtains to impede the view; Amelia had taken them.

He walked back to his tee near the door and tried a few practice swings. He was certain he could get the ball out of the window. And if he could, then he could set up some sort of a hole at the bottom of the garden. He could put a flag in it. He could, possibly, with practice, drive it back from the bottom of the garden to the living room again. Or perhaps not.

Anyway, the point was, he felt quietly confident.

He swung at the ball, hit it and watched it fly straight as a die out of the window.

He rushed to the window to see where it had gone. It wasn't visible from where he was standing but it was out there somewhere and he felt a very calm satisfaction at this.

He sat on the windowsill proprietorially, and he imagined setting up a golf course in his house. He could make Amelia's Jacuzzi into a bunker. He imagined inviting all his beleaguered, still-married friends to come for a round. He imagined their envy and what their wives would say.

And Jonathan Wade, every woman's idea of a romantic hero, felt sad, and wanted his own wife home again.

26

Marilyn was always one of the first in the school yard at the end of the day. It was a matter of pride to her to be there first for her boys. She quite liked the school; she liked the red bricks and the tarmacked playground and if she screwed up her eyes to blur out the graffiti, she could quite easily imagine that she was still there as a pupil.

She kicked a stone rather half-heartedly over the painted hopscotch. Those were the days. She'd been sorry to leave. She got three CSE's out of it – not bad for her family.

She looked at her watch. The playground was filling up with mothers and their younger children. They were mostly standing in groups, talking.

Yeah, she could have joined them if she'd wanted, but she didn't want. She pushed the strap of her bag further up her shoulder and began to walk towards the school's main door which was being opened.

Suddenly the children flowed out, a ramshackle bobbing sea of colour. She saw her boys and she craned her neck and seconds later they were running past her, one of them aiming a blow at the other as they went.

'Lee!' she shouted as his brother landed him a thump on the head in return. 'Wayne!' She turned towards the gates, knowing that they had seen her and would follow her.

'Mum, he hit me,' Lee said, acknowledging her at last. He pulled at her bag.

She pushed the strap of her bag up again. They quietened down once they were on their way home, once they were away from school.

'Behave you two,' she said.

'Yes, behave,' said a man's voice in her ear. Marilyn turned sharply and saw Arnold DaCosta standing behind her. He was wearing a purple tracksuit and running shoes but he wasn't sweating a bit.

Marilyn's first instinct was to look around for the boys. She saw them run. A rush of adrenaline brought on by fear made her skin prickle and she rubbed her arms agitatedly. Please, she thought, please let them keep away.

She looked at DaCosta dumbly.

'My sister says you've been causing her grief,' DaCosta said softly.

Marilyn swung her red hair away from her face. She saw the other mothers and their children trickle past noisily, comfortably, nothing on their minds.

'This isn't the time,' she said.

'I think that's up to me, don't you?'

Marilyn looked again for the boys. They were lying on top of each other, fighting joyously, happy not to be yelled at.

'What do you want?' she asked.

'Well, I could ask you to leave Harry alone. Fell off your friend's balcony, didn't he? Naughty boy. Still, Debbie can sort Harry out, I'm not worried about that.'

Marilyn looked at DaCosta and wished she hadn't.

The light in his small eyes frightened her but she couldn't look away. On the periphery of her sight, patterns of children bobbed about while she waited, patiently enough and scared to her bones.

'If you knew anything you'd know I'm not seeing him any more.'

'Yes, but I don't care, personally, about you and Harry. It's Debbie that cares. You could do it with anyone else until he bored you stiff, but Debbie's family. What I'm worried about is that you and Harry didn't care about my feelings in the matter.'

Amidst the flow of people Marilyn recognised one of the boy's teachers but couldn't return her smile. She was untouchable in a bubble of fright that DaCosta had created.

'What are you going to do?'

DaCosta took a packet of cigarettes out of his jogging pants and offered her one. She shook her head. DaCosta smiled. 'Got a little job for you,' he said, tapping the cigarette against the packet.

Marilyn's heart was racing. One of her sons came up to her, trailing his arm across her legs.

'Mum, can we go to McDonald's?'

'In a minute.'

'Can we go now?'

She looked down at him, making her expression fierce, making messages with her eyes. 'In a minute, I said. Go and keep an eye on Lee for me.'

He looked at her and frowned back fiercely for a moment, copying her expression. She watched him as he ran off and said, 'What is it, then?'

'A delivery. A package to a man in your local. His name's Ricky Enfield. He knows the guv'ner.' He gave her a small padded envelope. 'That's a good girl,' he said as she took it. He smiled at her, showing how nice he was, how easy life could be if only she behaved. 'I don't want to have to bother myself with you again. I won't have to, will I?'

'You won't,' she confirmed.

He nodded and for a fleeting second she found herself feeling grateful at his approval.

'Tell Harry ta-ta, will you? And tell him not to forget that I settle my debts.' He drew on the cigarette. The ash glowed for what seemed like an impossibly long time, and died to grey as he exhaled slowly and accurately in her face. 'Leave well alone in future, eh?'

Marilyn grabbed at her bag and stuffed the envelope inside it. 'Lee, Wayne,' she called. They were still racing around the playground, out of reach of her voice.

DaCosta was watching her benevolently.

She ran over to one of the boys and, as he raced past her, she grabbed the hood of his jacket. The momentum swung him around and he stumbled heavily and let out a cry as his knee struck the floor.

'That hurt!' he said indignantly. Tears were welling up in his eyes.

Fear kept her angry.

'Move. Now.'

'Mum?' Wayne had joined them warily.

'Come on,' she said, jerking her head. 'Quickly.'

'Who's that man?'

Had he gone? She couldn't bear to look at him. She could still feel the smoke in her nose. She wanted to retch.

'Let's go to McDonald's, shall we? I'll race you,' she

said jerkily. To hell with him. Let him see her running, just as long as she got the boys away.

They ran together through the park, leaping over dog dirt, the boys not laughing now. They knew a crisis when they saw one.

They didn't stop even when they reached the shops. Only when they got to McDonald's did they bunch together breathlessly and that was because they'd all leaned on the door at once and it opened not inwards but out.

They went inside and stood near the counter, frightened, all happy anticipation gone.

Marilyn opened her bag. She felt around the envelope for her purse and took it out and handed them a note. 'Get what you like,' she said. 'Look, they're giving away cars. Get a Happy Meal.'

Wayne held the money self-consciously. 'Can we really get anything?'

'Yes, as long as you eat it. I'm going to the toilet.'

She dashed upstairs, went into a cubicle and began to cry softly through gritted teeth. She hated him for bullying them. He was a low-grade gangster who'd put himself together from late night films on television; a boxing promoter-cum-self-made crook. And he'd frightened her. She hated him for that.

She took some toilet tissue and dabbed angrily at her eyes. She opened her bag and looked inside at the envelope that was making it bulge. She knew Ricky Enfield but he wasn't a regular; he turned up once or twice a month, a bread-and-cheese merchant who lived off other people's credit cards. The perfect kind of person to have as a friend.

It made her feel dirty, having the package in her

bag. DaCosta made her feel dirty, just the thought of him.

She shut her eyes and the tears squeezed through again and she wiped them off. The boys would be wondering about her. And to turn up at their school . . . he made her sick. He could at least have come up with something original.

For a moment, as she flushed the tissue away, she wanted Harry, but she wondered what good Harry could do, nothing, probably, apart from comfort her. She tossed her hair back. She could get comfort from anyone, she didn't need Harry for that.

She came out and ignored the queue that had formed in the cloakroom. She looked at herself in the mirror. Hell, she looked a mess.

She ran back downstairs to rejoin the boys.

They looked at her intently as she sat down. 'We got you a Big Mac.'

'Daft things, you know I don't eat them. Oh, go on, pass it here. Thanks.'

Lee looked at her, troubled. 'Who was that man at school?'

'Oh, him.' She took the lid off her tea and dipped the teabag up and down. 'Just someone I knew.' She opened the carton and looked down at her burger. The boys were looking at her. She took the biggest bite she could manage on the basis that she couldn't talk with her mouth full.

They were still watching her.

'What did he give you, Mum?'

Marilyn stopped chewing abruptly and swallowed her mouthful whole. Her eyes began to water. She put the burger back in its carton. Ribbons of lettuce dangled from it and she wiped her fingers on her jeans.

'Listen,' she said, as gently as she could manage, 'it's got nothing to do with you.'

She saw the boys look at each other.

'Did you owe him money, Mum?'

'Of course not,' she said indignantly. 'Why would he give me something if I owed him money? Eat your food, it'll go cold. Lee, you haven't even started your burger yet.'

They were still watching her with their steady eyes.

'Are you scared of him?'

Marilyn bowed her head and picked up her tea. Her hair flopped over her face and she left it there like a curtain through which she watched her sons. Their faces were transparent, there was no mistaking the expression on them. They were afraid for her because they loved her, and what was more, they were afraid for themselves. They had a right to be. It was the first rule of self-preservation. They had a right to worry about their parents' peace of mind.

'He's a bit of a loud-mouth,' she said at last. 'I didn't want him mouthing off in front of you two.'

'What's he got to do with us? Does he know Dad?'

Marilyn took the last couple of bites out of her burger and pushed her carton onto the next table. She looked at them and gave a short laugh. 'I'll tell you about it once and then I don't want to talk about it again, OK? You know Harry? You know Debbie? That man in the playground –'

'– in the purple tracksuit –'

'– yes, in the purple tracksuit, well, he's Debbie's brother. He thinks that because Debbie's married to Harry, Harry shouldn't have any other friends.'

She took another sip of her tea. She was doing quite well, considering.

'Debbie's his sister, then,' Lee said.

'Yep. That's right,' she said brightly.

They continued to watch her. The story hadn't gone down particularly well and they looked partly disbelieving and partly let-down.

Wayne picked up his cola and sucked at the ice-cubes with a straw. It was like the sound of a sink emptying. He shook the cup to see if there was any cola left and then put it back on the table before looking at her uneasily. 'Does it mean you're not going to see Harry again? I thought he was going to be our other dad.'

'Well he's not,' Marilyn said sharply. 'You've got one dad already, how many do you want?'

'Tom in our school's got three. He gets loads of pocket money.'

Marilyn sighed.

Later that night she was in her local, sipping a bottle of Pils and looking out for Ricky Enfield. She hated sitting in a pub on her own but the sooner she got rid of the package, the better. She could put it behind her.

She went over to the bar to have a word with the governor, who had just appeared from the back.

'Seen Ricky Enfield around lately?' she asked.

'You must be joking, he's been banged up. Mind you, he might be out by now. His missus came in with the visiting order a while back, that's how I know.'

'I'll have another Pils,' she said wearily.

'Go on, then. Terry might know where he is. Have you tried Theresa's Terry?'

She hadn't.

She pulled up a stool for herself and the governor called Terry over.

A small, pale man with wild red dreadlocks came up with his beer.

'Lady's looking for Ricky Enfield.'

The man looked at her appraisingly. 'Are you sure?' he asked. A compliment.

Marilyn tucked her hair behind her ear and tilted her head. 'I've got something for him.'

The man smiled. 'Wish you had something for me,' he said. 'Terry Jamieson.' He held out his hand.

'Marilyn Northwood,' she said.

'Have you ever had a massage?'

'Hey,' she said, 'hold on!'

He grinned. He had the nicest teeth she'd ever seen. 'It's me homework,' he said. 'I'm doing one of these courses for the jobless. This one's aromatherapy. Ever heard of it?'

'Of course I have.'

'I do them all. The only thing I didn't do was the one where you had to make umbrella stands out of corrugated cardboard. I couldn't get into that. What did you say you wanted Ricky Enfield for?'

She knew he'd come back to it. She reached down to feel for her handbag and felt the bulge of it with her fingertips. She straightened up.

'I've got something to give him.'

'Oh, yeah, you said. He's not on the bread and butter any more, you know that, don't you?'

Marilyn reared back, offended. 'I work for a living, me,' she said.

'Sorry. He's a bad lad, is Ricky. Don't tell him I said so. How about coming home with me?'

'He's out of prison, is he?'

'Saw him last week. He's in here some nights.'

'But not tonight.'

'Are you coming home with me?'

The boys were at a friend's house. Another Harry-less night loomed dark and empty.

'Not tonight,' she said, 'but don't give up hope.'

'I won't.' He turned to the bar and then turned back. 'I'll tell Ricky you're looking for him,' he said.

27

Catrin and Frances came out of their Friday-morning meeting together. Catrin glanced with raised eyebrows at Frances's mug of what looked like Ribena with something floating in it.

'I keep being sick,' Frances complained. 'I've gone off everything I like.'

'Sort of makes sense, I suppose,' Catrin said, popping another two Anadin out of the bubble pack on her desk.

Frances pulled the piece of string on the tea bag and played it like a fish. 'I've bought all the magazines I can find on babies,' she said. 'And nowhere does it mention it's fun.'

They walked into Catrin's office and sat down.

Frances stared into the mug doubtfully. Then she pulled out the tea bag and flung it towards Catrin's wastepaper bin. A small trail of purple drips arced across the carpet.

'I don't think anyone has a baby for fun, as such,' Catrin said.

'Exactly.'

'But there are other reasons, you know.'

'Don't say dresses with huge white collars.'

'Wouldn't dream of it. But it would be someone to love you.'

'I need a man for that,' Frances said.

'How about little tiny vests with ribbons to keep them closed?'

'No,' Frances said, 'vests aren't enough.' Her voice was stubborn and Catrin wondered whether the truth was that she had made up her mind.

'You could always try making the best of it,' Catrin said softly.

'Why should I?' Frances asked. 'I'm not on the path of no return yet.'

'Aren't you?'

'No.' Frances looked at her steadily. 'I don't want any of your moralistic Welsh stuff here,' she said, 'we're living in today. In Russia abortion is a form of contraception. Doctors who are geared to saving lives perform them, it's not a wicked thing to do.'

Catrin picked up two paper clips and linked them together absently.

'What are the reasons against having the baby?'

'Everything. I don't think I could manage. I know I couldn't.'

Catrin's phone rang. Her hand hovered over it while her eyes stayed on Frances. 'You could, you know. You'd get maternity leave, your job will still be here when you're ready to come back, you can be one of these people who has everything,' she said persuasively. 'Talk it over with personnel. Don't make a decision yet.'

Frances shook her head and flicked back the blonde hair that had fallen across her face. 'I don't want to discuss it with anyone at the moment. Keep it to yourself, will you?'

Catrin nodded. Her hand still hovered. 'Really,' she

said above the phone, 'this is the only good thing to come out of Alex's death, if you think about it.'

Frances got to her feet. 'That's easy for you to say.' She walked to the door and stopped, her hand on the handle. 'Tell me one thing. When you're walking down the street and you see women with pushchairs – do they ever look happy to you?'

'Well . . .'

'There you have it,' Frances said and closed the door.

William had seen Jenna looking wan and washed out in reception.

For a fraction of a second he thought she looked wan and washed out because of him but the watery smile she gave him made him realise that she was wan and washed out because of Jeff.

He got in the lift and went upstairs. He went to get a coffee and was joined by Hugh who looked nothing if not disapproving. William noticed that Hugh had copied Jeff and brought in his own cup, but in Hugh's case it was a large, earthenware pint mug. It took four average servings to fill.

'How are things?' Hugh asked him once the mug was full, patting his shoulder consolingly like a well-mannered uncle.

'Fine,' William said, slightly embarrassed by the personal approach. He opened a sachet of sugar and poured it into the plastic cup. He didn't take sugar – it was just something to do.

'Look, William, tell me to mind my own business if you like but if you must play away, keep it quiet, will you?'

William looked up from his coffee and stared at

Hugh. He was affronted at being given advice by a man whose private life was a bit of a blur to say the least.

He looked glumly at the coffee again. He hated man-to-man talks, he'd had enough of that from his father to last him a lifetime. He wasn't too keen on woman-to-man talks either – who was? Primitive man didn't talk, he acted. Talk was not something men were generally interested in.

'Not, of course,' Hugh added meaningfully, 'that she isn't good looking.'

William paid attention again. 'You started all that business,' he said morosely.

'What business?'

'With Jenna. Saying she was wonderful.'

Hugh's white eyelashes flickered rapidly above his dark eyes. 'Wasn't talking about Jenna,' he said, 'talking about your cleaning lady. Thought Jenna was going out with Jeff?'

'He finished with her,' William said, using Jenna's phraseology.

Hugh stared into the distance thoughtfully. 'He didn't mention it. When did he tell you?'

'Jenna told me. I found her crying . . .' he almost added that he'd taken her for a drink but it didn't seem the wisest of confessions bearing in mind Hugh's new avuncular attitude.

Hugh, however, seemed to have forgotten that he was lecturing William on the importance of moral standards when playing close to home. 'When was this?'

'A couple of nights ago. Why?'

Hugh looked at him blandly. 'No reason, old boy,

no reason. Anyway, you look after that wife of yours, you won't get one better.'

A sad comment on the wife-selection front, William thought, and he took his sweetened coffee slowly back to his desk.

28

It was cold the evening Marilyn walked to Catrin's house. Her left hand was icy. The right one was warmer, because she kept moving it over Harry's letter in her pocket. In his letter he asked her to fetch his jacket from Catrin's, where he'd left it the night of the party.

Marilyn looked up at the sky. She didn't usually notice it much, mainly because in London there wasn't much sky to see – just the odd square like a small canopy stretched over buildings. This night, though, was the sort of night for looking at skies, any sky, even streaky grey ones.

Her shoulder bag bounced against her hip as she walked. In the bag was the padded envelope containing the heroin.

Absent-mindedly she folded a corner of the letter with her thumb and finger, forward and back, forward and back, and wondered why Harry hadn't said in the letter that he loved her.

She smiled, remembering his startling shout of 'I LOVE YOU!' in the kitchen, but her smile quickly faded.

Things were supposed to get better between people, not worse; after what she'd put up with for him she'd expected anything but this short, bossy letter telling her to pick his jacket up.

She walked up the path and pressed Catrin's bell.

The door opened and Catrin appeared; unsmiling, cold, superior, still wearing one of the suits she wore for work.

'Hello, Marilyn,' she said, looking as though her face would crack. Well, it wasn't a social call.

'Hello, Catrin. I've come for Harry's coat,' Marilyn said, equally coldly.

'It's in the cupboard.'

'I'll get it,' Marilyn said quickly and before Catrin could answer, she pushed past her and went to the cupboard where Catrin kept the cleaning things. Cow! she thought, opening the cupboard door. She could at least have put Harry's coat in her wardrobe.

She unhooked it. It was huge, well-padded, like Harry. It felt as big as a sleeping bag in her hands.

She looked at the vacuum cleaner on the floor and bent down. It was a good vacuum cleaner and it took re-usable cleaner bags, too. She unhooked her handbag from her shoulder and opened the top of it and unclipped the cleaner bag. Into the cleaner bag she put the padded envelope. She couldn't hear Catrin but she thought she might still be in the hall, by the door. She stood up and bundled Harry's coat underneath her arm, picking up her rubber gloves as she did so. Then she closed the cupboard door behind her.

'Got it,' she said to Catrin who was waiting by the door, like a security guard, for her to leave. 'When do you want me to start cleaning again?'

Catrin seemed to take a sudden interest in the door's

locking mechanism. She pressed the catch with her finger, in-out, in-out.

'I don't think it would be a good idea,' she said finally.

'Oh.' Marilyn looked at the door catch too. She felt something sink inside her. Four years and she was getting rid of her just like that, just as if she was nobody. 'I'll see you, then.'

'See you,' Catrin replied tonelessly and closed the door behind her.

Marilyn toyed with the idea of wearing the jacket home but decided against it. Bugger Catrin, she thought and hugged it to herself as she walked home, fancying she could smell Harry on it.

She went back into her flat, switched off the video to protests from the twins and sent them for a bath.

She sat down and rested the jacket on her knees, her thoughts touching on Harry and his letter.

It had been such a short note.

She wouldn't have minded not seeing him until things died down, as long as he'd given her something to hope for.

She got up and looked for a carrier bag to put the jacket in, but Harry's jacket was too big for any carrier bag and she stuffed it inside a bin-liner instead and put it down by the door. Bugger Harry, too.

'Come on boys, bed,' she said, going into the bathroom. They looked up, frowning. The bath was so full of toys it was hard to see how they could fit in themselves.

'Mum —'

'BED.'

Reluctantly they got out of the bath, glowering at her.

She glowered back and went into the lounge and put the television on.

Watching the tail-end of a film, the feeling she'd got when she'd looked at the sky came back. Tears began to trickle down her cheeks and gather on her chin to drip onto her denim-covered knees.

She always got the rough end of the deal. She had to do favours for DaCosta while Harry got away with a telling-off from his wife. And what was it all for?

She had a right to be fed up.

She looked at the bin bag by the door.

Uncurling herself from the sofa she went into the bathroom for some tissues and made a diversion into the kitchen for a pair of kitchen scissors. She blew her nose and felt brighter, much brighter, with the scissors in her hand.

She balanced them on her palm. It was a game, only a game. She just liked the thought of cutting up Harry's jacket. She glanced at the television. The film was still on. Cutting up Harry's jacket would give her something to do, joke, but she wouldn't actually do it. However, she could, if she wanted to.

She got the bin liner from beside the door and sat back down on the sofa with it on her knee. She opened it up and looked at Harry's jacket, lying quietly inside. Look at the care with which she had folded it! Annoyed, she pulled it out and spread it on her knee. It was huge. She bet if she washed one of Harry's shirts in her washing machine it would fill the whole tub! It would be like washing a sheet! Ironing it would be a nightmare. She'd have to iron it in twenty-three parts! Never marry a fat man, she told herself sternly, although chance would be a fine thing, and she ran her hands over his jacket which covered her knee like a rug.

She picked up the scissors and snipped at the air to limber up. And then she turned the jacket over so that it was frontwards-up and she snipped one of the buttons off. It had three buttons on it – one was already missing – and she snipped them all and let them roll onto the floor where they rocked individually like exhausted tops.

Marilyn brushed her hair away from her face and faked a yawn to stretch the skin that the tears had tightened.

There.

It was just a gesture, really.

She meant to stop, at that point. Buttons were easy to sew on, even men could do them. Even Harry? Well, probably.

She picked up the sleeve and began to cut. It was a much slower job than the buttons but she did it carefully and, with extra pressure at the seams, the sleeve was off. She held it up in front of her and let it dangle. A dead sleeve! He could always sew it back on. He could sew a zip into it and have detachable sleeves. Harry? Maybe not.

She cut off the other sleeve.

Anarchy is not really anarchy when it's neat.

Marilyn laid the severed sleeves side-by-side on the floor and attacked the limbless jacket from behind. It was not an easy task. The padded fabric was difficult to cut but she battled on until there was a blister on her thumb and then until it burst. She went to the bathroom and got out the plasters and stuck one on it and continued with her job. The stuffing was lying around in wodges. They had been very liberal with the stuffing, she would give them that. It was in her hair, on her eyelashes, and coating the sofa like the first fall of snow. Still, she hacked away with surprising lightness of heart. Harry would have been pleased to know that there was no vindictiveness in it whatsoever.

Eventually the unidentifiable remains of his jacket lay littered around. She gathered all the bits together and then piled them back into the bin bag. And then she vacuumed the floor, the sofa, and to a certain extent, herself.

She was just putting the cleaner away when there was a knock at the door.

Her instinct was not to open it but it had been a strange sort of evening so without even asking who it was she opened the door.

And it was Harry.

'Harry,' she said brightly and with a shiver of guilt she tried not to let her eyes drift to the bin liner on the floor. 'What are you doing here?'

Harry looked over his shoulder out at the hall. She didn't know why he bothered to act furtive, because for one thing he wasn't the kind of person you could miss, and for another, he couldn't move fast enough to hide from anyone, so it seemed rather futile.

'Just popping in for my coat,' he said loudly, and added, 'Aren't you going to let me in?'

'Well – no,' Marilyn said.

Harry pushed her inside her own flat and closed the

door behind him. Then he looked at her. 'What's the matter with you?' he asked.

Marilyn looked up at him innocently. She *felt* innocent. She felt – she felt free. 'Nothing,' she said.

Harry's frown deepened and he looked around him, trying to appear casual. 'Have you got someone here?'

Marilyn looked surprised. 'No. No, I haven't. Have a look if you like.'

Harry pondered on this. 'All right,' he said, 'I will,' and he wandered into the bedroom. She heard him open the wardrobe door.

He came back, looking more disgruntled than ever. 'All right, what's going on?' He looked at her curiously. 'What's that fluff in your hair?'

Marilyn flapped at her hair with her hand. All the time that he had been hunting around, Marilyn had been sitting on the arm of the chair waiting for him to say he loved her or to take her in his arms, but he hadn't.

She got up and looked at him full in the face. 'How are you, Harry?' she asked him, smiling.

Harry stepped away from her. 'How am I? What do you mean?'

'I just mean how are you; and where's Debbie tonight? I'm surprised she's let you out, you're not the most trustworthy of people.'

'I am,' Harry said, affronted. He looked worried again. 'She's gone to one of those parties. One of those sex parties.'

'An orgy?'

'Not an orgy, one of those parties that they sell, you know, sex things.'

'An Ann Summers party.'

Harry looked deeply troubled. 'I don't know what she'll come back with,' he said.

Marilyn grinned and she found that it hurt. 'Never mind,' she said, 'I suppose you're used to that sort of thing.'

He tried to put a brave face on it, then he put his hand in his back pocket and fiddled around with something behind his back.

It was a Sooty puppet.

'Hello, Marilyn,' he said in a squeaky voice, waggling the puppet's head at her, 'fancy a cuddle?'

Marilyn looked from the puppet to Harry. Then she looked at the puppet again. She couldn't take too much of Harry; at this rate she'd go off him for life. She was, on the other hand, happy to be won over.

Harry was waving the puppet's arms around. Then he made a grab for her breast.

'Gettoff!' Marilyn shrieked, 'You kinky bugger!'

A small voice called out from the bedroom. 'Mum? Are you OK? Who's there?'

Marilyn clasped her hand over her mouth. 'It's only Harry, babes. He's got a Sooty with him.'

Sooty was creeping up to her breast again. Marilyn swatted him away.

'Can I come and see him?'

Marilyn put her hand over her mouth then caught Harry's eye and giggled. 'Harry'll come and show you.'

She led the way to the bedroom and giggled again as Sooty grabbed her bottom.

Harry filled the bedroom. Lee was awake but Wayne was still fast asleep, his arms outflung.

'Let me see him then,' Lee whispered.

Harry waved the puppet's hands and waggled its

head. 'Hello, little boy,' he said in a squeaky voice.

Lee's expression was one of disgust. 'You're hopeless,' he said.

Harry looked at the puppet and made it nod its head at him. 'I can't do the voice, whispering,' he said.

'Sooty doesn't even talk. Goodnight.' He turned over and buried his head under the blankets.

Dismissed, Marilyn and Harry tiptoed back out again.

Harry looked at the puppet intently. 'It's a miracle! He can speak!' he said.

Sooty gave a bow.

'And now, to bed.'

'Thought you didn't like sex aids.'

'Bloody hell,' Harry said, springing up. 'Debbie will be back soon.'

Marilyn looked at him. 'Why does she trust you at all? If it were me, I wouldn't let you out of my sight.' She entwined her legs with his. He laughed and jerked away.

'You'll get me going again,' he warned.

'Where's Sooty?'

'Down here, somewhere,' Harry said, diving under the duvet and letting a draught in. 'Found him.' He threw off the duvet. Sooty was covering his erection.

'Oh, Harry,' Marilyn said, and laughed. 'Why does she trust you?'

Harry shrugged and threw the puppet on the floor. 'I'm convincing, aren't I?'

Marilyn felt for her earring and twisted it between her fingers. 'You mean you're a convincing liar.'

Harry had the grace to look uncomfortable. 'Yeah,

I suppose so. It's for us, though, isn't it.' He took a long hank of her slippery red hair in his hand.

Marilyn gave a long sigh. 'It doesn't feel right though, does it?' she said, feeling disgruntled. 'We have to think more about her and her family than we do about us.'

'Not any more. She trusts me now.'

Marilyn moved her head away from him and her hair pulled out of his hand.

She kneeled on the bed, facing him. 'Why does she trust you?' she asked suspiciously.

Harry used his thumbnail to prise up a scab on the back of his hand. It opened like a small trap door and a glob of blood swelled up behind it. He put it to his mouth and sucked. 'Why are you asking me?' he said.

'Does she know you're here?'

He met her eyes. 'I told her I'd call in to collect my jacket, that's all.' He looked at her closely and shifted his shoulders uneasily. 'Look, I told her you'd slept with me once and then you'd blackmailed me. I had to do it, you should know that. It was to keep her off our backs.'

Marilyn felt her scalp crawl, she felt it contracting, teeming with a million fears. 'Off your back, you mean,' she said.

He didn't even look abashed. 'We can carry on meeting like this, can't we? When she's out?'

'So you get off scot-free? DaCosta's given me some horse to deliver for him – you make up with Debbie while I run around doing DaCosta's dirty work for him?'

'Yeah, well, I wouldn't know anything about that. And you can take it, can't you.' He said it too hurriedly; it would have been better, he realised, if he hadn't said anything at all. He got up out of bed and began to put on his clothes.

'And what about my kids?' she demanded of him, holding his jeans behind her back.

'What about them? Send them to Dave. You manage well enough when you want to.'

Marilyn felt a rise of terrible anger. She swung his jeans round and the belt buckle caught him on his cheek with a jangle of metal. 'Get out,' she said in a tight voice, 'get out of here and take your things before I burn them.' She picked up the Sooty which had fallen on the floor and she flung it at him. 'You're not worth a shit, you know that? Not worth a shit. Don't you dare come back.'

'Silly bitch,' Harry said, feeling the side of his face, 'I don't intend to.'

'Take that bag with you, it's got your jacket in it.'

Wordlessly he picked it up, left the flat and slammed the door.

Marilyn put on her dressing gown and walked slowly to the television and turned the sound up.

The credits were rolling.

Some stories had happy endings. Never hers, though; never hers.

29

It was a sunny March morning.

Catrin was brushing her hair, ready to leave for work.

William was sitting on the bed, putting his socks on. He glanced at her with his pure grey eyes and looked at his stockinged feet.

Catrin threw her hairbrush onto the bed. 'This is intolerable.'

William glanced up.

'Why won't you speak to me?'

'I can't think of anything to say,' William said, slipping his shoe on.

Catrin stared at him bitterly. 'Which means you're not going to try and put things right,' she said. 'Ignoring it won't make it go away.'

'Ignoring what?'

Catrin tightened her lips.

'That was a joke,' William said, getting to his feet. 'You would have laughed at it once.' He took his jacket off the hanger and put it on. 'We'll talk tonight.'

Catrin looked at her fair, handsome husband. In a suit, he always looked good, good but untouchable, and never more so than now.

'You sound as if there's hope,' she said, smiling to

show it was nothing heavy, although the thought of there being hope at all made her light-headed.

'There's always hope,' William said.

That evening Catrin laid the table using her Irish linen tablecloth and napkins – yet another lot of things she couldn't bear to iron – and the crystal candlesticks with slender white candles. Wine – Chateau Margeaux. They were going to need the wine.

And she went upstairs to shower and change. She put on a fine grey chiffon shirt over loose crêpe trousers, nothing too obviously dressed-up.

She opened one of the bottles of wine and she checked the time and found that it was five past eight.

She poured herself a drink.

The old William was never late, on principle; the new William – well, who knew what the new William was capable of. Anything, it seemed. It was like some mid-life crisis he was going through, asserting his independence, proving to himself he was still attractive to the opposite sex.

It didn't matter at all that William was late, five minutes was a held-up-in-the-traffic sort of late, nothing to get worked up about, if she was getting worked up, which she wasn't.

She went to sit on the sofa and carried on waiting. It was ridiculous to feel nervous waiting for her own husband in her own house, but she couldn't help it. She switched the television on and switched it off again and picked up a magazine. She rang the office but after six rings she knew that he was not going to answer; but each time she made to put the phone down she changed her mind, just in case, just in case.

She walked around the living room rather aimlessly, adjusting a photograph frame, and thought she would light the candles.

She watched them flicker and she sat at the table and shook out her napkin and poured herself another glass.

She could see why emotion was said to come from the heart because that was where she could feel the emptiness as she waited for him. She wondered whether this nervous, alarming pain was bearable for any length of time and how other people survived it.

She rang the office again and listened to the phone ring hollowly. She put it down and went back to her wine.

She thought of him with Marilyn. It must, she thought running her fingers along the chain around her neck, be strange being William, or indeed any man. They had such a hard time of it, there were so many opportunities for losing face. Men could lose face in so many different ways — for instance she'd never known a man to confess that he didn't know where somewhere was, if asked. She'd known men send people off in totally the wrong direction rather than tell them they didn't know the way.

It was the same with asking for directions. Men never would ask, at least, none of the men she'd ever known. They preferred to drive around in the hope of finding the place they wanted by accident, never mind that they were going miles out of their way and getting more lost all the time. To ask for directions was to lose face. So in a way, unforgivable though it had seemed at the time, she could understand why William had done what he'd done with Marilyn.

After the articles in the trade press it had helped him to save face in front of his friends.

But understanding it didn't mean it didn't hurt.

Catrin made to pour herself another glass and found that she'd finished the bottle.

She went to fetch the corkscrew and she opened another and stared at the burning candles flickering gently. Candles were so romantic. She wished William would come so that they could talk although she wasn't sure any longer what it was she wanted to talk about.

She poured herself another glass of wine, resting the neck of the bottle against her glass. It slipped, knocking the glass over. A small, purpley-red patch crept towards her.

'Ooops.' She watched it spreading and it looked very pretty. She felt good; pleasantly numb. 'William, where are you?' she asked aloud.

She poured herself a replacement, holding the glass firmly in one hand and the bottle in the other. She drank quickly and glared at the candles and suddenly the black hole of her nightmares opened up inside her.

'Where is he?' she asked, frightened.

The candle flames danced riotously in the draught of her breath.

'He's left me.'

The flames danced again. She sat very still, feeling the words. There was a strange, high-pitched humming in her ears, the sound of silence.

'Forget him,' William said to Jenna firmly for the umpteenth time. She'd found him by the coffee machine where he'd been looking for a caffeine hit before going home.

He tried surreptitiously to look at his watch. He could hear the phone ringing in his office but Jenna, tears blurring her scorching blue eyes, needed comforting and he didn't move. Needed comforting. Needed him.

She really did have no-one else.

Her parents, she said, ignored her. They had their own lives. She'd only ever loved Jeff. She said it with such pathos that he wanted to take her in his arms, prove to her that he was lovable too.

Jenna seemed to read his mind. She put her hand up to her fleece of white-blonde hair and tugged a curl.

It was the most natural thing in the world to put his arms around her small, slim body. Her perfume filled his head.

She looked up at him, her pink lips sparkling and he was tempted, so tempted, just to taste them. Hardly a kiss; he just wanted to try them, as he would try some delicacy, he just wanted the flavour of her on his tongue.

He dipped his head to sip her nectar.

It wasn't, he told himself sternly as they hugged by the coffee machine, anything as base as a kiss, at all.

Catrin fetched her wedding album and opened it out on the table and scrutinised the photographs in surprise, as though she herself hadn't been there at all.

The longer you were married, she thought, the harder you cried at other people's weddings. It was like a law. She wondered whether it had been thought of before. Catrin's Law. The dampness of the guest's handkerchief increases in direct proportion to the length of her marriage.

Or in other words, you knew it was such an enormous act of faith to promise that death was the only thing that would split you up despite the other minuses – sickness, poverty, deterioration of the relationship – that it made you cry.

She put her finger on a photograph of the two of them and rubbed it against the smooth surface of his face and traced him, down his shoulder to his arm, which was curving around her waist.

She felt drunk all of a sudden – it seemed to have crept up on her. She felt drunk and rather ill.

'I do love you,' she told the William in the photograph. And suddenly the utter futility of loving someone who didn't love back washed over her. She could almost see her love pouring into nothingness, into space, wasted, like fresh water soaking into hot sand, useless, unwanted, undesired.

Anger heated up in her, a black pain.

He didn't value her any more. She was nothing to him. She was worse than nothing, she was an irritation.

'Crash,' she said angrily, imagining him on the way home. 'Crash, crash, crash . . .'

She began to sob loudly in despair, racking ugly sobs that were wrenched from somewhere deep inside her. She put her head in her hands and slumped forwards over the wedding album that was stretched out on the purple stain of wine.

She cried until her stomach hurt from crying.

She raised her head and heard the sound of crackling close by and, through her hot and swollen eyes, she saw a bright light above her. Putting her hand up curiously, she found that her hair was on fire, lit by the candles that had now burnt down. She beat at the flame frantically with her hands and the appalling, pungent smell of burnt hair filled the room. Her hand was full of her hair, shrivelled and crispy and she got up from the table unsteadily and put it in the bin, aghast, and raked at her damaged hair with her fingers.

Her hands were burning from the flames and she put them under the cold tap until they ached with cold.

The smell. The smell was ugly.

Drying her hands she touched her head again. Her hair was stiff and brittle.

She went to the dining room and blew out the candles, just wicks now in small pools of wax.

She felt sick and empty and afraid.

She heard a noise behind her and William came into the room looking white. The room was thick with candle smoke and the ugly, sulphurous smell of burnt hair.

William looked around the room, at Catrin, wiping her mascara-smudged cheeks and his scared eyes went to her face.

'I've just crashed the car,' he said.

That night they went to bed afraid.

For the first time in weeks they clung to each other in the comforting dark.

William held her tightly to him. In the aftermath of the accident – only a slight one, a car had carved him up, crushing the wheel arch – he had decided that he would ask her to give up her job, have a baby with him, start again. He didn't want to hate her any more, he wanted her to save him from himself.

He'd kissed Jenna but he wasn't an unfaithful man, nothing like his father, never ever like his father had been.

He'd crashed because he'd been with Jenna and when it came to it, Jenna meant nothing to him at all or at least, very little. He wanted the safety of what he knew. He was looking for comfort in the familiar. He wanted to come home.

He clutched Catrin tight for comfort, closing his eyes in the relief of being where he belonged. But burying his face in her usually soft and fragrant hair he encountered a strange texture and an appalling smell.

Catrin, pressed against William's hot, hard body, smelled in the hair of his chest cigarette smoke and perfume and the smell of red wine on her own hot breath. She felt no relief at being held by him. What hatred there must be in her, to have wanted him to crash. She lifted her head and with her lips against the bristles underneath his chin she said, 'I can smell perfume on you.'

'Rubbish,' he replied crossly and his arms held her a little less tightly.

Maybe it was.

30

The following day, hung over, Catrin received a phonecall from Roger.

'Lunch?' she repeated in surprise, her head not feeling so dense that she couldn't detect a strange languor in Roger's normally brisk voice. 'Why? Is there anything wrong?'

The question was followed by a disconcerting silence.

Then Roger said in his newly drawling voice: 'I thought you might be in need of some male company.'

Catrin glanced at the clock in the outer office. It was ten-thirty; far too early for intrigue of any kind. The effort of adjusting her vision made her head throb.

'Can't, Roger, sorry; have to go to the hairdresser lunchtime.' Heavens – she used to use a variation of that excuse when she was sixteen. 'I mean, I genuinely have to,' she said.

It was a mistake. Encouraged, Roger lowered his voice a tone. 'How about Monday?'

'Roger – I'm not misunderstanding you, am I?'

Roger chuckled.

She wasn't.

'Let me run this past you once more,' he said. 'We've both had rough deals from our partners.

Sarah's cheated on me with I don't know how many men –'

'What? She said you'd cheated on her,' Catrin protested, feeling that she was losing the thread of this tangled conversation, 'often.'

'Never have,' Roger said glumly. 'Who'd have me?'

Just in time, Catrin stopped herself from falling into it. 'Honestly, Roger,' she said, 'it's not one of your better ideas.'

'No?' He coughed rather dismally. Catrin winced. 'Oh well.' He brightened. 'It's Lottie's birthday in two weeks. A Barbie party.'

Despite her headache, Catrin grinned. 'Barbie? Isn't that a bit sexist?'

'Lottie hacked the dining room table to bits with the tool kit we gave her. Sarah said she's all for her expressing herself but wanton destruction's something else entirely. Anyway, if you come to the Barbie party –'

'Yes?'

'You can let me know if you've changed your mind.'

There was no answer to that, but as Roger seemed to be expecting one, she murmured: 'Thanks.'

'When Sarah rings you, don't let on I've spoken to you, will you?'

'Of course not, Roger.'

'And think about it. There's no rush. We're talking adult behaviour, here.'

Catrin replaced the phone and rubbed her eyes.

She felt she'd been made a fool of, somehow.

At lunchtime she went to the hairdresser to have her singed hair cut off.

'Hello, I'm Sinbad your stylist,' stated a man with a crew cut and faded denim dungarees, smugly. He flicked her hair in the dismissive manner of hairdressers and swore expressively as he rolled the burnt strands between his forefinger and thumb.

'You're going to ask me who did it last time, aren't you,' Catrin said.

'Actually darling, I'd say it was in the same shape as Joan of Arc's after the English had had her.'

Catrin peered at herself in the mirror. Her eyes were still puffy from the effects of the previous night and apathy made her reckless. 'Listen, just cut it as short as you need to. I've reconciled myself to the fact that it's irretrievable.'

'Good girl. You'll suit it short. Maybe a bit of length here at the nape of the neck? Michelle will wash it. Michelle, when you're ready . . .'

Catrin got up reluctantly from the seat, her head feeling like a concrete block balanced on her shoulders.

'Er – Sinbad – you haven't got any aspirin, have you?'

'Aspirin, Michelle,' he called calmly. 'A coffee to wash it down?'

'Great, thanks.'

She sat by the washbasin and was swathed in towels.

'You won't rub too hard, will you?'

The first cut was the worst because after that there was no going back.

Catrin watched great hanks of hair fall to the ground with sudden consternation and then thought – so what? If she were to look different it would be less confusing for everyone. She wasn't the same person she had been, she wasn't, any longer, the Catrin of the long hair whose life was under control. The truth was, she didn't quite know who she was, but she was finding out.

She watched the stylist as he cut with precision, snipping away such tiny amounts, evening it up, shaping it, blow drying it, ruffling it, dampening it again.

He brushed the front of her hair and cut that too and finally he stood back, and Catrin looked at herself curiously, at the person she had now become.

A heavy dark fringe hung over her eyes, making them look larger, brighter, despite the hangover which was only slightly dented by the aspirin. He'd layered her hair as he'd promised, into the nape of her neck, its shortness drawing her eyes to the shape of her face, emphasising cheekbones she'd never really been aware of. She stroked it. It was soft and smooth and – strange. Very strange.

'What do you think?' Sinbad asked, holding up a mirror so that she could see the back of it.

'Hmm.' Catrin nodded. 'It's growing on me.' She paused and shot him a glance.

He shuddered with distaste. 'That's what they all say.'

With Sinbad's aspirins and a heady sense of liberation she felt well enough afterwards to pop into Hamley's for a present for Lottie.

She headed for the Barbie section, but the sight of the Kens all neatly packaged with their Lurex jackets and vacant smiles depressed her. In some strange way they reminded her of Roger. The more she thought of their conversation, the more she felt she ought to feel insulted. It seemed as if Sarah's remarks about his infidelities might have come more from wishful thinking than regret.

So in the end she bought Lottie's Barbie not a Ken but a convertible. Give her a bit of independence, she thought.

Satisfied, she waited an age for the lift and went down to the basement for a sustaining coffee before returning to work.

The basement was a mistake; it gibbered with noise and she looked with disbelief at the restaurant on one side and the wealth of electronic gamery on the other.

Chips and microchips.

She was aware of someone standing next to her.

'Any idea where the outdoor toys have gone?' he asked.

Catrin looked up at the owner of the voice. His face was familiar and yet she was sure she'd never spoken to him before. 'Sorry,' she said, and shrugged.

He smiled, and laughter lines crinkled at the edge of his deep blue eyes, but only his mouth was smiling. 'Look at it,' he said, his gaze drifting over the flashing lights of the games, 'all that virtual reality, as if the genuine thing wasn't bad enough.'

Catrin looked at him again, recognising the voice of a kindred spirit.

He nodded towards the carrier bag in her hand. 'Someone's going to be happy tonight.'

'Oh, it's for a friend's daughter,' she said, too quickly. 'What are you looking for?'

'Silver sand. I'm making a golf course out of my

house.' He looked from Catrin to the empty table beside her. 'Shall we sit here?'

Before Catrin could reply he held out his hand, not as though he was going to shake it, but more as though they were making a deal.

'Jonathan Wade,' he said.

And of course she knew him at once; chief executive of Midlands TV.

'Catrin Howden.'

He didn't smile this time, but the crinkles from the previous smile seemed to have lingered at the corner of his eyes.

'Ah, yes – the woman who rid this world of Alex Martin,' he said, and went to join the queue.

When he came back with the coffees and two jam doughnuts, Catrin found herself saying, as though there had been no break in the talk, 'You knew him, then?'

'He used to work for me. Decent enough chap.' He pushed the sugar bowl towards her. 'You've been through a bad time.'

Catrin felt something catch in her throat. She could handle anything but sympathy. And, as though he sensed it, Jonathan Wade gave her a sudden grin; a proper one now in that it reached his eyes. He looked, thought Catrin, incredibly handsome and the fact that it was the kind of fixed grin that denoted hours of practice in front of the mirror didn't detract from it one bit.

'Feeling a bit dodgy myself,' he said. 'Some bastard's run off with my wife.'

'Oh.' Catrin took a bite of doughnut. The sugar that

had frosted the top adhered itself to her upper lip. As she reached for a napkin the jam began to leak out and she caught it with her tongue, rather niftily, considering, enjoying the sensation of the sweet, comforting strawberry stickiness despite being conscious of the mess she was making of it.

Jonathan Wade took a bite of his and as he wiped the sugar off his nose she saw with some relief that there was no way of eating a doughnut gracefully.

It created a sort of bond between them. It was to consolidate this bond that she decided to say what she did.

'My husband,' she said, 'has slept with our cleaning lady.'

She was rewarded with that sudden, polished grin. 'Join the club,' he said.

The combination of the attentions of Roger and then Jonathan put her in a buoyant mood for the rest of the afternoon.

When she got home the mood was still with her until William came in.

He looked at her for a long moment with cool, unblinking eyes. Then he went into the kitchen and she heard the top come off the Scotch. After a few moments Catrin went in after him. She watched him pick up his glass and gulp half its contents down. She watched his Adam's apple jump as he swallowed over and over the mellow fumes until finally he could speak and when he did it was only one word.

'Why?'

For a moment she was baffled. She stuffed her hands in the opposite sleeves of her sweater as she had when she was young and playing at being a Chinaman or, she remembered, as she had when she was young and she'd done something wrong. She took her hands out again. They felt large and awkward by her side and she felt the resentment build up in her, that he should make her feel like this. She touched her hair.

'Why not?'

William swirled his drink around his glass. 'Why not? I liked it as it was. I've always liked your hair long.'

A number of answers to that one drifted up but she held her tongue and said, instead, the only one that was true.

'I know. But it was time for a change.'

31

The following day William strode into reception at *Media News* and leaned over the desk towards Jenna. He grabbed her arm. 'I have to talk to you,' he said under his breath, 'it's terribly urgent.'

Jenna looked up at him with her bland and trusting stare.

'Now?'

'Yes, now. Can you fix that thing?' he said pointing at the switchboard as though it was a Dalek. It was lit up. Some of the lights were flashing.

'You want me to sort this out first?'

William remembered he'd rung the office on the day of Martin's funeral and hadn't been able to get through. Now he knew why. 'I think you ought to,' he said.

'OK,' she whispered. She flicked some switches and said 'Hello, Media News,' several times and finally she got up and came out from behind the desk. 'Something's wrong,' she said. 'Not bad news, I hope?'

William looked down at her small, pure, unlined face and he wanted to cup it in his hands and kiss her gently, small kisses as you'd give a child. She brought out the tenderness in him. How could he tell her of the complications of marriage? She ought to be spared it, kept innocent. He didn't answer her. Maybe he wouldn't confide in her after all. She was so young.

'It's your wife, isn't it?' she said. Her pretty, bland face remained expressionless. He wondered, fleetingly, whether anything really did touch her. 'You can tell me,' she said.

He looked at her naked blue eyes and her pink-lipsticked lips mouthing the words, and a fierce sickness welled up in him and made a lump in his heart. 'I need someone to talk to,' he said.

'Where shall we go?'

She was so trusting, he thought. He could take her anywhere, push her into the men's lavatories – '– the stairwell,' he said, propelling her gently with his hand and knowing all the time that he must be insane. How could he explain it if Hugh caught them there? They would be caught, caught was the right word, even if they were yards apart, guilt would be admitted by their hiding there at all. He followed her to the door that led to the stairs. No-one used the stairs. They were uncarpeted, gloomy. There were other stairs, carpeted, on the other side of the building but people mostly used the lifts. As he pushed open the door for her he felt foolish. Foolish but desperate.

Jenna went to lean against one of the cream walls. She kept her head down as she looked up at him and the effect was of a naughty child about to be told off. William was disconcerted, but his need to talk overcame his desire to leave and he stood, slightly chilly in his shirtsleeves, and shoved his hands into his trouser pockets. He wondered whether he would seem petty to her but was powerless to keep it to himself.

'Catrin's had her hair cut,' he said.

Jenna's fine eyebrows lifted and her smooth brow crumpled slightly then smoothed out again.

'Seriously,' he said. 'It's short. It's shorter than mine.' He glanced up the stairwell, wondering whether the acoustics were such that his words would travel. They probably would. Someone was probably listening now, and suddenly he didn't care.

He took his hands out of his pockets and leaned against the banister at the bottom of the stairs. It was icy cold, a wrought-iron affair, but, having struck the pose, he thought he ought to keep it, at least for a minute or two.

'You can even see her scalp, at the back.'

This, at least provoked a reaction.

Jenna made a face, grimaced and hugged herself. She lifted her hand to her own hair and entwined a section around her finger. 'That's so strange,' she said. 'Why did she have it cut?'

William closed his eyes wearily. 'Why? he echoed. 'Don't ask me. I loved her hair. She knew I loved it. Why would she have it cut? She didn't even mention it to me.'

Jenna chewed her pearly-pink lower lip and lifted her eyes to his. A jolt shot through William. It didn't work every time, only when he forgot about their sparkling brightness and was suddenly reacquainted with it.

'Has she joined a women's group?' Jenna was asking him.

He looked at her, surprised. 'No. I'm pretty sure she hasn't.'

He watched Jenna lapse into thought again. Then she reached out her hands to him. He stood upright rather awkwardly. The hand that had been resting on the wrought iron banister rail was icy cold but in response to her he held out his hands too.

She took them in hers. Her hands were warm and dry and felt, surprisingly, wrinkled.

William took refuge in conversation. 'Her hair was one of her best features,' he said. 'The smell, the feel –' Ah, that had been indiscreet of him. 'Mind you, it smelled jolly strange the other night. Like wet wool. We used to go to a farm in the summer –' He stopped again. He wanted to talk. He missed talking to Catrin, the old Catrin. They used to be able to say anything they liked to each other, that had been part of the fun. 'That's in the past,' he said lamely. He'd loved her as she was. He'd loved her when she was his.

He noticed, now, that he was holding Jenna's hands and that hers were lying limply in his.

'Women,' she said softly, 'have their hair cut when affairs are over.' Her sympathetic, vivid eyes sought his, and then flicked swiftly away, the shy messengers of bad news.

'Do they?' William said sharply, as though it was something that was untrue, but Jenna's blameless eyes wandered back to his again and something clicked inside him and he knew it was the truth. 'Yes,' he said slowly to himself,' they do.' A parade of women with broken relationships and shorn hair walked defiantly through his mind.

He looked at Jenna in despair. 'I loved her,' he said. 'I loved her as she was.'

He'd raised his voice and it seemed to rise slowly in an echo and he looked up the stairwell anxiously. No-one was that busy that they couldn't wait for the lift. Still, he didn't want to be caught unawares.

He looked at the pale cream wall and saw only Catrin's startled face as he'd found her in the kitchen. Pink-cheeked, she'd looked like a guilty choirboy. His heart had gone out to her, until he stopped it.

'I asked her why she'd had it cut,' he said to Jenna, 'and she had nothing to say.'

'You know,' Jenna said, 'I'm not trying to say that your wife has been unfaithful. I'd never say that – it's only what Jeff's told me, but . . .'

William let out a sharp breath of air. 'It's all right,' he said. He looked at his watch. The interview was at an end. He wanted to go now. He wanted to judge Catrin himself but he didn't want her judged by anyone else, not even by the unjudgmental Jenna. It was astute of her, wasn't it, to have talked about the connection between hair-cuts and broken relationships. He wondered whose side she was on, after all. Her own probably, like most people.

'I'll have to get back,' she said softly. 'I could lose my job.'

Protectiveness welled up in him. He certainly hadn't forgotten the small voice in the car that had told him it thought it loved him, and if there was one thing he needed it was to be loved.

'You're so beautiful,' he said. The words sounded terribly loud and forced but they worked because she looked at him shyly and he thought he saw the beginnings of a blush. 'You're the only person who understands,' he said, not for a moment recognising that the words gave him membership of the worldwide My-Wife-Doesn't-Understand-Me club. 'Can I see you after work tonight?'

Jenna lowered her eyes. She put her hand to her throat. 'I can't,' she said, 'I'm seeing Jeff.' Her voice softened. 'He wants to talk.'

William felt his heart crush up. 'Oh,' he said, and leaned against the banister. Its coldness cut through him. Some other time, then, he wanted to say, but found he couldn't say anything.

'I could see you afterwards,' she said, 'about nine or so. Would that be all right?'

Of course it wouldn't. It would involve lies and deceit. It would involve ignoring Catrin and her newly shaven head. It would involve –

'Are you going to tell Jeff?'

Jenna looked startled. 'No, of course not,' she said, rather sharply.

It would involve deceiving Jeff.

'You're on,' William said.

Catrin wasn't really regretting it. She'd had no choice. But having short hair wasn't simple a matter of having short hair. Everything had to change. For instance, very feminine clothes looked silly with such a masculine look, but masculine clothes looked fine, made her look more feminine. Dangly earrings, good with long hair, looked appalling now. Small stud earrings looked awful too. The only earrings she liked were pearls, so she wore them with a cream lambswool sweater and cream trousers and black lace-up shoes.

Frances came into her office with two cups of black coffee.

'Is that supposed to be the career woman look?' Frances asked in horror. 'It's rather extreme.' She shuddered: her whole femininity was centred around her long blonde hair. 'I take it you're trying to make a statement. Like shoulder pads.'

Catrin opened her mouth to defend shoulder pads, which she still wore secretly, and then tried to defend her hairstyle, but as she could find no defence she ended up agreeing. 'No, I set it on fire,' she said.

Frances gave her a withering look and considered her from one angle, then another. 'That's your crowning glory gone then,' she said. 'I'd never have my hair cut. It's part of me.'

Catrin was stung. 'A dead part,' she said. 'Hair is dead, after all.' And anyway, it would all fall out after pregnancy, she consoled herself with thinking. In fact, it consoled her so well that she managed to be polite again.

'Thanks for the coffee,' she said, 'I really fancied a cup. What can I do for you?'

'This baby,' Frances said. 'I hate being poked inside, don't you? Smear tests, that sort of thing? Cold, fiddly things going up you and you don't know what's going on at all? Plus, there's the thought of people actually seeing parts of you that you haven't seen yourself and you can't tell me that's natural.'

Catrin picked up her coffee and hid her face in the mug and grinned to herself. She put it down without drinking anything.

'They are doctors,' she said, lifting her hand to play with her hair and finding only thin air. It was rather gratifying to see Frances discomfited. 'Once when I was being fitted for a cap they put in one that was too small and because I have a high pubic bone,' – she liked that, it made up sexually for not having high cheekbones – 'when the time came to take it out, I

287

couldn't reach it. Nor could the doctor. In the end it was the caretaker who did it as he had the longest fingers.'

It happened to be true. The effect on Frances was riveting. 'The *caretaker?* I would have sued,' she shrieked, putting down her coffee cup. It splashed onto some papers that Catrin had been looking at and she dabbed at them with her fingertips and spread the coffee around a little bit more.

'Anyway,' Frances continued, 'that's the sort of thing I'm talking about. I need support. Sisterhood. Look at me!'

Catrin looked. 'I thought I was supporting you,' she said.

'Yes, but look at me,' Frances said, 'I'm so fat.'

Catrin couldn't see fat. 'You've never been fat,' she said reasonably.

'Ever seen a thin pregnant woman? My waist's thickening already. I'm in the bathroom thirty times a day. If only Alex hadn't been killed . . .'

Catrin rubbed her forehead. She had the peculiar feeling that Frances only had a limited amount of lines in the script of life and she kept having to regurgitate the same ones.

'You've still got your job,' she said brightly. Just.

'I hate it!' Frances looked around for her handbag and peered inside it for cigarettes. 'I'd give up working tomorrow if I could. I've never wanted a career but I've had to have one, it's the only thing to do, isn't it, when you're not married. It's a trap we've fallen into, Catrin.'

Speak for yourself, Catrin thought.

'We've liberated ourselves from men and made ourselves slaves to our bosses instead. I brought you a coffee. Where's the difference? I'd rather be making coffee for my husband! I'd rather have a husband than a boss.'

'You didn't put any milk in it,' Catrin said. Frances's words had made her feel chauvinistic. 'I didn't know you felt like that. Work is meant to be fulfilling. And you never usually make me coffee.' She felt she'd lost the thread of the argument somewhere.

Frances rubbed the desk with her damp handker-chief and the grey surface smeared. Catrin felt a quiver of distaste. Thanks, Frances. She'd never known how to cope with her and she didn't now. If she had any authority at all she would tell her to get back to work but she had to remember that she was pregnant and it did make people emotional, or so her mother always told her. Had to remember she was pregnant? She laughed to herself. How could she forget? But the thought of Alex's baby softened her.

'See how it goes,' she said, finishing her drink. It was the wrong thing to say.

Frances's eyes filled with tears again. 'It's all right for you,' she said, 'you love it. And you've got a hus-band. You don't have to work, for you it's just a way of having everything. Alex shouldn't have been killed,' she said chastisingly.

'I haven't got everything,' Catrin said. 'I'm sorry you're so unhappy. I wish I could put things right.'

Abracadabra, Frances's tears seemed to drain back into her eyes.

'I'm sorry,' Catrin repeated. It came out automati-cally and she no longer even had to think about it.

She felt as though guilt had become moulded onto her like a second skin.

William was sitting in his office, wondering how to rearrange his desk so that he could keep an eye on Jeff without Jeff being aware of it.

He felt more kindly disposed towards him now that he was, in effect, stealing his girlfriend.

He liked this primitive, girl-stealing part of himself, he liked it very much indeed. He felt as though it was a new friend he'd instantly taken to. Mind you, a small part of him, the new man in him, quietly disapproved. It was just, though, wasn't it, he could see that, that it was just for him to take someone else's woman as his had been taken, and it was just for him to be unfaithful as his wife had been unfaithful. His conscience was clear.

He drowned out the small voice of disapproval and planned how he would meet Jenna after work.

The contrast between Catrin and Jenna was more acute than ever. Apart from Jenna's amazing bright blue eyes, she still had some hair left. She was feminine, malleable. She loved him. She was not worldly, like Catrin – the Catrin of the dead lover – Jenna was innocent, undemanding. He didn't love her, of course; there was no question of that. But he couldn't help it if women happened to fall for him.

He would tell Catrin he was going to the nets. There was only a couple of months to go before the beginning of the cricket season. Who knows – he could even go, get up a bit of a sweat, meet Jenna in his whites. Catrin loved him in his whites, loved him when he rubbed the red ball against his upper thigh.

Wasn't so pleased at trying to get the mark off them afterwards but that was marriage for you. He deserved a girlfriend. He deserved everything he got. Yes! He deserved everything he got.

William's smile faded as he wondered why the phrase didn't comfort him as it ought to.

32

That lunchtime, Frances cancelled her third business lunch in a row. She was tired. Business lunches made her nauseous. Work made her nauseous. The only thing that didn't make her nauseous was eating sandwiches of smoked salmon and Jelly Tots, with the Jelly Tots pressed hard into the smoked salmon. Try, she thought glumly, asking for that at Chez Nico.

She looked up from her desk and caught one of her execs. staring at her. Frances stared back and the girl dropped her eyes and went back to the calculator. Frances smoothed back her pale hair and stretched exaggeratedly in the hope that the girl would see she was preoccupied and not ask her anything that might tax her. In other words, anything at all.

'Er, Frances –' the girl began hesitantly, and Frances dropped her arms and looked at her impatiently . . . '– there seems to be something wrong here. The numbers don't add up,' she ended lamely.

'See if you can get it sorted, will you?' Frances said; that, she thought, was what they were there for. She stood up and made for Catrin's office where she knew she would get some sympathy. Catrin had always been a soft touch.

Catrin was on the phone when she entered her office and, looking at her, Frances did something of a double take. She looked young, fit, good. Surely, she mused, sitting in one of the swivel chairs, it couldn't just be the hair. Perhaps, after all, she should have hers cut. She stroked a section of it and folded it over itself, trying to imagine how it would look, short.

Catrin put the phone down and smiled.

Frances looked at her suspiciously. 'What's up with you?'

Catrin's face looked suddenly blank. 'Nothing,' she said, 'nothing at all.' She put her hand to her hair for a second. 'Did you want something?'

'I'm not feeling too good,' Frances said tragically. 'Sick, you know. I think I'll have to go home and lie down for a while.

'Sure,' Catrin said, and picked up a spreadsheet. When she looked up again she seemed to be surprised to see Frances still there.

Frances wasn't used to being dismissed so easily. She made herself more comfortable and leaned her elbows on Catrin's desk and sighed deeply. 'I don't know what I'm going to do,' she said morosely, in the hope of some attention.

'Oh –' Catrin opened the top drawer of her desk and took out a small glossy carton with a rainbow on it. 'Just in case,' she said lightly, pushing it across the desk towards Frances.

Frances picked it up suspiciously and turned it over in her hands. She glanced at Catrin's face but could read nothing in her expression so she opened the box and took out the contents. Wrapped in white tissue was a tiny lace jacket with little bows embroidered on it. It was feather-light and she held it up against the light, imagining a tiny figure in it.

'Is this how small they come?' she said in surprise.

Catrin smiled diffidently. 'Apparently,' she said.

Frances smoothed out the tissue on the desk and laid the jacket on it. She stared at it before wrapping it up again carefully.

It's real, she thought as she pushed the small package back into the box. And then she felt sick again. She really was going to have to do something . . .

'You do look a bit – peaky,' Catrin said, breaking through her thoughts. 'It's a good idea to go home.'

All Frances had wanted was to be taken seriously.

'Thanks, Catrin,' she said, picking up the box. She saluted her with it. 'Thanks.'

She rallied as she went to her desk and cleared her things away. By the time she'd finished she felt her usual self again.

'I'm off for some retail therapy,' she said when she saw she had her group's attention. 'Hold the fort for me.'

She smiled insincerely at them, scooped up her bag and gave them a wave. 'See you later!'

She caught a taxi from outside the office and headed for Harvey Nichols, with the growing feeling of having scored a hollow victory; it wasn't, she thought, like her at all. She poked her stomach a couple of times but her heart wasn't in it and it was more as a gesture than in the hope of any result. This seed of Zephyr's had well and truly taken root and it was beyond being damaged by a prod.

She stared out of the window of the cab at the passing traffic and tried not to think of the tiny jacket that Catrin had given her and which was now in her bag. She preferred to keep on thinking of the thing inside her as a seed – it made it easier for her to live with it. As a child she'd often grown mustard and cress on blotting paper and her greatest satisfaction hadn't come from seeing the seeds start to sprout their pale green shoots but from cutting them, snip, snip, snip; felling them with a pair of kitchen scissors. She'd loved the snipping bit. So, bearing in mind that Zephyr's seed's fate was undecided, she preferred to think of it as cress rather than something which might actually wear an embroidered jacket.

But even despite the jacket, she sometimes thought of it as a baby.

When she thought of it as a baby, she couldn't breathe.

She curved her hand around her throat.

The cab drew up at Harvey Nichols and she looked at the dazzling windows with something like despair. She rummaged through her bag for money and by the time she got out she felt totally dispirited and immediately the familiar lethargy took over.

She went up the escalators to the first floor and flicked disinterestedly and automatically through a rack of clothes and wondered bitterly why nothing was much fun any more. The truth was, she thought, nothing had been any fun since Alex had died. She missed dressing up for him. She missed arguing with him. She missed their scenes and their bickering. And what was more, she missed being looked after.

She felt the warning sting of tears behind the bridge of her nose. Alex had always been good at looking after her, he'd always been proud of her. He had loved her and now he was dead and she had no-one.

She saw a chair and she sat down rather heavily

and dropped her handbag by her feet, self-pity weighing her down.

She was staring at the carpet when she felt someone watching her and she turned her head, to find a sales assistant hovering uncertainly a few feet away.

Frances looked at her, daring her to speak.

The assistant seemed to have been struck dumb.

'Could you get me a glass of water,' Frances said, partly to get rid of her. She knew that they liked to feel useful.

'All right,' the assistant said, rather grudgingly, and disappeared between the displays.

Frances leaned back in her chair. It had a badly designed cold wrought-iron back to it which was digging into her spine. She frowned and sat forward on the edge of the chair, feeling even more depressed. The carpet was quivering before her eyes.

The assistant came back with the water, looking hard-done-by.

Frances took the glass and sniffed it suspiciously. It smelled like a goldfish bowl. She sipped it and the water was warm in her mouth.

The assistant was still standing next to her.

'Did you get this from the restaurant?' Frances asked her.

'No, from the cloakroom.'

Frances made a face and gave her the glass back practically untouched. She didn't bother to thank her – she wouldn't have thanked anyone for a glass of warm water.

The girl went away with the glass and when she came back she stood by the counter and Frances looked at her pityingly, thinking that she would have hated to have been as plain as that.

The assistant, probably sensing she was watching her, turned with a querying look on her face.

'Actually,' Frances said to her, as though a question had been asked, 'I'm pregnant.'

'Are you?' The assistant leaned back against the counter and sounded incredulous. Too incredulous. Frances was about to take umbrage when the assistant went on, 'you look so slim!'

'Only a couple of months,' Frances said negligently. 'It would be due –' she did some quick calculations in her head – 'October.'

'October! My birthday's in October. October the second.'

Frances didn't share her excitement at the coincidence. She was beginning to feel sick again.

'What do you want?' the assistant went on, as if it mattered, 'a boy or a girl?'

For Frances, who hadn't gone beyond the choice of a baby or a cress seed, the thought of preferring one sex or another came as rather a novelty.

'I haven't the vaguest idea,' she said, looking up at the ceiling. 'I suppose it doesn't matter, does it?'

'Girls are easier. My sister's got one of each and she thinks girls are easier. Hers slept through the night at three weeks.'

Frances, who was sleeping through the nights perfectly well at nine, wasn't interested in the assistant's sister's baby. She was bored. She wished she'd stayed at work.

'You ought to look at the Nicole Farhi rack,' the assistant said. 'They can take you right through, especially if you've got the right figure, like you. And you can wear them after the baby's born.'

Frances felt herself perk up again. This was the sort of thing she liked. Yes, Nicole Farhi all the way through was just the kind of idea that appealed to her. It appealed to her very much. She smiled, but the assistant was looking through the clothes.

'Most people don't get their figures back straight away; they stay baggy,' she was saying, 'a stone for every baby, they say.'

Frances looked at her with distaste. 'It sounds utterly grotesque,' she said, making a face. Baggy. She imagined herself being blown up slowly and unwillingly like a new balloon . . . a slow, tight, painful process. Then she imagined all the air being let out again, puff! and the feel, afterwards, of the overstretched balloon, papery, thin, all tautness gone, loose bulges in misshapen latex. No thanks. She could buy all the Nicole Farhi clothes she wanted without being pregnant. In her mind's eye she could see the balloon, her stomach, and she shuddered.

She leant down to pick up her handbag. 'Thank you so much for your advice,' she said.

The assistant looked surprised, but pleased. She was holding up a jacket in her hand and she slowly reached back towards the rack.

'Oh – you're welcome. And – good luck with the baby.'

Frances smiled. It was a beaming smile and she bestowed it like the kiss of death on the plain assistant.

'You've decided me. I'm not having it,' Frances said.

33

Catrin wasn't surprised to receive the call at work from Jonathan Wade. In fact she'd been expecting it. She'd have been more surprised had he not rung.

She showered as soon as she got home, and standing under the needle-sharp spray she thought, I've suffered, anyway, for an affair I didn't have, justifying herself, although she needed no justification – what she needed was fun.

Fun was terribly underrated, she thought, especially in marriage. Where did it go to, that elusive commodity that made life worth living? It wasn't even mentioned in the marriage service so little was it thought of. But fun was what she needed.

I deserve it, she said to herself.

And Jonathan Wade was fun. He must be, she thought, towelling herself dry and trying to imagine the indoor golf course.

Whereas William wasn't fun at all.

A night with Roger would be more fun than a night with William, heaven forbid.

'It's just for fun,' she emphasised, thinking of that gleaming smile. 'I deserve some fun.'

She folded her arms, braced herself and looked heavenwards ruefully. She was getting accustomed to the way the fates worked and they didn't take much tempting any more.

William was in the kitchen and Catrin heard him opening the fridge door. 'We haven't any food,' he called.

Catrin crouched down by the fire and watched the flames lick the logs as she towel-dried her hair.

'Look in the freezer,' she called, 'I'm going out tonight.'

She waited for him to ask her where. He would have once but tonight he didn't.

She heard him go upstairs and she went into the kitchen to make herself a coffee. She heard the shower run and a few minutes later William, his dark blond hair still damp, came back downstairs in his jogging gear, the smell of his aftershave knocking her out.

'I might go to Lords next week,' he said casually, 'use the nets. Have to keep fit.'

Get fit, Catrin thought, because he hadn't been fit to start with and despite his newly acquired enthusiasm for exercise he didn't seem to be getting any healthier. His face was drawn as though he hadn't slept for weeks. She saw him take his watch out of his pocket and look at it anxiously as it lay curled in his hand. Then he slipped it on his wrist.

'Right,' he said.

'William . . .' For a moment it seemed a good idea to come clean about where she was going; telling him would ensure that nothing would happen at Jonathan's, but she changed her mind as she saw him wince. 'Oh, it doesn't matter,' she said and she saw his tense shoulders relax.

He flexed his arms extravagantly. 'I'm off,' he said after a few stretches and he hurried out of the door, his aftershave hovering in the room long after he'd gone.

See, it's alright to go, she told herself in the humming silence of the house.

She went up to the bathroom and stood on his damp footprints that were pressed into the bath mat.

Nudging away a pang for him she went into the bedroom.

What should you wear for a date? she wondered. What should you wear for a date that you shouldn't be on when your husband is out jogging?

She looked in her wardrobe.

She wasn't sure what Jonathan had meant when he said it was a golfing evening, but entering into the spirit of it she pulled out a pink lambswool golfing sweater and pink-and-black-checked trousers.

She ruffled her hair with her hand and finished drying it with the hairdryer in a fair imitation of Sinbad, and applauded all his finicky cutting when it looked pretty well as it had done when she'd left his salon.

A sense of excitement rose up in her. She sprayed herself liberally with Sheer Scent and stood in front of the mirror.

It was just a golf evening. Whatever that was.

As she dressed she felt her spirits lift. Buoyant with the idea of seeing him again she ran down the stairs and was surprised to see the door open and William come in, looking more weary than ever.

Her heart sank with dismay. She hadn't expected him to come back so soon.

He looked just as surprised to see her. He looked

her up and down briefly, taking in her appearance, and looked away.

Catrin hesitated, feeling as though he had caught her out. She tried to smile. 'You're back early.'

'Catrin –' his voice caught in his throat like a sob.

'What is it?' She could overlook his appearance but his tone of voice gave her cause for alarm and she felt something close up inside her. No, she rebelled, not now. Normality struggled to surface. He'd sounded as though he were being torn apart and she tried against her will to feel some sympathy for him, for whatever might be wrong.

'Are you all right?'

He held onto the banister with both hands and shook his head slowly. He was deathly pale.

'Are you ill?' she asked him urgently, knowing that the urgency wasn't for himself but for her – she could call an ambulance, have him taken away –

'Catrin – what is going to happen?' he asked her as though the end of the world had come.

She held her bag tighter.

Tonight of all nights, she thought, staring at him. It was almost as if he knew.

She looked into his slate-grey eyes and looked immediately away. 'Can we talk about this when I get back?' she asked, her voice sounding reasonable, efficient. She glanced at her watch so that he would take the hint.

He didn't reply, he just stared into the distance with an air of desperation, before turning and going upstairs.

Catrin checked her handbag for her keys.

She'd got what she wanted. He'd left her alone, he'd got the message, he wasn't going to pursue it. Good. She didn't want to give up the pleasure of Jonathan Wade's smiling face.

Why should she? It would all be to the good. His humour would rub off on her; they would mock their bad luck; they would conspire together against it and she would come home refreshed, able to face her stricken husband, this haunted William who at the moment frightened her.

She just wanted some fun . . . she deserved it.

She put on her pink lipstick and practised a smile in the mirror, the smile she would give to Jonathan Wade.

She would go for a short time, she thought, and then come home. She would stay an hour, just an hour. An hour wouldn't make any difference to William, but it would to her. She would tell him. She wouldn't leave him for long.

She ran up the stairs to say goodbye and heard the shower running again. Standing close to the bathroom door she could hear him soaping himself, she could hear the sucking sound of him washing his armpits. She stood motionless, imagining his hands rubbing the hairs on his chest with the easy familiarity of someone at home in his skin.

Leaning against the door she shut her eyes as images of them in the days – not long before – when they'd showered together flooded into her head. She could almost feel her hands stroking the lather from the coarse hairs on his chest, sweeping it down his belly to his pubic hair.

'William?'

He heard her above the shower and replied, 'The door's locked.'

Catrin blew out a sigh of air, part relief, part regret. 'I'm going,' she said.

'I won't be a moment –'

But she wasn't going to wait. He'd had his chance. She ran down the stairs as though he was chasing her – she ran as she had when she young and afraid of demons in the dark. And oh, the feeling of relief as she got into the car and started the engine; she was going to see Jonathan!

She smiled. It was a lovely feeling, to smile.

Whatever William wanted, it could wait.

William sensed she had gone.

He was leaning against the white-tiled walls of the shower, his face raised to the shower-head and screwed up from the stinging, needle-like assault of the pressure of the water.

His mind was crying Jenna, Jenna, Jenna. He wanted her with him, he wanted to be with her now. He should have waited longer for her. He'd been so calm when he'd first got to the street corner, calm in the dark, not guilty about Catrin as he felt he ought to have been. He'd waited happily for Jenna, feeling good. He'd waited and waited until he'd started wondering whether his watch had stopped or whether he'd got her message wrong. Had he missed her? Had he misunderstood what she'd said? She hadn't come.

Who was he?

On that street corner he hadn't been the editor of *Media News*; he'd been a thug, he'd been a stranger, loitering, he'd been a lad waiting for a girl, a man waiting for a woman, a man waiting to be an adulterer.

'No,' he groaned and the pelting water filled his mouth and gushed in a torrent over him. He didn't want to be his father all over again. He'd always prided himself on being different, but he'd waited eagerly as his father must have waited for his women in the night. His head ached.

Jenna, he thought, seeing her remarkable, naked eyes looking at him.

Silently he began to cry.

He cried for Jenna and he cried for his lovely wife.

As he washed the feel of the cold night air from his body he cried for himself, because out of the two of them she had chosen Jeff.

Catrin reached the gates at the bottom of the drive and got out of her car.

She pressed a button and Jonathan's voice drifted out in greeting. The gates opened slowly and she got back into the car and drove through, up to the front of the house.

As the security lights came on she noticed golf balls scattered about the drive and she began to gather them helpfully, feeling slightly bemused. When she looked at the house again, Jonathan was leaning against a statue, watching her in the porchlight, with a lazy grin on his face.

'Hullo,' he said, in a friendly way.

Catrin walked towards him with her outstretched hands full of golf balls. 'Here you are.'

'Thanks,' he said, and picked up a wire basket for her to drop them into. 'They've come out of that window up there. That's the second hole. Come inside.

Come and see the world's first indoor golf course.'

Catrin followed him in and passed a red flag. She raised her eyebrows and stared at the acreage of emerald green carpet that filled the lobby and disappeared up the twin staircase at the top of which another flag could be seen.

She looked at the walls, bare except for a single portrait of a striking-looking woman who, uncannily, seemed to be sneering at her. Not only did the eyes follow her around the room, so did the sneer.

'Drink?' Jonathan asked but he saw where her gaze was and he looked up at the portrait too. 'That's Amelia,' he said, 'my wife.'

'Coffee, please.'

'Drink, drink?'

'A glass of red wine.'

Jonathan went away and came back with two huge glasses like soup bowls on stems which seemed to contain about half a bottle each. He stood next to Catrin, who felt mesmerised.

'What do you think of her?'

'She looks very striking,' Catrin said.

'Striking.' He mused on the word. 'Do you remember that film, two men were talking, one says to the other: "Which would you like best, a homely woman or a beautiful woman?" The other man says: "Oh, a homely woman. A beautiful woman might leave you." "So might a homely woman." "Yes but who cares."' Jonathan laughed and looked at the picture. 'I do,' he said ruefully. 'Do you want to come and see the bunker?'

Catrin nodded, and still holding her glass she followed him up the stairs and into a bathroom. There was a Jacuzzi below the open window and it was full of silver sand. It looked incongruous in the gleaming room. Catrin stood in the doorway and looked from it to Jonathan and back to the bath again.

'You managed to get some,' she said. As though she'd been there watching him she understood the effort it had taken to carry the bags of sand up the stairs. She could see him staggering with them, cursing the weight of them and emptying them out into the pristine bath.

It wasn't, she knew, anything to do with having the world's first indoor golf course at all. It was just for revenge, or for the sake of a good story, or simply so that he would have something to do to fill in the long hollow future left him by his wife.

Catrin rubbed her arms absently and glanced at Jonathan.

She recognised the tactics. If it hurts, make a joke of it. It didn't mean it would hurt any less but there was a useless satisfaction in mocking what hurt.

After her father had died the rambling club he had belonged to had organised for a wooden seat to be placed at his favourite spot, with an inscription to his memory. 'Lose a father, gain a bench,' she had said at the time. Her flippancy hadn't gone down too well; they'd have preferred tears but then the tears they had to cope with weren't their own.

She looked up at Jonathan and grinned. 'And you can always use it as a sandpit.'

Jonathan with his shiny dark hair and his incredible good looks gave her his polished, comradely grin in return.

He moved in close and she stood with one arm still

outstretched, holding her glass, and hardly breathed as he kissed her gently on the lips.

She didn't close her eyes; and neither did he, so she found herself looking into the dark blue depths of his irises as she tasted the wine on his lips. And when they stopped kissing they continued to look at each other.

Jonathan was the first to look away. 'Get your clubs,' he said briskly, 'and we'll try it out.'

'No.' Where had that come from? She went to the Jacuzzi and kneeled down and levelled off some sand. 'It's like brown sugar, always moving.' It clung to the palm of her hand and she stared at it and put her wine glass down and straightened up. 'I'd like to go to bed. Please.'

For a moment, nothing happened. Catrin heard her words hang in the air. There, she'd said it, she'd given permission, she'd taken control.

She dusted her hand on her pink and black trousers and wanted to cry.

Then Jonathan took her hand as William used to and led her down to the sweet calmness of his room.

They undressed hurriedly and she got into the cold bed and shivered with fright, but he kissed her properly and the feeling of warmth, contact, smooth skin, a person in her arms, was a relief, such a wonderful relief after the aridity of the last weeks; it was like a coming home.

They made love very gently as befitting brittle people and as he came she stroked his fine dark hair, and feeling warm and happy to be in someone's arms again, she fell asleep.

34

Life without a cleaning lady, Catrin thought as she arrived home from work, was a pretty tedious business.

She looked at the dust which had accumulated since Marilyn had last cleaned. If dust really was made up mostly of dead skin cells then how come she hadn't lost any weight? She should be visibly shrinking if the state of the furniture was anything to go by.

She went into the kitchen and switched the kettle on. It was one thing to keep the place tidy when one was happy there and quite another when one couldn't stand the sight of it. And why should she clear up William's mess? Half those skin cells were his. The problem was identifying which ones.

The windows were another problem. Why was it that the marks only showed up on the reverse side of the one she was cleaning?

How had Marilyn dealt with that?

Catrin made herself a coffee and leant against the kitchen table, bored even with the thought of cleaning.

Reluctantly she rolled up her sleeves and took the vacuum cleaner out of the cleaning cupboard.

She switched the machine on and nothing happened. Bending down she saw that the red light was on, which meant that the cleaner bag was full.

She took it to the kitchen and unclipped the bottom of it to empty it into the bin. Amidst the dust a padded envelope fell out sending up clouds of grey – more skin cells, no doubt.

Catrin stepped back, fanning the air with her hand until the dust died down. Then she looked into the bin and reached for the package.

It was a small, padded Jiffy Bag. It had no name on the front.

Catrin frowned. The envelope was sealed but she opened it and with a feeling of foreboding put her hand inside and found a small, self-sealing polythene bag of brownish powder. She put it back into the envelope hurriedly, feeling her skin prickle with adrenaline.

She put the packet back into the cleaner bag and clipped it up and replaced it in the vacuum cleaner, her mind racing.

Drugs.

William?

She rubbed her eyes. William *had* been acting oddly recently. There was his paranoia, his mood swings . . .

She fled into the kitchen and picked up her coffee and sat at the table, staring at the patterns in the wood grain. Sure, she thought, running her nail around a knot, he had been behaving oddly but then, she supposed, so had she.

She felt almost calm but she had a desperate need to talk to William. Funny how it was he she wanted and not Jonathan; definitely not Jonathan. She gave a weak laugh. Odd how in this moment of crisis he was the last person she would dream of telling.

She hurried to the phone to ring William at the office.

Her hand was shaking; she was afraid of speaking to him and equally afraid of his not being there but as the phone rang it was picked up almost immediately and a man's voice answered.

'William?' Catrin asked, realising almost at once that it wasn't him at all.

'He's left,' the voice said. 'Can I help you in any way?'

'Oh, I don't know – who is that?'

'It's Jeff. Is that Catrin?'

'Yes. Jeff . . .' Catrin found herself exhaling his name in a sigh of relief. Jeff was a friend. 'You came with him to the hospital after the accident,' she recalled thankfully.

'That's right. I was glad to help,' he said.

He sounded to Catrin both amused and friendly and she warmed to him immediately. He was a friend of William's. More than a friend, a colleague. He'd see him every day.

'Was it important?' Jeff asked casually as if it was just a matter of bringing milk home or picking up a *Standard*.

Catrin took a deep breath. 'You know him well,' she said softly. 'Do you think he would take cocaine?'

Jeff didn't miss a beat; he didn't even sound surprised. 'You know the business,' he said cryptically.

Well no, she didn't; not that side of it. There was a great division between the creative side and advertising, between the wild ones and the respectable. She and William had never been wild. Or at least, she hadn't.

'So you think it's possible?' she said. 'Or do you actually know?'

He turned the question back on her. 'What makes you think he might be?'

'I've just found some in the house,' she said.

Even Jeff was hushed into silence.

After a moment's thought he asked her whether William was going straight home.

'I don't know,' she said. It sounded odd for her not to know, so she added, 'He's been jogging lately –'

'Jogging? Hah!'

There was no mistaking the bitterness in Jeff's voice but Catrin didn't know what the source of it was.

'Well, I'm sorry to have bothered you,' she said. She held the phone to her ear for a little longer, but Jeff did not reply.

She was on her third coffee when William came in. He had hardly shut the door when the bell rang.

He opened it as Catrin got to her feet. She heard the murmur of voices and went into the hall.

Two policemen were standing inside, unsmiling. Fear returned more strongly than ever, along with a heady sense of unreality, Catrin found herself staring at them and she wanted to howl.

'We've had a report that Class A substances are being distributed from this address,' she heard one of them say to William.

She heard William laugh and she found herself wondering: was that wise?

She realised that she didn't know how to be inno-cent about it, she couldn't even imagine how someone innocent would feel at having that statement put to them. Was William innocent?

'I think you've got the wrong people,' she heard him say confidently, but the officers weren't easily put off.

'Would you mind if my colleague had a look round?'

William shrugged.

He needed help.

'No, we don't mind – if you think you ought to,' Catrin spoke up loudly in what she hoped was a helpful way. Her fringe was flopping into her eyes and she pushed it away. The officer was looking at her interestedly and she wished she hadn't drawn his attention.

'I can't understand it,' she said. That, at least, was true.

The older of the men moved round the house silently – she heard a single creak above them and that was all.

They walked past the vacuum cleaner which lay abandoned on the floor.

William sat down, still incredulous. 'Whatever is this about?'

'We received information which, as you'll understand, we are obliged to act on.'

'From whom?'

'A member of the public.'

Catrin stared at the carpet. They should, she felt, be indignant and offended. Instead they were trying to appease. If only they'd come before she'd known so that she could be angry . . .

Was William selling it?

She raised her head and saw the policeman watching her. 'I can't understand it,' she said helplessly.

The other officer came back. 'No sign of equipment,' he said to his colleague, ignoring them.

'Thank you for your time,' the younger one said and they all stood up together.

'I understand,' William said.

It was more than she did.

William went with them to the door.

Catrin heard the crackle of a radio and a few moments later she heard a car engine start up.

William wandered back looking bemused.

Catrin, her relief turning swiftly to anger, picked up the vacuum cleaner in both hands as though it was weightless and dropped it in front of him with a mighty bang.

'Catrin,' William said, jumping, his hand on his heart, 'you scared the life out of me!'

Catrin glared at him. She kicked the vacuum cleaner towards him violently.

'What are you up to, William? Don't you think things are bad enough as they are?'

William glanced at her. She could see the guilt in his eyes.

'I know I haven't been doing my share,' he said, 'but I did take the rubbish out last night.'

'The drugs,' Catrin said.

'Drugs? What drugs?'

Her anger left her as quickly as it had come and alarm took its place. This was malevolence over and above the normal quirks of fate. For a moment she was uncertain. 'The drugs in the vacuum cleaner,' she said expressionlessly.

'There are drugs in the vacuum cleaner?' William stared at it. It was lying on its side on the floor.

'In that?' He pushed it tentatively with his foot as though it might explode. 'They've been planted on us?'

The thought of a human, rather than fate, having a hand in it was, if anything, worse.

'By whom?' she asked. She couldn't bring herself to trust him. 'Nobody hates us, do they?'

'How long have they been there? When did you last vacuum?'

Catrin shrugged. 'I don't know. Ages.' She added defensively: 'It hasn't needed it, has it?'

They both fell silent.

William said, 'It could have been anyone.'

Catrin looked at him.

'It could have been Marilyn,' he said. 'Who else knows where the vacuum cleaner is?'

'You don't need a degree to work out it might be in the cleaning cupboard,' Catrin said.

'She's getting back at us,' William stated, warming to the theme. 'I bet she rang the police.'

'No,' Catrin said, 'why would she do that? She hates the police.'

'She told the police where the drugs were.'

Catrin turned her wedding ring round on her finger. 'But she didn't, did she? They didn't find them.'

'Who knew about them?'

Catrin looked at him suddenly. For a moment she couldn't find the words to tell him but the answer was so obvious that once she'd thought of it she knew there was no other explanation.

'I told Jeff,' she said hesitantly, 'but that's all.'

'Jeff?' William seemed about to blow up. 'What did you tell Jeff for?'

'He's your friend, isn't he? I tried to get you at the office, I panicked when I found them. I've never even smoked.' She should have told the police that; it seemed to have an authentic ring of indignation to it. 'Why would he have rung the police?'

William pushed his fingers through his wiry hair.

'He's crazy,' he snapped, 'that's why.' He buried his face in his hands. 'I can't believe you told Jeff.'

'I thought he was your friend,' Catrin said, baffled by William's behaviour.

'Well he isn't.'

'You didn't mention it.'

William went over to the window and pulled the curtain back and looked out. 'Do you think they'll be back?'

Catrin didn't reply.

'We'll flush it away,' William said decisively. 'Where did you say it was?'

'In the bag.'

She watched him take it out and she followed him as he led the way to the lavatory. He sprinkled some of the powder in and it puffed up around the pan and floated on top of the water . . .

'Drape a sheet of toilet paper over it,' Catrin said over his shoulder.

So William submerged it by means of the toilet paper and flushed it away. Catrin got the bleach and squirted it around the pan and wiped the seat. It took seconds, but still, they looked at each other with the appreciation of a job well done. Catrin smiled at William and William grinned back.

'What a team,' he said.

They were pleased with themselves, they had got themselves out of trouble.

And for the first time in weeks they'd found they were on the same side.

35

Jonathan Wade decided to shave in the dining room – he could shave anywhere now that there was no-one to care – and as he did so he marvelled at the coming of Catrin into his life.

Unlike Amelia she was pretty and that counted for a lot. In bed with her he often imagined they were a set of celestial bookends with their matching short dark hair and good looks.

Sometimes he fantasised that she would move in with him and he imagined pretending to Amelia that they'd been having an affair all along. Catrin Howden was an infinitely better catch than old Henry even if Henry did have several children to his name.

Jonathan ran his fingers over his face and went over his jaw-line again.

Basically he wanted another wife.

It didn't suit him any longer to wander around his empty house with his golf clubs – the novelty had worn off now and the occasional ricochet meant the glazier was becoming a bit of a problem. The married friends whom he'd hoped would be envious seemed to be giving him, not support, but a wide berth.

He switched the shaver off.

He wanted Catrin to marry him.

Strange, he thought, knocking the bristles out onto the Wilton, how easily he forgot about Amelia when Catrin was around. In bed with Catrin he hardly remembered Amelia at all, and kissing Catrin he couldn't for the life of him remember how Amelia had kissed.

He'd always thought that if one married again one would start afresh and that everything would be new, would feel new as it had done when he'd been young.

He thought differently now.

He felt he would take up where he'd left off. Not, of course, with red-asterisked charts on the door, but in a sort of easy companionship.

He stood up and stretched, feeling satisfied with himself.

He had a board meeting later that day and after that – after that he would pursue his new mission in life.

The wooing of Catrin Howden.

It was ten o'clock in the morning and Frances couldn't keep her news to herself any longer. More importantly she felt like having a bit of drama in her life – a bit of drama was twice as effective as black coffee for giving her a lift.

And Catrin was looking a little too cheerful for her own good these days. Actually, Frances mused, it was probably all for the best that she'd kept her news until Catrin was feeling better. Never kick a woman when she's down and all that, although she wasn't quite sure why not.

Catrin looked up as she entered her office. 'Hello, Frances,' she said. 'Are you feeling better?'

Frances thought she could sense some scepticism in Catrin's tone of voice. She felt a little less charitable.

'Actually, no.' Frances pulled a long blonde strand of her hair between her fingers and sat up straighter, facing Catrin with a certain relish. 'There's something I want to say to you. I've come to a decision. I'm not having the baby after all.'

Bombshell dropped, she sat back and awaited the results.

But it seemed she'd dropped a dud.

Catrin merely carried on looking at her, with little or no emotion in her dark eyes. After a while, she breathed out slowly, as though she'd been holding her breath for a long time.

'Don't try and talk me out of it,' Frances said swiftly, raising her hand to fend her off, 'it's final.' She kept her hand up, but Catrin seemed for once to take her at her word and the silence fell between them once again.

Frances fidgeted slightly as she began to feel the slow disappointment of anticlimax. 'Catrin,' she asked, 'don't you care?'

Catrin rubbed her forehead slowly with her knuckles, as though her brains hurt. 'You know I do,' she said, 'but I'm trying to give up worrying about things I can't control.'

'Since when? First you want to adopt, then you tell me about maternity benefit, then you buy baby clothes –'

'I know. I only gave it up yesterday.'

Frances stared at her moodily. She hated people who gave things up. She never gave things up herself and she didn't see why anyone else should.

'It'll be like smoking,' she said, 'you'll last a week and it will get too much for you.'

Catrin, the non-smoker, didn't reply.

'You're like everyone else,' Frances said, 'you're selfish. You only think about yourself.' Weetabix and all its connotations drifted in and out of her mind; she'd been happy knowing someone was fighting for the life inside her even though she herself wasn't.

She liked the thought of someone worrying about her actions as though it mattered. She'd liked the old Catrin, the one with the guilt. It was a great deal nicer than this stolid indifference.

She stood up and leaned over Catrin's desk, filled with an energetic desire to wound. 'It might cheer you up to know it's not Alex's baby in any case,' she sneered, 'and I don't believe for one minute you were having an affair with him. You're absolutely not his type,' and for emphasis she banged her fist on the desk.

It hurt, but as she saw Catrin flinch she was cheered by her retaliatory blow and, head high, she stalked out of the office to make herself a herbal tea.

Catrin sat staring at nothing.

So that was that, she thought. There had been no divine plan, after all.

The accident hadn't happened to test her or so that she could help save Alex's baby – the accident had just been an accident.

It flashed into her head like neon – LIFE WAS NOT SOMETHING SHE COULD CONTROL.

She jumped to her feet, so strongly did it hit her that this was so; propelled by the fear that comes with knowledge she stood and stared and held on to the top of her computer with both hands as though it was her very last link with reality.

In truth, it was her first. Slowly, gradually, the fear slid off her. It felt so physical that she could feel the fine hair on her arms move on her skin. Without the fear she felt naked.

She waited for something to take its place but nothing did. She felt light, light-headed, weightless. Weightless! That's what it was! And liberated. Liberated from her guilt. She was responsible for no-one any more.

For a moment she felt a brief sense of loss and her heart quickened.

But what can I control, then? she wondered.

She let go of the computer and the answer came back at once: only myself.

PART FOUR

For Want of a Horse

36

The answer to the vacuum cleaner episode came sooner than they'd expected.

That evening, as Catrin was getting ready to go to Jonathan's, the doorbell rang. Catrin already had her jacket on as she opened it and was surprised to find Marilyn standing there, with a pair of rubber gloves in her hand.

'I've taken the wrong ones,' Marilyn said, brandishing them feebly at Catrin. 'I thought I'd put them back.'

To Catrin they looked disgustingly like severed hands and she backed away. 'No, you haven't,' she stated definitely, 'those are yours. I don't use them.' She'd never needed to; she'd always had Marilyn and the dishwasher.

'Oh,' Marilyn said. 'My mistake.'

Catrin gave a smile and little shrug and was beginning to shut the door when she saw Marilyn's fingers wrap themselves around it.

'Catrin,' Marilyn said with anguish through the gap, 'you don't even close the door on Jehovah's Witnesses.'

Which was true.

Catrin opened the door again and looked at Marilyn expectantly but Marilyn looked so uncomfortable, so ill at ease that Catrin took pity on her. Whatever else this visit was about, it wasn't about rubber gloves.

'You'd better come in.' Glancing at the gloves she added, with an attempt at lightness, 'Remember the Addams Family?'

Marilyn looked at her blankly and then glanced at the gloves which she had replaced hurriedly and not very efficiently into her bag. One pink, air-filled finger poked out of the corner, pointing accusingly towards the ceiling.

'It's just that I've left something in the cleaning cupboard,' Marilyn said, changing tactics. 'Harry's wallet – it might have fallen out of his jacket pocket.'

She hurried down the hall and Catrin went after her. 'What you actually left there was an envelope,' she said. 'It was yours, wasn't it?'

Marilyn turned sharply towards her. Her face seemed drained of colour and the large freckles stood out in harsh relief. 'You've found it then,' she said.

Catrin gave a humourless laugh. 'Come on,' she said, 'I was bound to, eventually, wasn't I?'

She went into the living room, Marilyn trailing behind.

The late-evening sun was shining in. A couple of spring flies danced around each other under the lampshade and darted away.

She glanced at Marilyn.

Marilyn's expression was changing so quickly it seemed as though a film was projecting itself onto her face.

'Where's the envelope?' she asked.

'What was in it? Cocaine?'

'It's not cocaine, it's horse. Heroin. It's not mine, if

that's what you're thinking.' She put her hand to her throat and rubbed her thumb over the nub of her collarbone.

Catrin raised her face to the sunlight and asked curiously, 'How did you expect the vacuum cleaner to work with that lump in it?'

Marilyn swung her hair away from her face. She looked suddenly hurt. 'I thought you'd want me back,' she said. 'I thought you'd ring me. I know what you're like, you're soft-hearted, you. Usually.'

She made it sound like an insult. Catrin raised her eyebrows but Marilyn went on: 'I was going to come before, but I didn't know what to say. Anyway, it doesn't matter now, you know. Can I have it?'

Catrin put her hands up her sleeves and held her elbows. 'Marilyn, you don't seem to understand,' she said, feeling that the tables had turned. She had no need to be on the defensive but she looked at Marilyn's quizzical face and felt suddenly as though it was she who was in the wrong. 'We couldn't possibly keep it, could we? We didn't even know whose it was.'

'What do you mean, you couldn't keep it?'

'Look, the police came here, you know,' Catrin said, trying to sound reasonable. 'What if they'd found it?'

Marilyn's face seemed to go a pale shade of grey.

'Catrin – why would they –'

'I know they didn't find it,' Catrin said, 'but it's hardly the point, is it?'

Marilyn the atheist crossed herself briefly with heartfelt fervour. 'You know where it is, though, don't you?' she said.

Catrin squinted at the sun which was sliding down behind the houses. She shivered briefly. Yes, she knew where it was. She remembered herself leaning over William's shoulder, fear mingling thrillingly with glee.

'We got rid of it, William and I.' Letting it be known she hadn't done it of her own volition, that it was a joint household decision. Letting her know that she wasn't going to take the blame on her own. 'What did you expect us to do? The police might have come back with dogs – I mean, that sort of thing, it's not a game, is it?'

Marilyn's face was so pale it was a green-white, the fluorescent shade of skin no longer warmed by blood. 'Where did you get rid of it?' she asked calmly for the last time.

'We flushed it away.'

Marilyn looked at her. 'You're right, it's not a game,' she said.

The bitterness in her voice roused Catrin again. 'I don't feel we're in the wrong,' she said. 'We could have told the police, but we didn't.'

'Well thanks.' Sarcastic now. 'After all I've done for you.'

'Slept with William?'

'In the state he was in? He could hardly stand, he'd had a skinful –' Suddenly the green, hard little face broke up as her thoughts came back to reality. 'Da-Costa'll kill me,' she said, and her voice seemed to squeak.

Unease made Catrin laugh. 'Don't be silly,' she said uncertainly. 'Who is he anyway?'

'He's Harry's brother-in-law, getting his own back on me for upsetting poor old Debbie. He told me to take that stuff to a bloke, Ricky Enfield, but I haven't got hold of him yet. I just put it in the cleaner for storage.' She grabbed the front of her hair in a fist. 'DaCosta will kill me. He'll take my kids away. I couldn't have them found on me, it's possession.'

Her agitation unnerved Catrin. Marilyn's frightened eyes were beginning to frighten her and suddenly she was afraid for her husband and for herself for nervously flushing DaCosta's heroin down the loo, as if it was a game.

'Look, all we have to do is replace the stuff.'

Marilyn was staring at her so hard that Catrin thought she saw herself in Marilyn's eyes.

'You know where to get it from, don't you?' Catrin asked reasonably.

'Yeah, we'll replace it.' Marilyn said, and gave her a sudden, pitying smile.

'Can you think of a better way?' She went into the kitchen brushing off a shower of fridge magnets with her jacket in passing.

Marilyn followed her. 'He's going to kill me,' she said.

'Do you have to be so matter-of-fact?'

'I was supposed to deliver it,' she said, ignoring Catrin, 'he was never there.' She was shaking her head quickly from side to side so that her hair was slipping first off one shoulder then another. 'What am I going to do? What am I going to do?'

Her voice made Catrin feel ill. 'This is England,' she said. 'This DaCosta –' she jerked her head, '– if we explain what happened –'

Marilyn's face lit up for a moment with humour. 'Explain?'

Catrin felt a smile flicker across her own face, a reflection of Marilyn's, but it just as swiftly died.

Marilyn shook her head morosely. 'Oh, sod it. I knew what I was getting into. Mind you, the funny thing is that he hasn't been after me before now.' She sniffed and picked up her bag from the floor. 'It's not as if he can't keep track of me.'

'Have you rung this Ricky Enfield?' Catrin asked.

Marilyn gave a laugh. 'How can I? I haven't got his number.'

'Look him up in the phone book,' Catrin said and felt again the pity in the smile that was bestowed on her.

They looked awkwardly at each other then Marilyn's face took on an expression of philosophical resignation. 'I'll have to wait for what's coming to me,' she said. 'The boys can stay with their dad.' She pushed the strap of her bag higher up her shoulder. 'Better go,' she said.

She went through the kitchen door and into the hall and Catrin followed her and opened the door to let her out.

She watched Marilyn as she walked down the road, a small figure whose hair was flying in the breeze like a burning veil. She looked noble and brave.

Once she was out of sight Catrin wanted to get out. Marilyn's panic was clinging to her like cigarette smoke. She picked up her car keys and hesitated just for a moment. On impulse she got out the telephone directory and found, under E, five Enfields with the initial 'R'. Only one lived in NW1. She rang the number and let it ring. There was no reply.

Catrin drove to Jonathan's with Marilyn on her mind. She wanted to believe that her ex-cleaning lady was exaggerating, but the green face hovered on the edge of her memory like a stray balloon.

When she reached Jonathan's, the stray balloon floated away.

Catrin smiled to herself as the gates opened for her to drive in.

This was the part she loved. She loved driving through his gates and entering his house with its green sea of calm carpets and golf clubs everywhere and the amazing drapes that were never closed.

It was only when Jonathan greeted her with his wonderful smile and a glass in his hand that something in her balked. She always felt she ought to be looking behind him, looking for someone else. Forget it, she thought, taking the glass and smiling into the handsome, dimpled face.

With his usual warmth, Jonathan dragged her into the drawing room and pulled her down onto his knee, mmm, mmm, mmm, nuzzling her neck and putting his head between her breasts.

Catrin, used to a more subtle form of foreplay, closed her eyes and tried to lose herself in the sensation but her mind was on l: what Marilyn was going to do, 2: whether she'd brought any spermicide with her, 3: whether she could use forgetting it as an excuse for not making love even if she hadn't. She felt detached, as though she wasn't really there. She only wanted to talk. She put her arm around Jonathan's neck and kissed the top of Jonathan's soft fine hair and shut her eyes to get herself into the mood. She should be enjoying herself. He was every woman's ideal man. Where had that come from? She had the idea he had told her so.

Jonathan stopped his nuzzling and raised his head. 'Catrin?'

'Yes?' she said, attentive suddenly and slightly guilty.

'Will you marry me?'

Ha ha ha, she thought, putting her mouth back on his soft black hair. She kissed his head and took some of his hair in her mouth and smoothed it through her lips.

'I'm married,' she said regretfully.

'Leave him.' Jonathan looked up at her with dark and pleading eyes. He raised one eyebrow, seemed undecided, then changed to a glower. He gripped her shoulders and, to Catrin, looked more than ever like a character in a film. 'I'm serious,' he said. 'Get a quickie divorce and marry me. I can't wait any longer. I hate being on my own.'

Of course, he wasn't a character in a film, he was real. Still, Catrin found herself looking at him with growing amazement. 'Are you serious?'

'Of course I am. It's as if it was meant to be, don't you think so? Meeting at Hamley's like that, when we never normally go there. Don't you think it's fate?'

'I've had it up to here with fate,' Catrin said, trying to make a joke of it, but Jonathan wouldn't be put off.

'Come with me to Paris will you, Catrin? Let's spend some time together.' His passion and persistence were, to an extent, soothing. It was nice to be wanted. She looked into his eyes and he smiled; his teeth gleamed, his skin reflected the light, his hair flopped disarmingly over eyes she could drown in. No woman in her right mind would say no, or even think twice. Catrin drew her hand down the side of his face and felt the smoothness of her newly-shaved suitor. She felt like crying. She was terribly touched that he had shaved for her.

Still – 'It's too sudden,' she said.

'No,' he said, 'it isn't. You left your husband when you had the car crash. Or he left you. Think about it.' He smiled at her gently.

Catrin felt that she ought to be impressed with his perception but the truth was that she felt resentful. It was all right for her to mention William but she resented it when he did. After all, he didn't even know him.

She made to get up off his knee but he pulled her back down.

She turned to look at him with her head to one side, thinking: he's not really saying it to me. He's saying it to Amelia.

'What's the rush?' she asked him softly.

'I love you,' he said and she was struck by the sincerity in his voice. 'I love you.'

Catrin looked at his slim, shapely lips and at his blue eyes and at the whole of his tanned face and watched his lips as they formed the words 'I love you,' and all that she could wonder was – why?

She smiled and touched his mouth with her fingertip, tracing the shape of his lips. She could feel the warm breath from his nose on the back of her hand.

'You're on the rebound, that's all.'

He stood up, spilling her from his lap. Just as she was about to fall he grabbed her, jerking her up. As she caught her balance she pulled away from him but he held her by the elbows urgently and pulled her to him and her face was so close to his that their noses were touching.

'Don't say that. I'm asking you to marry me,' he said, 'and I want the answer to be yes.'

Catrin pushed him away from her, afraid of his closeness, and turned her head, but a little voice inside her was saying – Look at him! Look at his house! Look at his job! Grab him while you can!

Disturbed by his seriousness she started moving away from him and he fell at her feet with a mock growl and began to take off her shoes. She hopped on the spot and began to giggle. She was wearing court shoes which only required a tug but still she felt obliged to stand on one foot while he lay on the floor. She knew he should look ridiculous but he didn't, and she stopped laughing as he began kissing her stockinged foot. She felt herself wobble and give in although she wanted to stand and laugh and get away – she twirled her arms to achieve some balance but too late – she toppled down onto the floor and gasped loudly as the fall knocked the breath out of her.

'Ouch,' she said, rubbing her coccyx.

She gave him a sideways glance.

He began laughing and she joined him, couldn't help it, and he pulled down her skirt and her Marks & Spencer white cotton briefs and wrapped his warm arms around her and she found herself undressing him with a sigh of pleasure at the feel of him. Catrin and he made love on the rug beside the Lillywhite's golfing machine that was the third hole.

'Don't go,' he insisted later, after they'd made love again, this time in his bed.

Catrin was pulling on her panties. She looked at him over her shoulder. 'I have to,' she said. After sex she almost loved him, but she longed to be home. 'It's my Welsh Methodist upbringing.'

'Look at me.'

'I can't,' she said honestly, 'I might want to stay.'

'Good. Look at me, Catrin . . .'

And she did. He was such a good sight, such a very good, good-looking sight, lying back against the pillows, with his hands behind his head. He wasn't smiling now but it made no difference to his looks. In fact he was even better looking in repose. She wanted to kiss him but instead she got off the bed and began looking around for her shoes.

'Why are women so strong-minded?' he asked her plaintively.

Catrin straightened up and shrugged. 'Maybe they've got no choice.' She was relieved when he didn't reply. 'Sleep well,' she said, leaning over the bed to kiss him. She knew it was a dangerous manoeuvre but he lay still, allowing her to kiss him, and then he smiled. 'Will you come to Paris?' he asked her.

And because he was making it easy for her to leave, she liked him again. 'I may do.'

He got out of bed, stood behind her and put his arms around her, hugging her so hard that she felt her spine crunch.

'Do you think you might get to love me?'

She tilted her head back to look at the face of the ideal man, the romantic hero, Amelia's husband with a broken heart and said: 'I do! How could I possibly not?' Which was what she was saying to herself.

'We'll have fun in Paris,' he said, 'just you and me, all night.'

'If I ask William –'

'Don't ask him, tell him. Tell him soon, won't you,' he said.

Yes, she would tell him soon, she would tell him soon; he made her promise him all the way down the stairs.

As usual he said goodbye to her by the door and, as soon as she'd left, he shut it, leaving her alone in the cold still garden, in the glare of the security light.

She turned back to look at the house and wondered whether it was some plot to make her long for re-entry to the warm, gilded interior of his golf-coursed home. It should have been because that was exactly the effect it had; she always wanted re-admittance once he'd closed the door against her.

This time, like all the others, she half turned away and then turned back again, looking at the gleaming brass knocker which fell so heavily against the old wood and which was just waiting for her to use it again. But she didn't. She walked towards her car whose roof was emerging like a small shining island out of the darkness and got in it and began the drive home.

He wanted to take her to Paris, she thought, shivering from the cold.

He wanted to marry her, did he.

William had too, once, and the thought made her want to cry.

37

William entered the *Media News* building with his head averted.

He hated walking into the office and seeing a temp where Jenna had once sat; he hated more than anything the leap of his hopeful heart when he thought the figure at the desk might just be her. So, most mornings he got in early, just to avoid seeing anyone there at all.

He missed Jenna more than he could say, or, as he admitted occasionally to himself, he missed the dream of her. He missed her innocence, he missed her fragility, he missed her startling blue eyes and her wiry blonde hair. He missed having someone for himself.

He looked constantly at Jeff for signs of triumph – of gloating – ah, he had been a great detector of gloating a long time ago – but he saw none in Jeff. Jeff was the same as he'd always been. He looked as though emotions never touched him. He was young and cool.

William looked at his watch. It was early and, as he walked into the air-conditioned calm of reception with his averted head and averted eyes, he braced himself for the long day ahead.

'William?'

He stopped by the lift and turned slowly and his spirits rose, without him even thinking twice. He didn't have to think, because in his soul he knew it was her. Her gentle voice seemed to float over him like a mist.

'Jenna,' he said and it was less a name than a thankful sigh of relief. He stared at her. She was sitting there as usual, looking a little pale but at least and at last she was back, looking at him with her vivid blue eyes.

He felt himself smile inanely at her. 'You're back,' he said unnecessarily.

'I've had flu.' She lowered her eyes and gazed somewhere down the front of him, at his tie. 'You didn't call me,' she said, flicking her gaze towards him and away again.

'No, no,' he said and his heart was rejoicing – he could hear it drum in triumph! She'd expected him to call! 'I hadn't realised you were ill.'

Her face was raised to him like – like a sunflower towards the sun, he thought, and he wanted to kiss her. He contented himself with looking at her and with the sum of all the good things that he now had to cling on to – she'd been ill! she'd missed him!

'I've missed you,' he said.

He wanted to tell her things, he wanted to tell her how Catrin was never at home any more. He wanted to kiss her young lips and be young again himself.

'I was just going up for a coffee,' she said. 'I'll come up with you.'

William smiled at her. The lift came, pinging for attention.

They walked into it together and he could smell the perfume rise from her warm body into the air. He recognised it as Lauren. He'd bought it for Catrin once, some long time ago. He looked at her but they didn't speak. There was no need for urgency now, the time for panic was over. She was his again.

When the lift stopped and they stepped out, William took a deep breath. He liked being the first there, the first to breathe the waxy vapour of polish the cleaners left behind.

He got them a coffee each and they walked to his office to drink it.

She leaned against the thin partition wall that gave him the illusion he had a place of his own. He hoped she realised it wasn't very sturdy.

She drank her coffee and looked at him over the top of the cup.

William put his drink down. She put her drink down, too.

William got to his feet.

He felt reckless – to the victor the spoils! His mouth still tingled from the toothpaste that he'd used not half an hour before. His hands still smelled of after-shave.

He put his arms around Jenna and she lifted up her pink lips for him to kiss. They were such small lips . . . he put his hand on her breast . . . how erotic it was to do such a thing in the office. The primitiveness of it! The primitiveness of him!

He wondered if he could manoeuvre her to his desk, he was opening his eyes when suddenly the door opened. He leapt around, shielding Jenna with his body. He felt her hands against his back.

'Hugh,' he said with forced bonhomie, 'a little warning next time, maybe?'

Surprisingly, Hugh did not take the hint. He stood with his arms folded, looking over William's shoulder angrily. William turned to look at Jenna. She was flushed and a stray wisp of blonde hair was lying across her face.

'I'll see you later,' William said to her with what he hoped was an encouraging smile. Jenna went out through the door and left it open behind her.

William closed it with his foot. 'Are you mad, you fool?' bellowed Hugh, red in the face.

'Sit down,' William said with a frown. 'She was upset.' He looked at Hugh. 'Anyway, you're a man of the world.'

'And you're a fool,' Hugh said again. 'You know what she's up to, don't you?'

'What do you mean?'

'She doesn't want you. She wants our boy Jeffrey.'

William felt he was being put in an intolerable position. 'I really don't want to discuss this with you, Hugh,' he said stiffly.

'Be warned. She'll have you up for sexual harassment. Think, man! Your marriage will be up the spout.'

'Already is,' William said.

'You're a fool, then. And think of the talk! I could have been anyone.'

William was annoyed at being called a fool again. He pulled down his cuffs and examined his cufflinks. 'What did you come for?' he asked.

'Oh, yes,' he said, pressing his hand on his heart. For a moment he was distracted, and then he collected himself. 'Jonathan Wade said he saw your wife last night. Catrin being headhunted, do you think?'

William shot him a glance. 'I wouldn't know. She seems quite happy where she is.'

'Make it your business to find out. I like you both, you know that.'

'I know,' William said glumly.

As Hugh walked out of the door, William put his hand very carefully into his jacket pocket; if he thought about it he could still feel the sensation of Jenna's breast against his palm.

PART FIVE

For Want of a Rider

38

A week after Frances's announcement about her intention of having a termination, Catrin was on the phone to one of her clients.

'There's always a rider,' Catrin was saying; 'VAT.' She felt the receiver hot in her hand. 'You were quoted net of. If Frances didn't make that clear to you, then I'm sorry. She's got a lot on her mind.' At least that was true; an impending termination was enough to mess anyone's figures up. Frank Taylor was coming to the end of his tirade. 'I'll sort it out,' she said wearily. Her head was aching from the argument. 'Yes, I'll get back to you.'

She was about to replace the receiver when it slipped out of her hand and fell onto the desk. She grimaced, then hoped that he'd still had the phone to his ear.

She replaced the handset and picked it up again almost immediately to speak to her secretary. 'Get Frances to come and see me, will you?'

She picked up her handbag and rifled through it for her Nurofen. She opened the packet and it was empty. Great. She got up to look in her jacket pocket and Frances came in sulkily, tossing her hair.

'You wanted to see me?' she asked.

Catrin sat down again and rubbed her temples with her fingertips. 'I've had Frank Taylor on the phone about their campaign.'

'And?'

Catrin frowned. She could do without this. 'I'm not talking to you while you're standing up there,' she said irritably, 'sit down, will you.'

Frances slid into the chair.

'Right. They're arguing about the cost. You know why, don't you?'

Frances raised her eyebrows. They were the same dark blonde as her widow's peak. She looked towards the phone. 'They always argue about the cost,' she said carelessly.

'This time with cause. You quoted them net of VAT. They took it as the total cost and they've got it in writing from us. They don't want to pay the difference.'

'And that's my fault?'

Catrin hooked her foot beneath the crossbar of her chair and pulled it nearer the desk. She could feel anger and dislike in her chest as heavy as a fist. 'Yes,' she said. 'It is your fault.'

'It could have been a typo.'

'I've seen the original. You left out the rider.' Now, thought Catrin; apologise. She watched Frances shift in her seat.

'I don't know what you want me to say,' Frances said haughtily.

'Oh, don't you?'

'I suppose you're waiting for me to say sorry?'

Up to that moment it was exactly what Catrin had wanted but the derision in Frances's voice made it worthless. Catrin's ever-tightening headache was giving her trouble.

'I'm sure you'll be able to think of someone else to take the blame,' she said softly.

Frances pushed her chair back and it rasped on the carpet. 'This isn't about the rider at all,' she said, 'this is personal, isn't it. Because you don't want me to get rid of the baby.' She made as if to get up.

'Sit down,' Catrin said sharply.

Frances sat, an expression of surprise on her face.

'I think you should take some time off,' Catrin said coolly. She looked at the things on her desk and the colours hurt her eyes. Black and white computer print-out, blue paperclips, yellow memo pads.

Frances slouched in the chair. For once, she looked troubled. 'I don't think it's necessary,' she said. She hesitated before asking awkwardly: 'Er – what's going to happen about Frank Taylor?'

'We'll have to let it go but it'll be dependent on you taking some leave.'

Frances leaned back in her chair. Then she shrugged. 'OK. You're not giving me much choice.'

'That's the idea.'

Frances shrugged again and grudgingly and got up to go.

Catrin stood up too, and suddenly they caught each other's eyes.

'I was thinking,' Catrin said, 'if the father isn't Alex – couldn't he support you and the baby?'

'He's too young,' Frances said off-handedly. 'And I don't know where he is.'

'I see.'

Frances looked at her curiously. Then she gave one

of her rare smiles. It was touched with sadness. 'Told you you couldn't give it up easily.' She paused. 'Was that your last shot?'

Catrin smiled ruefully. 'It seemed worth a try,' she said.

'Thanks,' Frances said and turned to go.

Catrin turned back to the figures she'd been working on before Frank Taylor had rung. Her headache was worsening and she seemed to see them through a dazzling haze of pain.

The phone buzzed and she picked it up. 'Catrin Howden.'

'Jonathan Wade's here to see you.'

'Thanks,' she said but her heart sank. She rubbed her forehead vigorously and put her papers back on the table. What did Jonathan want, coming here in the middle of the day? She felt in her handbag for a lipstick and she was putting it on when he barged in, dressed in black and wearing his ideal-man grin.

'Happened to be passing,' he said, dropping his briefcase on her desk. The noise made her wince. 'I've got the tickets.'

He took her hand in his and squeezed it warmly. Catrin let him. It lay on his palm like a dead thing and she couldn't bring herself to squeeze back. He massaged it gently as though artificial resuscitation would bring it back to life.

She peered at him through eyes that she dared not open too wide for fear of letting in too much light. 'This isn't a good time,' she said. 'Can't we talk about this later? I've a meeting to prepare for.'

'With Midlands TV,' he said persuasively, bending

over her desk to look into her eyes. 'Or at least with its Chief Executive.'

The ease with which he thought he could persuade her made her more irritable still. 'I'm not coming to Paris,' she warned him, 'it's out of the question while William and I are still together.'

'Are we talking morals, Mrs Howden?'

'Not morals; logistics.'

'Is that your final word?'

Catrin looked despairingly into his eyes. 'On Paris, yes. And obviously I can't consider marriage when I'm still married myself.'

'Oh, my.' Jonathan wasn't laughing now. 'You can't half sound officious when you try. Lady, you're no fun any more.' He picked up his briefcase. 'Have a nice life with your husband as that is obviously what you want. Goodbye.'

He bowed his way out of her office.

Catrin stared after him in astonishment. Was that it? No tears, no pleading, just goodbye?

Catrin picked up her papers again, but the hurt was hard to ignore.

The neon lit up again in her head and began to flash bolts of agony into her eyes.

Frances was clearing her desk.

She was delegating. It was her favourite word. She was glad to; some of the things she was delegating were long overdue for attention.

Still, she wasn't delegating so hard that she missed Jonathan Wade walking into Catrin's office happy and coming out again looking mad.

She waylaid him as he headed for the door and

smiled at him charmingly. 'I think you knew my fiancé,' she said. 'Alex Martin.'

Jonathan Wade scowled at her. He was wearing a black polo shirt under a black jacket and it brought out his tan. Still, he wasn't in the mood.

'Vaguely,' he said. 'Once. Prat.'

To his surprise Frances laughed and tossed her blonde hair away from her magnificent face like a wild horse. 'Well, the fates freed me from him,' she said.

Jonathan Wade began to look interested. 'So you're not another Alex groupie?'

'Are there any?' she asked, separating herself rather effectively from Catrin.

Jonathan pushed up the sleeves of his jacket and sat on the edge of her desk. His bad mood seemed to have left him and he watched her pack up with interest. 'Clearing out?'

'I'm on leave.'

Jonathan wasn't interested. Or at least, he wasn't just interested. He was riveted. A blonde! Better looking than Catrin! Single! He held out his hand. 'Jonathan Wade.'

'I know. Frances Bennett.' She looked up at him from under her lashes.

'And where are you going for your holiday?'

Frances weighed up the possible answers. 'It's a pin in the atlas trip.'

Jonathan Wade smiled his brightest. His teeth gleamed and his tanned skin caught the light and his blue eyes seemed to shine through star filters.

'Come with me to Paris,' he said, 'all expenses paid.'

And with a moment's thought, for propriety's sake, Frances said she would.

39

Marilyn had ruined things for herself. Ever since Catrin had broken the news to her, she'd been living on the edge of a volcano that was likely at any minute to erupt and bury her forever beneath the lava of Arnold DaCosta's anger.

'It's no way to live,' she said to herself in her darkened flat.

Opposite the flat a small dog barked from a balcony. It had been barking all morning, an incessant and indignant yelping at being trapped; Marilyn went to her window and opened the curtains just enough to see out.

The dog on the balcony was a little, sandy runt of a thing. His head was aimed skywards in desperation and the yelps were jerking his small body as though they were being wrenched from deep inside him. As Marilyn watched him he stopped for a moment to listen, but finding no evidence that he was anything other than utterly alone, he returned to his lonely protest.

'Poor sod,' she said; and she said it for herself as much as for the dog.

She'd brought it on herself.

Here she was, locked in her flat just like him on his balcony.

There was only one difference. She was getting out.

'I'll make amends,' she said. The phrase sounded old in her mouth but it was a good phrase for all that. It smacked of hope. But making amends was something for the future. She had to sort out the present first.

Remembering Catrin's suggestion, she got out the telephone directory and looked up Enfield. There was only one in Camden. She copied out the address and put on her coat and went out, locking the door behind her.

It was just beginning to rain. She turned up her coat collar and walked down the road, the dog's yapping echoing off the buildings as she walked.

Two men stood smoking outside the entrance to the flats where Ricky lived.

'Could you let me in?' Marilyn asked one of them. He shrugged and pressed one of the buzzers.

'Get lost,' crackled a belligerent voice through the intercom, but the door buzzed and Marilyn pushed it open.

The graffiti-ridden entrance hall was dark. Unwilling to take her chance in the lift, she ran up the stairs to the first landing. Ricky Enfield's flat was behind the last door on the walkway; the door itself was in a state of decay. One of the panels had been kicked out and replaced by plywood.

Marilyn tapped on the door. The house inside sounded empty and unlived-in. A free-sheet was sticking out of the letter box and she pushed it in and looked through the letter box into the dark hall. Scattered about on the floor were letters and papers; it was about all she could make out. And the bin liner. She wrinkled her nose at the smell. Pigs, she thought, to leave a bin liner there in the hall.

Her eyes were getting accustomed to the lack of light and she looked more intently at the bag on the floor.

It's not a bin liner, she thought idly, it's a man.

Her heart heaved in her chest suddenly and she dropped the letter-box flap and backed away, her hands outstretched to keep the image away.

She ran down the stairs, her shoes clattering like a stampede underneath her. She pushed open the door in the lobby and ran out into the open air.

'There's a man dead up there,' she said; DaCosta seemed to curse everything he touched.

That same Saturday morning William was still in bed.

He couldn't bring himself to get up because if he did he'd be forced to keep the promise he'd solemnly made to Jenna and tell Catrin he was having a relationship with a girl from work.

He didn't want to tell her because it sounded so bloody sordid and yet it wasn't – it wasn't any old girl from work, it was Jenna, pure and perfect, the trophy he had won from Jeff.

Girl from work! The thought almost made him laugh.

If he could never quite see Catrin as the 'your wife' of Jenna's contempt then he couldn't see his relationship with Jenna as an affair with a girl from work.

And it wasn't an affair, it was a liaison.

It was not yet an indiscretion.

He'd not yet succumbed to his father's genes, despite Jenna's coaxing.

He relaxed on the pillow a little. Pillow, yes. He only had the one, now. Curled poultry feather. Catrin was using the down, all of them, for herself, as particular as the princess and the pea.

On with the daydream. He would take Jenna places, places Catrin wouldn't go. He could take her to Greek restaurants – Catrin hated Greek. One day perhaps he could introduce her to cricket. He liked the thought of that. He could imagine Jenna in florals, her little face tanned and her blonde, wayward hair wafting in the wind, because cricket pitches were always windy. Other men, his friends, would admire him and women would vie to be chosen too. It was a good daydream so far as daydreams went.

Then he imagined himself telling Catrin and the day-dream began to wobble rather violently, because now this was no dream but real life. He was going to have to tell her.

Why?

Because Jenna had told him to and he'd said that he would.

He wondered whether he wanted to and what would be gained by it. Well, for one thing, it would be putting her in the picture. It wouldn't be deceit, not quite, not really; not like his father's deceit. Not like that. But he couldn't pretend to himself that he was doing it for Catrin's sake. No, it was all for Jenna. His first show of commitment. He shied away from the thought of Catrin's reaction. It wasn't that he could imagine the horror on her face, he couldn't see anything like that – what he could see was some sort of bloody explosion, the fallout of which would be devastating. That was what Jenna could not understand.

William looked at the clock again. Twelve-fifteen. He heard a sound he hadn't heard for a while, singing, and thought of Jenna, but this was different singing, it was Catrin singing hymns in Welsh.

A feeling of relief took him by surprise and he had a sudden glimpse of a world put right again, but it didn't last for long because of course the world hadn't been put right.

The singing troubled him. Her happiness troubled him. It troubled him more the longer he heard her sing. Sometimes she'd go into another room and he thought she'd stopped but she hadn't. She was happy again and he was going to destroy it.

He was going to destroy it for Jenna.

The thought was so shocking that it propelled him out of bed and he put on his dressing gown and went to find her.

She was surprised to see him. She had a band around her hair and no make-up on, but she was beautiful without make-up as dark-haired people tend to be. She was wearing a very baggy pale blue T-shirt with white bleach marks down the front and she was wrapping something up in Barbie wrapping paper.

It was all too incongruous – the smile, the wrapping paper and the terrible T-shirt. She used to use old T-shirts for dusters once; now she wore them!

'Morning,' she said brightly.

'Morning,' William said back. He braced himself for the recoil of his confession. She tore a piece of Sellotape from the roll and sealed one end neatly. 'It's for Lottie,' she said.

He couldn't tell her now, not when she was happy. He put the shotgun of his confession away and hung around a little longer in a state of confusion and anticlimax and when she turned around again, obviously surprised to see him still there, he felt that he ought to say something.

'She's five, is she?'

'Yes.'

She smiled at him, looking into his eyes and he was afraid again because she hadn't done that in a long time.

'Great,' he said, sticking his thumbs into the belt of his dressing gown. 'I heard you singing.'

'Did you?'

He saw the colour rise in her face and was sorry.

'It was nice,' he said.

She tore another segment of tape and kept her head down but he knew that she was pleased. What do you think of me? Do you love me? he wondered and wished he could ask her, he wanted to know. She was unwittingly confusing him, it seemed, so that he couldn't do what he had set his heart on doing. Now, when her old self had come back, he was going to leave her for somebody else.

'Are you going to take it there?' he asked her, searching for courage.

'Yes,' she said. 'Will you come with me?'

Why was she asking him like that, as though it was important?

He pinched the bridge of his nose and tried to think.

She looked at him and took the band from around her head. She picked up the present and gave him a pen for him to sign the label.

'You don't have to, of course.'

He could feel her eyes on him as he wrote down his name.

'Is there anything the matter?' she asked.

'No,' William said, rather too forcefully. 'No,' he said again and tried to make his voice softer, 'there's nothing the matter, there's nothing the matter,' he repeated and he sounded as though he was shouting the words at her. 'Nothing. I think I'll have a bath.'

She smiled at him, a warm, lovely smile.

He bathed, dressed in a hurry and left the house like an escapee, without, he hoped, Catrin seeing him.

Catrin, annoyed at finding that William had sneaked out, went to Lottie's party alone.

The din made by sixteen small girls was indescribable. Catrin ducked in under a cloud of pink helium balloons and found her leg clutched by the party girl, dressed in pink.

Catrin handed her the gift.

'Mummy says I'm not to open them until afterwards,' Lottie informed her.

'What a meany.'

She could see Sarah bashing her way through the balloons. When she got to her, she kissed her warmly. 'You're looking rather special,' she said, examining Catrin's face.

'Do you want a hand with the food?'

'Ah – Roger's getting it all from McDonald's. Those wholemeal baby quiches last year – they didn't go down too well if you remember. What's new?'

'Well – I suppose I've joined the club,' Catrin said.

'You're pregnant?'

Catrin fielded a ping-pong ball which had been shot at her out of a gun. 'Not pregnant – I've been having an affair.'

The news didn't produce the reaction she'd expected. Sarah stared at her, open mouthed. 'Oh, Catrin,' she said sadly. 'Why?'

'Well – because,' Catrin said. Sarah's reaction wasn't quite what she'd expected. 'I thought you'd be pleased.'

'It's not anything to be proud of,' Sarah said, pushing her blonde hair out of her eyes.

'But you've done it!'

'Not exactly. I mean, I've flirted – look, marriage is a long-term enterprise, it's a high-maintenance sort of a thing. You have to see it in the long term.'

'You make it sound like a time-share.'

Sarah looked up at her ruefully. Suddenly interest flickered in her pale eyes. 'Is it anyone we know?' she asked hopefully.

'Not really. And it's over now. He wanted me to go away with him, but I wouldn't.'

Sarah looked relieved. 'There's hope for you yet,' she said. 'The thing about marriage is that it's like a merry-go-round. Sometimes it's slow and effortless and sometimes it goes so fast that you have to cling on for dear life. But once you get off – the ride's over. Understand me? You can't change rides.' She paused. 'What was he like anyway?'

'Nice. Handsome. Just not William.'

'Well there you have it. Sort yourselves out; we don't want to have to explain divorce to Lottie. She's not ready for disillusionment yet.'

Catrin's gaze flickered towards Lottie who was sitting on the edge of the table with a doll in her hands.

'She's just bitten the head off Ken,' Catrin said.

'It's a metaphor, Catrin,' Sarah said. 'Ah, here's Roger. Fancy some fries?'

William was driving to Jenna's thinking, strangely enough, not of Jenna but of Catrin, happy in her faded T-shirt.

He knocked on Jenna's door and seconds later the door was flung wide. Jenna was smiling at him, her face pure as though she had been untouched by sleep and oh, fate, wearing a very large, pale blue T-shirt, just like Catrin's. There was something different about her that he couldn't put his finger on.

'William,' she said and rubbed her eyes. 'Come in. What time is it?'

William glanced at his watch.

'One-thirty.' He felt virtuous, having been up and about so much earlier than she. She put her arms around his neck and nuzzled him.

'Come into my bedroom,' she said.

'I think it's best if I don't,' he said, sounding priggish even to himself. 'It would be awful to spoil it now,' he added darkly.

He looked at Jenna. Surely she wasn't rolling her eyes at him?

'So what's happened?' she asked.

He couldn't avoid hearing the excitement in her voice and realised with sinking heart that his reason for seeing her was nothing to the one she'd worked out inside her head. He tried to erase his troubled look.

'Nothing,' he said, 'I couldn't tell her, not today. It

wasn't the right time. I just wanted to see you. Thought we could spend the day together.'

Her face didn't fall, not exactly. But then she didn't look thrilled either. She came close to him again and began to fiddle with his shirt buttons.

'I'm doing something,' she said.

'Oh?'

'You should have told me you were coming. I wouldn't have made plans.'

'I came on impulse.' For some reason she began to laugh at that. He was annoyed but made sure he didn't show it. 'I'll get off, then,' he said, turning towards the door.

'You're annoyed now, aren't you,' Jenna said. 'Don't go. I'm not going out until later.'

William didn't want to ask her where she was going but there again he wanted to know. And he was gratified that she wanted him to stay.

'Are you going anywhere special?' he asked her.

'Not really,' she said but she didn't seem inclined to tell him any more than that. 'Come into my room while I get dressed,' she said. 'I'll be quick. '

He went into her room.

She pulled on a pair of panties underneath the T-shirt and pulled a pair of jeans on after them.

William was surprised. He'd never get dressed without having a shower. He was surprised, and shocked.

He felt awkward and tried to think of something to say.

'What would make you terribly happy?' he asked her after a bit of thought.

She sat down on the bed.

'To have you jump on me,' she said. Her eyes were

wide and innocent, belying the statement. Her wide, blue eyes . . . strangely enough they were not so blue after all. Hardly blue at all, in fact. More of a greyish colour.

'Your eyes,' he said.

'Haven't put my lenses in, yet,' she said, still curled up on the bed.

His heart turned over with love at the sight of her but steadied itself as he looked at her eyes again.

'They're green, really,' she said. 'But blonde hair and green eyes don't really go, do they? A bit wishy-washy? I like being blue-eyed. I had a turquoise pair once but they were a bit obvious, you could tell at once they weren't real.'

William continued to look into her eyes which he realised were, now she'd said it, wishy-washy. Not even green. They definitely looked grey to him. Greeny-grey at best. It gave him a strange feeling, to look into her blue eyes and not see them blue any more. He felt terribly cheated. To cover it up, he said:

'Any more surprises? Not a brunette, are you?'

She giggled at that. 'I'm fair,' she said. 'But hair fades after you're twenty. There's no such thing as a blonde twenty-three-year-old. I have highlights every six weeks.'

'Do you?'

He felt as though she'd made a fool of him. The shock of those eyes . . .

'You're so innocent,' she said. 'That's why I love you.'

He didn't want to be innocent. He didn't feel innocent. All the same, he knew that he was. Suddenly he wondered if there was any primitive man in him at all, any small part of that species of man who knows women through and through. Or maybe it was just that he'd lived with Catrin for so long that he'd got used to honesty and lack of artifice. Or was he fooling himself again? Their lenses were clear, meant only for improving sight. Catrin herself needed no improving.

He thought of her singing that morning and wondered again if there was any way he could avoid losing her. Whilst keeping Jenna.

Women were a law unto themselves.

'I'm going,' he said.

Jenna gripped him around his chest, arms and all. He wanted to break free. He tensed his muscles and she let him go.

'What is it?' she said.

'Nothing.'

And the urge came upon him again to talk but just as he'd decided to stay she said: 'Don't bother then.' Dismissively.

He thought of Catrin singing in the house.

He felt afraid, suddenly, of being without a woman, of being without anyone. The fear came like a rabbit punch to his ribs.

He looked at Jenna and her wishy-washy eyes and her highlighted hair and remembered that she had seemed like the answer to a prayer, though how could she be? He gripped her wrist and looked into her wishy-washy eyes.

'Jenna,' he said, 'will you come away with me?'

40

Wives are the last to know.

Husbands are as well. It's a law that works both ways.

Hugh Gascoigne came for a friendly lean on William's desk. It was such a lean that the desk moved a couple of inches and William looked up in alarm. 'Watch it,' he said.

'Any news?' asked Hugh, beamingly. It was meant to be a joke, once, a long time ago but now it meant just that.

'BAS are axing some of their marketing people,' William said. 'Probably about time.'

'What's Jonathan Wade doing these days?' Hugh asked diffidently. So diffidently that William looked up with narrowed eyes.

'Go on,' he said.

Hugh shrugged his shoulders elaborately. 'It was a question,' he said.

William stared at him. Hugh hadn't been the same since he'd found him with his hand on Jenna's breast. He put it like that in his head to have the full value of the memory of it. And was secretly appalled.

'All right, since you ask, I haven't the slightest idea,' he said.

Hugh scratched indulgently behind his ear. 'Rumour has it he's got himself another woman.'

William continued to look at him as though he was crazy. After getting no clues at all from Gascoigne's face he said, 'So? His wife's left him.'

Hugh straightened himself up until his arms were taking the strain of his body which made him look as though he was going to begin press-ups where he stood. William was certain that his desk wouldn't take the pressure.

'Ah well, it's interesting, all the same. He bought airline tickets to Paris last week. We know his companion's name.'

William knew that he was being given a message of some description. What it was continued to elude him. Whatever it was, Hugh seemed to think that it was of interest to him.

They continued to look at each other.

Hugh then let his feet take his vast weight and rocked back from the table with a sombre expression on his face. He nodded. William nodded back.

'You know where I am if you want me,' Hugh said.

With this consoling message safely delivered he lumbered back to his chair.

William picked up the phone and rang Jenna. It seemed to be his answer to everything these days, to ring Jenna.

He was answered by her standard speech of, 'Hello, can I help you,' which peeved him a little because surely she could see whose phone it was from?

'It's me,' he whispered.

'Hello, can I help you,' she said again, impatience creeping into her voice.

'It's me,' he said, glancing at his door.

'Hello, can I put you on hold for a minute? The switchboard's like a laser show at the moment,' she said and before he could object he was thrust into the bleak silence of an unconnected telephone line.

He put the phone down at once. He was a man confused. What was it about him today? His wife had been happy again and his chief reporter had been nudge-nudging him while his lover-to-be put her laser show before him.

Lover-to-be? Jenna wanted him to buy her a ring. A ring! And him a married man. More or less. In law, anyway, and what was more, a married man in the eyes of his wife.

Nothing was easy. He was beginning to think that it wasn't worth the worry.

He got up from his desk and went to look for Hugh.

Hugh was laughing with Jeff rather raucously. They both shut up fairly quickly when they saw him which made him think they were laughing at him.

'Are you busy?' he asked Hugh coldly.

'What's up?'

William could see Jeff grinning behind Hugh's back.

'Want a coffee?'

Hugh got to his feet reluctantly – it was something he tried to rule out of his life if it could be helped. 'What is it, mate?'

William took his arm. 'What were you trying to tell me?' he said. 'Out with it, man.'

They were walking the length of the office. William hoped that to all intents and purposes it looked like a casual stroll. To Jeff, anyway. He didn't care about anyone else.

'Jonathan Wade's got a new woman,' Hugh said with his graveyard voice.

'Carry on,' William said encouragingly.

'They're going to Paris together.'

They had reached the far end of the office. Hugh was making it hard work.

William looked at him and saw that he was staring at the carpet. 'WHAT,' he said loudly, 'HAS IT GOT TO DO WITH ME?'

Hugh made a patting motion with his hands and William looked at him incredulously.

Hugh was by now looking pretty incredulous himself. 'Paris,' he said meaningfully. 'Do you know anyone else who is going to Paris?'

William had had enough. 'No, I bloody well don't,' he said. He stalked back to his office, and grabbed his coat.

Hugh was hurrying behind him.

'I'm going for lunch,' William said.

Hugh blocked his way.

William flung his jacket over his shoulder as Hugh shook his heavy head sadly. 'William, old son,' he said, 'sorry to be the one to break the news. He's having an affair with your wife.'

41

Frances's absence made the office a lot more peaceful.

In fact, Catrin felt her whole life was a lot more peaceful. The oddest thing was, she didn't miss Jonathan at all; she didn't even miss his smile. Her main response to his departure was one of relief. The endless circle of thoughts, as pointless as a dog chasing its tail, had been broken. In short, she'd found herself again, even if it was a rather more weatherbeaten version, and was happy.

Were it not for Marilyn, she would have felt she'd made her peace with the world.

She felt in a way that she shouldn't have taken the Marilyn thing personally. As Marilyn had pointed out, William was drunk and Marilyn was – well, Marilyn, and in any case, nothing had happened. She'd acted hastily.

It was ironical really that she'd, after all, been the one that was unfaithful.

She hoped it didn't matter. She wondered how many affairs began accidentally, almost; began because it seemed as though people were interchangeable, as though what was wrong in a relationship with one person could be put right in a relationship with someone else. It couldn't, of course.

If you wanted a William, then it was inconceivable that a Jonathan would do just as well.

Still, she knew now.

She wanted William back.

She looked up from her papers. 'I do still love him,' she said aloud. 'The trouble is, does he love me?'

William had left the office and was taking a taxi to Cartier.

His heart was flapping wildly. He felt as though he was doing some horrible dance with fear. He was twitching in the taxi; there was a flicker in his eye and his fingers tapped involuntarily against the leather seats.

He was going to be left!

The fear of being left alone, womanless, was like the fear of the dark. It was a bottomless swamp of nameless horror. He was a man grabbing at straws, at women.

The taxi driver didn't talk at all, which unnerved him, despite the fact that most of them now drove in thoughtful silence. William found himself glancing at the rear-view mirror to try to catch the driver's eye but his gaze didn't waver from the road. William, he who despised small talk, would have given a great deal for a chat about the weather.

Instead, he was forced to carry on dancing in his mind, dancing with fear. His partner was infidelity – Catrin's infidelity. Again. Again.

He felt as though the earth wasn't safe. He felt as though all his powers of judgement had deserted him, that he was an innocent, that all around him raged disloyalties, slyness, deviousness, evils and duplicities of every sort.

I'm getting paranoid, he thought for one hopeful moment, but no. He wasn't. It was all true.

What if he'd never known her! What if she'd been cheating on him with everyone, everyone they'd ever known, Tim, Roger, Hugh Gascoigne, the man who fell off the balcony, the milkman, the paperboy, the dry cleaner, Jehovah's Witnesses . . .

He started to dance again in his mind. But he wasn't dancing – he was avoiding, ducking, weaving because he couldn't bear to think -

Jonathan Wade.

The dancer gripped him by the throat.

Oh, hasn't she done well for herself.

She would divorce him, of that he was sure.

She was going out with the Midlands chief.

He, on the other hand, was going out with a receptionist. Shame on him! Oh, how innocent he was! He felt with sudden horror that he was about to cry for his own innocence.

'Can't go any further, mate. Want to get out here?'

William raised anguished eyes to the rear-view mirror. The cabbie at last looked at him back. There was nothing in his gaze at all, neither sympathy nor dislike. He was impartial. William didn't want him to be impartial! William wanted him to be on his side!

He realised that he must get out.

He ducked, to leave the cab, and yet still banged his head on the roof.

'Mind your head, mate.'

William gave him a note and hurried away. Then he tried to remember what the note had been. Five?

Ten? Twenty? He maybe hadn't left a tip in which case the driver would hate him. Or he'd given too much and would be despised. Another worry.

He worried his way to the jewellers.

He hurried through the displays, glancing at them, and realised that a man was watching him, an oldish man wearing a dark suit. He stared at the man and the man stared at him. The doors closed.

William turned and saw other people watching him.

He swayed on the balls of his feet to show how lighthearted he was, how guilt-free.

He found himself faced with showcases and desks. He sat down and the middle-aged man came to sit at the other side. 'And how can I help you?' he asked, in tones of gentle amicability.

The voice and the gentleness reminded William of his grandfather. 'A ring,' he said.

'What size?' his grandfather asked him.

'Not too big,' he said. 'Not tiny – ' lest the man who was like his grandfather should think him mean, '– but em – I'd like to see a selection.'

His grandfather's double looked benevolent. 'The size of the lady's finger,' he said, moving forward slightly in his seat in a sort of reverential sway.

'Ah, her finger,' William said, feeling that here he could be helpful, but he remembered in a flash sizes, ring sizes, and half sizes and Catrin's engagement ring, and he knew with sinking heart that complications had set in.

'Ah. J,' he hazarded.

'Yes,' said his grandfather gently. He understood. William knew that he was now in safe hands and was relieved. 'That's small.' He got up from his desk and fetched a tray and put it on the desk in front of William.

William looked at it and his eyes dazzled.

'An engagement?' his grandfather suggested.

'No,' said William. He'd already bought one of those. Of course, not for Jenna. 'Well,' he said, 'a token engagement ring.'

His grandfather nodded, shutting his eyes in deep understanding as he did so.

He took out three and laid them on a soft cloth in front of William.

William picked them up together and laid them on the palm of his hand.

'They go up in price,' his grandfather said.

'Ah.'

William was not sure that he knew which was which. He studied each of them closely without coming to any conclusions.

'The, er, medium priced?' he asked.

'The emerald and diamond. The smaller sapphire is cheaper. What colour are the lady's eyes?'

'Blue – er, grey,' William said.

'Ah,' said the jeweller, who seemed to have caught the 'ah's' from him, 'then either, really. If you would prefer diamonds –'

William decided that he wouldn't. 'The em – this one, the smaller sapphires, will be fine. Silver, is it?'

'White gold,' his grandfather said gently without the least sign of being offended.

William paid for the ring with his credit card, knowing that he was going to have to get to the bill first and hide it. The ring was produced gift-wrapped. It

371

was put in a bag for him and he went to Fortnum's for a waffle; his grandfather had always taken him there when he was small.

When he got back to the office later that day he found that Jenna had already gone home.

It was like a stay of execution although why he should feel like that he didn't know. He imagined giving her the box and he tried to imagine her joy and her gratitude. As he did so it occurred to him that as far as he remembered the ring was rather small.

The box was in the pocket of his raincoat, a huge box, which reassured him. He took it out and went with it back into his office. He opened the paper and the outer box and took out the jeweller's box with the furtiveness of one outsmarting Santa Claus. He opened up the jeweller's box and he looked at the ring. It was a nice ring, he told himself. Small.

He tried to wrap it all back up again but he couldn't get it to look the same. He put the wrapping in the bin, and replaced the smaller box in the larger box. He put it in his desk.

Catrin had decided to go home early. She would cook a meal for them both.

She wore red; red trousers and a red, short-sleeved sweater.

She heard William's car and stayed in the kitchen, nervous, which was ridiculous really.

She heard the door slam shut and she still waited in the kitchen, topping and tailing some sugar snap peas as though oblivious to the world.

She finished the peas. She swept the bits into the bin. She wiped the chopping board with the dishcloth. She put the peas into a pan.

Still no sign of William.

She took a large carving knife out of the block and checked her face in it.

And she went to look for William.

She found him sitting in the parlour looking straight ahead.

When he saw her he jumped violently and stared at her from the chair. 'What are you doing here?' he said in amazement.

Catrin took a swift look around the room. He sounded as though he'd been caught red-handed doing something or other.

'I decided to come home early,' she said in explanation. 'I haven't seen you for such a long time. Oh, William –'

'What?' he asked nervously.

'What are we doing?'

'I'm not doing anything,' William said. He got up out of the chair. 'I think I'll have a drink.'

Catrin followed him to the kitchen. 'I'll have one too,' she said.

'Will you?' He looked alarmed again.

'Is there anything wrong,' she asked finally. 'You seem – strange.'

'There's nothing wrong with me,' he said. He took a bottle out of the cupboard. 'I expect you've got some holidays owing to you.'

'Yes,' Catrin said. 'Why?'

Her reply seemed to pain William and he poured the whisky into a glass. He lifted it to his mouth without adding water, and swallowed it in one.

Catrin looked at him open-mouthed. She saw him swallow several times. She knew it was something serious.

Holding her elbow with her hand she said, 'I think that we should talk.'

William picked up the bottle again. He carefully poured some into his glass and went over to the tap and added some tap water. He put the glass to his lips and gulped.

'Oh, William –'

'No talking,' William said. 'Not yet. Just let me get my thoughts straight.'

Catrin looked at his glass and said, 'You're never going to get them straight like that.'

He wandered over to the cooker and looked in the pans. 'We're having supper together?' he asked her, loosening his tie.

'Yes, I thought it might be nice.'

'Did you?' he said, like one searching for approval.

'You're not all right, are you?'

'I'm fine,' William said, 'fine, fine, fine. Don't worry about me. Hah!'

The 'hah' came out so ferociously that Catrin stepped back involuntarily.

'You're not fine,' she said, 'you're weird. I'm worried about you.'

'As well you might be,' he said under his breath.

'I heard that. What's wrong?'

'What's wrong? What's wrong?' He looked wild for a moment. 'YOU'RE asking ME that? I'm going out,' he said.

'Don't go out,' Catrin said and she pulled at his shirt.

It came out of his trousers and she hung on to the end of it.

'I have to,' he replied piteously.'

'Then how is it all going to end?' she said, her voice rising. She bit her inside lip hard.

'Quickly, I hope,' he said. 'Quickly.'

They looked at each other, stricken.

The kitchen clock ticked loudly, like a countdown.

'Oh, William,' she said in a small voice.'

'Don't say that.' He closed his eyes as if he was in pain. 'I'm going.'

'No –' she put her hands out to him but she wasn't able to touch him. There was an electrified barrier between them. Her hands seemed frozen in the air. 'Everything's changed, you know,' she said, 'there's no baby now –'

'Baby?'

'It's different now, I know what I'm doing, I know what I want –'

'Don't say it. I've got to go.'

And William, the frightened man, rushed out of the house pursued by his dancing partner again.

Catrin too was dancing, little steps of indecision, back and forth on the kitchen floor.

'Well that's that,' she said, coming to a halt as the front door clicked shut.

She looked at the cooker and reached into the pan of sugar snap peas. She took out a pod.

'He's scared,' she said suddenly and popped the pod in her mouth. It was green and sweet and the sap and the rinse-water sweetened her mouth which was still rough from the whisky. Scared.

Like a revelation, the person who was the true William stepped forward from the dramatis personae of her mind.

All the incidents from the morning of the accident fast forwarded through her mind and she could see how it had been for him, from her guilt and confusion over Alex to the survivors' party to the drugs, she could see the reason for his increasing absences from home. He hadn't known what was happening and he was afraid of the unknown.

No more talking, then.

She would be utterly normal for him. They would go back to being a normal couple and they'd put all this behind them. She could do it. She would arrange things so that they were ordinary again. She had confidence that all would be well. She knew William. After seven years of marriage, she could stand up and say that she knew him.

She felt terribly proud.

PART SIX

The Battle Was Lost

42

The battle was lost.

It was Sunday lunchtime.

William went to the Friars Inn, the pub nearest the office where he had taken Jenna that first night and a few times more besides.

He rushed in and looked around him. The place was almost empty except for three chaps in the corner who were telling jokes about cannibals and looked as though they'd been there since the night before.

He went to the bar and ordered a Scotch. He asked the landlord if he could use the phone and he rang Jenna's number.

She answered the phone happily enough. It was only his frame of mind that made him think that she sounded less happy on hearing that it was he.

'What are you doing next weekend?' he asked rhetorically, his hand shielding his words from the landlord.

'Next weekend? she said. 'I'd have to check my diary.'

William realised that for some reason she was annoyed with him.

'I was going to ask you to come away with me,' he said.

This information was greeted with silence. William

looked up and saw the landlord's eyes on him. He'd said the incriminating bit anyway so he took his hand away and waited for her response. Really, he reflected, it was hardly what he'd expected. Whoops of jubilation maybe; fanfares, party poppers at least. And a bolt of lightning from above for his immorality. All he got was silence which stretched on. He wasn't going to be the first to talk. He knew that she was still there, he could hear her gentle breathing.

The pips went. He thrust in another coin.

'Where are you?' she asked him.

'The Friars.'

'Where do you want to go?' she asked.

'There's a marvellous place near Oxford.'

'Oxford?'

He could see he was going to have to sell her the idea. 'Swimming pool, gym, Jacuzzi, beauticians,' he was lying horribly, he would find something, he wasn't worried, 'log fires, four-poster beds . . . and I've got something for you. A present.'

'A present?' Warmth at last filtered though the small holes in the ear-piece; William felt it trickle through his head. Bingo! Her voice was fine now.

'All right, William,' she said. 'I'll cancel my other stuff.'

'Great,' he said and he felt great as he put down the phone.

He was primitive man, not saying goodbye.

Hang on – what did she mean – she'd cancel her other stuff? What other stuff?

As he was looking for more coins the landlord took the phone away which saved him from having to make a decision as to whether he should ring back.

He picked up his drink and sat at the opposite end of the room from the three cannibals. Cannibalism wasn't a laughing matter.

Oh, hell, he had done it.

The implications of his actions had sunk in.

There was no going back. He, William Howden, was going to have a mistress.

He drank some of his drink. 'Only,' he said softly into it, 'because my wife is leaving me for a chief executive.' And despite the mistress and the present that he'd bought for her the future seemed to hold very little at all.

Someone else came into the pub and he looked up automatically and saw to his surprise that it was Jeff. Jeff was his mortal enemy but he had won the fair maiden, at least for the weekend, and his triumph made him extravagant.

He stood up and called him over.

Jeff looked at him from the bar.

He said something to the landlord and the landlord smiled and gave him a bottle of beer and a glass and poured some in for him to show that he was being helpful.

Then he moseyed over towards William.

William stood up again. 'Jeff,' he said heartily. And he sat down again, with nothing else to say.

Jeff seemed to be looking at him ironically. 'William,' he said.

They had kept away from each other since the crash, as awkward as if they'd carried out some crime together which they now regretted. The drugs business had put the seal on their enmity. But whisky was quite helpful in dissolving barriers.

'How's your wife?' Jeff asked pointedly.

'Fine,' William said, 'I suppose.'

Jeff gave him a look of contempt.

William caught the diluted tail end of it and remembered Jenna crying in his office over Jeff.

The best man always wins, he thought, looking at him over his glass. The phrase satisfied him.

Frances leaned out of the hotel window and looked out onto the place de la Concorde and wondered how it would feel to be brought there to die.

Death. They had decided to go to the catacombs today, two healthy, well-off people whom death could never touch.

She was doing a fine job of putting it off touching her; still pregnant, she knew she was going to have to make a move soon.

She straightened up. She was wearing a black, fitted dress. She put her hand to her abdomen, not in the protective, inquiring way of a pregnant woman but like a crab, pinching the flesh. There was precious little to pinch. But still, she was acquiring a new shape.

She looked at the magnificent room Jonathan Wade had brought her to and at the twin beds with their rumpled covers. It was a game. She used to like playing games. Now she wished in a way that he would fling her into bed and have done with it.

Oh, it had all been effortlessly tasteful. She'd showered first, dressed for bed, he'd showered, wrapped a towel around his waist, made her tea, she'd read, he'd read and she'd fallen asleep before him. Just like a long-married couple.

They'd got up, used the bathroom in turn.

Now, she lay down on the bed, pulling her dress straight so that it would not be creased.

Her hair was heavy and glossy, either from the water or from pregnancy.

Jonathan came into the room dressed all in black too. Black polo shirt, black jacket, black trousers, his damp hair brushed back off his face. He was freshly shaved and his face was glowing slightly. He smiled that half-smile and it made him look slightly abashed.

'You look like Sleeping Beauty,' he said, looking down at her.

She only liked games on her own terms. 'Come here,' she said.

He lay down next to her on the bed, carefully, and looked at the ceiling.

It was all she wanted, really, someone to lie down next to her. But she reached out for him. He raised his head slightly to look at her and she slipped her arm underneath it. He rested his head back. She rolled over and looked at him and bent forward to kiss him. Her hair fell around his face and they were sheltered beneath it, kissing.

She pulled his polo shirt out of his trousers and slid her hand up over his lean stomach and to his chest, pushing her fingers through the hair.

He moved, rolling them over so that he was above her. Her hair spilled back from her face.

'It's not as simple as that,' he said.

She thought at first that he meant he had some impotence problem. She wanted to cry. She turned her face away from him but he reached for her chin and turned her back. She was unwilling but he was still holding her face and she was worried that she would look distorted to him.

'I don't want you to feel that in me you're laying the ghost of Alex Martin. As it were,' he said, stroking her hair gently away from her face.

She was silent for a moment. Then she said, 'Alex.' And laughed. 'Never occurred to me. He probably didn't love me anyway.'

It was the most honest thing she'd ever said to a man in her life.

Jonathan looked at her closely. 'Oh, I don't know,' he said. 'We're never really loved as we think we ought to be.'

'Not even you?' She was smiling. 'Look at us. God's gifts, both of us and where has it got us?'

'It's got us here,' he said.

He leaned over her and kissed her gently.

It started off gently. They helped take each other's clothes off and they got into bed to make love. It was that sort of a thing. More gentleness than passion. Or at least, the first time was.

Now that William's future was secure he could afford to be less afraid of Catrin.

The following morning he even lingered in the kitchen with her before breakfast.

'Have a coffee,' she said, 'it's fresh.'

'Thanks,' he said, sitting at the table. 'Listen, on Friday there's leaving party for one of our chaps. It's in Croydon. I'll probably stay there the night.'

'Can't you get a taxi back?'

'From Croydon? It's easier for me to stay.'

'If that's what you want.'

'It is.' He drank the coffee quickly, the evil deed done. 'What time will you be back this evening?'

'Seven — seven-thirty.'

'See you later.'

He drove to the office and without taking his coat off he took an hotel directory from his desk. After making a couple of phone calls, the room was booked.

Satisfied, he took the ring box out of his desk and opened it. It was going to be the start of a new life for him, although he still hankered after the old one.

Hugh Gascoigne came through the door without knocking. 'Owe you a bit of an apology,' he said. 'Jonathan Ward hasn't gone to Paris with your wife.'

'I know that,' William said, snapping the box shut. 'She's at home.'

'Hope it didn't cause any inconvenience.'

'None.' He thrust the box into the pocket of his raincoat.

'It wasn't entirely unjustified,' Hugh said, 'under the circumstances, to draw conclusions. Anyone can make mistakes.'

William nodded. 'Thanks, Hugh. I know.'

Catrin was listening to the news on the car radio as she was driving home from work.

It was beginning to rain and she switched wipers on and a name caught her attention.

'. . . DaCosta, a former boxing promoter, has been charged with making fraudulent claims . . .'

Catrin reached for the volume button but found herself listening to the traffic report.

The dominoes of bad luck were coming to the end of their run.

Indicating, she changed direction and headed for Marilyn's.

Once there she thought at first that Marilyn was out. The rain was worsening and she stood back from the house and looked up at Marilyn's window. A crack of light appeared between the curtains. Catrin put her hands in the pockets of her jacket and shivered. She was going back to the car when the door opened.

'Hurry up,' she heard Marilyn whisper.

Once inside, Marilyn refused to put on the light and told her to feel her way up the stairs.

'Actually,' Catrin said, 'I've just heard something on the radio. DaCosta's been arrested.'

She bumped into Marilyn in the dark. 'Sorry.'

Marilyn didn't speak until they were in her flat. There she faced Catrin. Her red hair had lost its lustre and she had shadows under her eyes. Her freckles looked like army camouflage on her pale face.

Catrin repeated what she'd heard. 'So you're safe,' she added. 'Can we put some more lights on?'

'I'll never be safe,' Marilyn said. 'I found Ricky Enfield's body . . .'

Catrin felt the hairs on her neck stand up. 'What had happened?'

'Heroin overdose. The governor at the Duke of Wellington told me. I thought DaCosta'd killed him.'

'It's solved your problem, hasn't it,' Catrin said brightly. 'Shame he should have overdosed on what DaCosta sent with you but it's hardly your fault.'

'It wasn't anything to do with me,' Marilyn said indignantly. 'Oh.'

She turned it over in her mind. 'Oh,' she said again. And she began to cry.

Catrin made her a cup of tea. She was learning. A bit late, but it couldn't be helped.

'Here you are,' she said, handing it to Marilyn. 'And you can have the boys back.'

Marilyn started to cry again.

'Look,' Catrin lied, 'there's something else. I can't cope with the house without you. It's such a mess, stuff everywhere. The laundry hasn't been sorted for ages and William's going mad because he hasn't got any shirts. I know you're busy yourself but we could pay you more money.'

Still Marilyn hesitated.

'And I can't get the oven clean – there's smoke coming out of it all the time . . .' That bit happened to be true.

'You want me to come back?' Marilyn said.

'Yes,' Catrin confirmed. 'I just don't know what to do about the oven . . .'

'All right, I'll come back.' She looked at Catrin. 'You didn't get a tea for yourself. No, no, I'll do it.'

When she came back she switched the main lights on. Catrin blinked in the brightness. 'Any sign of Harry?' she asked.

'Nah, that's over. What's your news?'

So Catrin told her the news, which was that she and William were going to patch things up. She was making sure of it.

'Are you sleeping with him again, then?' Marilyn asked.

'No, not yet,' Catrin said. 'I'm working on it.'

'Shouldn't be too difficult. He must be desperate for it by now.'

That was one way of looking at it, wasn't it.

'I'm sorry about Harry,' Catrin said.

'Yeah. Sometimes I hear a bit of shouting from up there,' Marilyn said, nodding upwards, 'but that's about all.'

The following morning, William had gone to work before her.

Because Marilyn was coming, and because of the lies she'd told her, all except the oven, Catrin set to work untidying the place. She washed as many of William's shirts as would fit in the washing machine and hung them on hangers on the line to dry.

She opened the coat cupboard and saw that William had left his raincoat behind. It was lying on the floor and she picked it up. She felt something bulky in the pocket and put her hand inside and found the ring box. She opened it up and looked at the sapphire and diamond ring inside.

43

William's plans were going wrong.

Finding that the ring box was no longer in his pocket he'd searched his car from bonnet to boot and even driven back to work to check in his desk. He'd turned the coat cupboard upside down.

Now he came back in to find his wife was waiting for him. Catrin smiled at him as he took off his jacket and threw it over the back of the chair.

What was in that smile?

It was the smile of someone who didn't want to show she was afraid.

William sat down but felt at a disadvantage sunk into the sofa so he moved to a chair instead, facing Catrin. He rested his forearms on it.

Catrin seemed so wound up she was almost humming with tension.

William couldn't stand it any longer.

'You've got my ring, in a ring box,' he said.

Catrin looked surprised and for a second he thought – she hasn't got it! – but she said yes.

'It's in my drawer,' she added.

William looked at her steadily. She held his gaze for minutes, neither of them flinching.

'You had no right to move it,' he said. 'It was in my pocket.'

'Who is it for?'

William knew that he had a choice of answers. Good answers, bad answers, lies. He was still flipping through the options when she asked in a small voice, suddenly doubtful, 'Was it for me?'

And there was a ready-made answer. William had spent practically the whole of his life trying to do the right thing. It was in his nature to do so. He didn't know that Catrin's nature was the same and he'd never realised that that was the thing that made them so close, or had done, once.

From her face, her eyes under the fringe of dark hair begged him for the right answer, which was the right answer for her, for Catrin, for her peace of mind. Yes. One small word.

But William was getting tired and he shook his head.

Catrin shook hers too, slightly, imitating him. 'No,' she said as though she'd uncovered a clue in Charades. She pondered for a moment. 'Who is it for?'

She was very calm still but William was not deceived. 'It's for a woman I know,' he said.

Catrin's huge eyes grew huger. She seemed to have shrunk to the proportions of a child, her eyes dominating her face, dominating his line of sight.

Somehow it had all changed around now, he didn't know when the balance had changed and couldn't believe that he'd missed it. *Catrin loved him.* How was it he hadn't realised this before? He realised it now. The power was his. But he didn't want the power, he merely wanted the truth. Lies had worn him out.

'Which woman?'

'You don't know her.'

'How do you know that? What's her name?'

'It's Jenna,' William said. 'Jenna Greenwood.'

'Jenna.' Catrin jerked the word out. She hugged her arms to her body and glared at him. 'It would have to be a Jenna, wouldn't it? I suppose she's younger than me.'

Too young.

'Yes,' William said.

'And you bought her a ring. I would have liked a ring . . .' She halted. Her face flushed slowly. 'I thought it was for me.'

William stretched out his arms so that they almost reached her.

'NO! DON'T TOUCH ME!' she shouted and covered her face with her hands.

William stood as still as he could but the force of her crying seemed to make him rock slightly on his heels. Back and forth. Back and forth.

Catrin's voice came echoing through the damp cave of her hands. He could hardly make out the words. 'Where did you meet her?'

'At work.'

'A secretary, I suppose,' she said, blinking through the tears.

'No, a receptionist.'

Fresh evidence of the reality of the woman for whom he'd bought a ring brought forth a renewed gush of tears. 'I wanted it all to come right!' she said, her voice rising.

She sounded almost petulant with grief. William looked at her, his small pretty wife whom he used to adore and then, whom he feared. Now he felt sorry for her.

'I don't know how to put it right,' he said.

'And you've given up trying?'

'I didn't know what else to do.' He started rocking again. He didn't seem to be able to stand still. He thought he might fall over. 'This isn't just my fault,' he said.

'I didn't think – after Marilyn –'

'Don't go back over all that stuff,' he said, suddenly angry. 'That was nothing and you know it. It's now that you should be worried about.'

'You're going to leave me?'

William felt as though his emotions were a sort of foreign currency that he couldn't work out the value of.

'I'm not saying that,' he said finally as though he was speaking through a mouthful of mud. 'But I'm glad you know.'

Where had that come from?

'I'd rather not have,' she said.

'I said that to you, once.'

Catrin became frightened again and cupped her hands over her face. He didn't know why, whether it was because she couldn't bear to see him or because she couldn't bear him to see her.

'What are we going to do,' she said, swallowing words, tears, sobs.

'I don't know,' he said. 'We can't go on as we are.'

'I know that.'

'The trust has gone.'

'We can bring it back. We can patch it back up again.'

Patching. She didn't know that it was beyond all hope, that there was a room booked and that he was going to start again with someone else.

'Come here,' he said. Having the upper hand made him kind towards her. She went to him obediently. He put his arms around her and she sobbed onto his chest. He felt the hot wetness of her tears through his shirt and felt blisters form from the agony. Oh, she was so small, he'd forgotten. Small and hurt. He kissed the top of her head, without thinking.

'What are we going to do?' she asked.

'I'll sort something out,' he said as though he was at work talking to someone awkward on the phone.

'Are you going to leave me for her?'

'I don't know,' he said, still striving to be honest although he knew she didn't want it.

'You don't know.' She pushed away from him, hanging her head. 'I've never seen us as divorced.'

Nor had he. He didn't say it. He had nothing to comfort her with except his arms and they weren't enough unless they were going to stay there, ready to put around her in the years ahead.

'Are you going out tonight?'

He hesitated for a moment, then said, 'Yes, it's that thing in Croydon, I told you about it . . .' Uh-oh, back to the lies again. 'Are you going to stay in by yourself?'

'No, I'm going out.'

'Where to?' he asked, concerned.

'Out with a friend,' she said. It made her cry even more.

William, to his surprise, was not distressed. Somehow it seemed right to have the fuss and the tears in a time when things were going badly. He, who always believed in being civilised, now did a complete about turn. Give things their due, he said to himself. It sounded like something that his grandmother might have said.

On the other hand, seeing his wife sobbing on her sofa over him did make him feel that he meant something to her after all. All the ducking and diving that he had done, hopping from stone to stone to cross a torrent of violent emotion and now he realised that he might have managed better had he jumped straight in. Of course, it wasn't his emotion they were talking about here, it was hers.

Still . . . he felt that he'd grown up.

He went up the stairs to pack a small bag. He looked at his room as though he was seeing it for the last time. Their bed with the fresh white bedcovers looked as virginal as a child's. The next time that he slept in it he would be different. And it might not be for long. If he married Jenna – he felt a surge of pleasure at the thought of Jeff's face when he found out.

Revenge was sweet.

Revenge was sweet for Debbie Buckley.

She stood in front of Harry wearing cut-off leggings and a high-neck leotard, in black. She was wearing white socks and black Reeboks. She had her arms folded. Her biceps were clearly defined. Where the light caught the leotard it highlighted her collarbone above her breasts.

Wow, thought Harry, she looked fit. And healthy.

'I'm leaving you,' she said, just like that, without any warning at all. Not even the folded arms came as a warning because she often stood like that to do bust exercises when she thought he wasn't looking.

She said it so casually that Harry didn't bother to

reply. They were always like that. Neither of them thought the other had anything of note to say. So his eyes went back to the television while the words relayed themselves slowly to his consciousness.

Harry reluctantly dragged his eyes from the screen to look at her. She didn't look any different from usual, which was her unamused, unsmiling self. So he thought that he must have misheard.

'What was that?' he said politely. He was less polite to strangers than to his wife.

'You heard. I'm leaving you,' Debbie said. She looked down at her folded arms and he saw her flex her biceps. Then he saw her press them with her thumbs. He bet they felt like half-bricks. She looked up again and he averted his eyes from her muscles.

'Where are you going?' he asked. 'I've got a right to know.'

'Islington,' she said smugly. 'He's a cabbie, if you must know.'

'Is he? You want to watch it, there are too many of them these days, all queuing up for hours for a five-minute fare. There's no money in it.'

She gave him a look of disgust. 'He's got a damn sight more money than you'll ever have, you waster.'

Well that hurt Harry. 'Money isn't everything,' he said. 'You've got a nice home here –'

'Yeah, and you with that leprosy-ridden resident bike downstairs.'

'I don't see her any more.'

'Chucked you out, has she? She's got more brains than you have, I'll say that for her.'

'What's going to happen to me?' Harry asked.

'How should I know?'

Harry was hurt again. 'Anyone'd think you didn't care,' he said.

'Funny, that. Anyway, I'm going tonight. I'll want all the things that are mine. That includes the stuff we got as wedding presents from our side of the family. The CD's mine, too.'

The thought of her taking his things made him feel worse. He'd be left with nothing.

'Isn't this a bit previous?' he asked.

'I've been seeing him for six months. Shows how much you notice, doesn't it. Robbie's bringing the van round later.'

'Van? I thought he was a cabbie?'

'Funny.' She managed a scornful laugh.

Harry sunk lower into his chair. It was ironical really. He'd been trying to make her laugh for years.

44

William drove to Finchley to pick Jenna up. He pulled up outside her house and sounded the horn.

Almost immediately the door opened. For a moment he saw her silhouetted there, her fair hair in a sort of drift around her shoulders. She turned her head towards the interior of the house, and picked up a bag and ran out to the car. She opened the door and slid in beside him, smelling of Lauren.

He looked at her in the shadows, thrilled by the outline of her perfect face.

'Hi,' she said shyly.

He liked that. 'Hello, you,' he said, drinking her in. She looked so new that she was like a present. And as soon as he thought that, he remembered the ring.

Catrin hadn't given it back to him.

He was briefly annoyed that his perfect plans had gone wrong but he stroked Jenna's hair and it stuck to his hand. He let it drop and put his hand on it again and watched it rise. Jenna turned her head to see what he was doing, and laughed. He put his arms around her and kissed her. She smelled of shampoo and of the perfume and he squeezed her tightly, impulsively and she gasped as he forced the air out of her lungs.

'Sorry,' he said, and laughed.

She shook her head, still shy, and her hair quivered

around her face. He was fascinated. He touched it again.

'I didn't have time to dry it properly,' she said.

It was a great thing to worry about. He would have given a lot to have had such a small worry. He loved her for her small worries. He kissed her again.

'Let's go,' she said.

'All right.'

He stroked her face which seemed powdery in the dark but which was smooth and cool as alabaster.

'Will there really be a beautician?'

'Everything you could want.' And William reversed the car and drove away proudly, his girl by his side.

He felt a little bit like he had on his honeymoon. Not too much, he hoped; hadn't been able to come despite the fact they had lived together for months. But the pride was the same now. The anticipation. It was better for waiting. The whole relationship was better, they were ready.

He glanced at her and the street lights washed over her as they drove. She looked very young and he wondered whether she was a virgin.

He hadn't any contraceptives.

He was more annoyed than he had been about forgetting the ring. He glanced at her again. This time she looked at him and gave him a very small smile.

So much for new man taking all the responsibility. But she was new woman, she probably had something in her handbag. It solved the problem, but it would mean she wasn't a virgin.

Not necessarily!

She could be a careful virgin.

Virgins didn't need to be careful.

She wasn't a virgin, she'd wanted to make love since the first night when he drove her back to Finchley from the pub. She couldn't be.

Unless he'd driven her to such depths of female desire that she was prepared not to be a careful virgin any longer.

William couldn't bring himself to wonder whether that was likely.

He'd driven Catrin to some ecstatic heights, once. Heights where she went beyond normal pleasure, where she would laugh or cry, it could go either way, but she'd do it with such abandon that yes, the power had been his, then.

He hadn't reached such heights himself, only as a sort of hanger-on. Sometimes physically. Clinging on to her shuddering body and hoping she would take him there with her. He didn't really know where. He didn't know where she went. He'd had good times himself, but they were always physical and he didn't arch or stretch or wallow in them, he sort of crunched up, grimaced against them.

What a time for nostalgia, he thought.

Jenna shifted in her seat beside him and he left the thoughts of Catrin behind.

'One of the tele-ad girls was so rude to me today,' Jenna said.

'Really?'

'She kept flashing her phone and I was on another call.' The light, clear voice was young, too.

He felt indulgent. 'What did you do?'

'I cried. She was horrible to me.'

'Poor baby.'

'Do you call –' she stopped abruptly and looked out of the window.

He was about to ask what but intuition provided the answer and he filled in the blank. 'Do you call your wife baby?' And she'd stopped because there was no need to fight any more. She was the victor and she knew it. She was there with him, wasn't she?

He realised that he hadn't asked Catrin where she was going that night. Not that it mattered. Still, perhaps he should have asked.

'I don't like being the receptionist any more,' Jenna said, staring through the windscreen.

'Oh?'

'I think I would be better doing something else?'

'Yes,' he said, 'you're probably right.' It would make things easier for them, being apart. She couldn't, for one thing, accost him in the office. And their relationship wouldn't have anything to do with Hugh Gascoigne and his shabby mind.

'I could become your secretary,' she said.

William roared with laughter, so forced that it took them both by surprise. He stopped, then chuckled once or twice to make it seem more natural. He gripped the steering wheel tightly. The girl was out of her mind.

'What's so funny?' she asked him, rather defensively.

'It's an excellent idea,' he said. Yes, he could see it now, her sitting on his knee while he was trying to fathom out someone's scribble.

'Do you really mean that?' she asked softly.

Now really wasn't the time. Or was it, for her? Now, whilst his mind was still on good things to come? He looked at her face. Why was it so difficult to think of

400

deviousness residing in someone beautiful? Beautiful was good, ugly was bad. Simple, wasn't it?

'William?' she said, prompting him.

'Can you type?' he asked her.

She put her little finger in her mouth. 'I could learn.' Which meant no.

'You don't want to be a secretary,' he said. 'Why not join tele-ads? They're always looking for people.'

'I hate them. I told you I hated them.' A frown had developed on her smooth forehead and he just managed to stop himself from trying to humour her out of it.

'I'll see what I can do,' he said. 'You're a good receptionist, though.' Not so good on the telephones. He'd had a few complaints. This wasn't the time to mention them.

The A40 was clear and the car picked up speed. Power was his. By his side his girl had fallen silent again.

'I bet you won't,' she said and it was such a long time later that he'd forgotten the subject for a moment.

'I will,' he promised.

He thought of the evening ahead. He hadn't before allowed his thoughts to dwell on her but now he did. They would have a couple of drinks, first, in their room. Have champagne in the bath together. And then dinner. More drinks. Brandy to follow. And they'd fall into bed or into the shower. A delicious shiver ran through him. It had been such a long time since he'd lain in naked arms.

'You're beautiful,' he said softly, glancing at her and then back to the road.

She smiled up at him sweetly as though in acknowledgement. 'What's the hotel going to be like?' she asked.

'Old,' he said. 'It's a manor. You'll like it.' He glanced at her again. 'It's haunted.'

'Is it?' she said, and giggled. 'Oh, William . . .'

William couldn't wait to get there. He touched her knee lightly with his hand. The power! The power of primitive man! He pressed his foot onto the accelerator to excite more power but instead of the usual surge of speed there was nothing. No sound of effort from the engine. If anything, the car seemed to be slowing down.

He pressed the accelerator to the floor and when he saw that nothing was happening he glanced in the rear-view mirror to where the dazzle of headlights met his eyes. There was something behind him. He flicked the indicator up but that was not working either and he slewed across the carriageway, aiming the car for the safety of the verge. Amidst the angry screech of brakes behind and the din of horns he pulled into the nearside lane. The car behind him pressed the horn a last time before accelerating past in a flash of headlights.

'What's the matter?' Jenna said. 'What's wrong?' There was fear in her voice.

They came to a halt at the side of the road. The interior lights had dimmed to nothing. He switched off the ignition and switched it on again. Nothing.

'Bloody hell,' he said.

'What's wrong, William?'

The car was still motionless. William was sitting, staring forward in the dark. Branches were rubbing against the window, screeching feebly. Cars whizzed past, lights ablaze, rocking the car in their slipstream. William felt again the ineffectual accelerator beneath his foot, the sensation of all power gone.

Jenna was tugging at his arm. 'Talk to me, will you?' she said and he slowly turned to her and there was nothing to say.

It had been the truth all along because here it was, his own car, his trustworthy car, broken down again out of the blue, just as she'd described.

He turned to Jenna again with the look of someone in shock.

'Don't just sit there,' she said, 'go and phone someone. We can get towed there. We're just wasting time.'

And he'd always been so utterly proud of his principles. Disliked girls who, sensing his diffidence, had thought intimacy was the answer. He'd loved Catrin because – because she was the same as him. In a way, to people like Marilyn, they hadn't lived. But they had lived, secure, they'd thought, because of their innocence. He looked back on himself and saw himself only a few months ago, as a child. But he'd loved that child and now the child had gone, grown up into this person here in a car with a girl who, for whatever reason she was with him, was not with him out of love.

He felt Jenna shake his arm. 'What's the matter with you?' she shrieked in frustration. 'I'm sick of sitting here! I'm getting cramp! I hate the dark . . . my hair's not even dry!'

And he looked at her, still dumb. And he saw her beautiful face and he still loved it.

And he knew that against his will, and just at the

right time, he had been saved. It wasn't too late. He knew that had he slept with her, this beautiful girl with brightly coloured eyes, he would have wanted her forever and he would never have got her, because they lived by different rules.

'I'm getting out,' she said finally. 'I'm not staying here all night.'

'No,' he said, 'don't. Not yet. Please don't push time.' He knew it would shortly all be over.

And she let her hand drop off the door handle and she waited.

After a while he said, 'I have to go back home now.'

'I knew it,' she said.

'No, no – it's not that –'

'She's always got to win, hasn't she.' Disappointment brought misery to her face.

'I don't know if she'll see it that way.'

'Just because the car broke down?'

'Yes,' he said. It summed it up. Just because the car broke down.

Jenna gave a sniff. She might have been crying.

'I'm going to ring the RAC. Do you want to come with me?'

'Yes. I don't want to stay by myself.'

So they got out of the car and he tried to lock it and found that the central locking had gone, and he suffered again the memory of his disbelief. And they hurried to the phone and returned to the car to wait.

'You said you'd brought me a present –' Jenna said. Maybe something could be salvaged after all.

'Catrin found it.'

'She has everything. Well, she's welcome to you,' she said with contempt.

'Yes,' he said.

'I hate you. I only wanted to make Jeff jealous. I told him where we were going. He loves me, you know.'

The light of passing cars bounced off her tears as they slid down her cheeks.

He loved her too. It was pointless to tell her. It would wear off, he knew, and he would recover and in a short space of time he would be able to look at her without feeling anything at all.

She carried on crying quietly.

He put his arms around her and she didn't push him away. He buried his face in her hair and smelled her shampoo mixed with the Lauren perfume that had held so much promise a lifetime ago.

45

Catrin woke slowly. She felt the warm body next to her and reached out her hand and touched his hair.

She had been dreaming about William.

Now, under her fingers she felt not his thick wiry hair but silky fine hair, thinning slightly she realised as her fingertips encountered his scalp.

She sat up in bed with a start.

Why had she thought that running to Jonathan would make things better? She looked down at him and as she did so Jonathan pulled the bedcovers back over himself.

Catrin stared at him with something like revulsion and the thought screamed into her mind: *what am I doing here?*

In the gloom she saw her clothes draped over a chair. She saw the empty champagne bottle and the glass by the side of the bed. Getting drunk hadn't altered the fact of the ring. It had just blurred it for a while.

Jonathan turned over to face her and looked at her through one eye. 'Can't you sleep?' he asked.

She could see his white teeth in the dark. 'I'm going home,' she said.

He sat up in bed and reached for his watch. 'Are

you crazy? It's just turned midnight. I thought you'd missed me.'

'Sorry.'

'Sorry? What's that supposed to mean?'

'I made a mistake,' she said. 'I panicked. I'm sorry.' She leapt out of bed and started to put on her bra.

'We're adults,' Jonathan protested. 'You're not a schoolgirl now, this is real life. You can't go messing about, leaping in and out of beds on the strength of a whim.'

It was the second time she'd heard him annoyed. 'Haven't you had your money's worth?' she asked coldly.

'Frankly,' he said, 'no.'

She pulled her blouse on over her head. It was inside-out. She pulled on her tights and skirt and put on her jacket and looked in her handbag for money.

'This should cover it,' she said.

Jonathan jumped out of bed and picked up a towel from the floor which he tied around his waist.

'Let's not be stupid about this,' he said.

'It was a mistake.'

'Too true,' he said, shaking his head. 'For both of us. I should have put you off. I had half a mind to but I've always believed I was irresistible and it's rather nice to have it confirmed.'

He switched on the bedside light and sat on the edge of the bed and gave her a swift grin. 'Your hair's sticking up,' he said.

Catrin combed her fingers through it. She hesitated with her hand still on her hair. 'You are irresistible, really,' she said. 'Otherwise it would never have happened.' She rubbed the corner of her eye.

His impassive face broke into a gentle smile. 'Then that's all right,' he said.

'I believe in marriage,' she said wistfully.

'So do I, oddly enough.'

'You'll understand, then. I hope things work out for you.'

He seemed to be about to say something. She hesitated but he raised his hand. A salute or a goodbye.

Marilyn came home from school with the boys and two Sainsbury's carriers to find Harry sitting outside her door, red-eyed. She looked at him coldly and said, 'Excuse me, please,' nudging him away with her foot.

One of the boys kicked a football to him. He knocked it back with his fist half-heartedly.

Marilyn put her shopping down and put her key in the lock.

Harry got to his feet and picked up the bags.

'Put those down,' Marilyn said sharply. 'Can't you go and sit on your own doorstep? You look like a stray.'

'I've been waiting for you,' he said piteously. 'Something awful's happened.'

Marilyn opened the door and ushered the boys inside. She heard the television being switched on. All she wanted was to have a cup of tea and sink into a chair and be with her children and stay mindless for a couple of hours.

She looked at Harry. 'Not now, eh?' she said pleadingly.

'Debbie's left me,' Harry said and the words came out in a gush so that there, lying before her, was the proof of his agony and his own wife's desertion.

'DaCosta's going down for fraud and she says she's off. Aren't you going to say anything?'

Marilyn began to laugh. 'I'm glad she left you. She's got sense.'

'She's gone to Islington to live with a cab driver. She's taken all our stuff. There's nothing left in there – she hasn't even left me a chair to sit on.'

'Poor Harry,' she said, still smiling. Harry wasn't sure he liked the smile. 'So that's why you're on my doorstep, is it? Well I've got no sympathy for you, Harry. You asked for it. You slept with everyone but her.'

'I didn't,' Harry said, shocked, 'only you.'

'You'll have to go, now. I've got the boys' food to get ready.'

Harry grabbed her by the arm. 'Don't you care about me?' he asked her in astonishment at her cold-heartedness.

'Course I do, Harry. But I've had enough of messing my life about. Don't say I'm cold-hearted though – I'll send the boys up with a spare chair. After they've finished supper.'

Catrin returned from Jonathan's to find the lights on in the house. There was no sign of William's car and, slightly alarmed, she looked through the window. There, lying on the sofa was William, his face distorted with grief.

Appalled, she was still aware enough of her bedraggled appearance to know that she ought to tidy herself up before seeing him. She slipped her jacket off and took her blouse off right there in the shadows at the front of the house. She turned the blouse the right way round, put the jacket back on and opened the door. She went straight into the room where William was and stood in the doorway awkwardly.

'I didn't expect you back tonight,' she said. 'What happened to Croydon?'

William stood up and walked over to her. There was some strange expression in his eyes. He reached out for her hands and held them, his eyes begging for understanding.

'The car broke down,' he said, his voice tight. 'Just like it did when you took a lift with Alex. Just like you said.'

Catrin's face relaxed slowly until her expression was one of wonderment.

She smiled slowly. 'I don't believe it.' After all this time. Then she shook her head. 'I do believe it.' Tears began to prickle at the back of her eyes as she smiled.

She looked at him again and saw that strange expression in his face.

'I'm sorry,' he said, 'for everything. For Jenna Greenwood. For not believing you. I should have known you'd never be unfaithful . . .' He looked ashamed but he kept his eyes on hers.

'Don't be,' she said quickly. They both had some apologising to do. If she hadn't come back tonight . . . 'Don't be sorry.' She thought that he looked older and she remembered the grief that she'd seen on his face as she'd looked through the window. There was no trace of it now.

'Was that all it took,' she asked him curiously, 'proof that the car broke down?'

'I should have believed you,' he said. 'Should have known you better.'

'You know me better now. It's been a shambles, hasn't it, these last few months? Insanity . . .'

He dropped her hands. She stood with them down by her side. Because of their actions that very night, neither of them wanted the other to take any blame; it seemed fairer to blame oneself.

'Shall we have a drink?' Catrin asked.

William nodded. 'I'll get them.'

'I'll just pop upstairs for a quick shower and put on something more comfortable.'

'Fine. By the way, where did you go tonight?'

But Catrin was out of the room, feigning deafness so that she could have some time to think up a reply.

It was Monday morning. The office was back to normal; Frances arrived late for their Monday-morning meeting.

Catrin was taking a call and out of the corner of her eye she saw Frances hang around when the rest of them had gone.

'Take a seat,' she mouthed. 'Fine,' she said to the voice on the phone. 'Wednesday's fine.'

She put the phone down and swivelled her chair to face Frances. 'You're looking better,' she said. 'Wonderful.' She lowered her voice. 'It was the right decision after all.'

Frances looked uncomfortable. She picked up her handbag from the floor and put it on her knee, making some sort of a defence between them. 'I had a holiday,' she said.

'Good,' Catrin said. It was meant to sound encouraging. 'That's great.'

It obviously wasn't great for Frances. She swung her

hair away from her face and for a second there was a trace of the old defiance. 'I mean,' she said, 'that a holiday was all I had.'

Catrin sat immobile. 'You changed your mind? You're still −' she finished the sentence with her eyes.

'Yes,' Frances said.

Catrin's mouth shaped an 'oh.' She waited for Frances to continue.

'I couldn't make the decision,' Frances said. 'But I look all right, don't I?'

'You look great. What's that got to do with it?'

'But do I look slim?'

Catrin leaned forward and tried to look over the top of the desk.

'You'll have to stand up,' she said.

Frances pushed the chair away. 'There.' She stood sideways.

Catrin looked her up and down. 'Most un-pregnant women would kill for a figure like that,' she said, 'but what's it got to do with anything? It's not something you can hide forever.'

'Sit down,' Frances said. 'I know this is going to come as a shock − I mean, you know him, I know you were friendly −'

'Who are we talking about?' Catrin asked her, puzzled.

'Jonathan Wade. I went to Paris with him.'

Catrin gave an incredulous laugh. 'You didn't,' she said after a moment.

'I did,' Frances said. She looked surprised and proud.

Catrin rubbed her temple. 'And you and he −'

The rat. Catrin stared at the desk. He could have saved them both from that − debacle − last night. She

412

blew through pursed lips. 'Now what's going to happen?' she asked.

'The thing is –' Frances glanced at the door then back at Catrin, '– I didn't take, you know, contraceptives. We didn't use anything at all. What's to stop me from saying it's his?'

Catrin looked incredulously at Frances. 'You think he'll believe you?'

'I hope he will. I'll say it's premature.'

Four months? Catrin wondered, impressed.

Frances looked at Catrin steadily and said, 'I think he'll marry me.'

Catrin thought she was probably right. Frances would make a great replacement Amelia.

'But you've only known him a couple of weeks.'

'I know,' Frances said calmly, 'but he seems to be serious.'

'Good luck, then.' Catrin meant it. Frances was having a whole new start in a direction she wanted.

'Thanks.' Frances got up from the table. She smiled suddenly at Catrin and she looked beautiful and Catrin was suddenly convinced. She smiled back. It was funny how things worked out.

William found himself in a practically empty office that morning.

Nine-thirty came and went. He wandered restlessly around, getting coffee from the machine and saying 'live it down, live it down,' over and over in his head. He knew that he was the villain of the piece and was ashamed. Most of the time. In unguarded moments a feeling of pride, primitive man, crept through and raised a fist in the air.

Where was everyone?

The phones were not even ringing.

Eventually he took the lift down to the ground floor and found the switchboard lit up like a Christmas tree and no sign of Jenna at all. He went back up the stairs and into the sales department. One of the girls agreed to man the switchboard until she turned up.

At about ten-thirty Jeff came in looking pale and ill at ease. He knocked on William's door.

'Come in,' William said and had to repeat it before Jeff came inside and shut the door behind him.

Jeff took his cigarette case out of his pocket and knocked one out. He searched in all his pockets for a lighter, then glanced up at William hopefully. 'I don't suppose?'

'Sorry,' William said. Disinclined to take the initiative, he studied Jeff, and was surprised at his pallor and the recent departure of his savoir faire.

'I've got some in my desk,' Jeff said, scraping along his mouth with his thumbnail. He stood up. 'I'll be back in a minute.'

William, automatically bracing himself for some reference to Jenna, now wondered whether he was on the wrong track.

He saw Jeff pass the window of the office, his cigarette already lit. He came back into the room and sat down once more.

'You've probably heard rumours,' he said, 'about Hugh.'

To ask what sort of rumours would betray his lack of knowledge. So William said that he had.

'He's been touching me,' Jeff said. 'You know . . .'

He took another puff of his cigarette. 'On the knee. That sort of thing.'

He looked up again at William's face. It betrayed nothing.

'I went out with him last night. We drank too much. I went back to his place. I know what you're thinking. I liked him, he was a good bloke, he was funny and we were drunk.' He took another pull of the cigarette. 'Messing about, that's all it was. We took our clothes off. He had some old tinsel around his neck. He started to sing this song he'd made up. Then he collapsed with the tinsel still around his neck. I got dressed again, I thought it was the drink, but he said he felt ill. He kept lifting his arm up in the air, I thought he wanted to touch me and I backed off. Then he went blue. Dark blue.'

William felt the blood drain out of him so that he was sure his colour matched Jeff's. Hugh, poor Hugh, he thought bitterly, ending his life with this waster by his side.

'Where is he now?'

Jeff stared. 'I didn't leave him there, if that's what you mean. I rang the hospital. There'll be an inquest, won't there? What am I going to say? What's going to happen to me?'

'I don't know,' William said.

'Is that all you've got to say?'

William considered.

'You could always sell the story to the trade papers,' he said.

PART SEVEN

Living it Down

46

The boys were in bed.

Marilyn was finishing the coffee-break crossword puzzle, the television was on, and the background conversation was just loud enough for her to feel that she had company. She was nearing the bottom of a packet of biscuits that she'd bought for the boys, choosing ones she didn't much care for in the hope it would put her off eating them. It hadn't.

The flat was quiet; for a flat. There was music playing below. Above her she could hear footsteps on the bare floorboards. Harry's footsteps. Debbie had been and taken the carpets. Whichever way you looked at it it was a funny thing to do, take the carpets off the floors, but it hadn't been much trouble because there hadn't been any furniture left to stand on them anyway. She'd heard shouting, of course. Most of it from Debbie. Some of it aimed at Marilyn but most of it directed towards Harry and his roving eye. Except that Debbie hadn't said eye, exactly.

For a month Marilyn, while she was in, had known pretty well every single one of Harry's movements. She could have followed his path around the house with a pencil on the ceiling, if she didn't mind pencil marks on the ceiling. One other thing she knew was that Harry hadn't had any visitors. Not a single one.

Apart from Debbie when she came to take the lightbulbs.

Poor Harry.

There were two biscuits left in the packet. One for me, one for you, Marilyn thought, and ate them both.

She went to check on the boys. They were both asleep. She'd read them a story and that had done it. She'd learnt fast that making stories interesting to children was fatal because firstly, they stayed awake to the end and secondly, they wanted another because the first had been so good. Now she read them Mills & Boons in a monotone.

She crushed up the packet in her hand and went into the kitchen and put it in the bin.

She went into her bedroom and looked at herself in the mirror and put some lipstick on and blotted it well with tissues to stop it from looking too fresh.

She went out of her flat, pulling the door to, and went upstairs to Harry's.

She pressed the bell but it wasn't working, so she knocked on the door, hard.

She heard Harry's heavy tread on the floorboards and imagined it as it would sound from her flat.

Harry opened the door wide with an expression that seemed to say, 'Here I am. Take me.'

His expression didn't alter on seeing that it was Marilyn. He merely stood aside for her to come in.

She walked through into what had been the lounge. A garden chair was in the centre of the room, surrounded by newspapers. That was all there was. Without a word she went into his bedroom. There was a mattress on the floor with a radio next to it.

In the kitchen was the sink and gaps underneath

the cupboards from where the appliances had been taken.

'Oh, Harry,' she said and began to laugh.

Harry was still standing by the door with a certain amount of dignity. 'Satisfied?' he asked her.

'Don't be like that.' She wanted to sit down but there was nowhere to sit. The house was all echoey like an empty house except that it wasn't empty, both she and Harry were in it. 'She's cleaned you out good and proper, hasn't she?'

Harry was still standing very straight by the door. 'I like it like this, ' he said. 'She did me a favour.'

'What do you mean, you like it like this?'

'It's minimalistic.'

'Minimalistic.' Marilyn shook her head in disbelief. 'It's empty, that's what it is. Why don't you buy yourself some more stuff?'

Harry's nose remained in the air.

'How do you eat?' Marilyn asked him, going back into the kitchen again. She opened the cupboard doors. The cupboards were empty. She slammed them shut.

'I'm on a diet,' Harry said.

'You're round the bend, that's what you are.' She started to laugh again. 'Tell me you're round the bend.'

'As a matter of fact I've never been happier,' he said solemnly. 'I've had peace and quiet for the first time in my life.'

'Oh, have you? It's more than what I've had. Thump, thump, thump, every time you move out of your chair. Where's that chair from, anyway?'

'It was on the balcony. Debbie'll be here any day now to collect it.'

'You loony. Will she? I said I'd give you a chair. Mean cow. What have you been living on?'

Harry was still by the door looking noble. 'Pot Noodles.'

'You can't live off those, they're a snack. Poor Harry, has it been awful for you?'

'I've done my share of suffering, yes.'

Marilyn went by the door and stood next to him. He towered above her. He didn't move his head but he moved his eyes. He looked like an Indian chief.

'Well I'm glad to hear you've suffered,' she said frankly. 'I always said you had life too easy. Fancy a take-away?'

'Is the Pope Catholic?'

'Come downstairs, I've got a menu and we can ring them. Where are you off to, Harry?'

Harry went into the lounge and reappeared with the garden chair.'

'I never leave home without it,' he said.

'I think Debbie's made you mental.'

'You say the nicest things.'

They went to Marilyn's flat.

The food was delivered and Marilyn got out a bottle of wine. They spent twenty minutes looking for the corkscrew before giving up and then they found it was a screw-top bottle anyway.

They discussed the future. They discussed opening a sandwich bar together. They discussed making a hole in the floor of Harry's flat and inserting a spiral staircase so that they would have a maisonette to share. And after the take-away they went to bed.

Why not? Marilyn thought as she took off her clothes. Harry had suffered enough. And Harry was ready, reluctantly – he knew Marilyn by now – to agree with her.

Frances came into Catrin's office in the afternoon and put her hand flat on the table.

Catrin looked at the hand and smiled slowly.

'A ring,' she said. She looked up at Frances who was wearing the dazed expression of one who couldn't believe her luck.

'He knows about the baby and we're getting married.'

Catrin's smile grew bigger. 'Great,' she said. 'I'm really pleased.'

'It was so easy,' Frances said incredulously. 'I told him I was pregnant, and he just sat there looking happy. And then he said that he knew. That he could tell from my face that I had good news.'

'He thinks that it's his, then?'

Frances held out her hands, palms upwards. 'He thinks that it's his.' Tears came into her eyes suddenly. 'It will be his,' she said.

'Yes . . .' They looked at each other, friends, some-how, strangely enough.

Catrin ducked down and got the magazine that Frances had skimmed over the desk at her four months ago. 'You'll need this now,' she said.

Frances smiled again, a somewhat watery smile. 'What about you?' she asked softly.

'Oh, I'm working on it. Poor William.'

'Why poor?'

'I feel sorry for him, that's all. He feels so guilty.'

A head popped round Catrin's door. 'There's a call for Frances at her desk.'

'Coming,' Frances said. 'There's one other thing,' she said to Catrin, 'he doesn't want me to come back to work after the baby.'

'He's your ideal man.'

She watched Frances leave the office and she thought about rings, more importantly about the ring that she'd found in William's overcoat.

Things were mending between them now. There came a time when you had to move forward and just let some of the stuff that life throws at you go. Can't carry it all with you through life. Well, letting it go was what they were doing. They'd begun to love each other again. Who said the spark could never come back? It was coming back; as Sarah had said, you just had to hang on in there. Life wasn't a straight line, it was a spiral and if you hung on long enough you began to recognise the pattern.

The tragedy of life and the miracle of life was the same thing, which was, everything changed, whether you wanted it to or not. You just had to hang on.

Love and forgiveness were the important things; both for themselves and for each other.

The ring.

She hadn't known what to do with it.

The ring had been a shock but whatever had gone on between him and his receptionist had fizzled out, now. He'd mentioned that she'd left – she'd only been a temp, anyway.

So what was she to have done with the ring?

She hadn't wanted to keep it. It hadn't been hers.

It hadn't been hers to wear and it hadn't been hers to give away.

That morning she'd taken it to a pawnbroker's.

Chosen one of the doors and gone up to the counter and spoken through the grille and handed over the ring in its beautiful box. She'd never redeem it, that was all; and in doing that she would neither be selling it nor giving it away.

The jeweller had looked at it carefully, admired the stones and offered a paltry amount, 'bearing in mind the current economic climate.'

'I'll take it,' she'd said.

On the way home she'd dropped the money into a polystyrene cup held by a beggar with a dog on a string.

She no longer wanted scars to pick at. She just wanted to be healed.

And suddenly she'd felt light as air; it was finished.

Jonathan rang his ex-wife with the news that, when the divorce came through, he was getting married again. His voice was jubilant.

'What's the rush?' she asked in her superior voice.

'She's expecting a baby. It's due in February.' He, too, was happy to collude in the story of the premature birth.

There was a long, long silence from his ex-wife's end which after a while seemed to hum with anger.

'How did you manage that?'

Jonathan put the phone down with quiet satisfaction.

Score one to him. Alex Martin was never going to be able to claim paternity and Frances wasn't going to mention it to anyone, was she. It had all been worth it, just for that one call . . .

*   *   *

William was looking at Catrin over dinner when suddenly she looked up and for a minute their eyes locked in a look of understanding and not a little lust.

William was aware that he had a lot to be forgiven for. He had apologised about the car, and about her supposed infidelity with Alex. The time for apologies was over; now was the time for consolidation.

He was grateful for one thing – that he hadn't slept with Jenna. He was better than his father after all; he hadn't succumbed in the end. He looked at Catrin. And that made them quits.

Catrin looked at William.

He'd been with Jenna Greenwood and she'd been with Jonathan. As Sarah had said, it was nothing to be proud of, but still, she didn't regret it. It had brought the balance back to the relationship. They were evens.

William looked at Catrin.

It was about time, he thought, that they had a baby. A boy, preferably; it was bound to be, all those primitive genes in him. Boys were hereditary in his family. And he'd have someone to explain cricket to.

They got up together from the table and to Catrin's glee he smacked her on her bottom and chased her up the stairs.

Primitive man had regained his kingdom against the odds and was taking his woman to bed.